CHAPTER

13

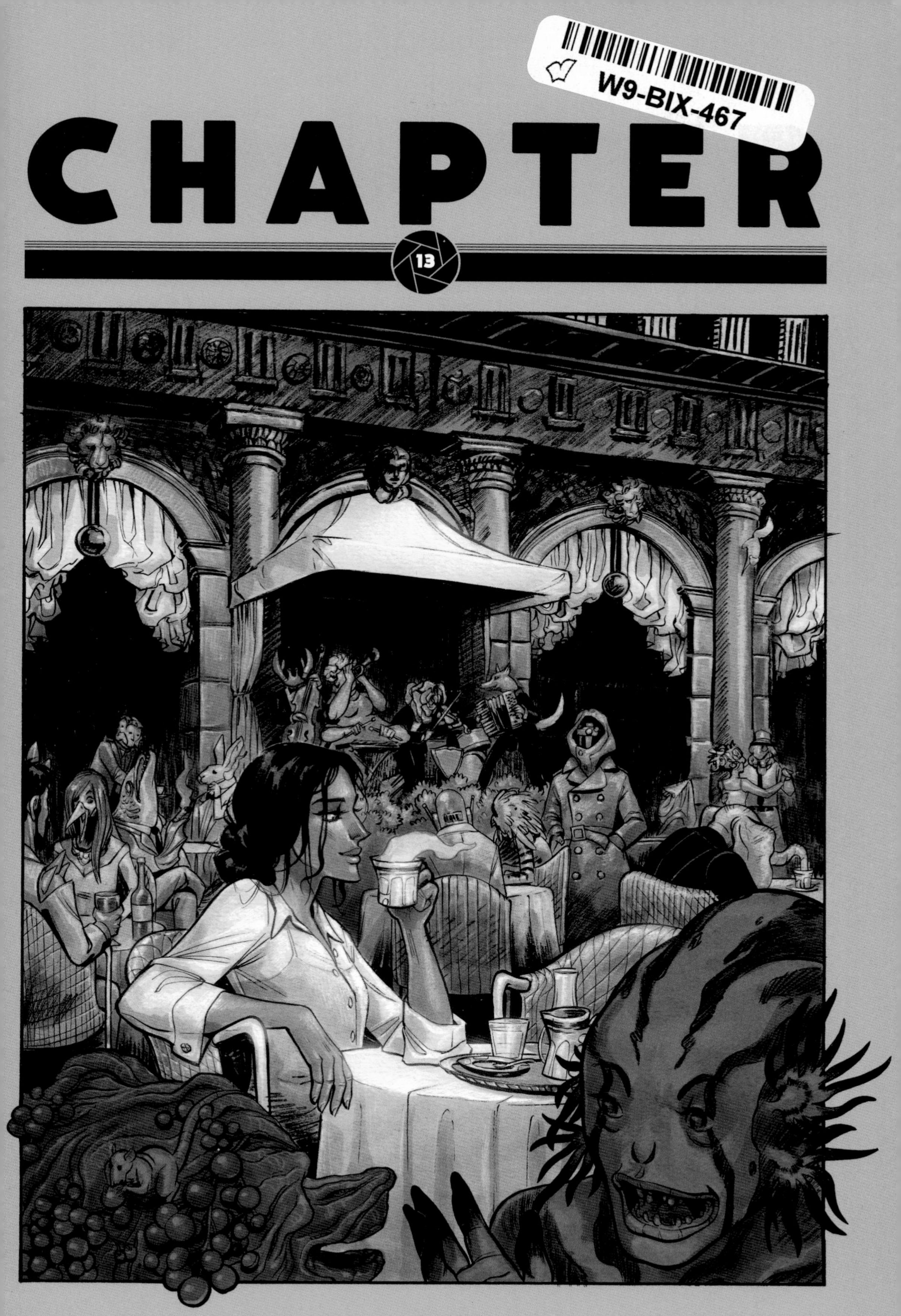

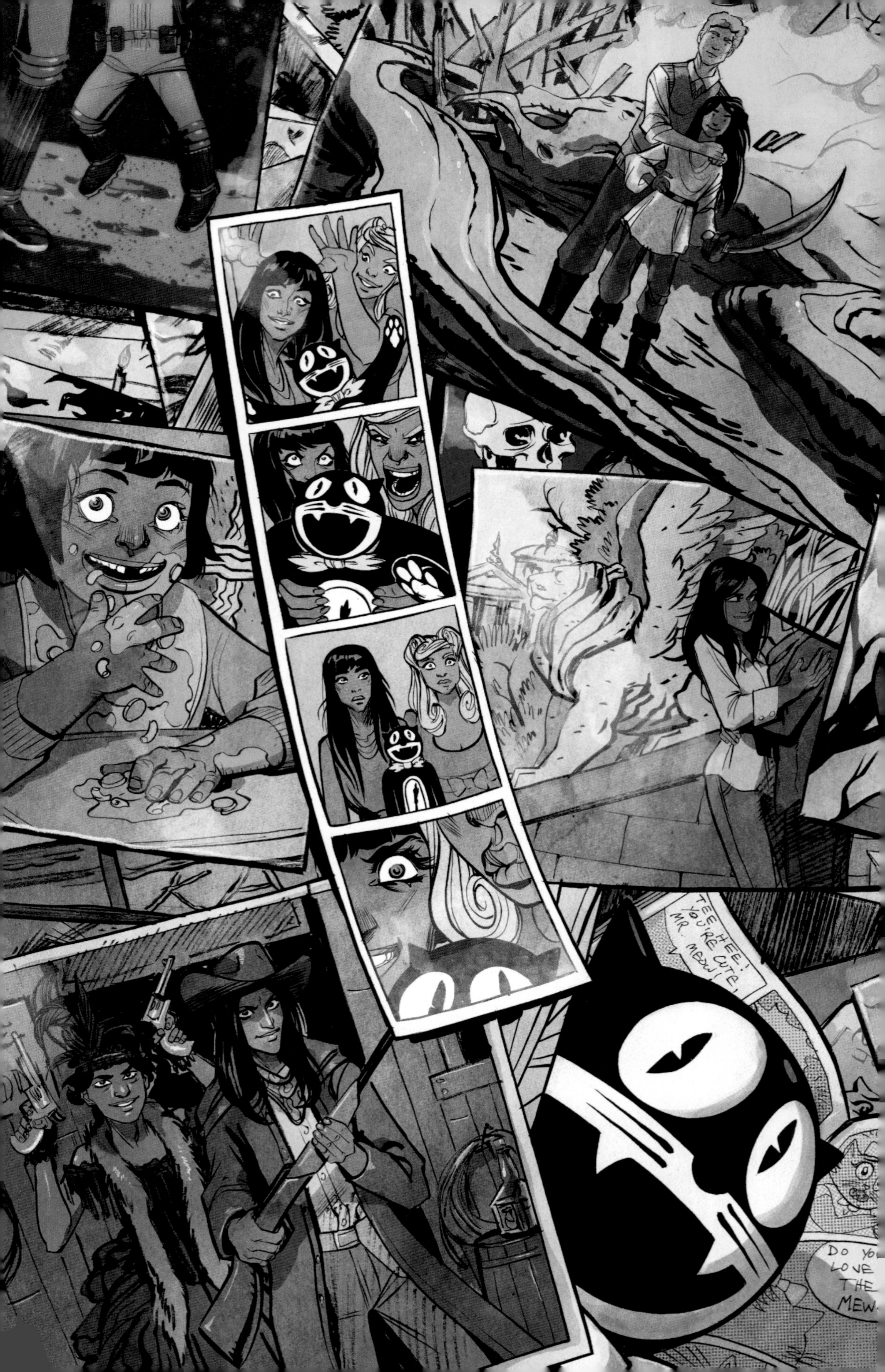
TEE HEE! YOU'RE CUTE, MR. MEOW!
DO YO LOVE THE MEW

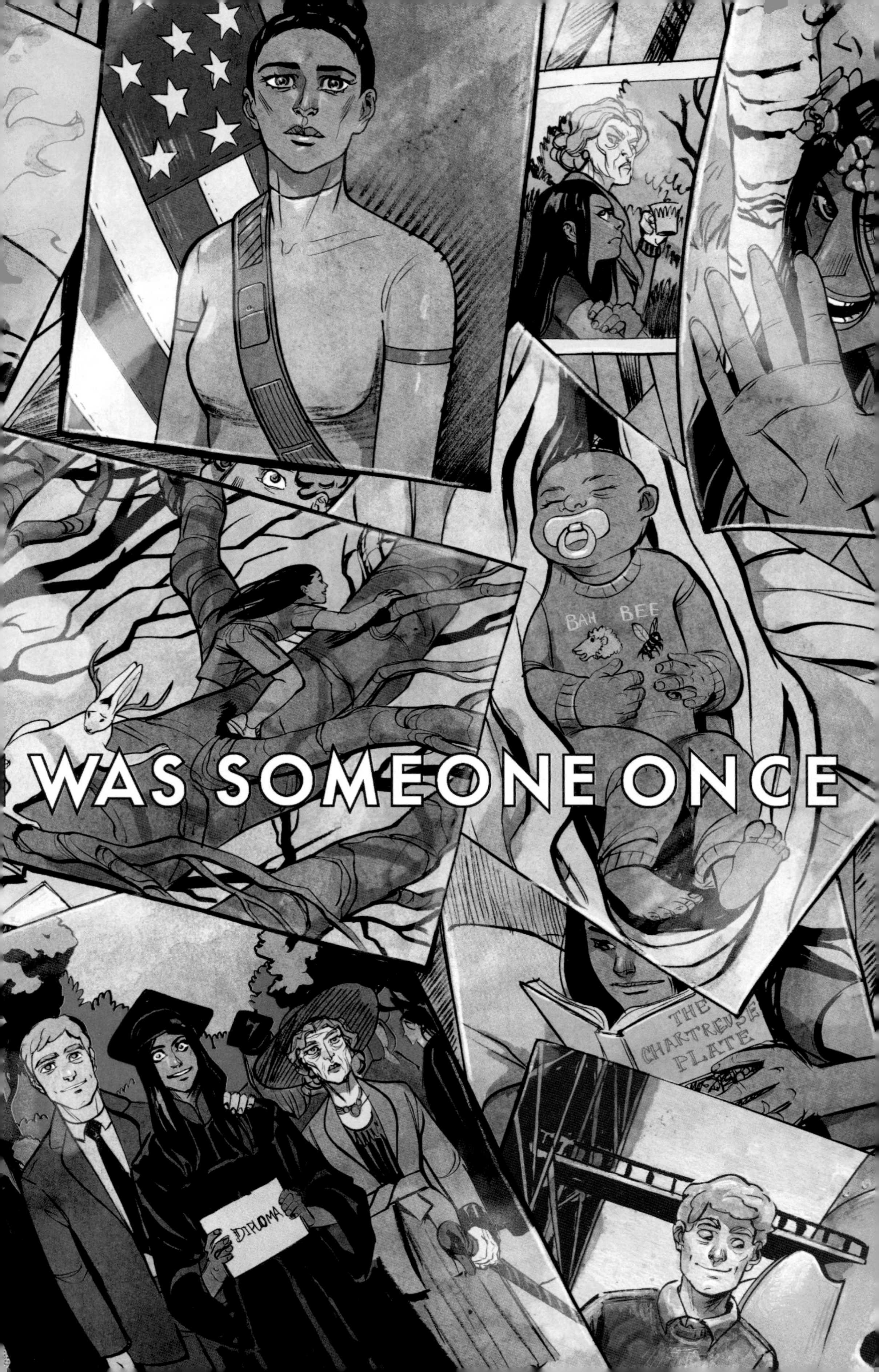
WAS SOMEONE ONCE
BAH BEE
THE CHARTREUSE PLATE
DIPLOMA

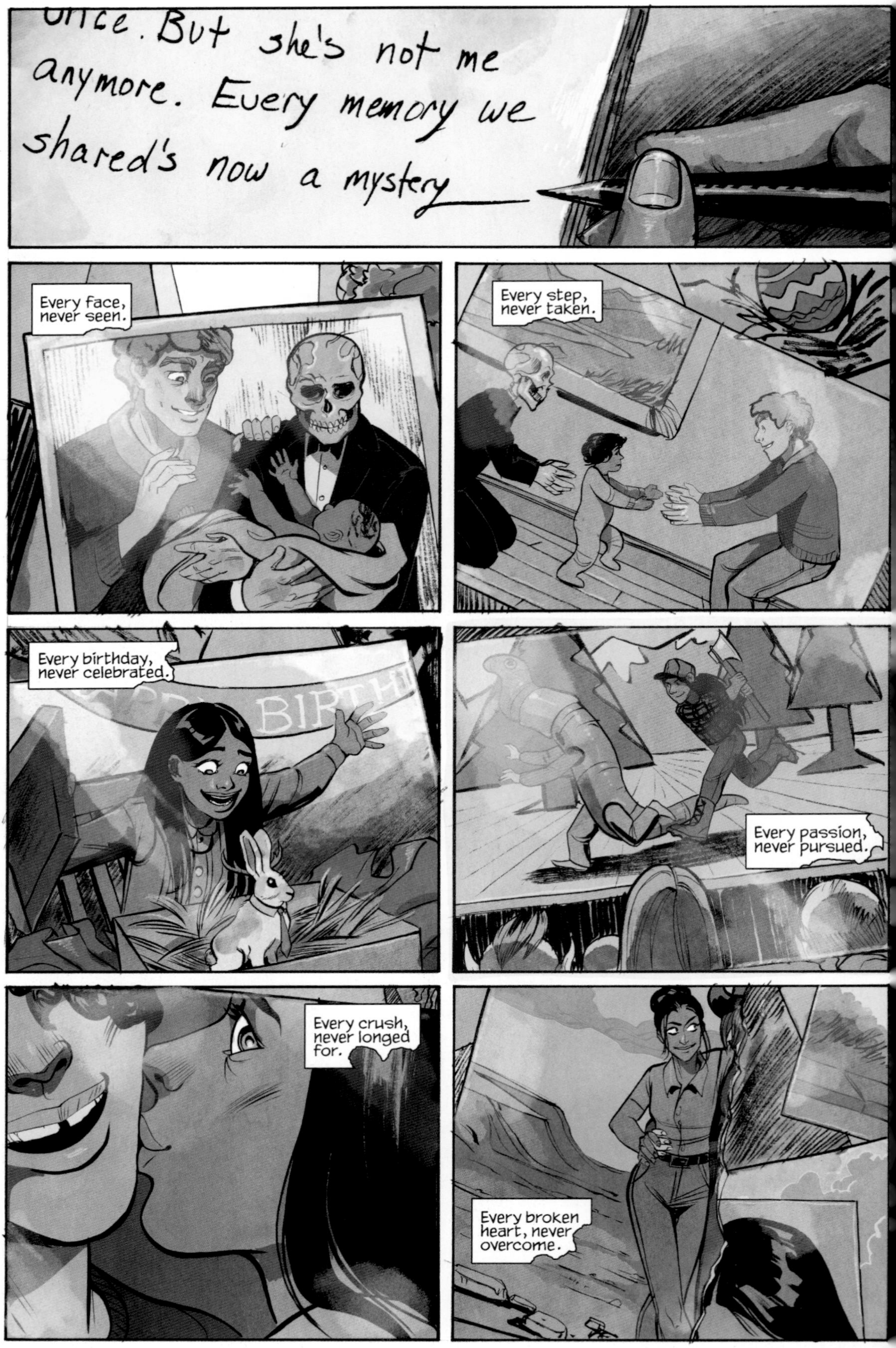
once. But she's not me anymore. Every memory we shared's now a mystery
Every face, never seen.
Every step, never taken.
Every birthday, never celebrated.
BIRTH
Every passion, never pursued.
Every crush, never longed for.
Every broken heart, never overcome.

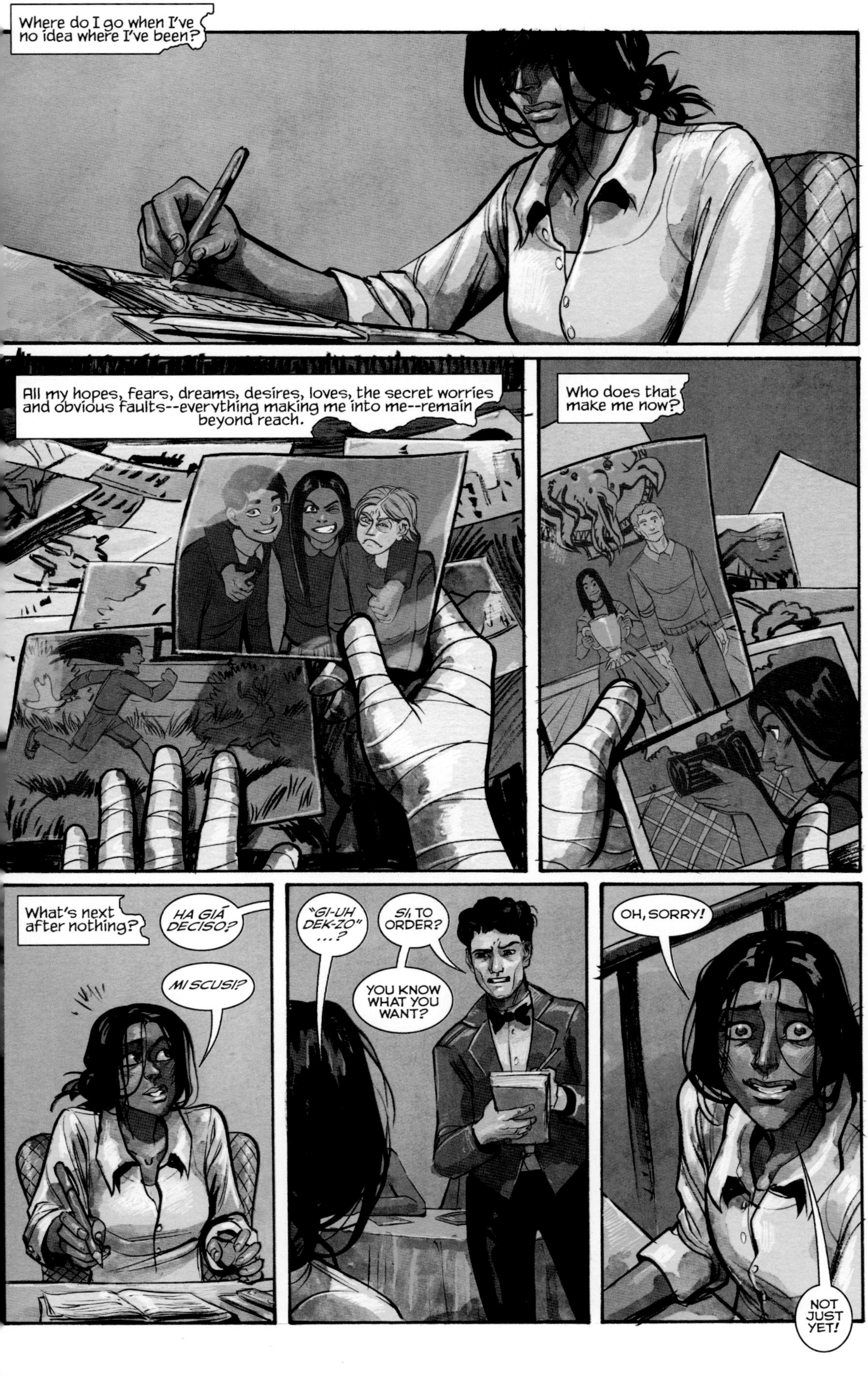

Where do I go when I've no idea where I've been?
All my hopes, fears, dreams, desires, loves, the secret worries and obvious faults--everything making me into me--remain beyond reach.
Who does that make me now?
What's next after nothing?
HA GIÁ DECISO?
MI SCUSI?
"GI-UH DEK-ZO" ...?
SI, TO ORDER?
YOU KNOW WHAT YOU WANT?
OH, SORRY!
NOT JUST YET!

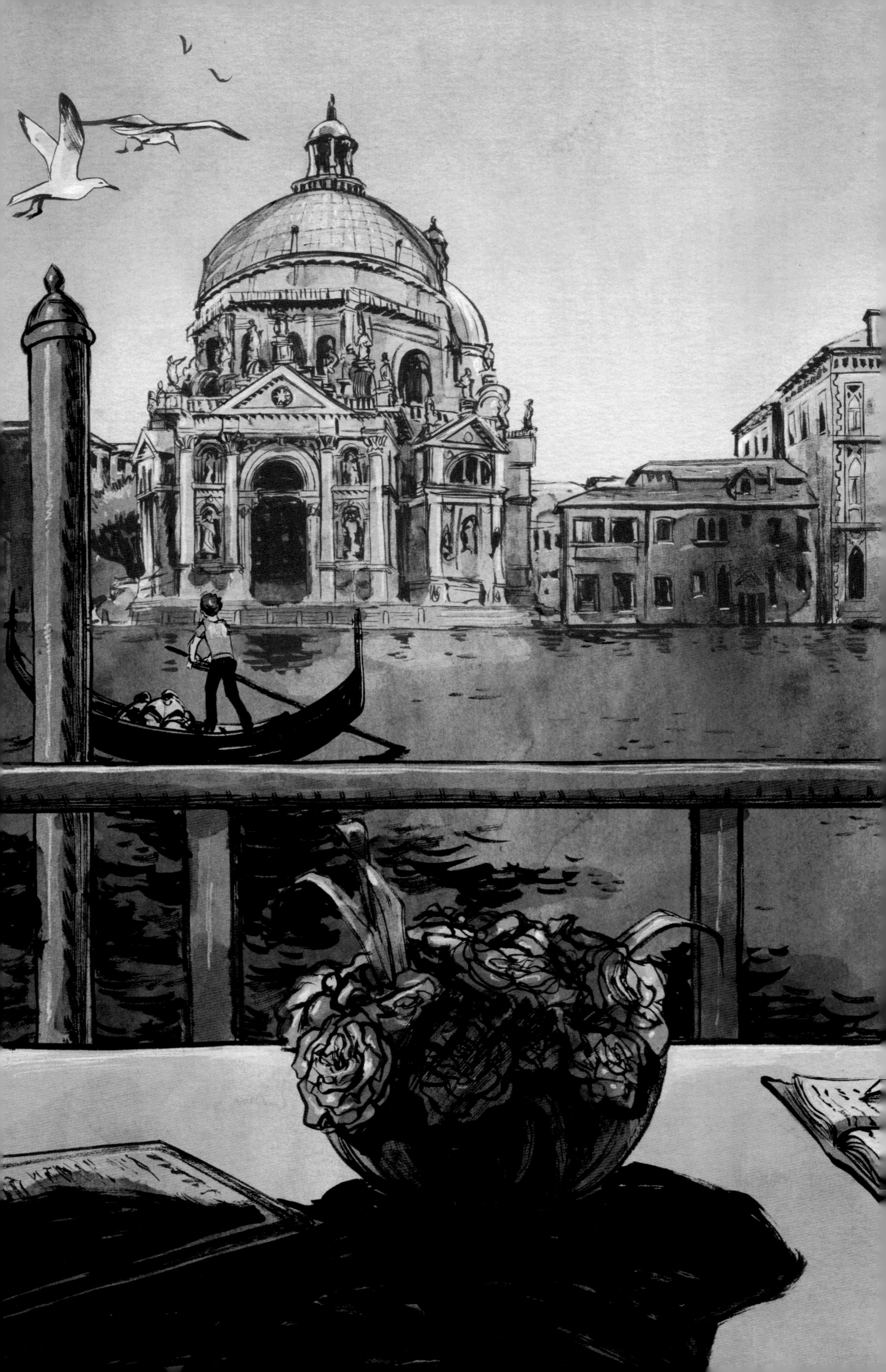

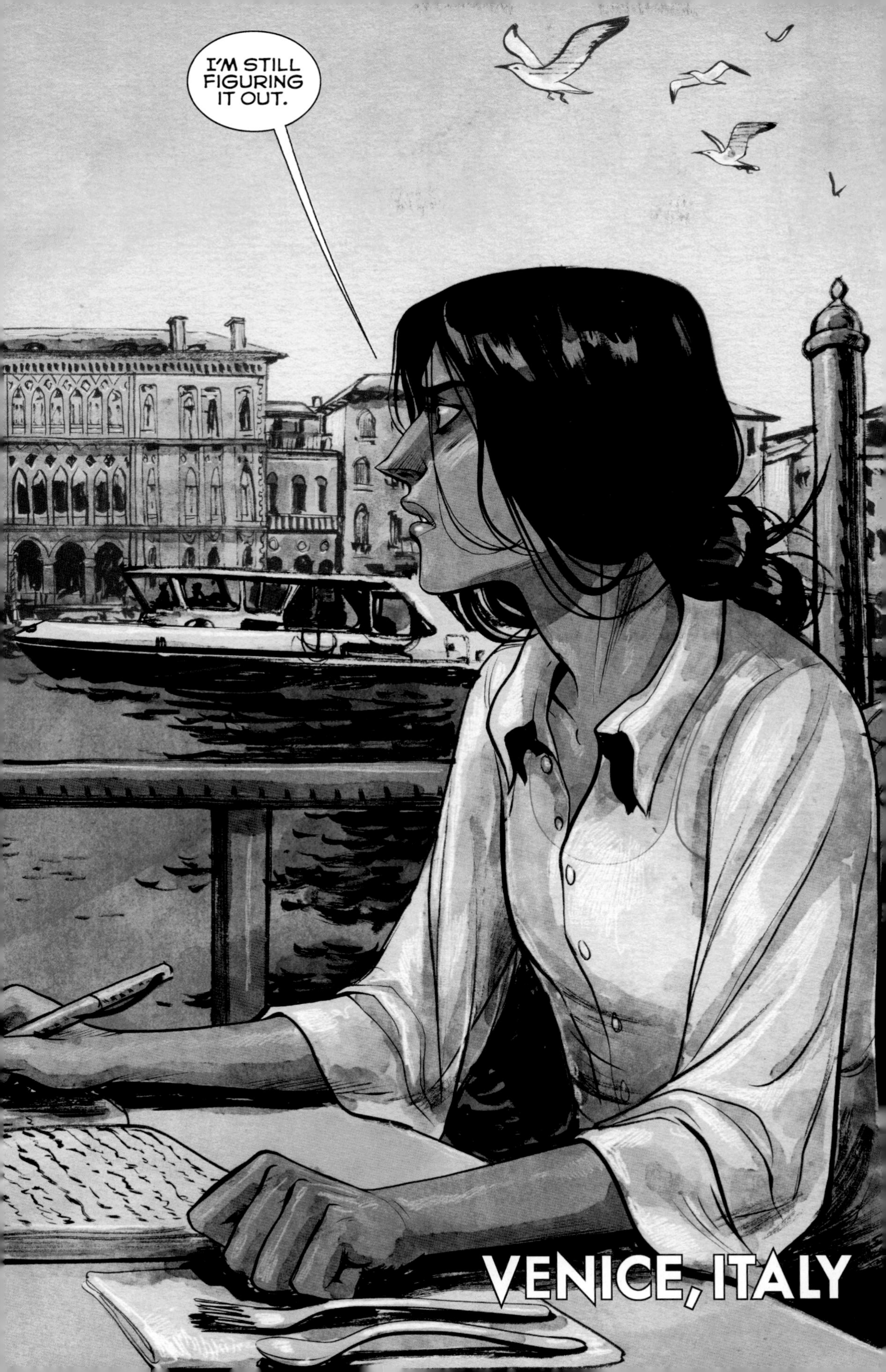
I'M STILL FIGURING IT OUT.
VENICE, ITALY

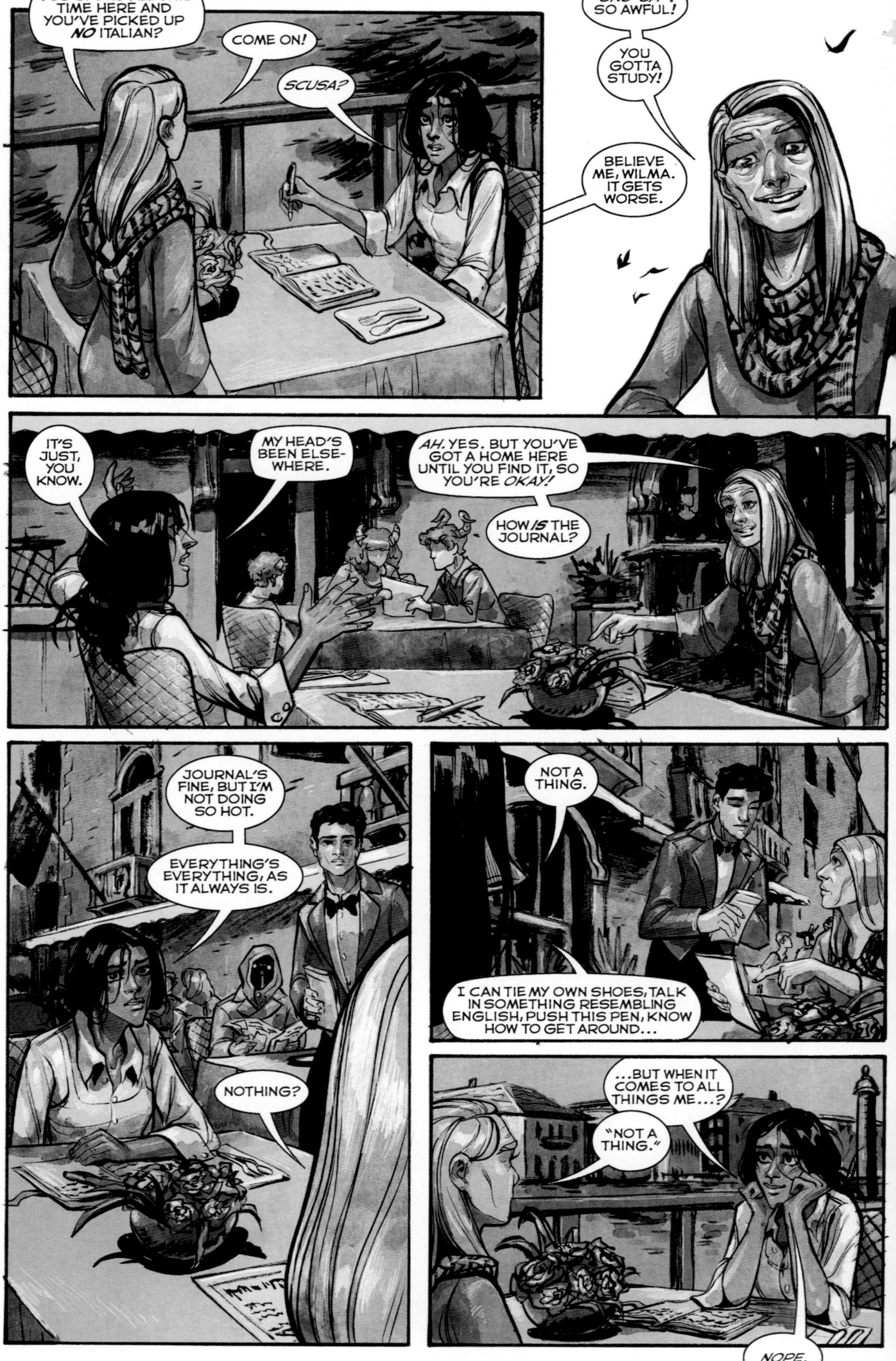
YOU SPEND ALL THIS TIME HERE AND YOU'VE PICKED UP *NO* ITALIAN?
COME ON!
SCUSA?
"*SKO-SA*"? SO AWFUL!
YOU GOTTA STUDY!
BELIEVE ME, WILMA. IT GETS WORSE.
IT'S JUST, YOU KNOW.
MY HEAD'S BEEN ELSE-WHERE.
AH. YES. BUT YOU'VE GOT A HOME HERE UNTIL YOU FIND IT, SO YOU'RE *OKAY!*
HOW *IS* THE JOURNAL?
JOURNAL'S FINE, BUT I'M NOT DOING SO HOT.
EVERYTHING'S EVERYTHING, AS IT ALWAYS IS.
NOTHING?
NOT A THING.
I CAN TIE MY OWN SHOES, TALK IN SOMETHING RESEMBLING ENGLISH, PUSH THIS PEN, KNOW HOW TO GET AROUND...
...BUT WHEN IT COMES TO ALL THINGS ME...?
"NOT A THING."
NOPE.

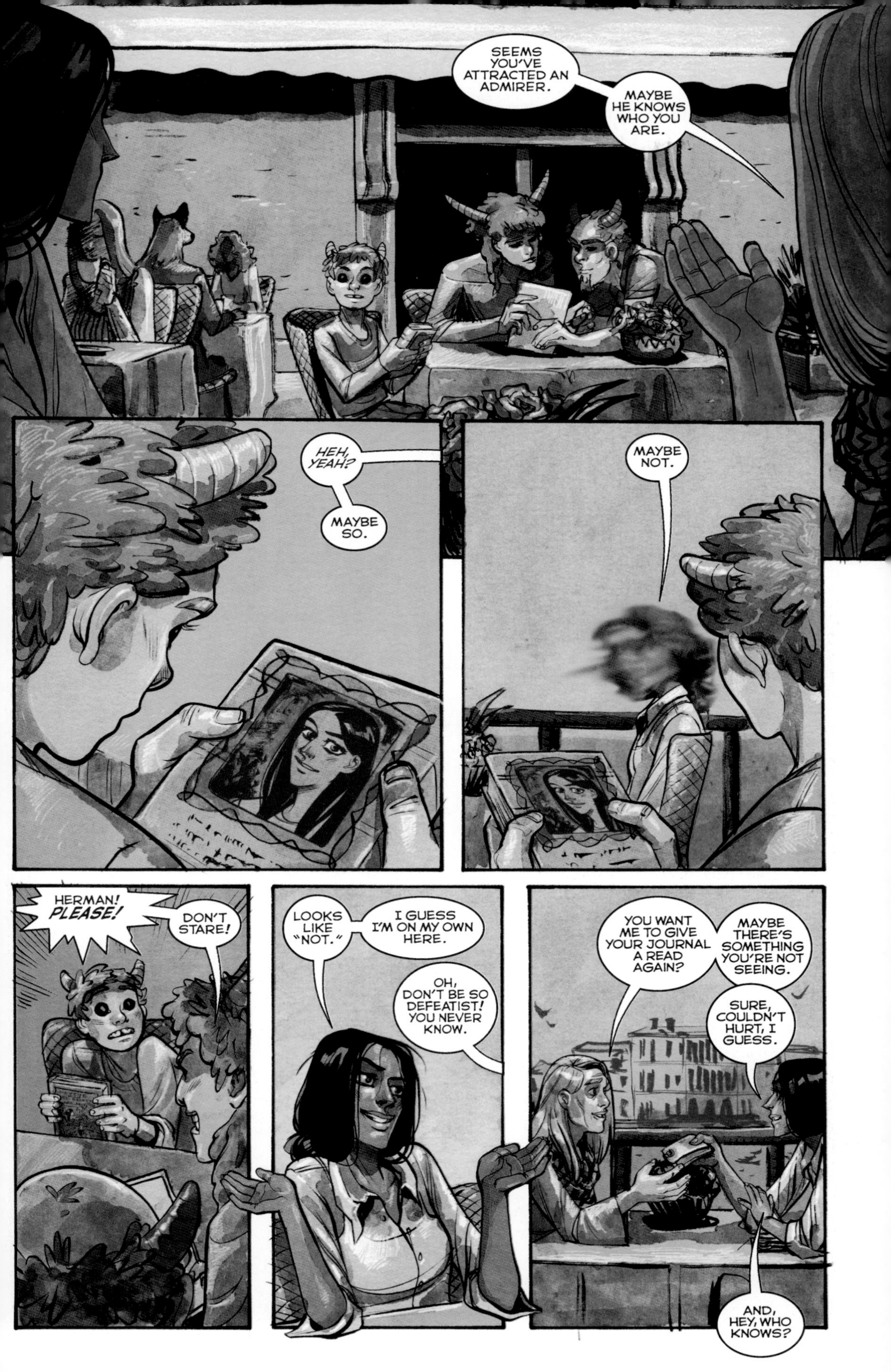
SEEMS YOU'VE ATTRACTED AN ADMIRER.
MAYBE HE KNOWS WHO YOU ARE.
HEH, YEAH?
MAYBE SO.
MAYBE NOT.
HERMAN! PLEASE!
DON'T STARE!
LOOKS LIKE "NOT."
I GUESS I'M ON MY OWN HERE.
OH, DON'T BE SO DEFEATIST! YOU NEVER KNOW.
YOU WANT ME TO GIVE YOUR JOURNAL A READ AGAIN?
MAYBE THERE'S SOMETHING YOU'RE NOT SEEING.
SURE, COULDN'T HURT, I GUESS.
AND, HEY, WHO KNOWS?

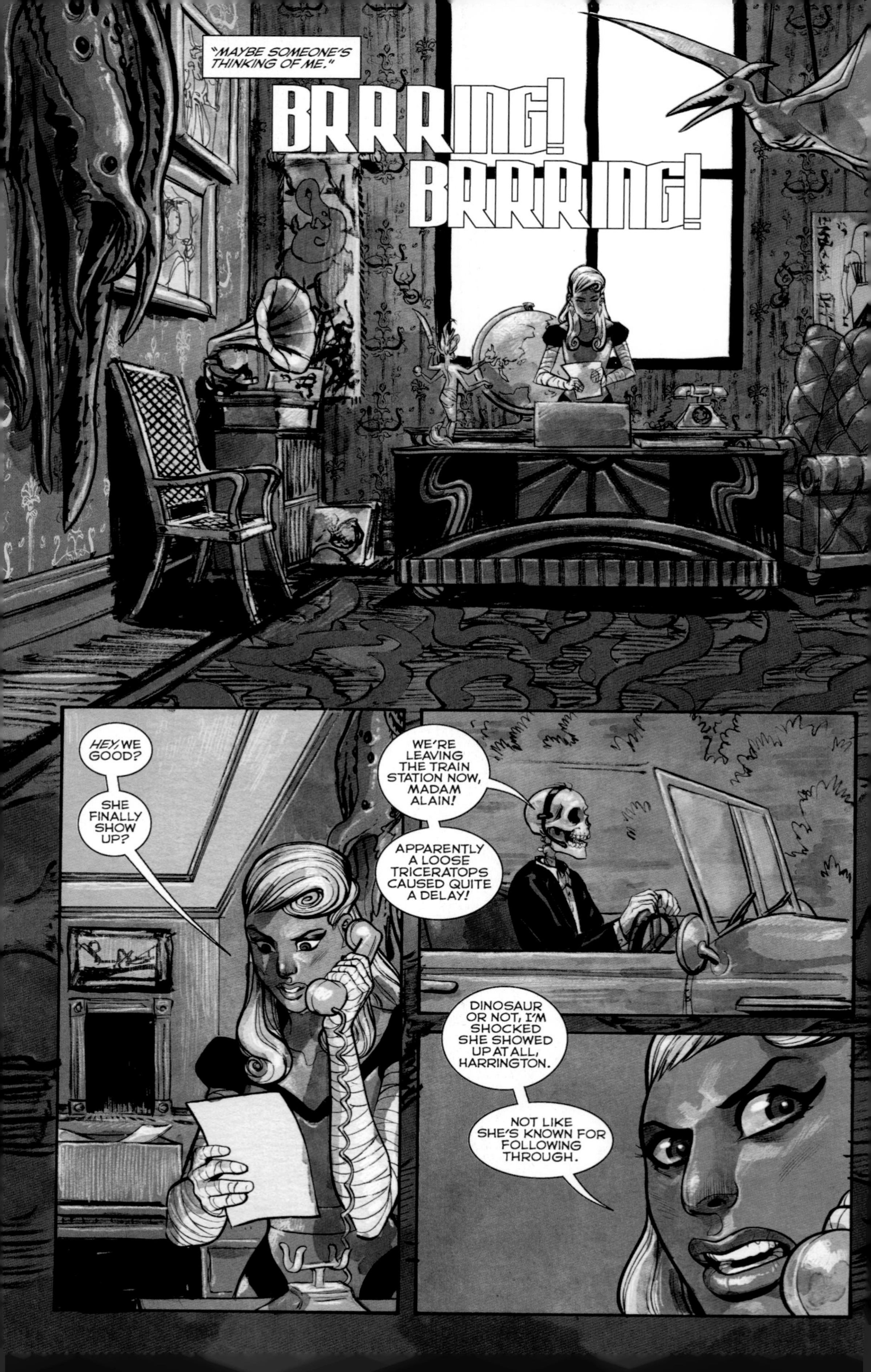
"MAYBE SOMEONE'S THINKING OF ME."
BRRRING!
BRRRING!
HEY, WE GOOD?
SHE FINALLY SHOW UP?
WE'RE LEAVING THE TRAIN STATION NOW, MADAM ALAIN!
APPARENTLY A LOOSE TRICERATOPS CAUSED QUITE A DELAY!
DINOSAUR OR NOT, I'M SHOCKED SHE SHOWED UP AT ALL, HARRINGTON.
NOT LIKE SHE'S KNOWN FOR FOLLOWING THROUGH.

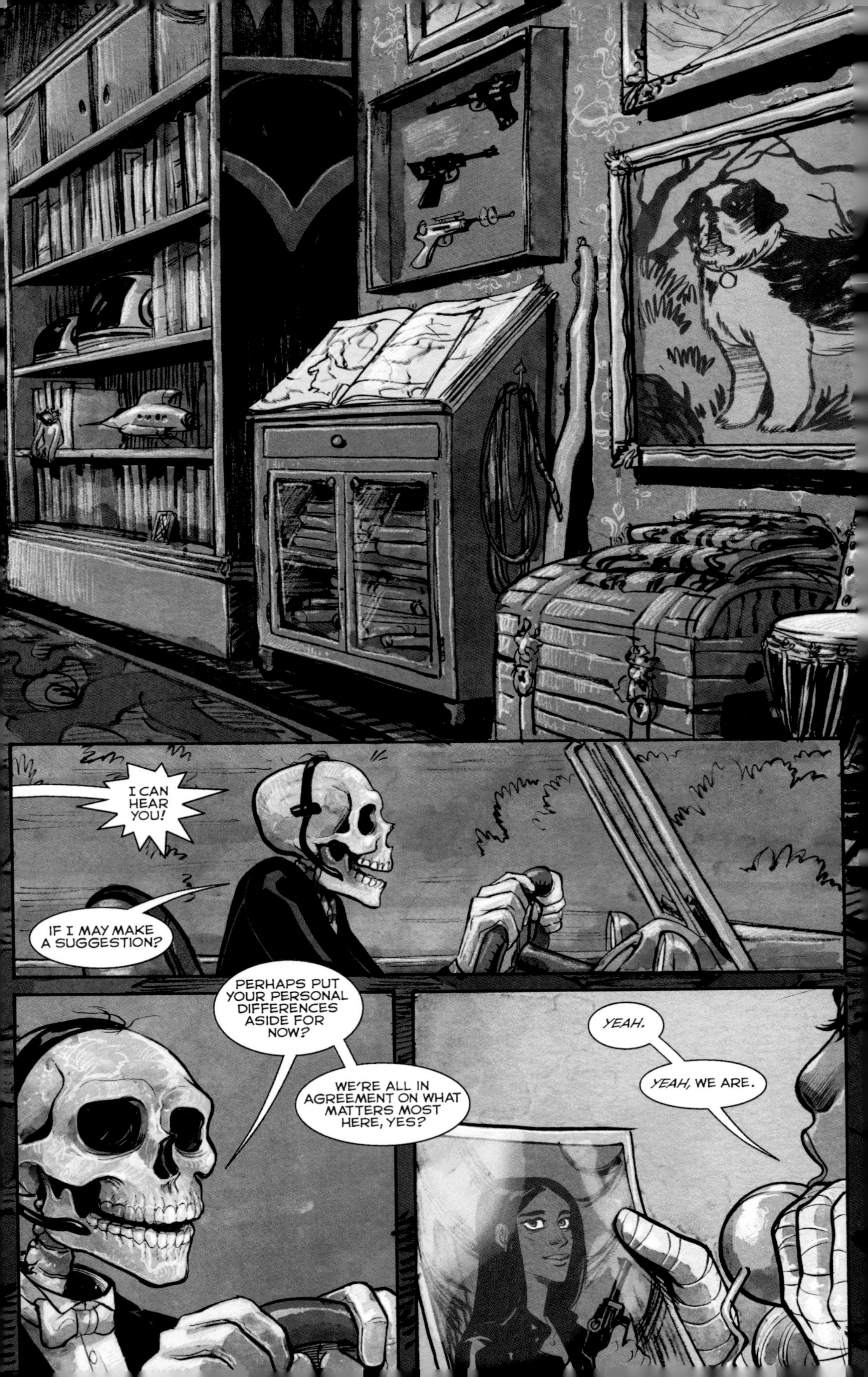
I CAN HEAR YOU!
IF I MAY MAKE A SUGGESTION?
PERHAPS PUT YOUR PERSONAL DIFFERENCES ASIDE FOR NOW?
WE'RE ALL IN AGREEMENT ON WHAT MATTERS MOST HERE, YES?
YEAH.
YEAH, WE ARE.

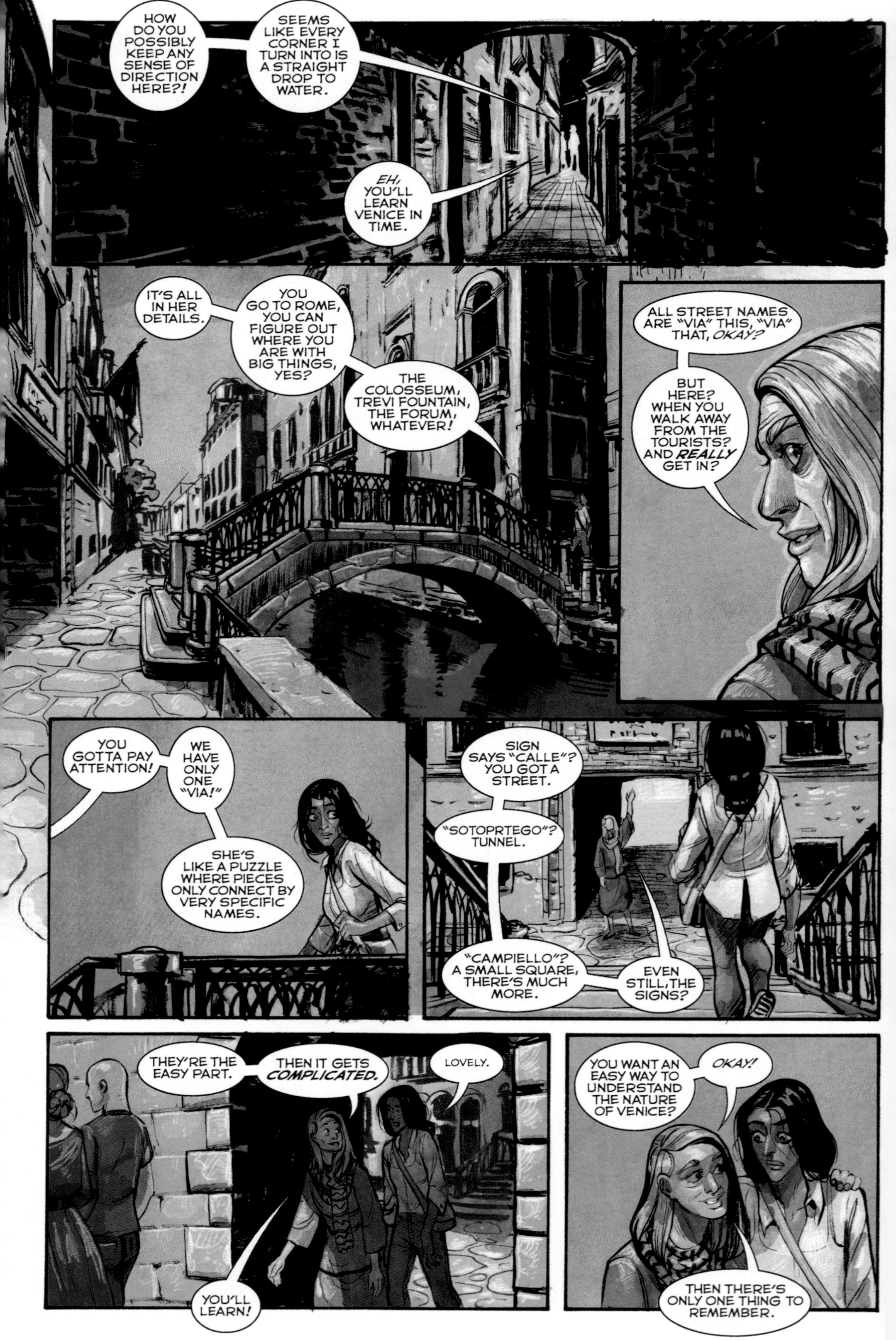
HOW DO YOU POSSIBLY KEEP ANY SENSE OF DIRECTION HERE?!
SEEMS LIKE EVERY CORNER I TURN INTO IS A STRAIGHT DROP TO WATER.
EH, YOU'LL LEARN VENICE IN TIME.
IT'S ALL IN HER DETAILS.
YOU GO TO ROME, YOU CAN FIGURE OUT WHERE YOU ARE WITH BIG THINGS, YES?
THE COLOSSEUM, TREVI FOUNTAIN, THE FORUM, WHATEVER!
ALL STREET NAMES ARE "VIA" THIS, "VIA" THAT, OKAY?
BUT HERE? WHEN YOU WALK AWAY FROM THE TOURISTS? AND REALLY GET IN?
YOU GOTTA PAY ATTENTION!
WE HAVE ONLY ONE "VIA!"
SHE'S LIKE A PUZZLE WHERE PIECES ONLY CONNECT BY VERY SPECIFIC NAMES.
SIGN SAYS "CALLE"? YOU GOT A STREET.
"SOTOPRTEGO"? TUNNEL.
"CAMPIELLO"? A SMALL SQUARE, THERE'S MUCH MORE.
EVEN STILL, THE SIGNS?
THEY'RE THE EASY PART.
THEN IT GETS COMPLICATED.
LOVELY.
YOU'LL LEARN!
YOU WANT AN EASY WAY TO UNDERSTAND THE NATURE OF VENICE?
OKAY!
THEN THERE'S ONLY ONE THING TO REMEMBER.

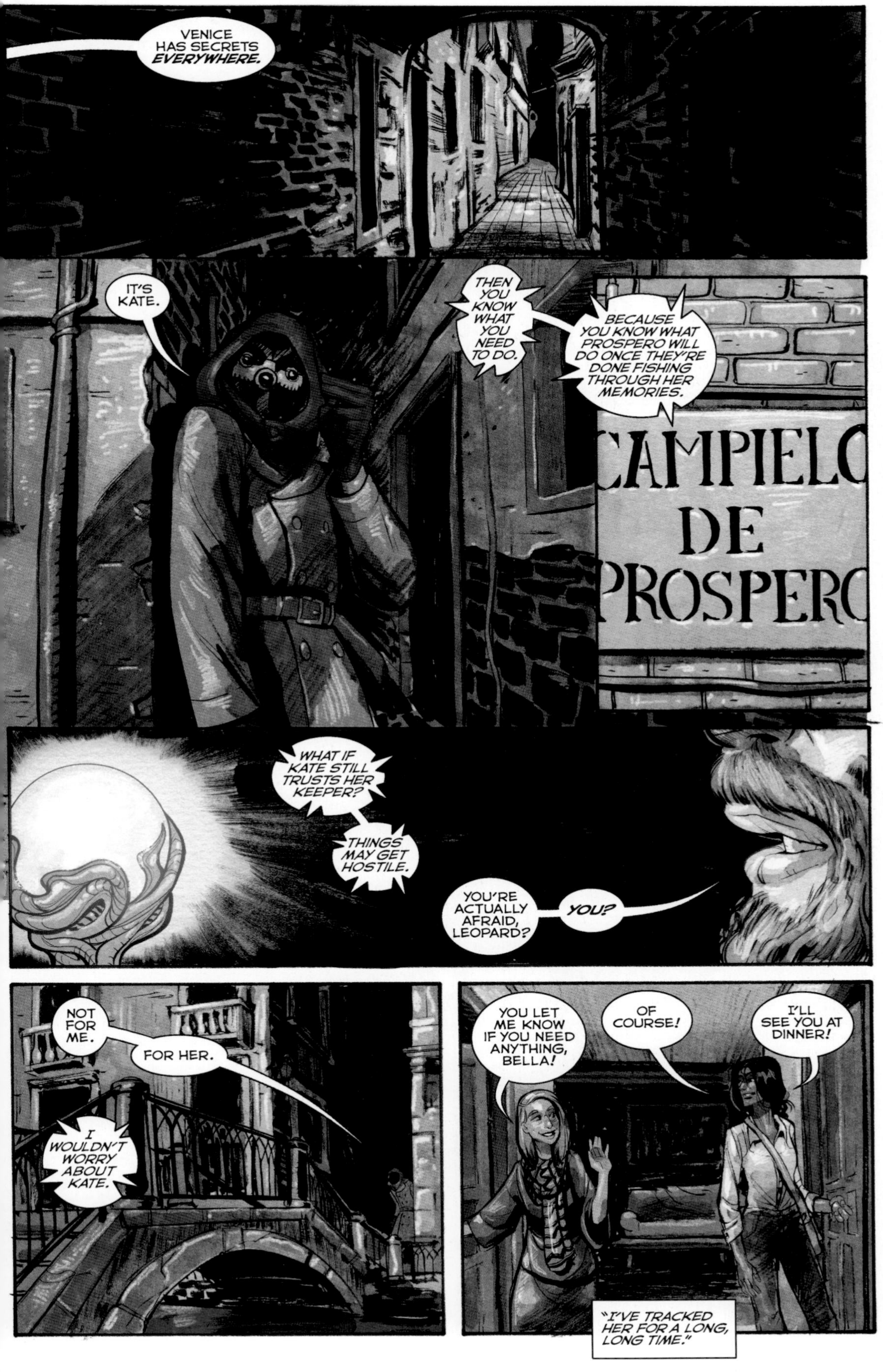
VENICE HAS SECRETS EVERYWHERE.
IT'S KATE.
THEN YOU KNOW WHAT YOU NEED TO DO.
BECAUSE YOU KNOW WHAT PROSPERO WILL DO ONCE THEY'RE DONE FISHING THROUGH HER MEMORIES.
CAMPIELO DE PROSPERO
WHAT IF KATE STILL TRUSTS HER KEEPER?
THINGS MAY GET HOSTILE.
YOU'RE ACTUALLY AFRAID, LEOPARD?
YOU?
NOT FOR ME.
FOR HER.
I WOULDN'T WORRY ABOUT KATE.
YOU LET ME KNOW IF YOU NEED ANYTHING, BELLA!
OF COURSE!
I'LL SEE YOU AT DINNER!
"I'VE TRACKED HER FOR A LONG, LONG TIME."

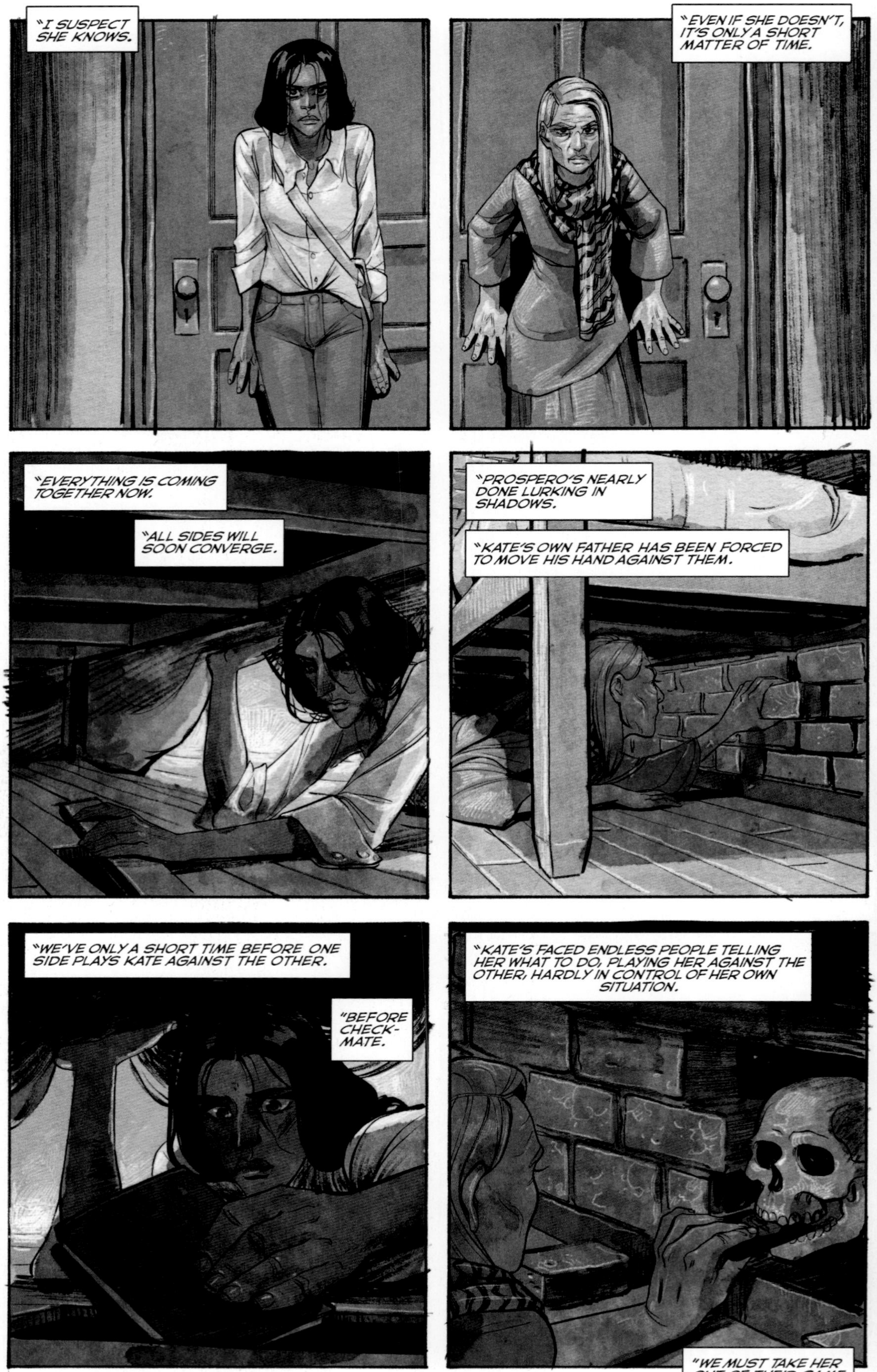
"I SUSPECT SHE KNOWS.
"EVEN IF SHE DOESN'T, IT'S ONLY A SHORT MATTER OF TIME.
"EVERYTHING IS COMING TOGETHER NOW.
"ALL SIDES WILL SOON CONVERGE.
"PROSPERO'S NEARLY DONE LURKING IN SHADOWS.
"KATE'S OWN FATHER HAS BEEN FORCED TO MOVE HIS HAND AGAINST THEM.
"WE'VE ONLY A SHORT TIME BEFORE ONE SIDE PLAYS KATE AGAINST THE OTHER.
"BEFORE CHECK-MATE.
"KATE'S FACED ENDLESS PEOPLE TELLING HER WHAT TO DO, PLAYING HER AGAINST THE OTHER, HARDLY IN CONTROL OF HER OWN SITUATION.
"WE MUST TAKE HER OUT OF THEIR GAME.

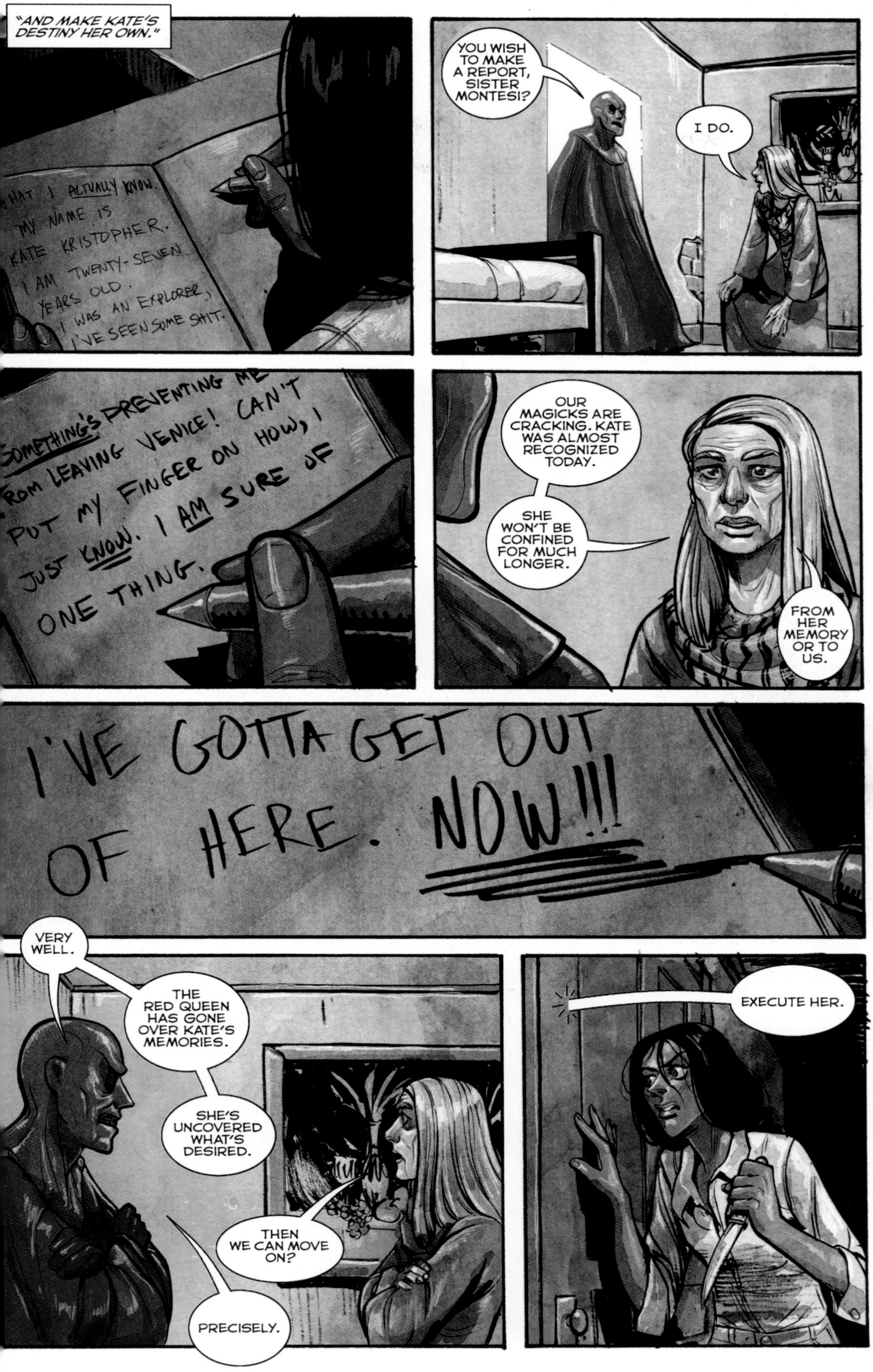
"AND MAKE KATE'S DESTINY HER OWN."
WHAT I ACTUALLY KNOW. MY NAME IS KATE KRISTOPHER. I AM TWENTY-SEVEN YEARS OLD. I WAS AN EXPLORER, I'VE SEEN SOME SHIT.
YOU WISH TO MAKE A REPORT, SISTER MONTESI?
I DO.
SOMETHING'S PREVENTING ME FROM LEAVING VENICE! CAN'T PUT MY FINGER ON HOW, I JUST KNOW. I AM SURE OF ONE THING.
OUR MAGICKS ARE CRACKING. KATE WAS ALMOST RECOGNIZED TODAY.
SHE WON'T BE CONFINED FOR MUCH LONGER.
FROM HER MEMORY OR TO US.
I'VE GOTTA GET OUT OF HERE. NOW!!!
VERY WELL.
THE RED QUEEN HAS GONE OVER KATE'S MEMORIES.
SHE'S UNCOVERED WHAT'S DESIRED.
THEN WE CAN MOVE ON?
PRECISELY.
EXECUTE HER.

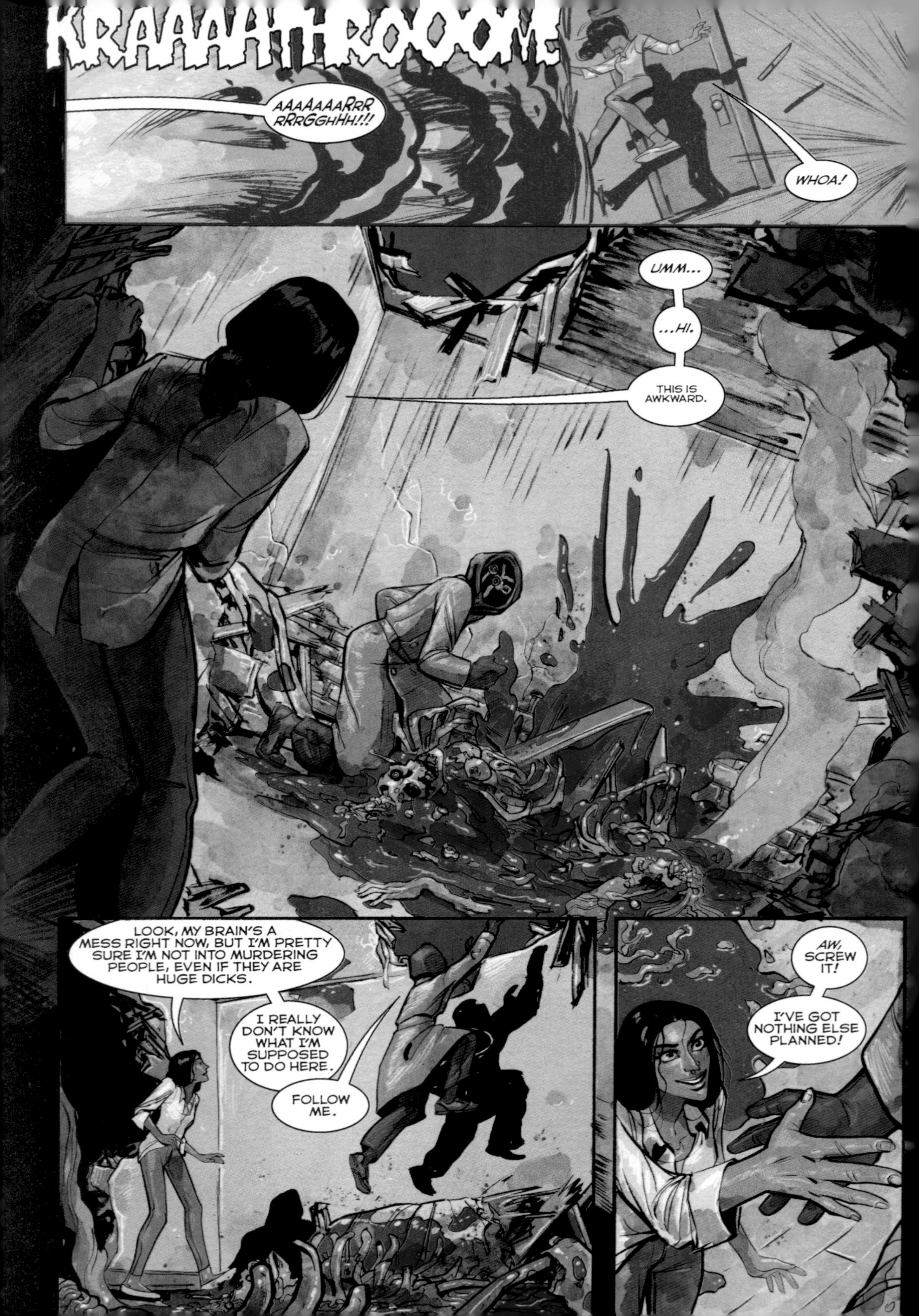
KRAAAHTROOOM!
AAAAAAARRR RRRGHHH!!!
WHOA!
UMM...
...HI.
THIS IS AWKWARD.
LOOK, MY BRAIN'S A MESS RIGHT NOW, BUT I'M PRETTY SURE I'M NOT INTO MURDERING PEOPLE, EVEN IF THEY ARE HUGE DICKS.
I REALLY DON'T KNOW WHAT I'M SUPPOSED TO DO HERE.
FOLLOW ME.
AW, SCREW IT!
I'VE GOT NOTHING ELSE PLANNED!

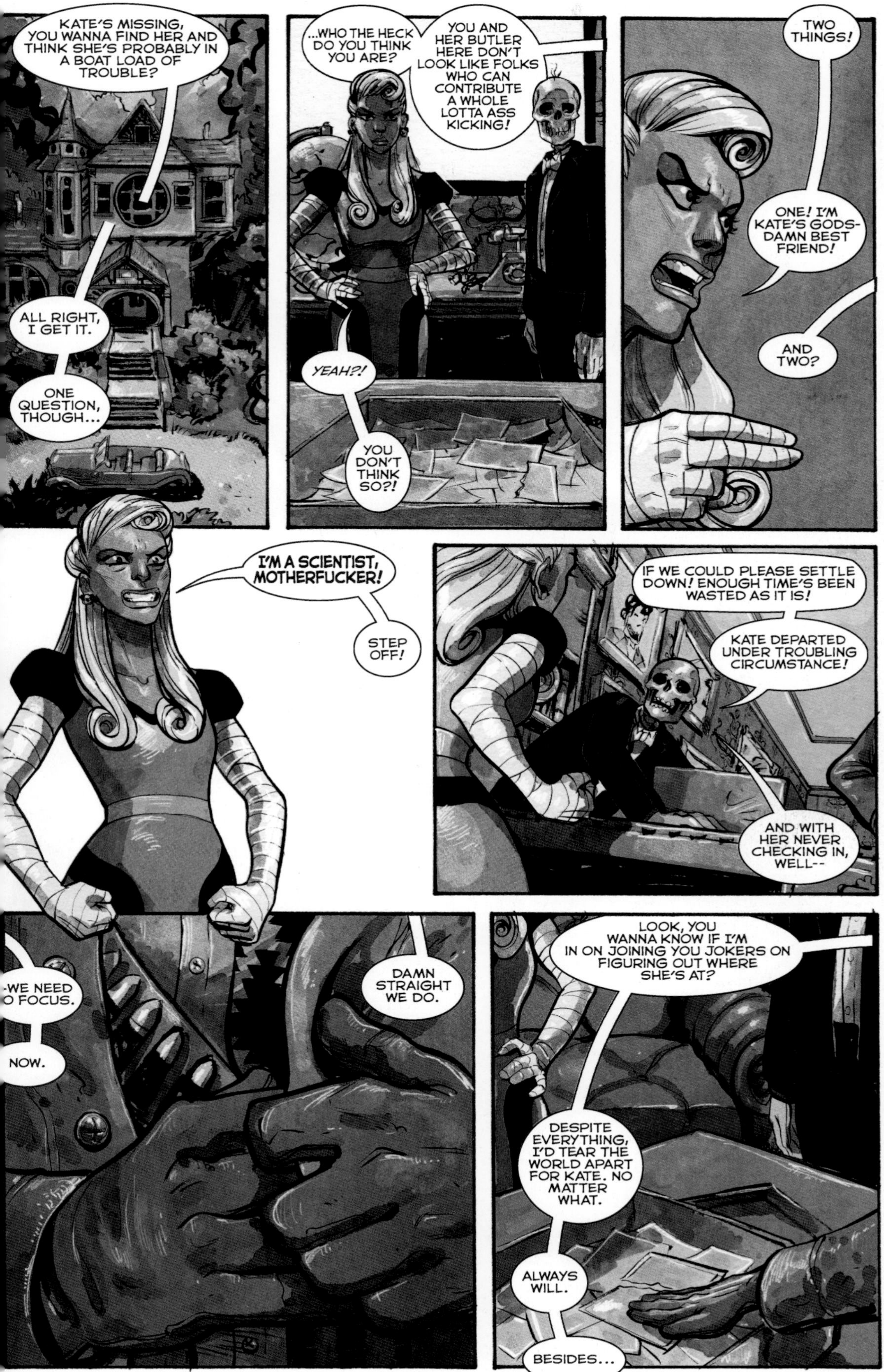

KATE'S MISSING, YOU WANNA FIND HER AND THINK SHE'S PROBABLY IN A BOAT LOAD OF TROUBLE?
ALL RIGHT, I GET IT.
ONE QUESTION, THOUGH...
...WHO THE HECK DO YOU THINK YOU ARE?
YOU AND HER BUTLER HERE DON'T LOOK LIKE FOLKS WHO CAN CONTRIBUTE A WHOLE LOTTA ASS KICKING!
YEAH?!
YOU DON'T THINK SO?!
TWO THINGS!
ONE! I'M KATE'S GODS-DAMN BEST FRIEND!
AND TWO?
I'M A SCIENTIST, MOTHERFUCKER!
STEP OFF!
IF WE COULD PLEASE SETTLE DOWN! ENOUGH TIME'S BEEN WASTED AS IT IS!
KATE DEPARTED UNDER TROUBLING CIRCUMSTANCE!
AND WITH HER NEVER CHECKING IN, WELL--
-WE NEED O FOCUS.
NOW.
DAMN STRAIGHT WE DO.
LOOK, YOU WANNA KNOW IF I'M IN ON JOINING YOU JOKERS ON FIGURING OUT WHERE SHE'S AT?
DESPITE EVERYTHING, I'D TEAR THE WORLD APART FOR KATE. NO MATTER WHAT.
ALWAYS WILL.
BESIDES...

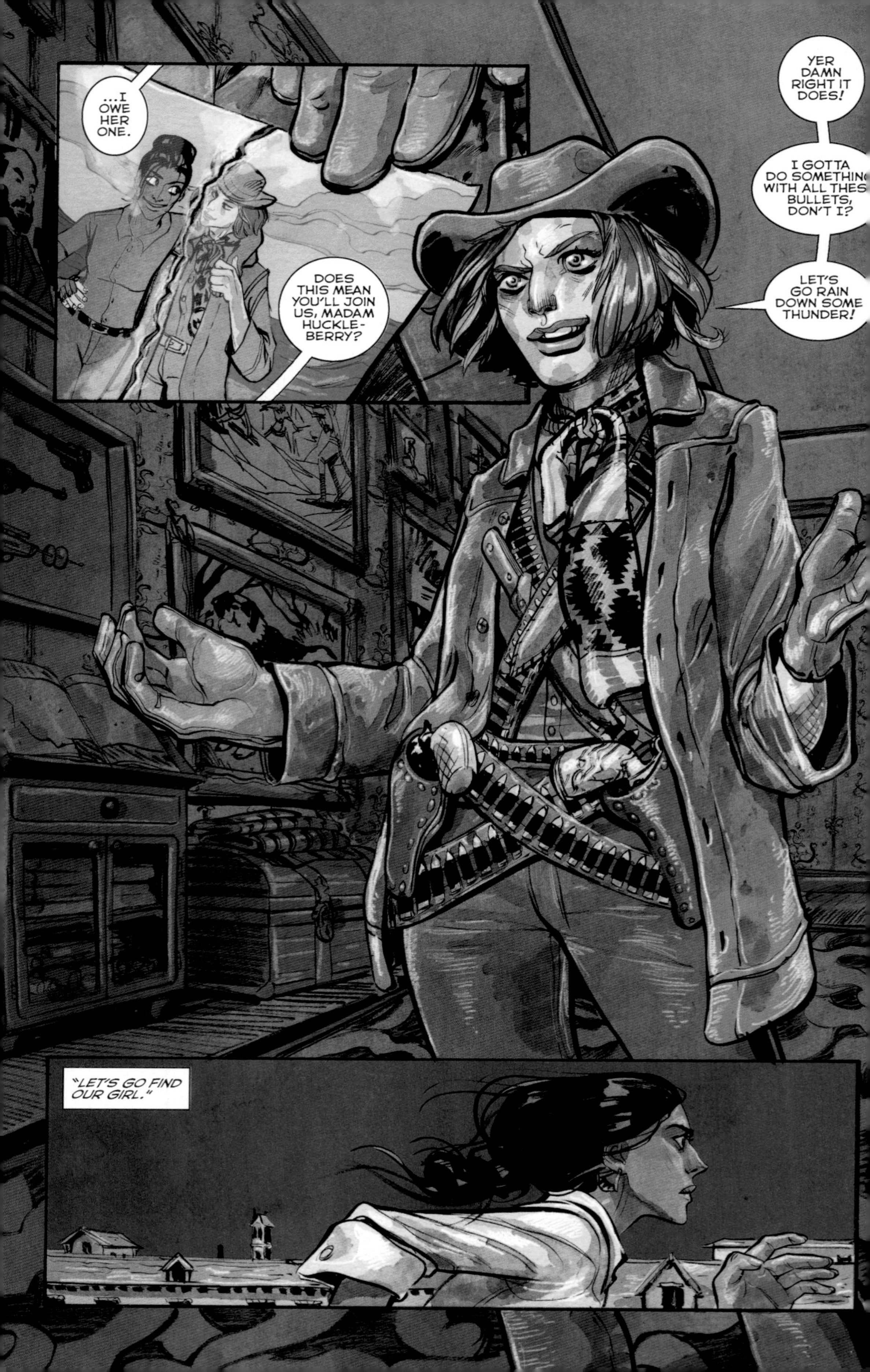
...I OWE HER ONE.
DOES THIS MEAN YOU'LL JOIN US, MADAM HUCKLE-BERRY?
YER DAMN RIGHT IT DOES!
I GOTTA DO SOMETHIN WITH ALL THES BULLETS, DON'T I?
LET'S GO RAIN DOWN SOME THUNDER!
"LET'S GO FIND OUR GIRL."

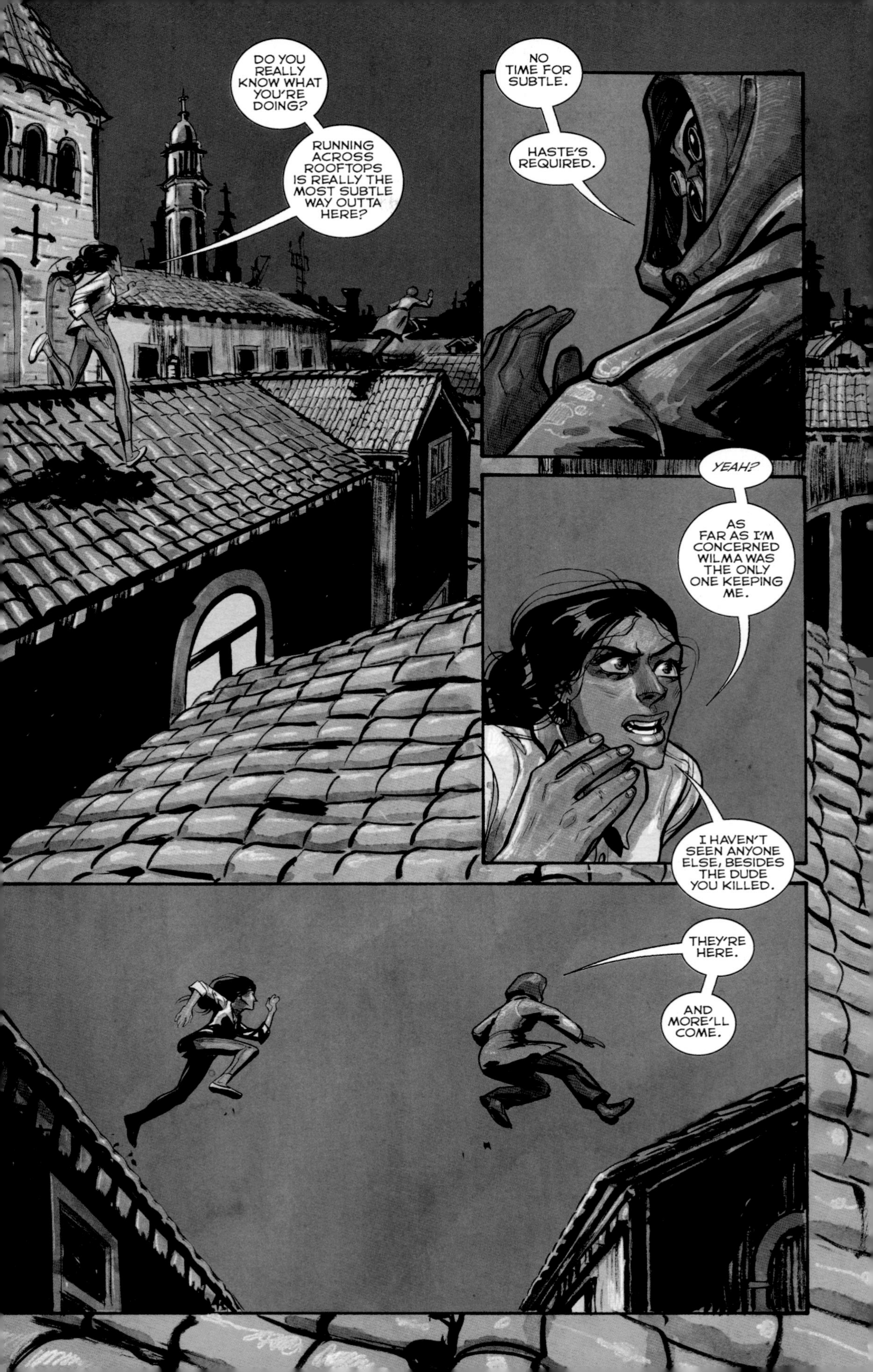
DO YOU REALLY KNOW WHAT YOU'RE DOING?
RUNNING ACROSS ROOFTOPS IS REALLY THE MOST SUBTLE WAY OUTTA HERE?
NO TIME FOR SUBTLE.
HASTE'S REQUIRED.
YEAH?
AS FAR AS I'M CONCERNED WILMA WAS THE ONLY ONE KEEPING ME.
I HAVEN'T SEEN ANYONE ELSE, BESIDES THE DUDE YOU KILLED.
THEY'RE HERE.
AND MORE'LL COME.

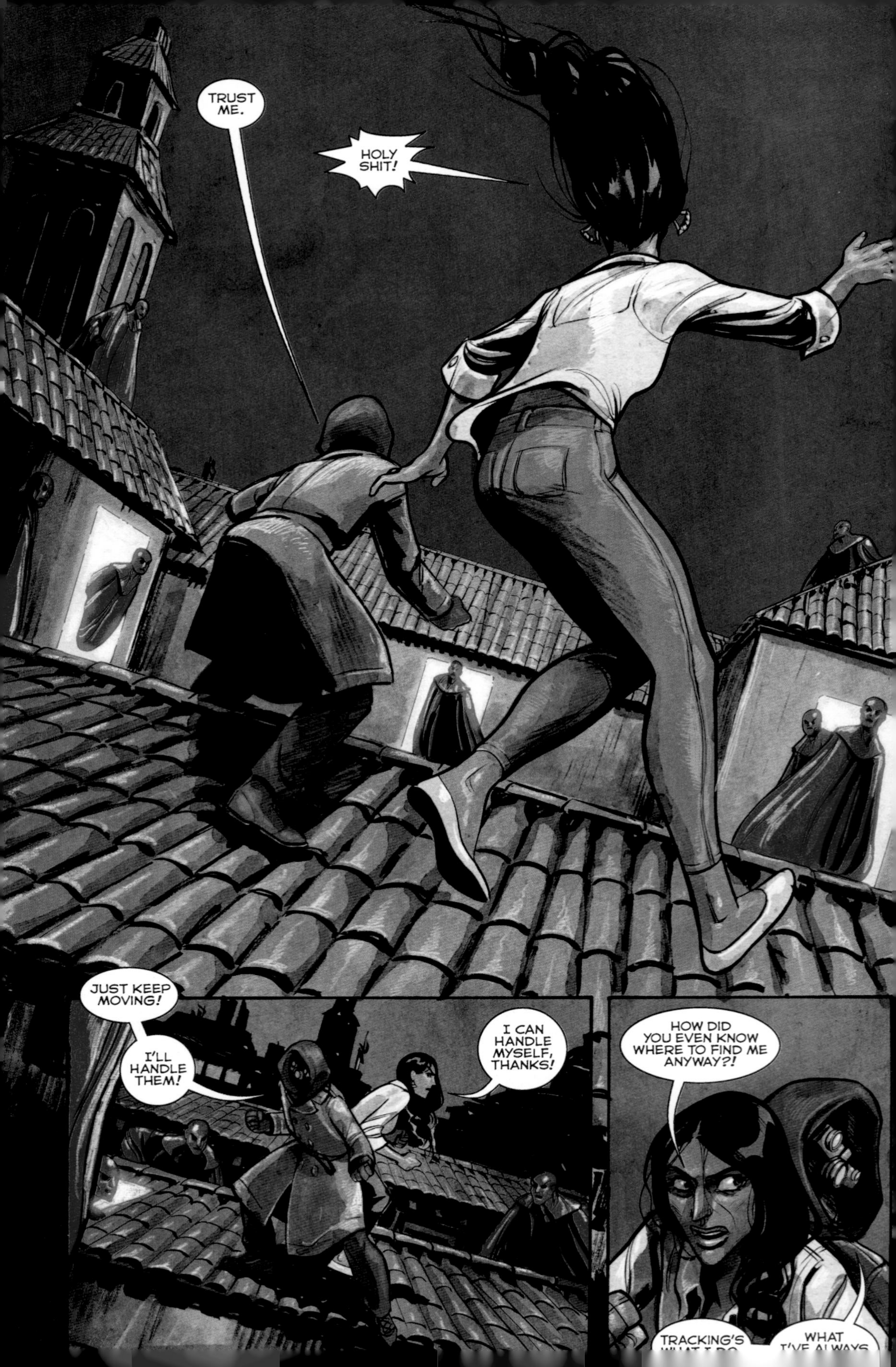
TRUST ME.
HOLY SHIT!
JUST KEEP MOVING!
I'LL HANDLE THEM!
I CAN HANDLE MYSELF, THANKS!
HOW DID YOU EVEN KNOW WHERE TO FIND ME ANYWAY?!
TRACKING'S
WHAT

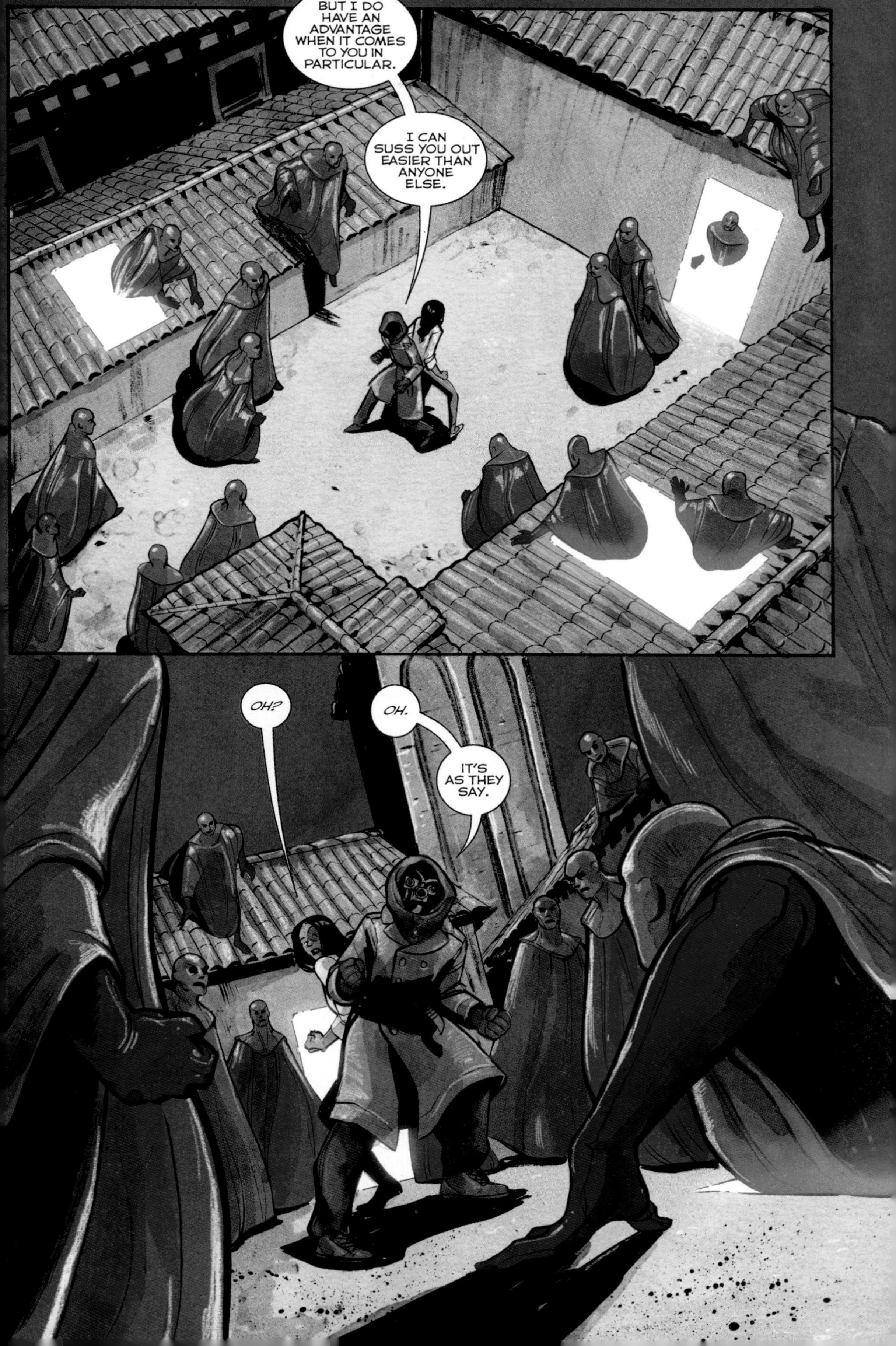
BUT I DO HAVE AN ADVANTAGE WHEN IT COMES TO YOU IN PARTICULAR.
I CAN SUSS YOU OUT EASIER THAN ANYONE ELSE.
OH?
OH.
IT'S AS THEY SAY.

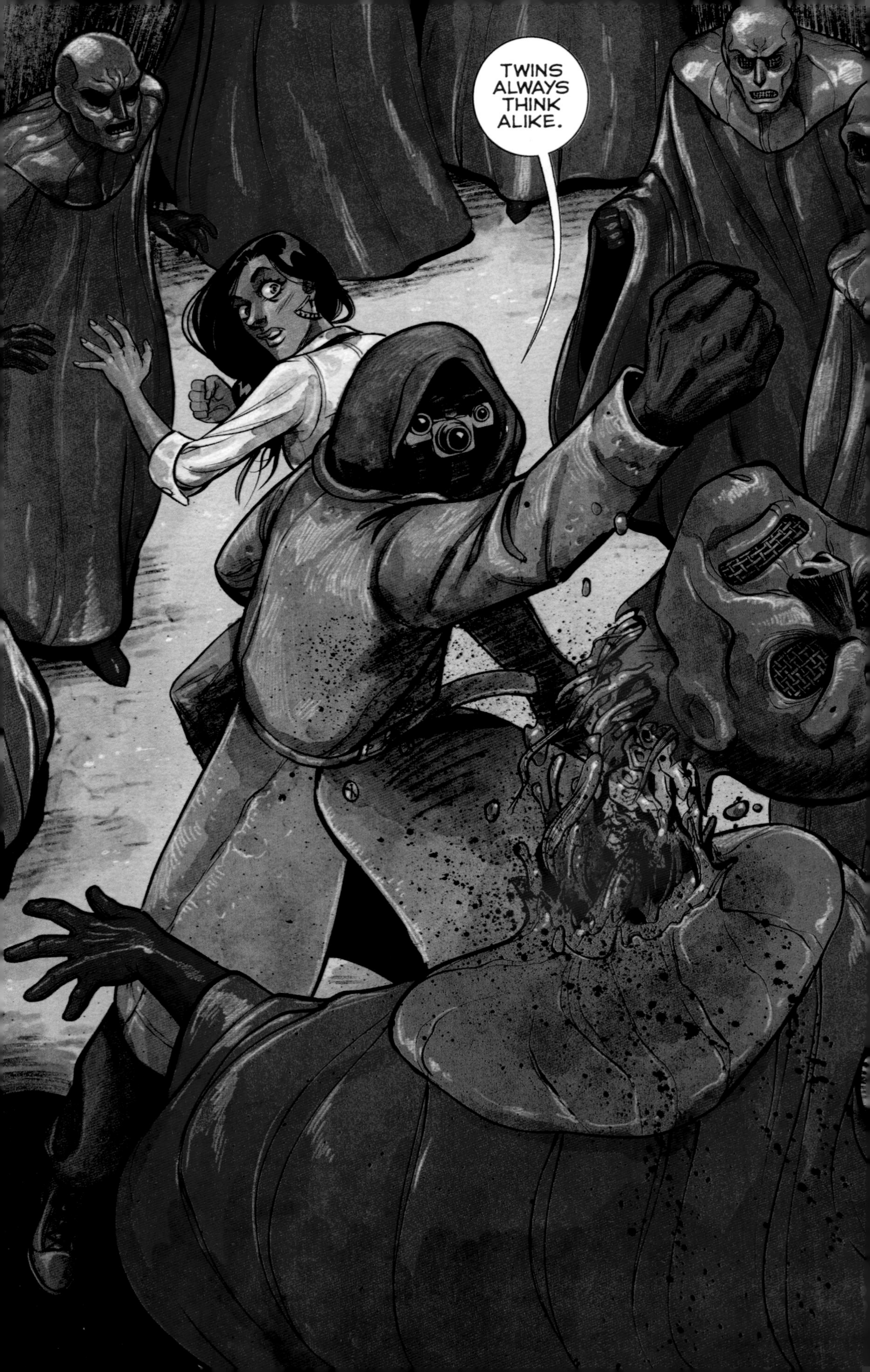
TWINS ALWAYS THINK ALIKE.

CHAPTER 14

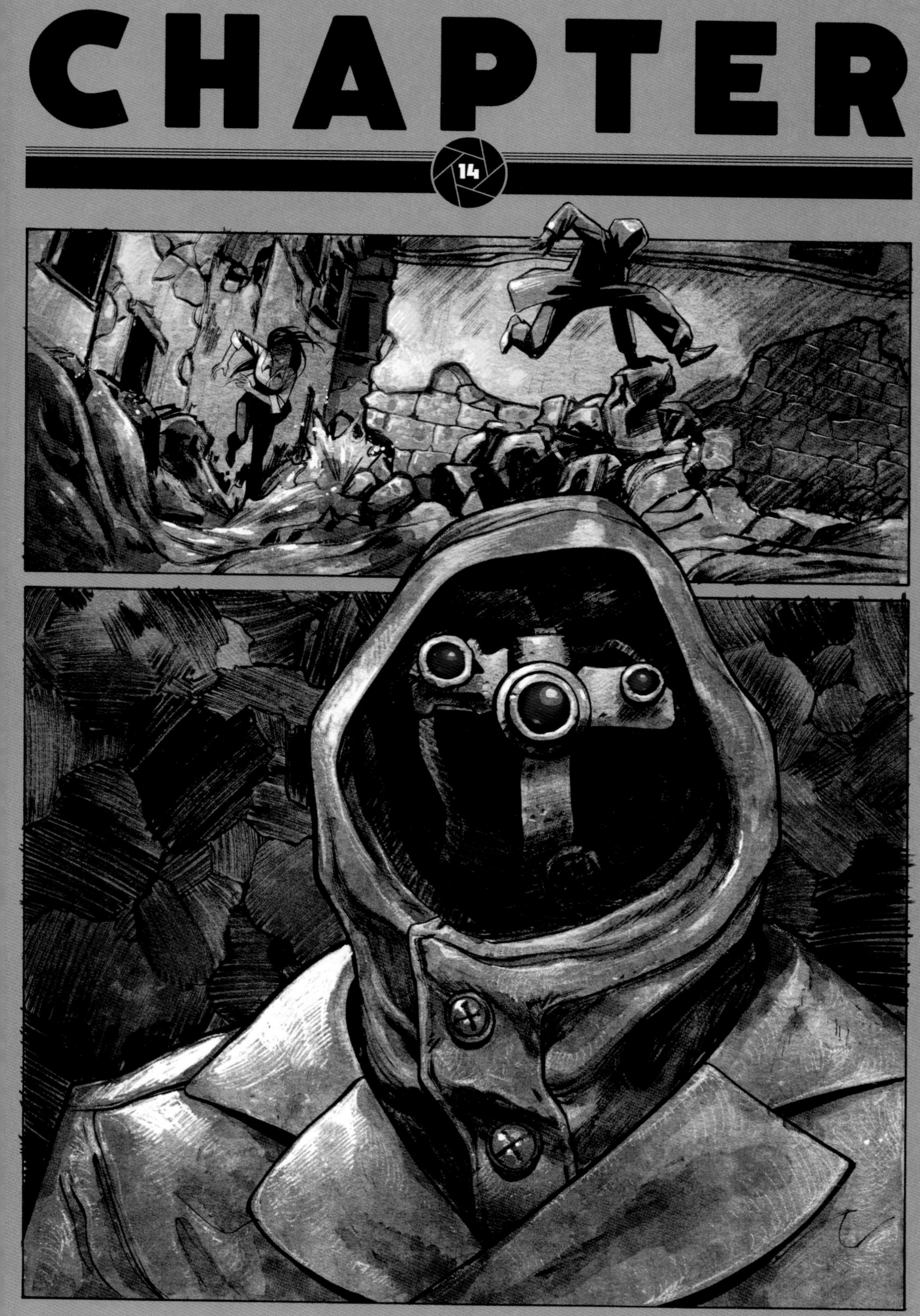

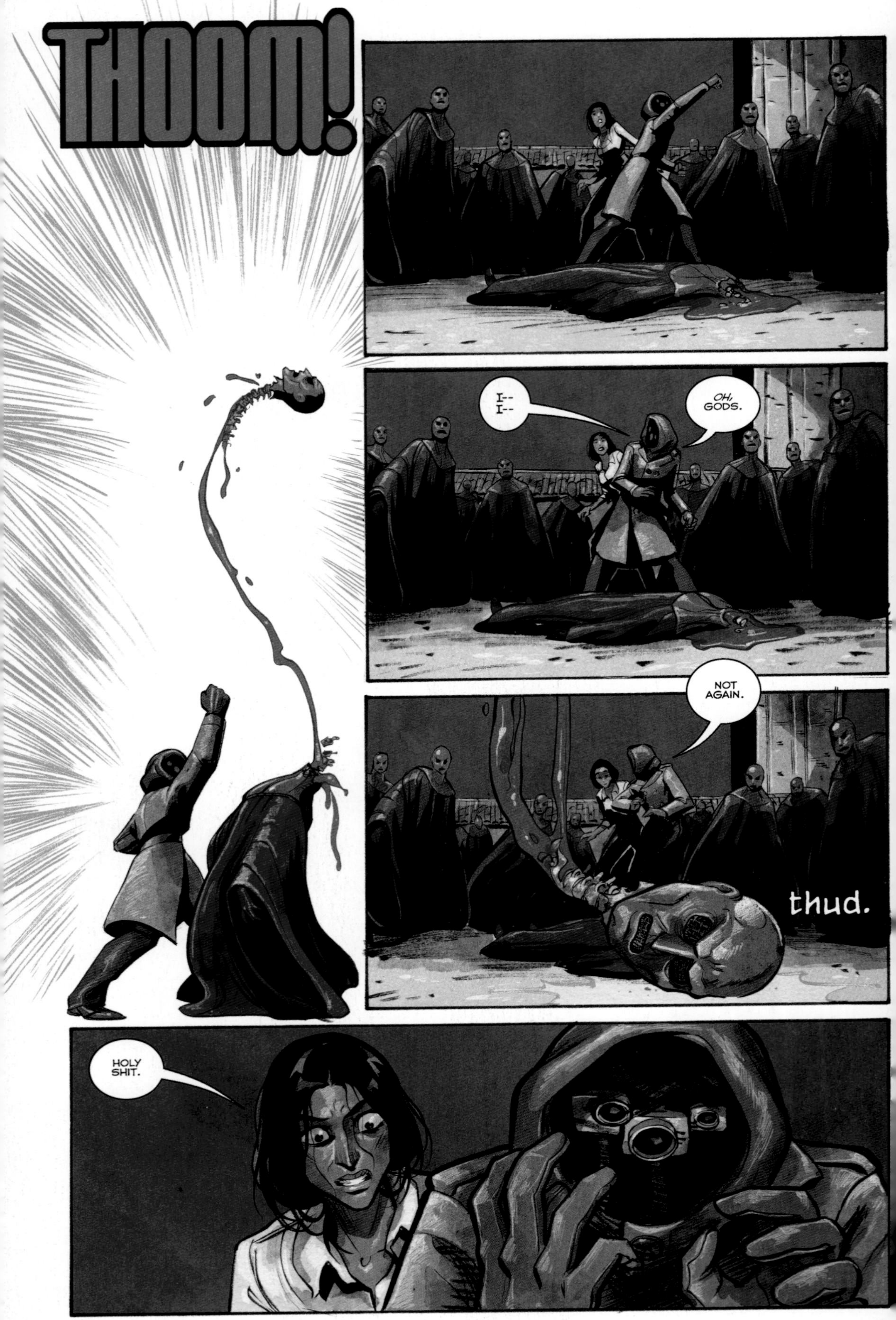
THOOM!
I--
I--
OH, GODS.
NOT AGAIN.
thud.
HOLY SHIT.

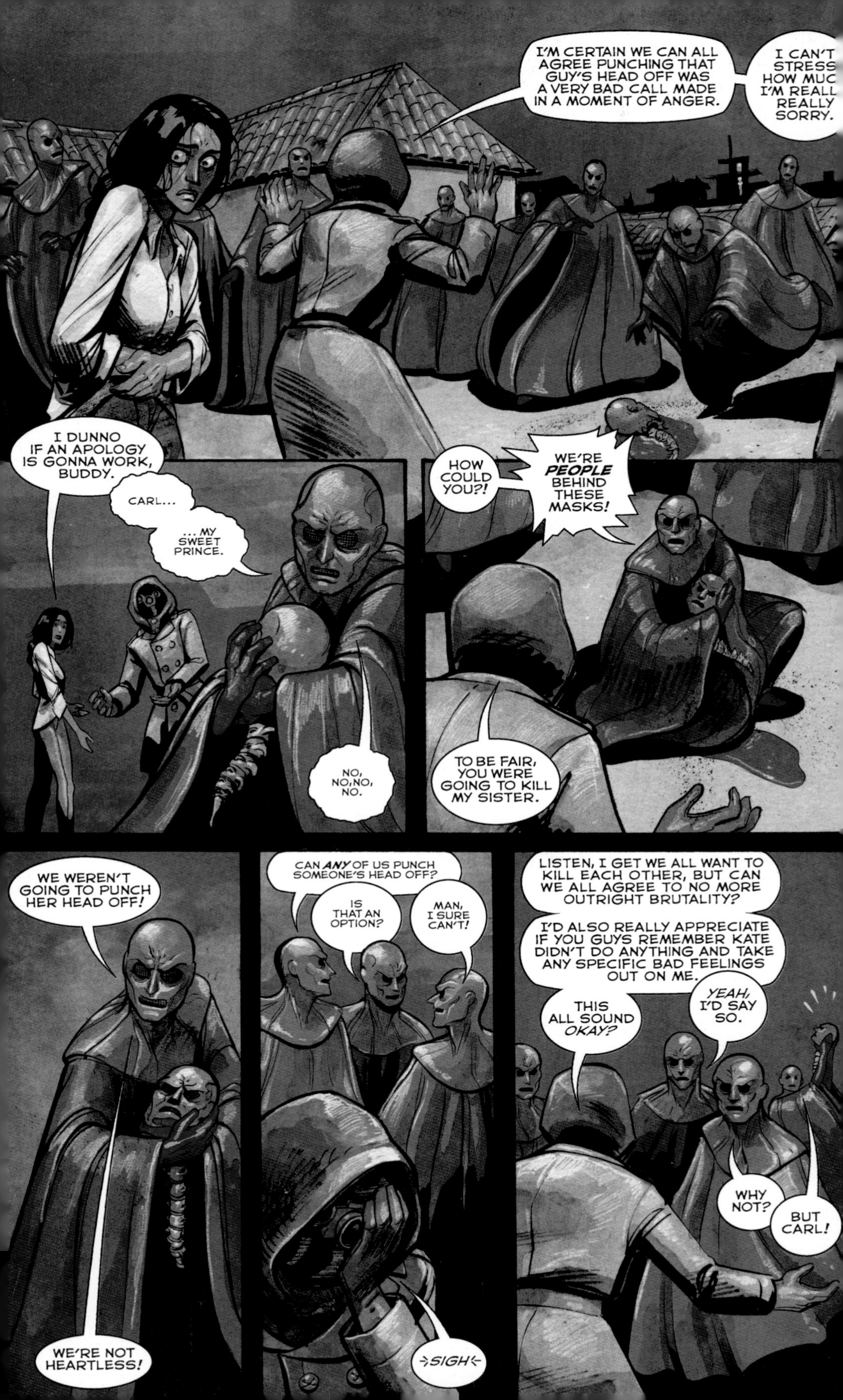
I'M CERTAIN WE CAN ALL AGREE PUNCHING THAT GUY'S HEAD OFF WAS A VERY BAD CALL MADE IN A MOMENT OF ANGER.
I CAN'T STRESS HOW MUC I'M REALL REALLY SORRY.
I DUNNO IF AN APOLOGY IS GONNA WORK, BUDDY.
CARL...
...MY SWEET PRINCE.
NO, NO, NO, NO.
HOW COULD YOU?!
WE'RE *PEOPLE* BEHIND THESE MASKS!
TO BE FAIR, YOU WERE GOING TO KILL MY SISTER.
WE WEREN'T GOING TO PUNCH HER HEAD OFF!
WE'RE NOT HEARTLESS!
CAN *ANY* OF US PUNCH SOMEONE'S HEAD OFF?
IS THAT AN OPTION?
MAN, I SURE CAN'T!
SIGH
LISTEN, I GET WE ALL WANT TO KILL EACH OTHER, BUT CAN WE ALL AGREE TO NO MORE OUTRIGHT BRUTALITY?
I'D ALSO REALLY APPRECIATE IF YOU GUYS REMEMBER KATE DIDN'T DO ANYTHING AND TAKE ANY SPECIFIC BAD FEELINGS OUT ON ME.
THIS ALL SOUND *OKAY?*
YEAH, I'D SAY SO.
WHY NOT?
BUT CARL!

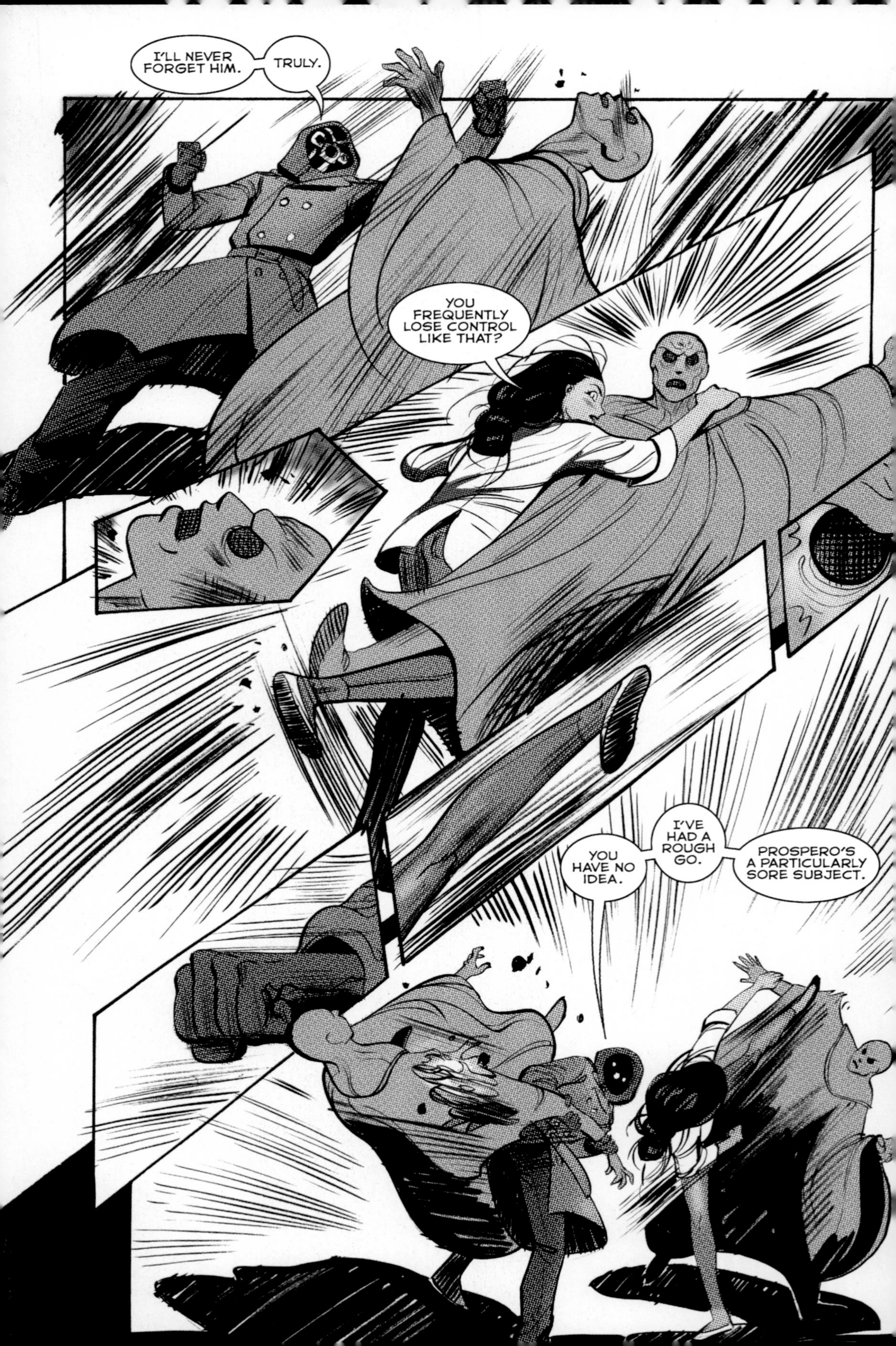
I'LL NEVER FORGET HIM.
TRULY.
YOU FREQUENTLY LOSE CONTROL LIKE THAT?
YOU HAVE NO IDEA.
I'VE HAD A ROUGH GO.
PROSPERO'S A PARTICULARLY SORE SUBJECT.

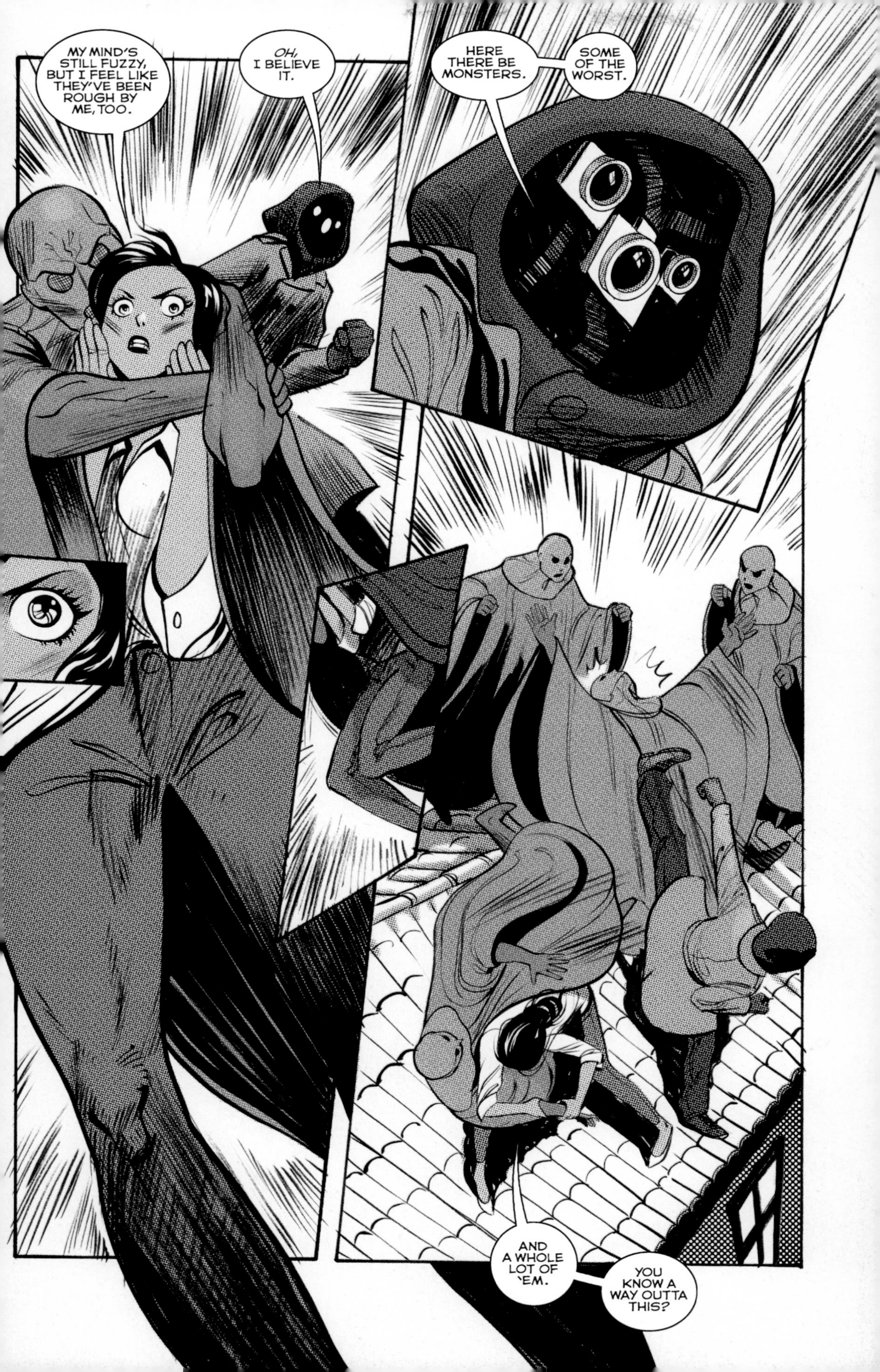
MY MIND'S STILL FUZZY, BUT I FEEL LIKE THEY'VE BEEN ROUGH BY ME, TOO.
OH, I BELIEVE IT.
HERE THERE BE MONSTERS.
SOME OF THE WORST.
AND A WHOLE LOT OF 'EM.
YOU KNOW A WAY OUTTA THIS?

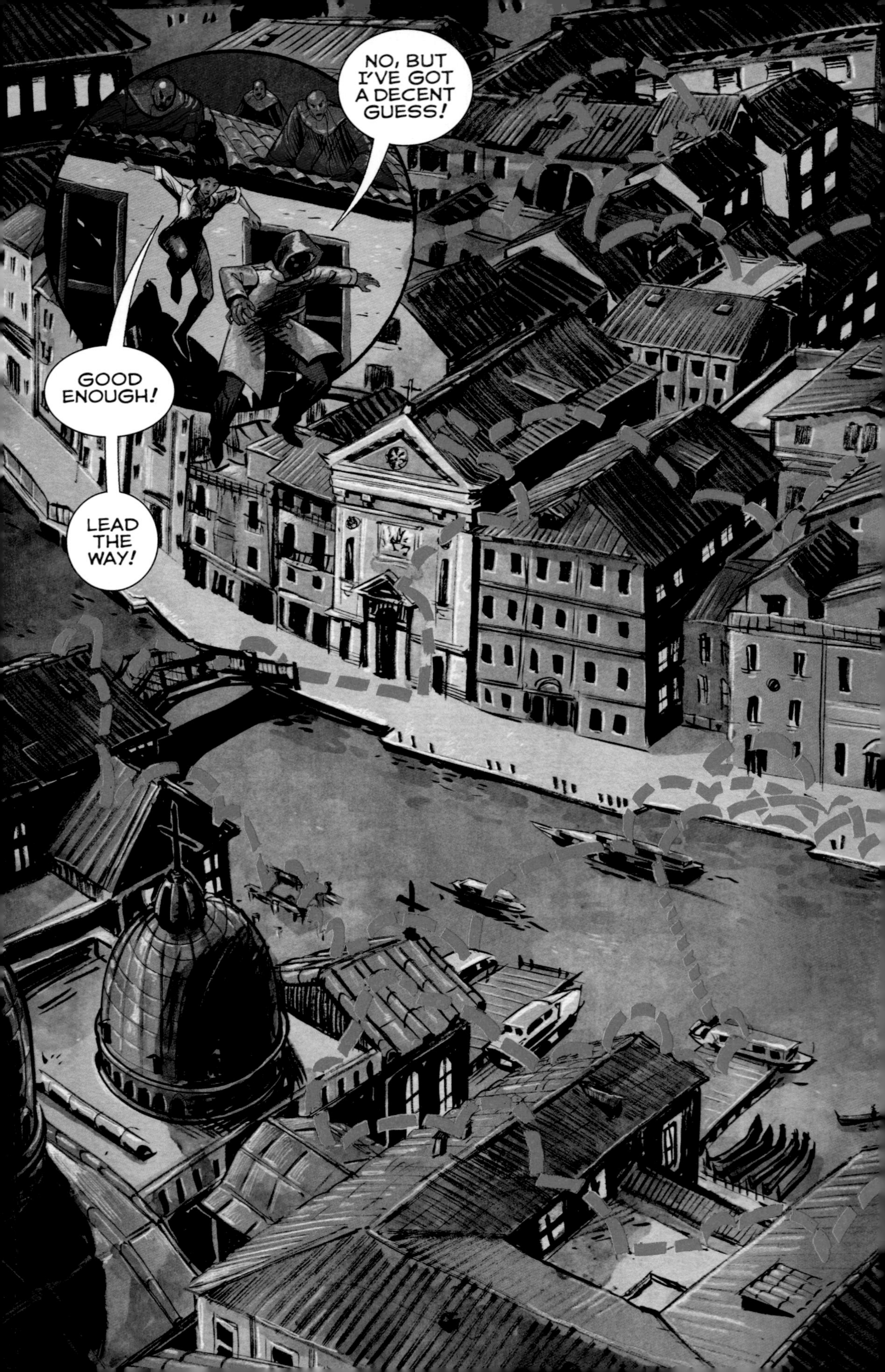
NO, BUT I'VE GOT A DECENT GUESS!
GOOD ENOUGH!
LEAD THE WAY!

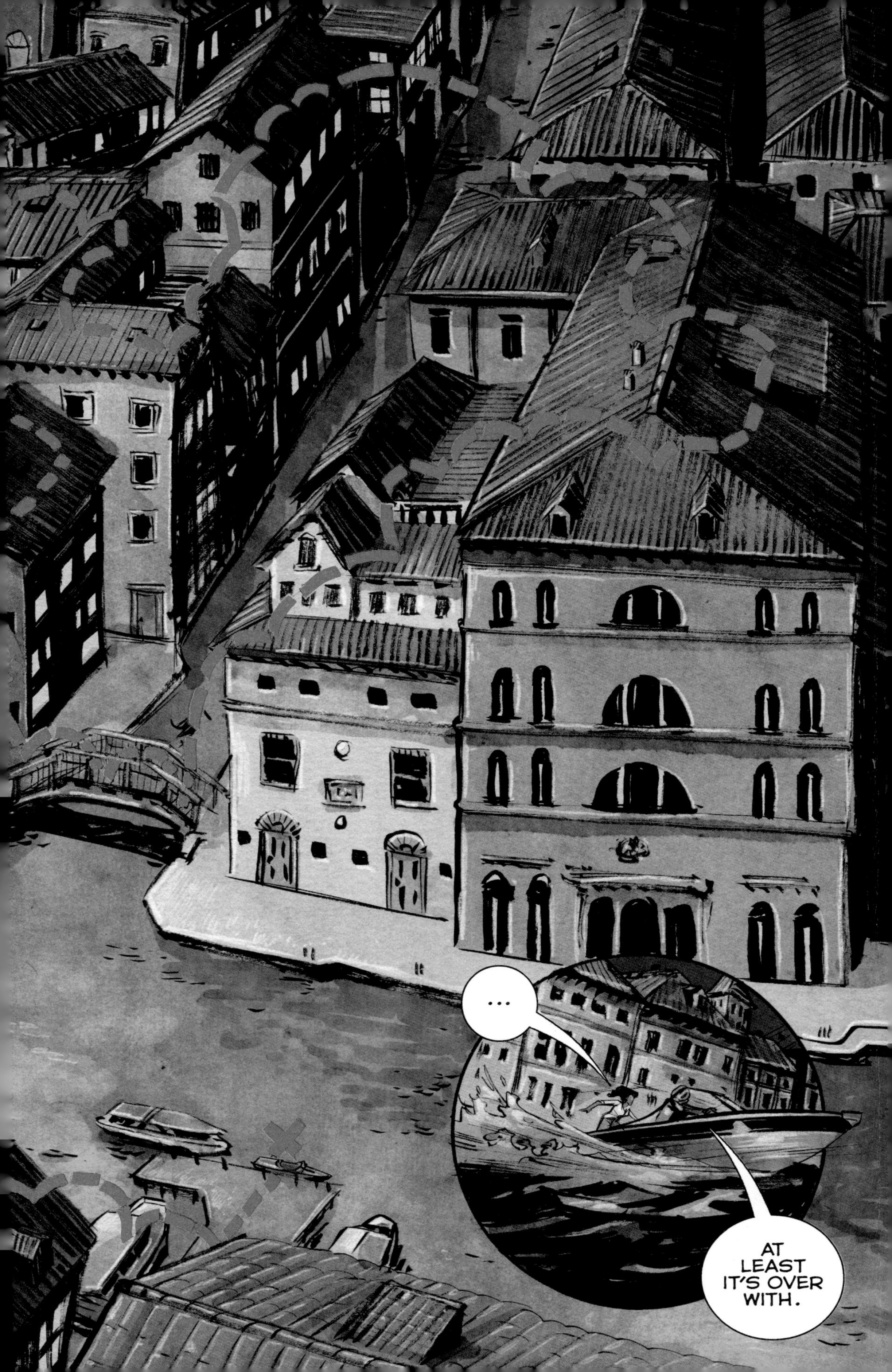
...
AT LEAST IT'S OVER WITH.

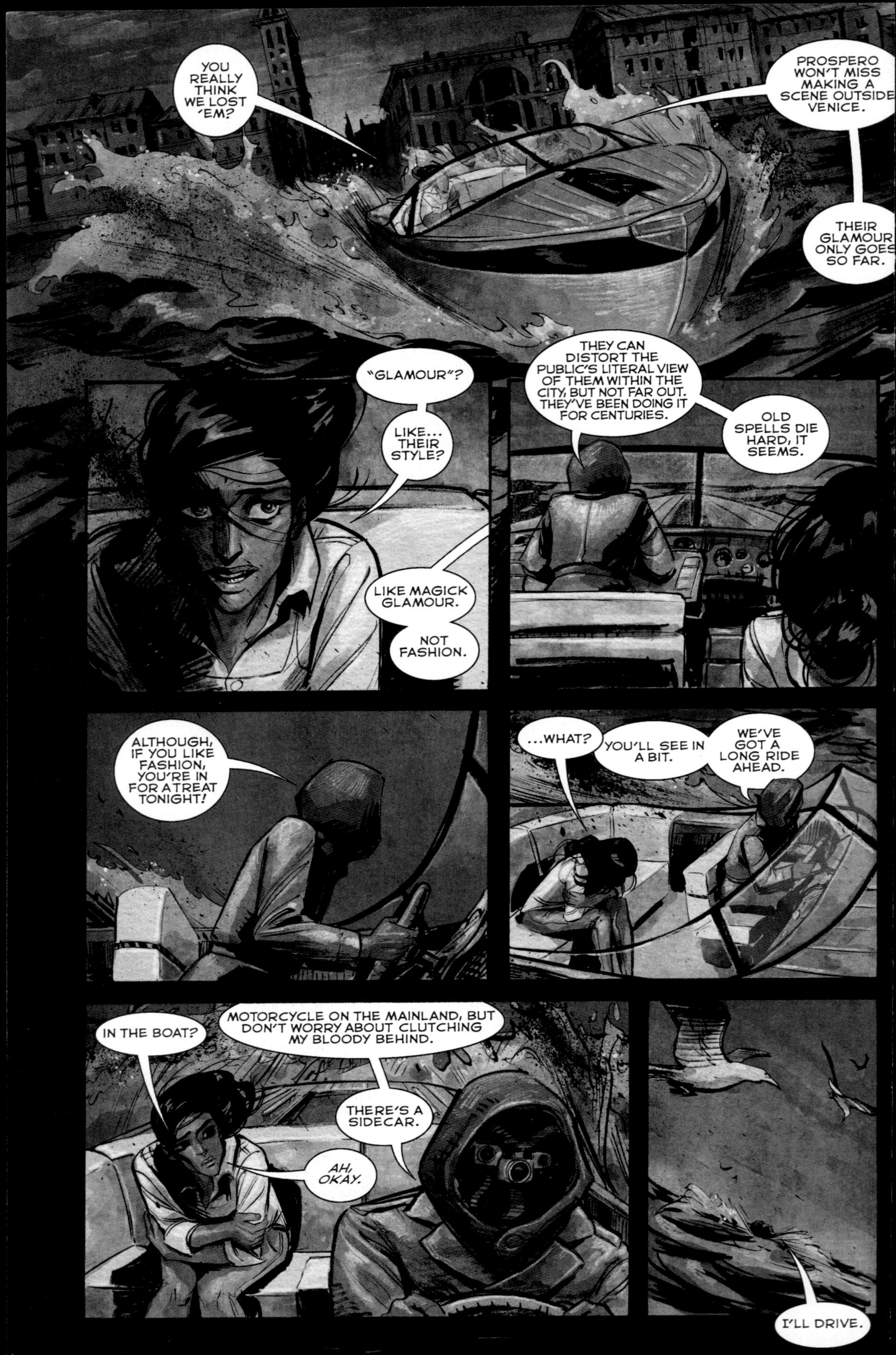

YOU REALLY THINK WE LOST 'EM?
PROSPERO WON'T MISS MAKING A SCENE OUTSIDE VENICE.
THEIR GLAMOUR ONLY GOES SO FAR.
"GLAMOUR"?
LIKE... THEIR STYLE?
LIKE MAGICK GLAMOUR.
NOT FASHION.
THEY CAN DISTORT THE PUBLIC'S LITERAL VIEW OF THEM WITHIN THE CITY, BUT NOT FAR OUT. THEY'VE BEEN DOING IT FOR CENTURIES.
OLD SPELLS DIE HARD, IT SEEMS.
ALTHOUGH, IF YOU LIKE FASHION, YOU'RE IN FOR A TREAT TONIGHT!
...WHAT?
YOU'LL SEE IN A BIT.
WE'VE GOT A LONG RIDE AHEAD.
IN THE BOAT?
MOTORCYCLE ON THE MAINLAND, BUT DON'T WORRY ABOUT CLUTCHING MY BLOODY BEHIND.
THERE'S A SIDECAR.
AH, OKAY.
I'LL DRIVE.

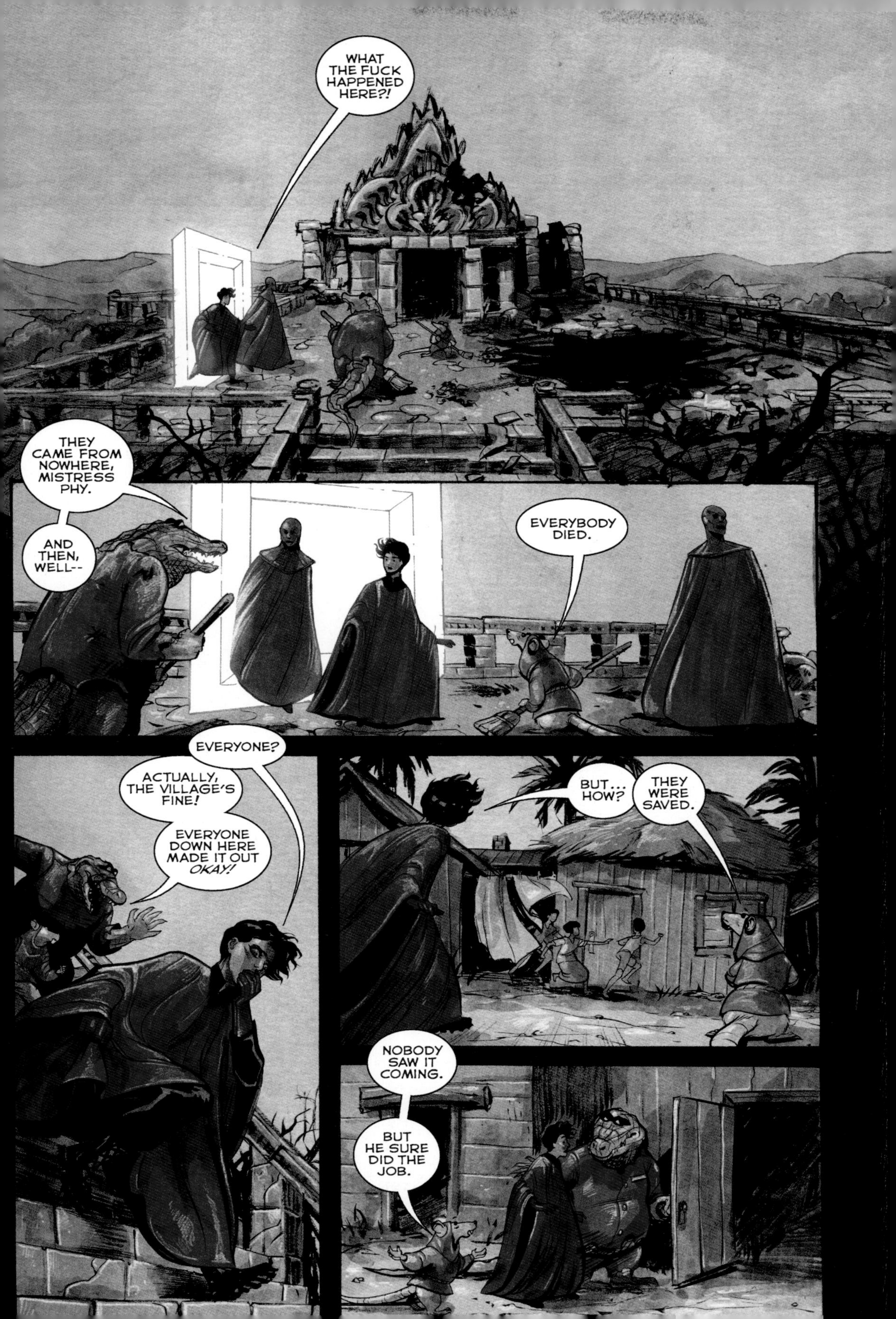
WHAT THE FUCK HAPPENED HERE?!
THEY CAME FROM NOWHERE, MISTRESS PHY.
AND THEN, WELL--
EVERYBODY DIED.
EVERYONE?
ACTUALLY, THE VILLAGE'S FINE!
EVERYONE DOWN HERE MADE IT OUT *OKAY!*
BUT... HOW?
THEY WERE SAVED.
NOBODY SAW IT COMING.
BUT HE SURE DID THE JOB.

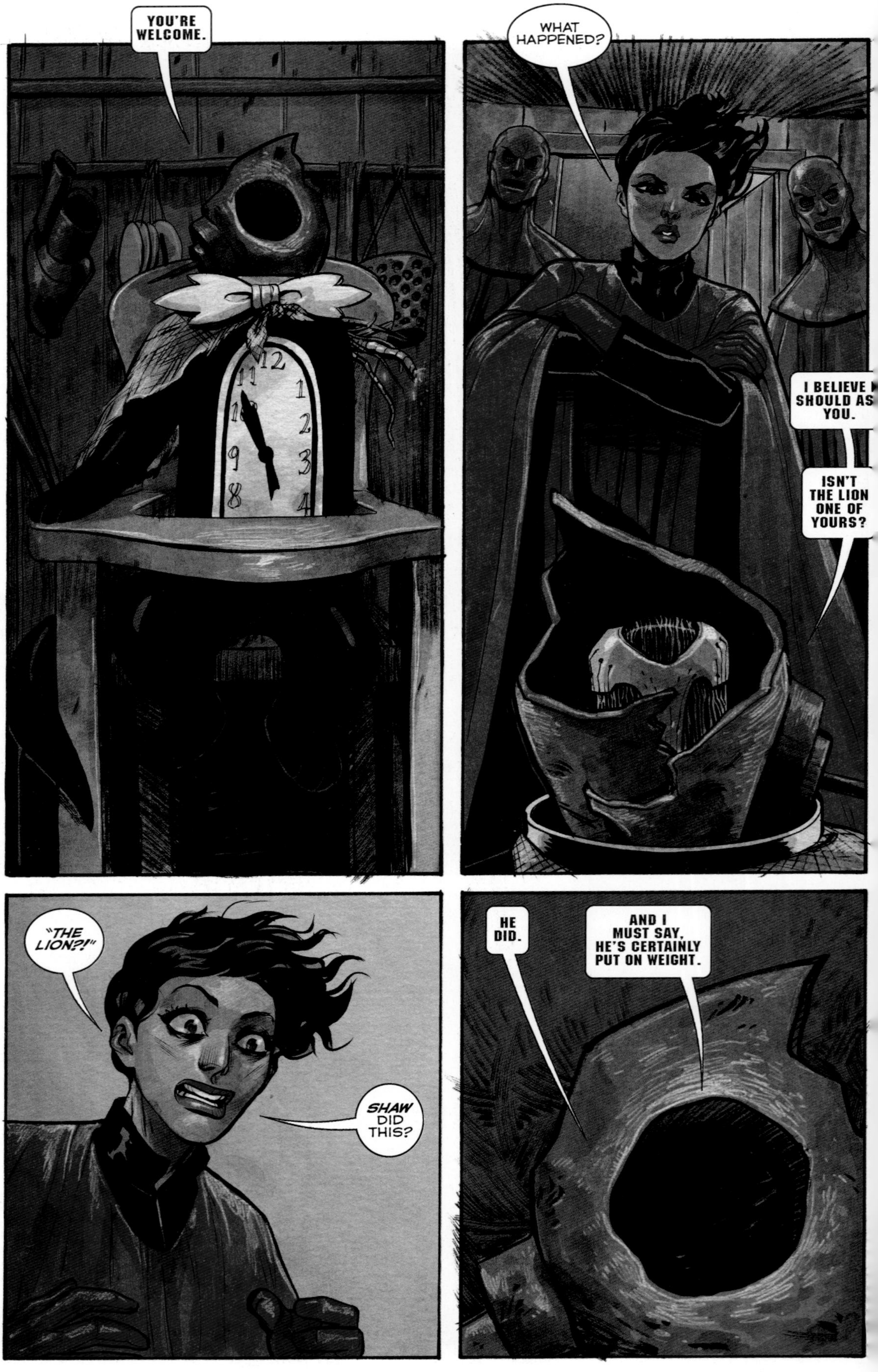
YOU'RE WELCOME.
WHAT HAPPENED?
I BELIEVE I SHOULD AS YOU.
ISN'T THE LION ONE OF YOURS?
"THE LION?!"
SHAW DID THIS?
HE DID.
AND I MUST SAY, HE'S CERTAINLY PUT ON WEIGHT.

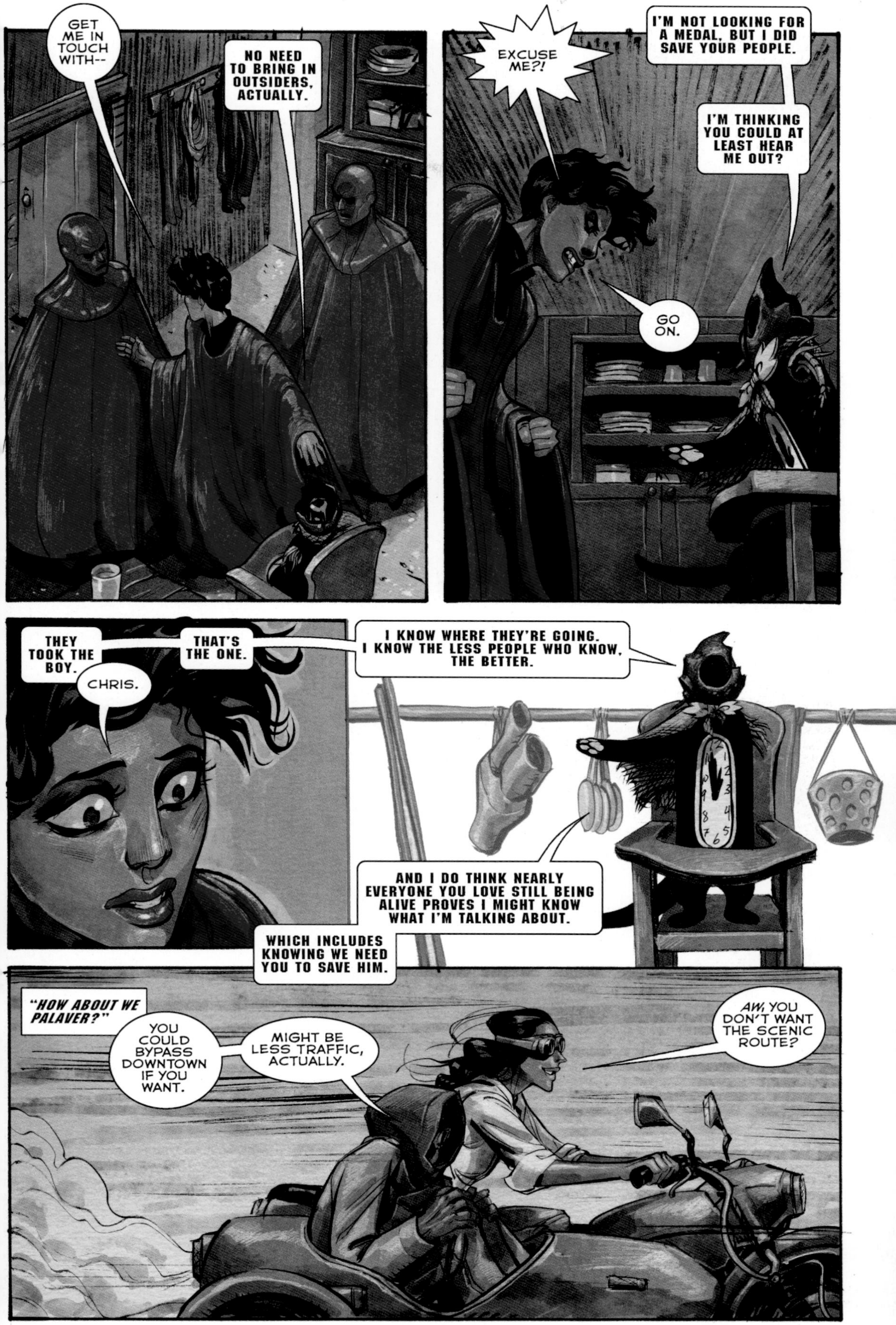
GET ME IN TOUCH WITH--
NO NEED TO BRING IN OUTSIDERS, ACTUALLY.
EXCUSE ME?!
I'M NOT LOOKING FOR A MEDAL, BUT I DID SAVE YOUR PEOPLE.
I'M THINKING YOU COULD AT LEAST HEAR ME OUT?
GO ON.
THEY TOOK THE BOY.
CHRIS.
THAT'S THE ONE.
I KNOW WHERE THEY'RE GOING. I KNOW THE LESS PEOPLE WHO KNOW, THE BETTER.
AND I DO THINK NEARLY EVERYONE YOU LOVE STILL BEING ALIVE PROVES I MIGHT KNOW WHAT I'M TALKING ABOUT.
WHICH INCLUDES KNOWING WE NEED YOU TO SAVE HIM.
"HOW ABOUT WE PALAVER?"
YOU COULD BYPASS DOWNTOWN IF YOU WANT.
MIGHT BE LESS TRAFFIC, ACTUALLY.
AW, YOU DON'T WANT THE SCENIC ROUTE?

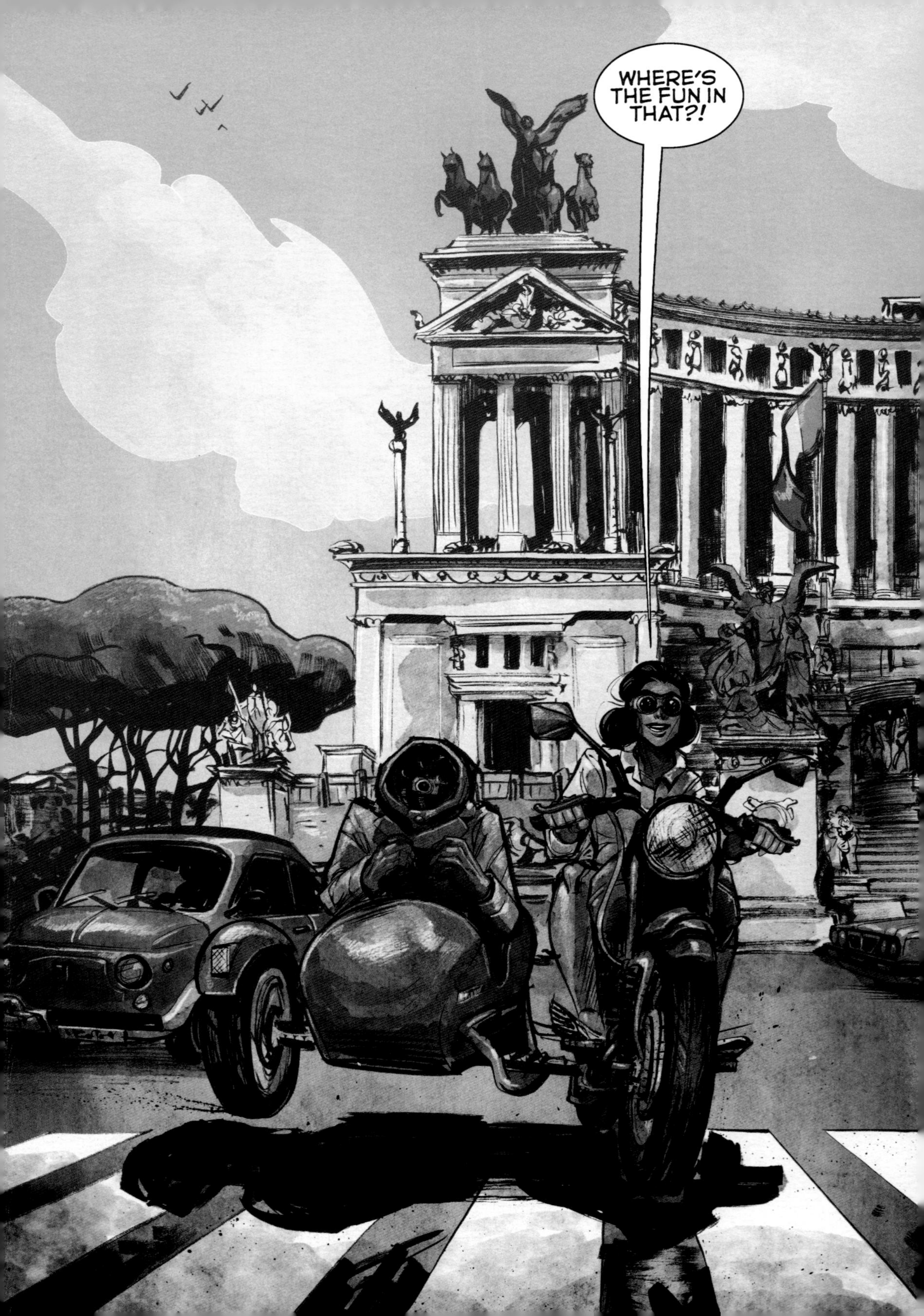
WHERE'S THE FUN IN THAT?!

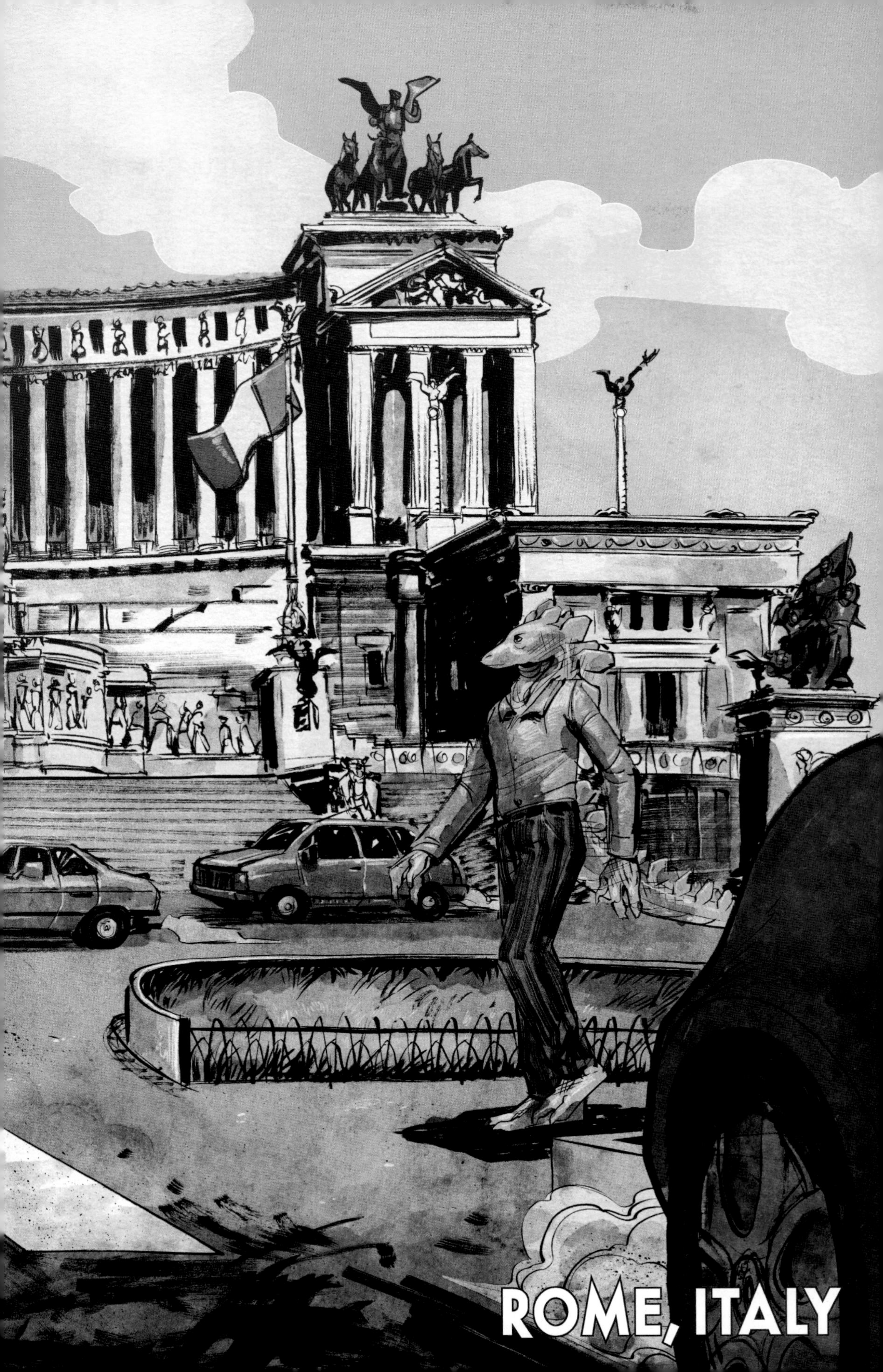
ROME, ITALY

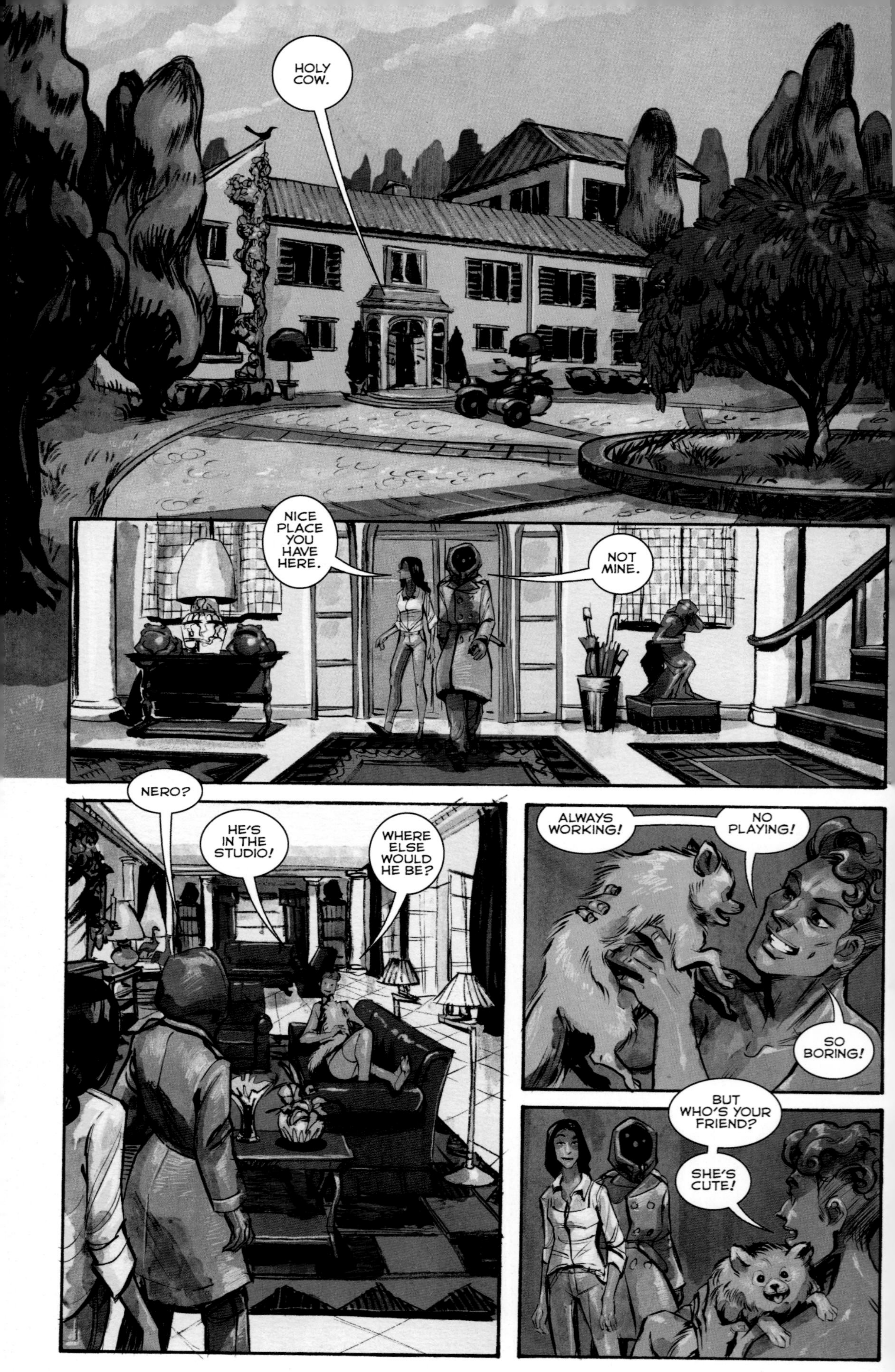
HOLY COW.
NICE PLACE YOU HAVE HERE.
NOT MINE.
NERO?
HE'S IN THE STUDIO!
WHERE ELSE WOULD HE BE?
ALWAYS WORKING!
NO PLAYING!
SO BORING!
BUT WHO'S YOUR FRIEND?
SHE'S CUTE!

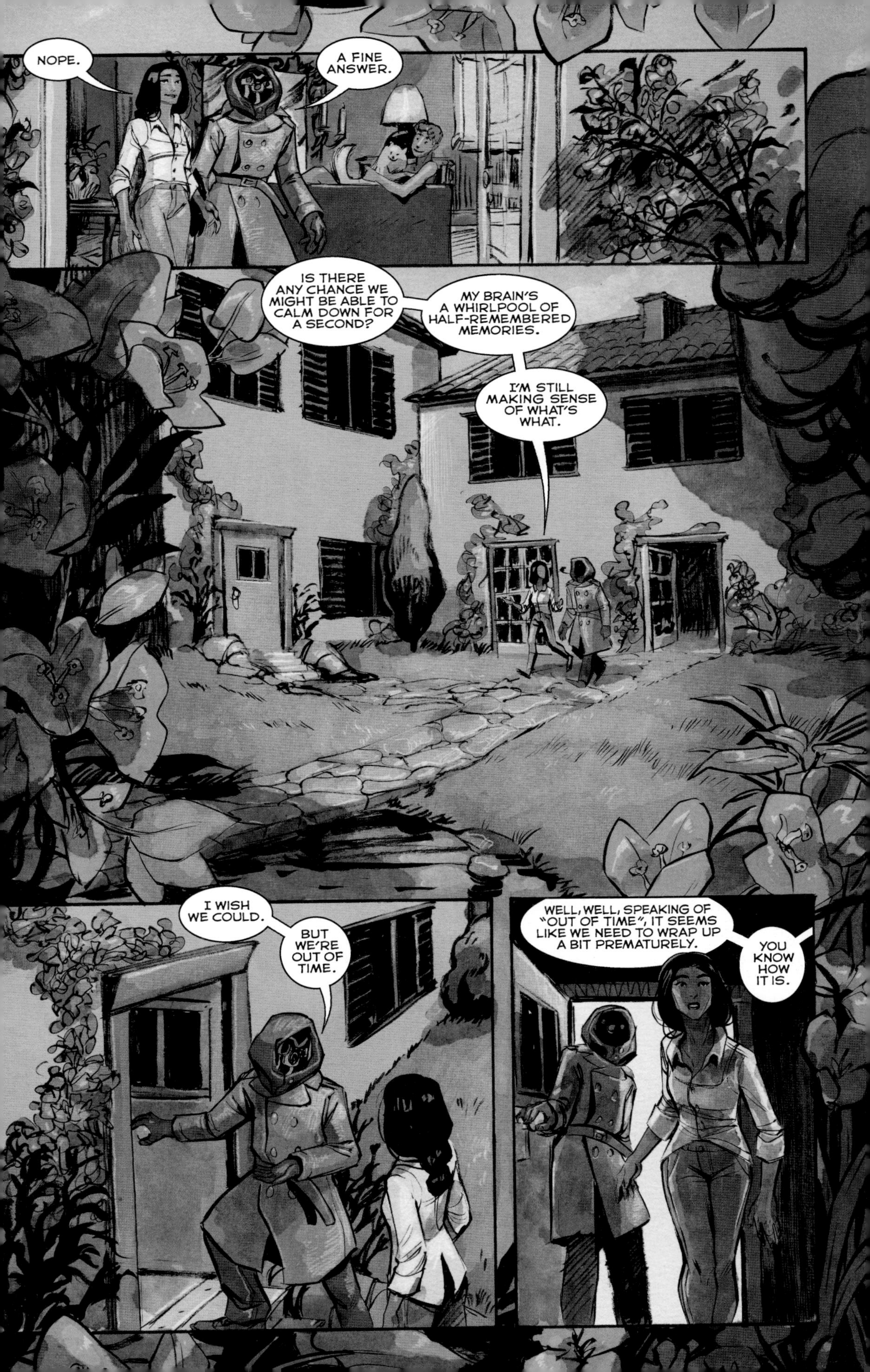
NOPE.
A FINE ANSWER.
IS THERE ANY CHANCE WE MIGHT BE ABLE TO CALM DOWN FOR A SECOND?
MY BRAIN'S A WHIRLPOOL OF HALF-REMEMBERED MEMORIES.
I'M STILL MAKING SENSE OF WHAT'S WHAT.
I WISH WE COULD.
BUT WE'RE OUT OF TIME.
WELL, WELL, SPEAKING OF "OUT OF TIME", IT SEEMS LIKE WE NEED TO WRAP UP A BIT PREMATURELY.
YOU KNOW HOW IT IS.

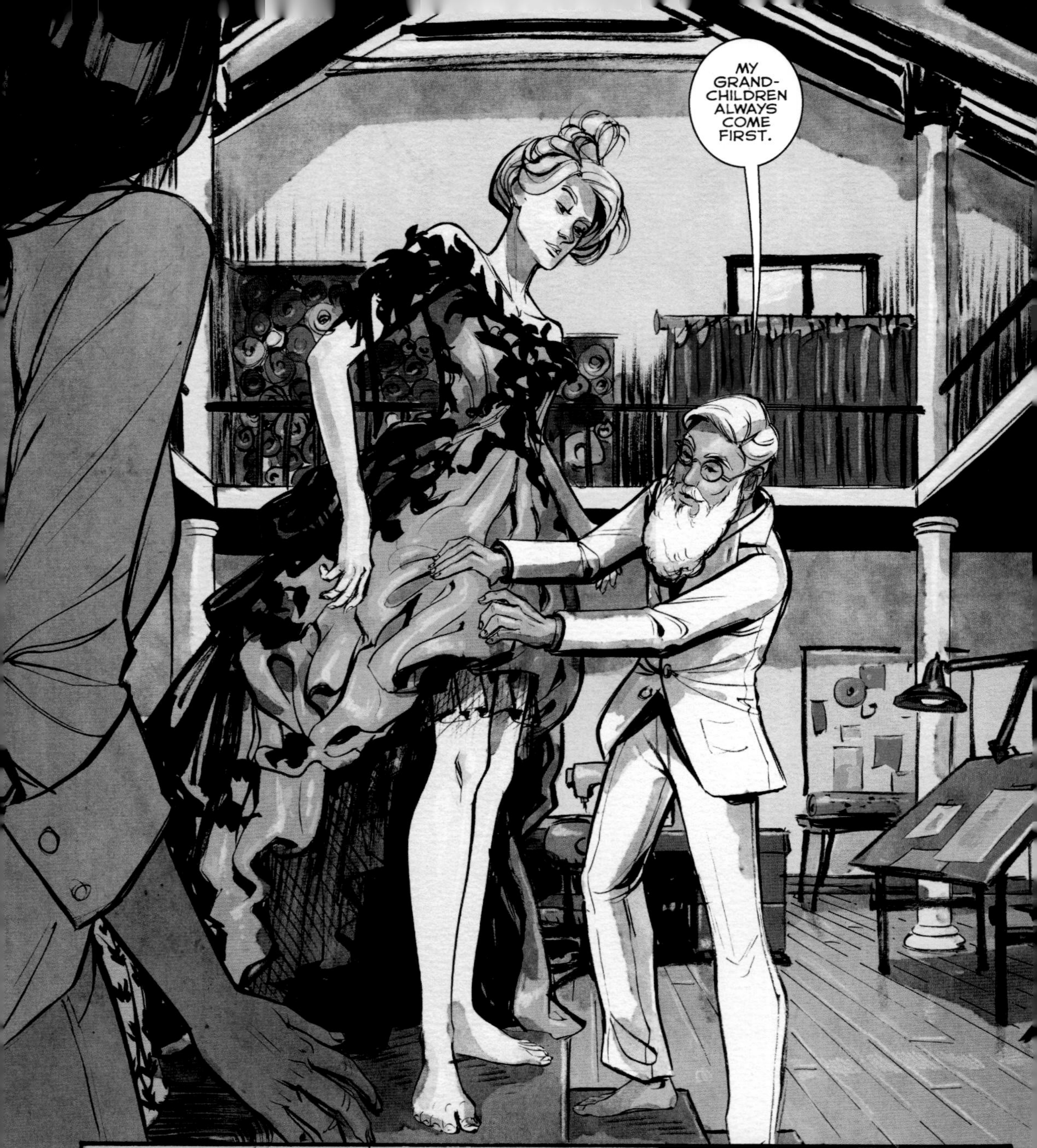
MY GRAND-CHILDREN ALWAYS COME FIRST.

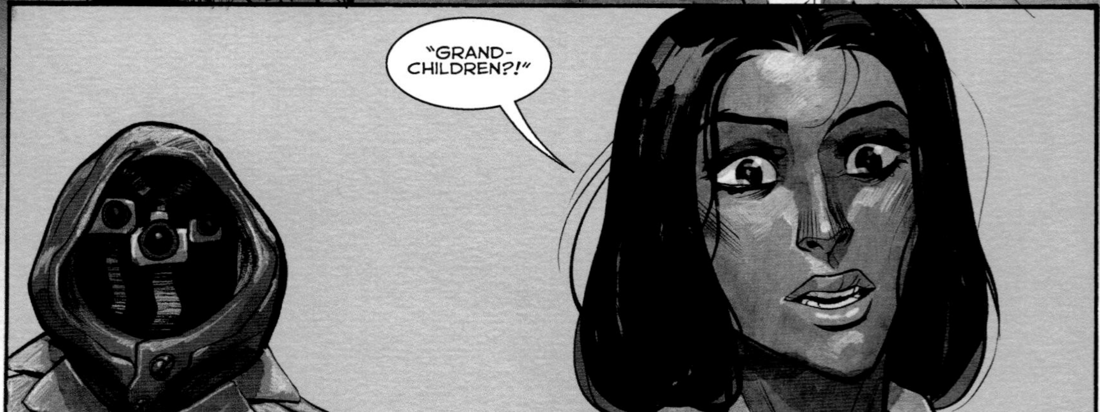
"GRAND-CHILDREN?!"

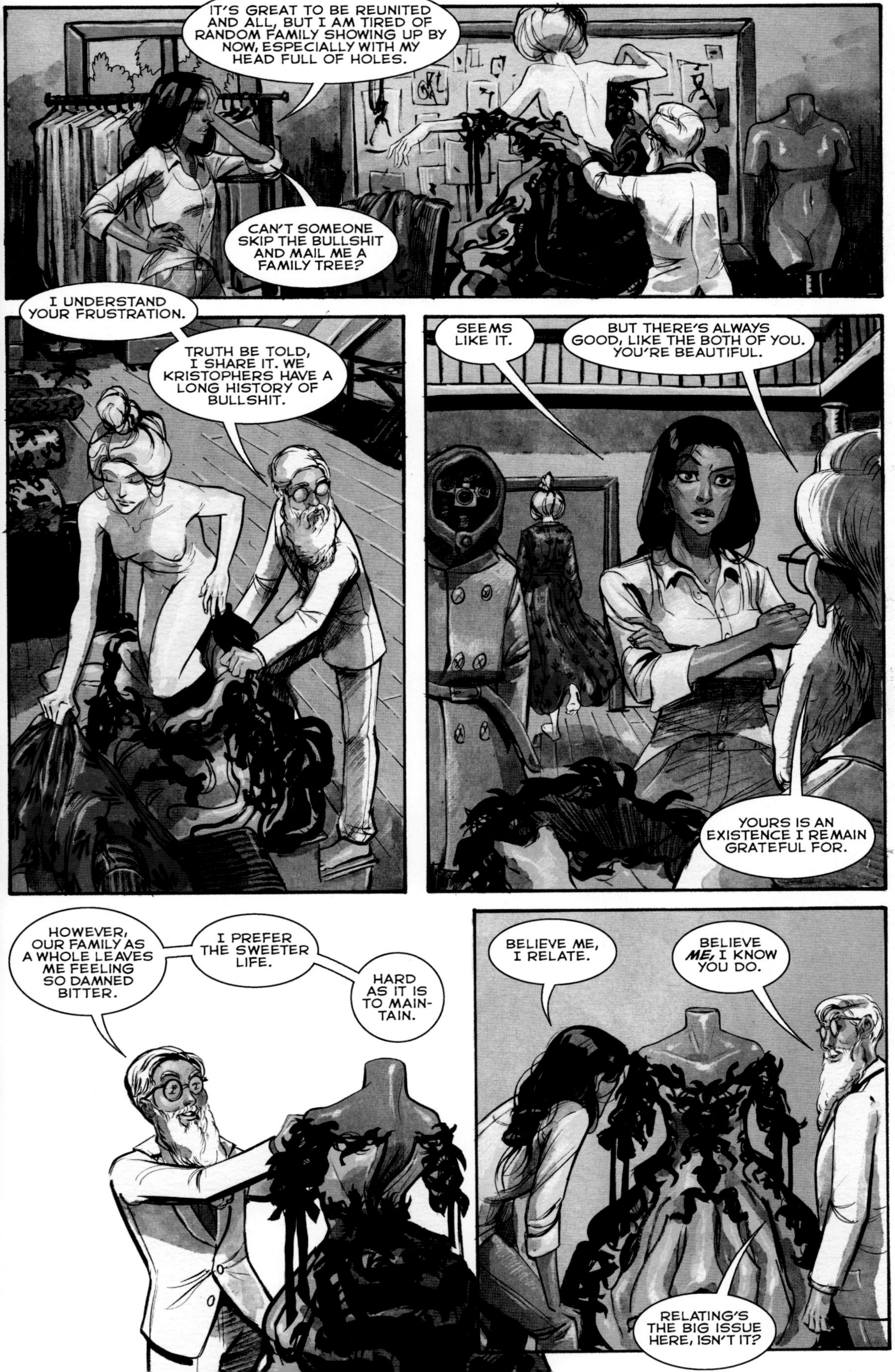
IT'S GREAT TO BE REUNITED AND ALL, BUT I AM TIRED OF RANDOM FAMILY SHOWING UP BY NOW, ESPECIALLY WITH MY HEAD FULL OF HOLES.
CAN'T SOMEONE SKIP THE BULLSHIT AND MAIL ME A FAMILY TREE?
I UNDERSTAND YOUR FRUSTRATION.
TRUTH BE TOLD, I SHARE IT. WE KRISTOPHERS HAVE A LONG HISTORY OF BULLSHIT.
SEEMS LIKE IT.
BUT THERE'S ALWAYS GOOD, LIKE THE BOTH OF YOU. YOU'RE BEAUTIFUL.
YOURS IS AN EXISTENCE I REMAIN GRATEFUL FOR.
HOWEVER, OUR FAMILY AS A WHOLE LEAVES ME FEELING SO DAMNED BITTER.
I PREFER THE SWEETER LIFE.
HARD AS IT IS TO MAIN-TAIN.
BELIEVE ME, I RELATE.
BELIEVE ME, I KNOW YOU DO.
RELATING'S THE BIG ISSUE HERE, ISN'T IT?

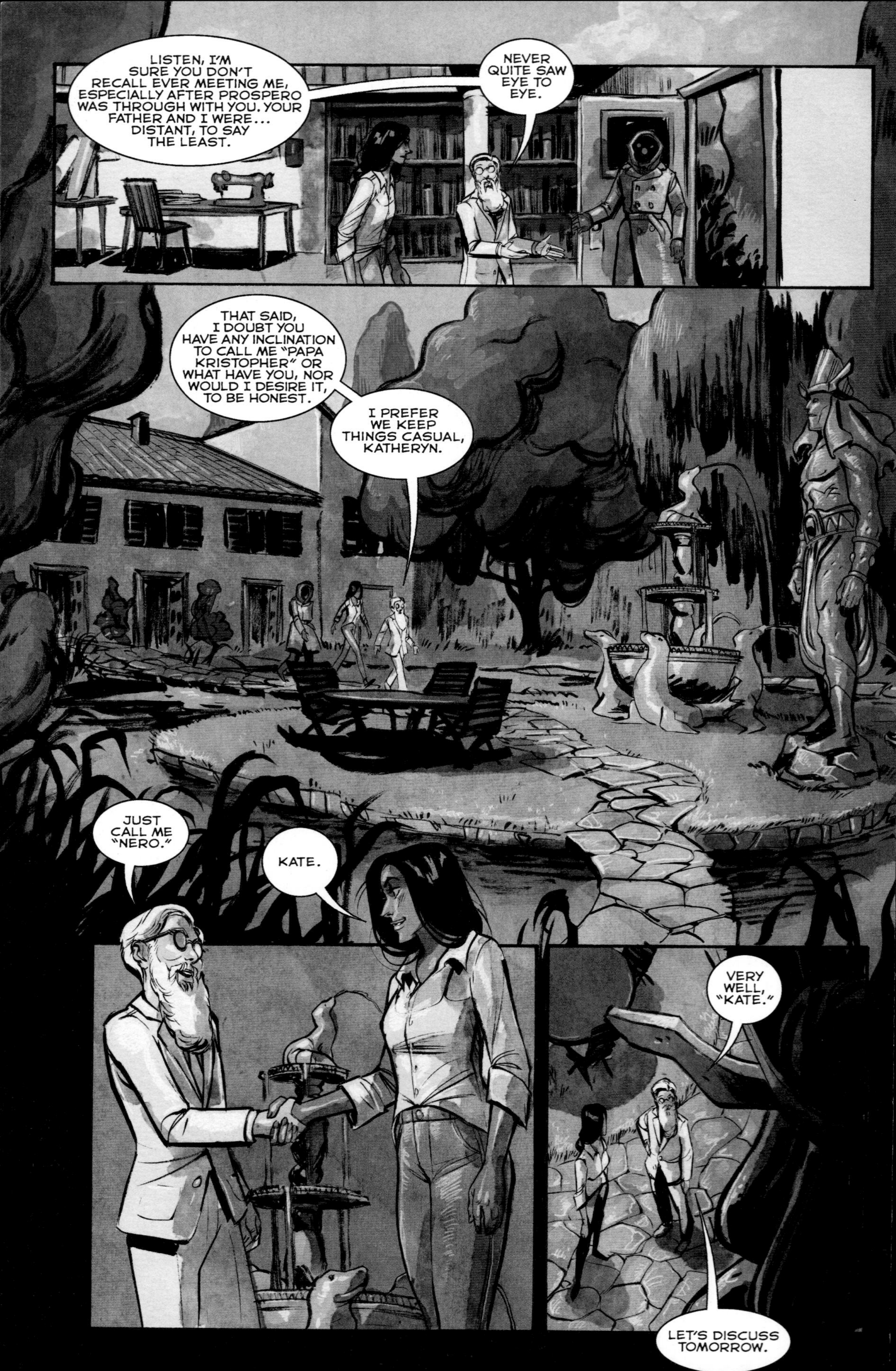
LISTEN, I'M SURE YOU DON'T RECALL EVER MEETING ME, ESPECIALLY AFTER PROSPERO WAS THROUGH WITH YOU. YOUR FATHER AND I WERE... DISTANT, TO SAY THE LEAST.
NEVER QUITE SAW EYE TO EYE.
THAT SAID, I DOUBT YOU HAVE ANY INCLINATION TO CALL ME "PAPA KRISTOPHER" OR WHAT HAVE YOU, NOR WOULD I DESIRE IT, TO BE HONEST.
I PREFER WE KEEP THINGS CASUAL, KATHERYN.
JUST CALL ME "NERO."
KATE.
VERY WELL, "KATE."
LET'S DISCUSS TOMORROW.

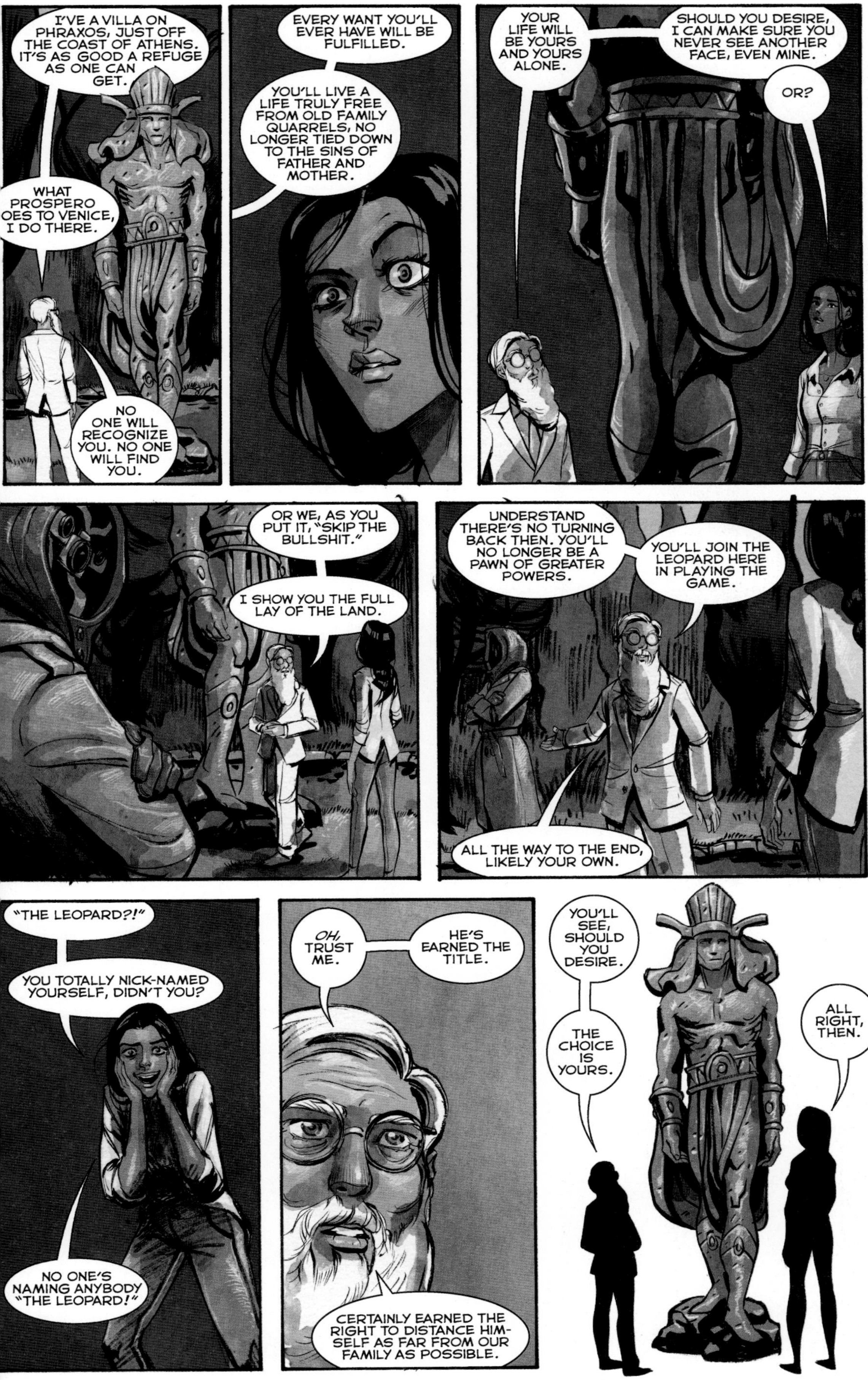
I'VE A VILLA ON PHRAXOS, JUST OFF THE COAST OF ATHENS. IT'S AS GOOD A REFUGE AS ONE CAN GET.
WHAT PROSPERO OES TO VENICE, I DO THERE.
NO ONE WILL RECOGNIZE YOU. NO ONE WILL FIND YOU.
EVERY WANT YOU'LL EVER HAVE WILL BE FULFILLED.
YOU'LL LIVE A LIFE TRULY FREE FROM OLD FAMILY QUARRELS, NO LONGER TIED DOWN TO THE SINS OF FATHER AND MOTHER.
YOUR LIFE WILL BE YOURS AND YOURS ALONE.
SHOULD YOU DESIRE, I CAN MAKE SURE YOU NEVER SEE ANOTHER FACE, EVEN MINE.
OR?
OR WE, AS YOU PUT IT, "SKIP THE BULLSHIT."
I SHOW YOU THE FULL LAY OF THE LAND.
UNDERSTAND THERE'S NO TURNING BACK THEN. YOU'LL NO LONGER BE A PAWN OF GREATER POWERS.
YOU'LL JOIN THE LEOPARD HERE IN PLAYING THE GAME.
ALL THE WAY TO THE END, LIKELY YOUR OWN.
"THE LEOPARD?!"
YOU TOTALLY NICK-NAMED YOURSELF, DIDN'T YOU?
NO ONE'S NAMING ANYBODY "THE LEOPARD!"
OH, TRUST ME.
HE'S EARNED THE TITLE.
CERTAINLY EARNED THE RIGHT TO DISTANCE HIM-SELF AS FAR FROM OUR FAMILY AS POSSIBLE.
YOU'LL SEE, SHOULD YOU DESIRE.
THE CHOICE IS YOURS.
ALL RIGHT, THEN.

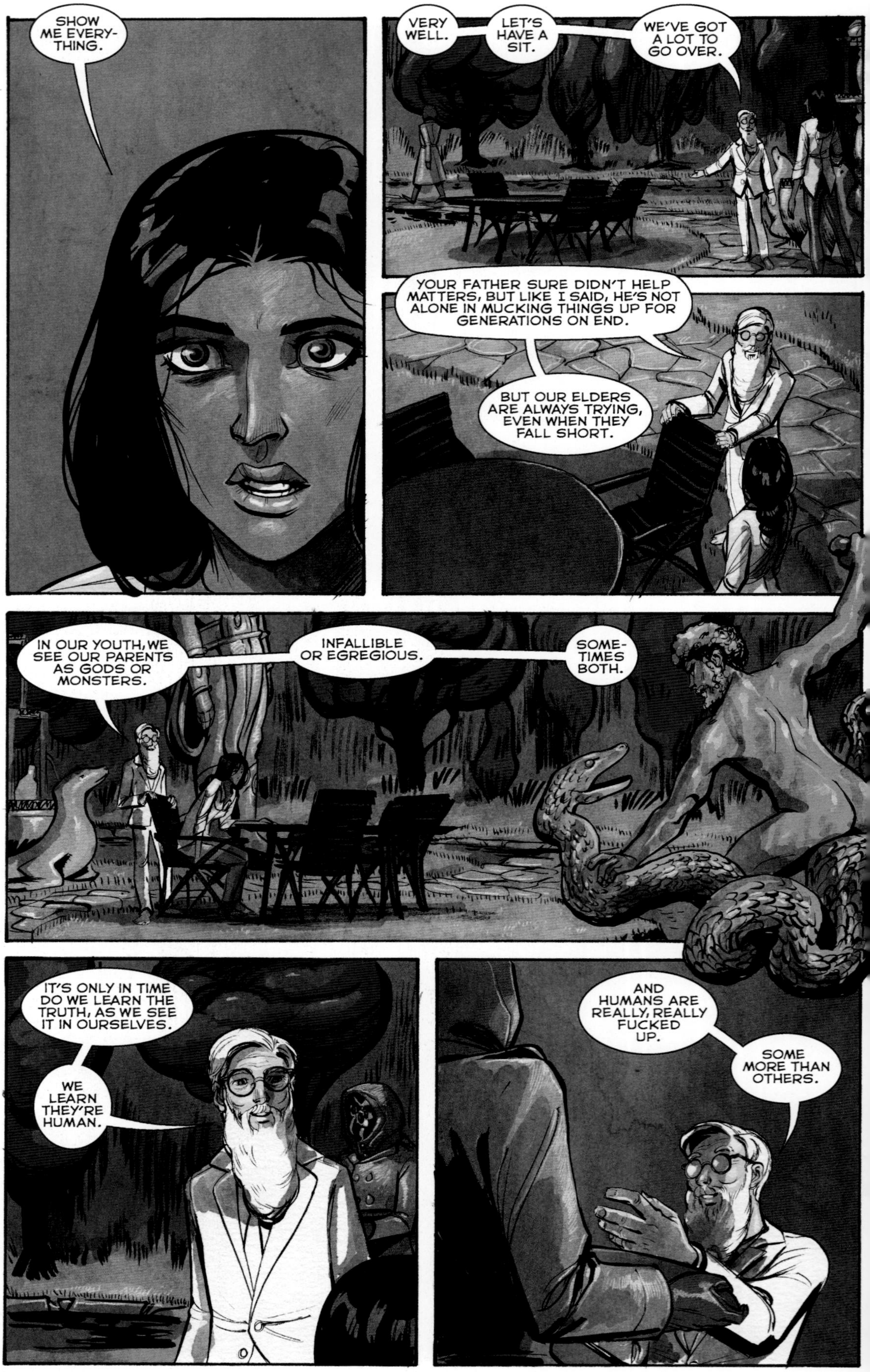
SHOW ME EVERY-THING.
VERY WELL.
LET'S HAVE A SIT.
WE'VE GOT A LOT TO GO OVER.
YOUR FATHER SURE DIDN'T HELP MATTERS, BUT LIKE I SAID, HE'S NOT ALONE IN MUCKING THINGS UP FOR GENERATIONS ON END.
BUT OUR ELDERS ARE ALWAYS TRYING, EVEN WHEN THEY FALL SHORT.
IN OUR YOUTH, WE SEE OUR PARENTS AS GODS OR MONSTERS.
INFALLIBLE OR EGREGIOUS.
SOME-TIMES BOTH.
IT'S ONLY IN TIME DO WE LEARN THE TRUTH, AS WE SEE IT IN OURSELVES.
WE LEARN THEY'RE HUMAN.
AND HUMANS ARE REALLY, REALLY FUCKED UP.
SOME MORE THAN OTHERS.

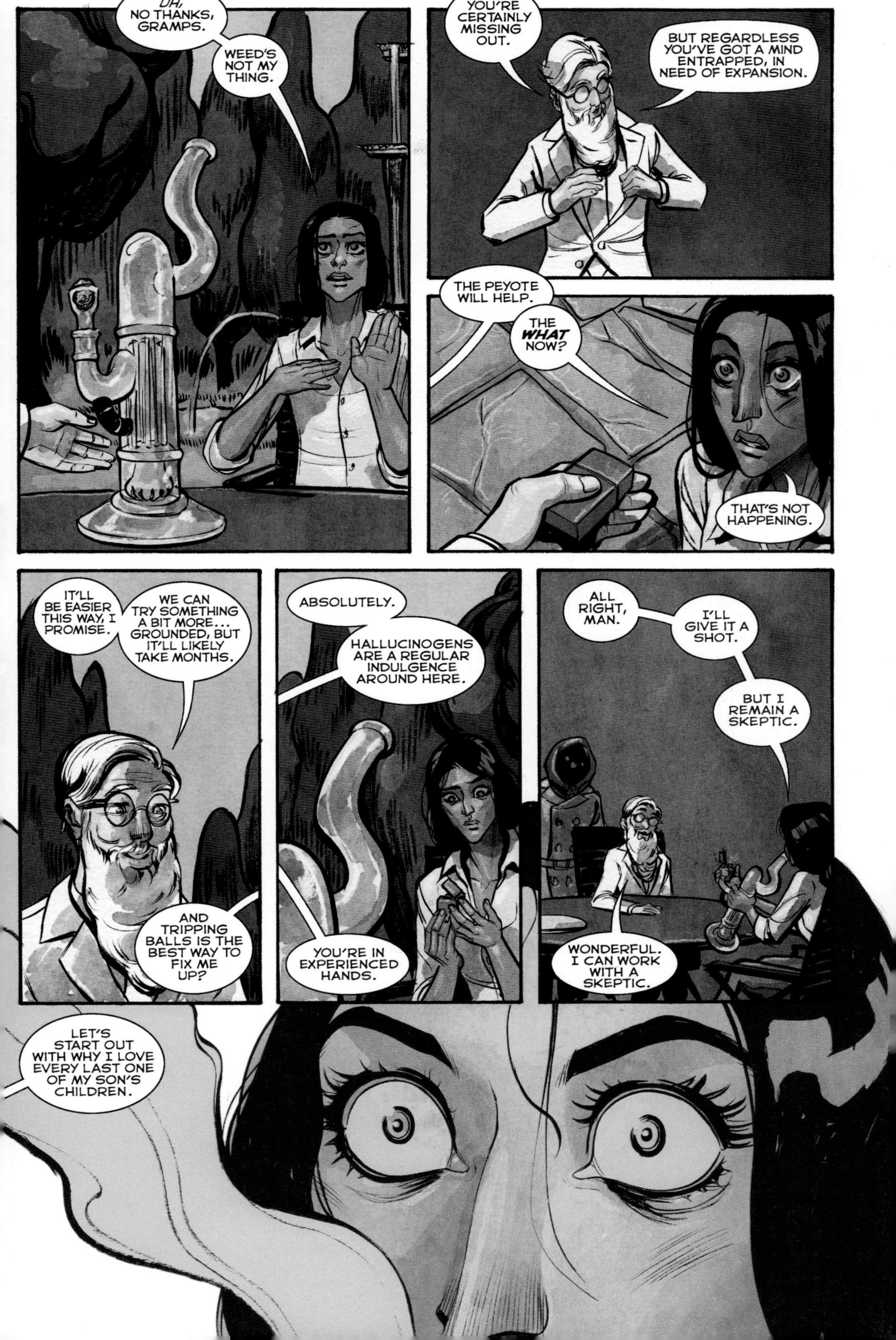
UH, NO THANKS, GRAMPS.
WEED'S NOT MY THING.
YOU'RE CERTAINLY MISSING OUT.
BUT REGARDLESS YOU'VE GOT A MIND ENTRAPPED, IN NEED OF EXPANSION.
THE PEYOTE WILL HELP.
THE WHAT NOW?
THAT'S NOT HAPPENING.
IT'LL BE EASIER THIS WAY, I PROMISE.
WE CAN TRY SOMETHING A BIT MORE... GROUNDED, BUT IT'LL LIKELY TAKE MONTHS.
AND TRIPPING BALLS IS THE BEST WAY TO FIX ME UP?
ABSOLUTELY.
HALLUCINOGENS ARE A REGULAR INDULGENCE AROUND HERE.
YOU'RE IN EXPERIENCED HANDS.
ALL RIGHT, MAN.
I'LL GIVE IT A SHOT.
BUT I REMAIN A SKEPTIC.
WONDERFUL. I CAN WORK WITH A SKEPTIC.
LET'S START OUT WITH WHY I LOVE EVERY LAST ONE OF MY SON'S CHILDREN.

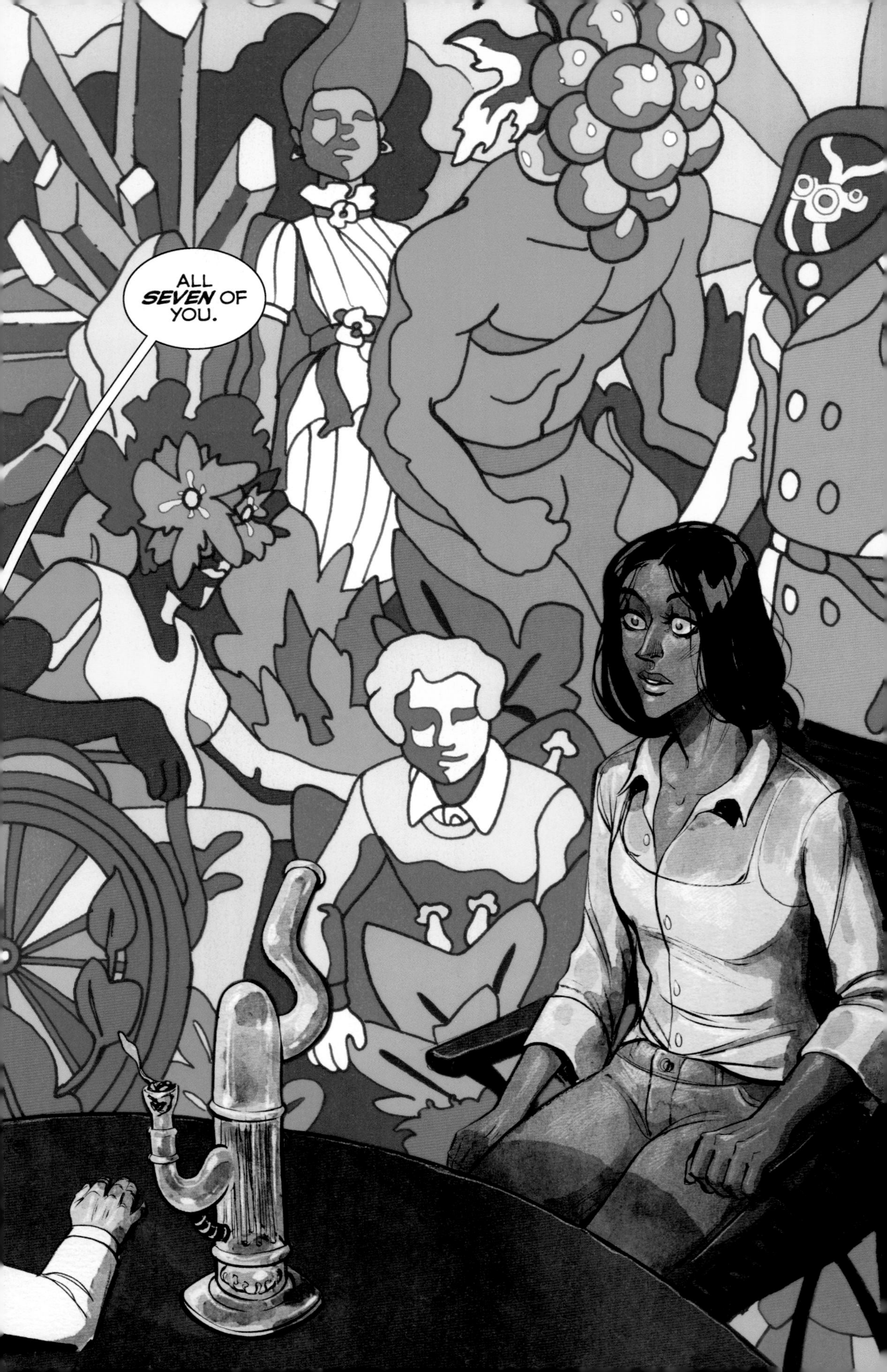
ALL *SEVEN* OF YOU.

CHAPTER 15

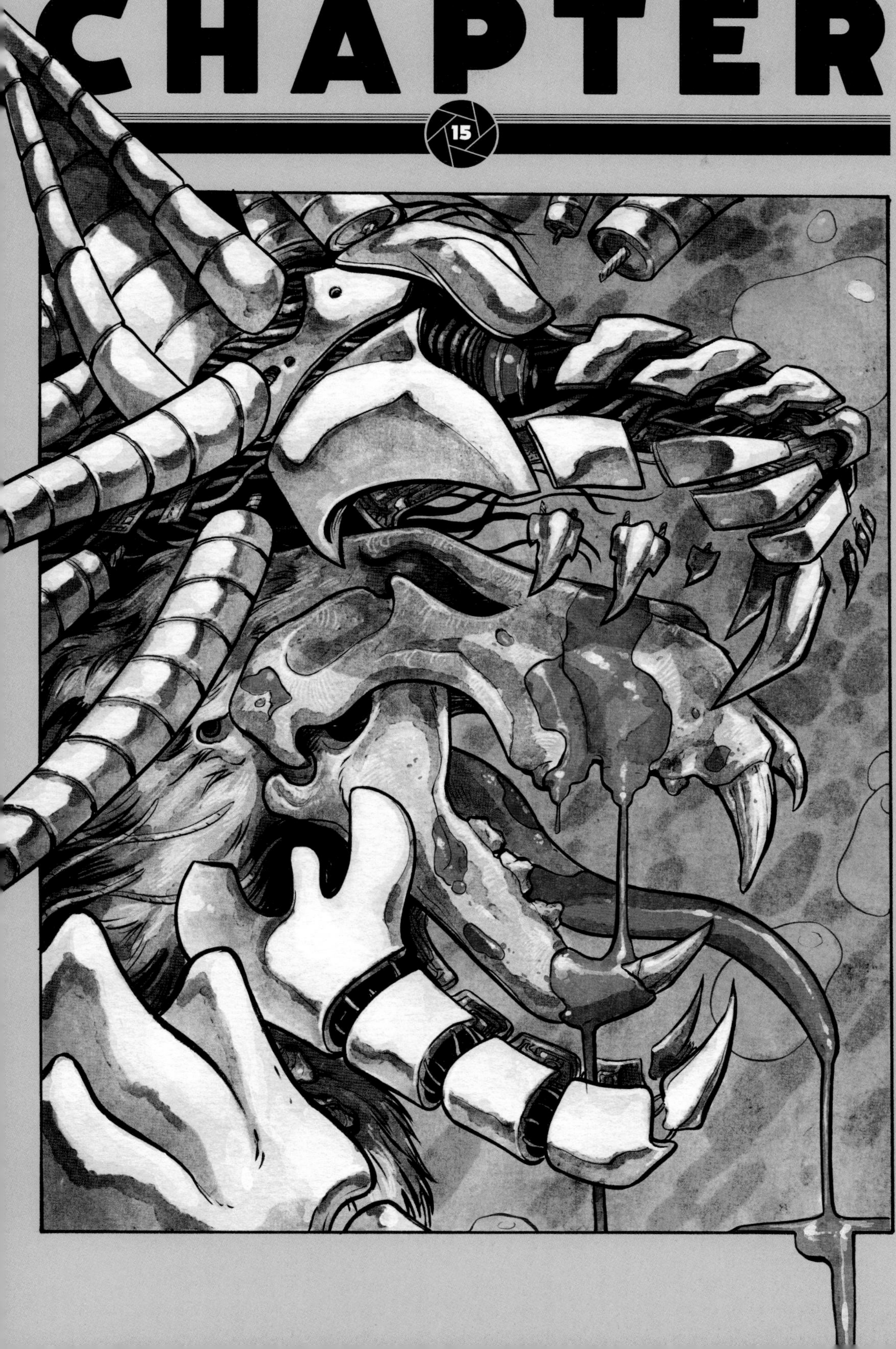

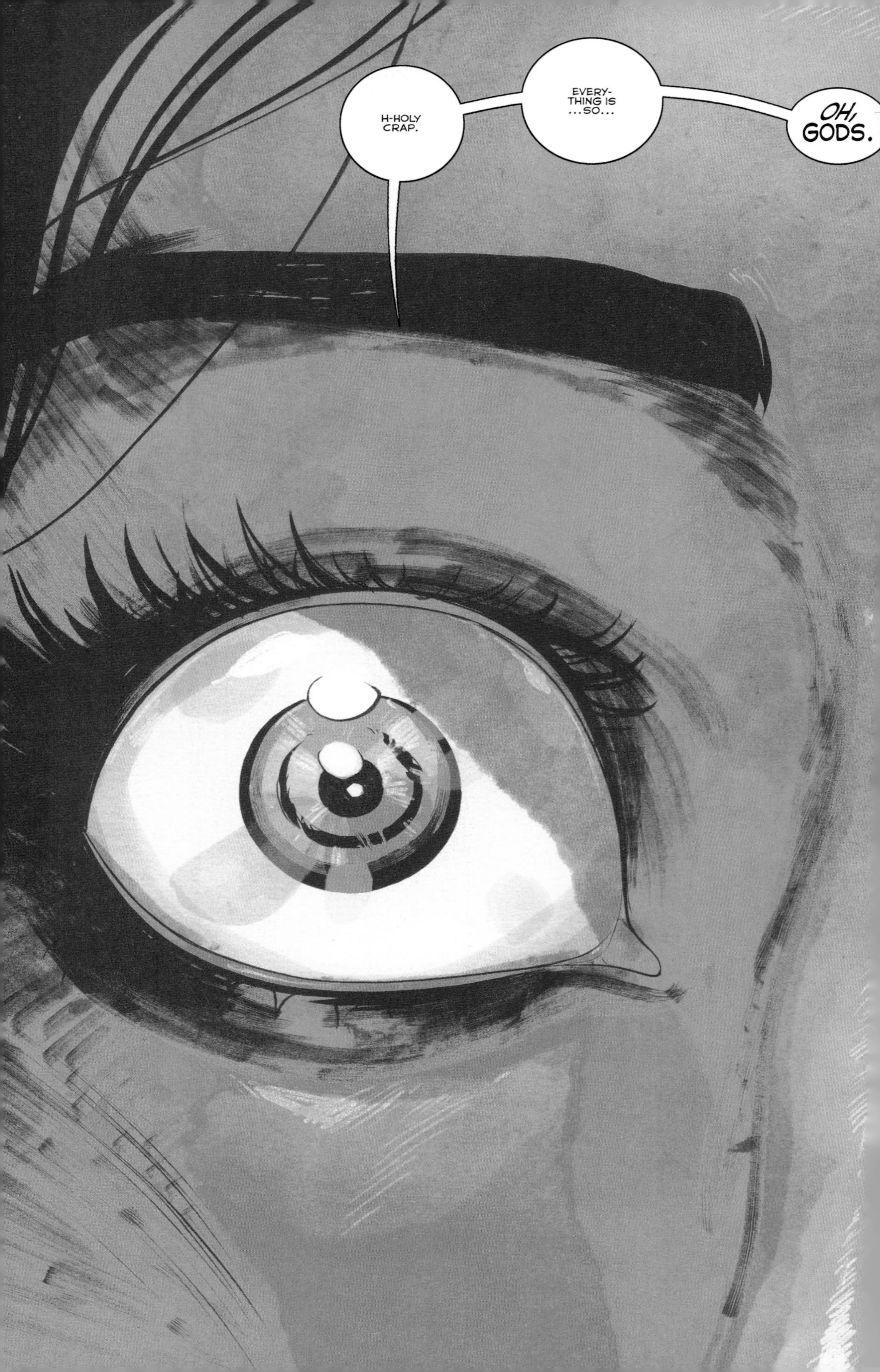
H-HOLY CRAP.
EVERY-THING IS ...SO...
OH, GODS.

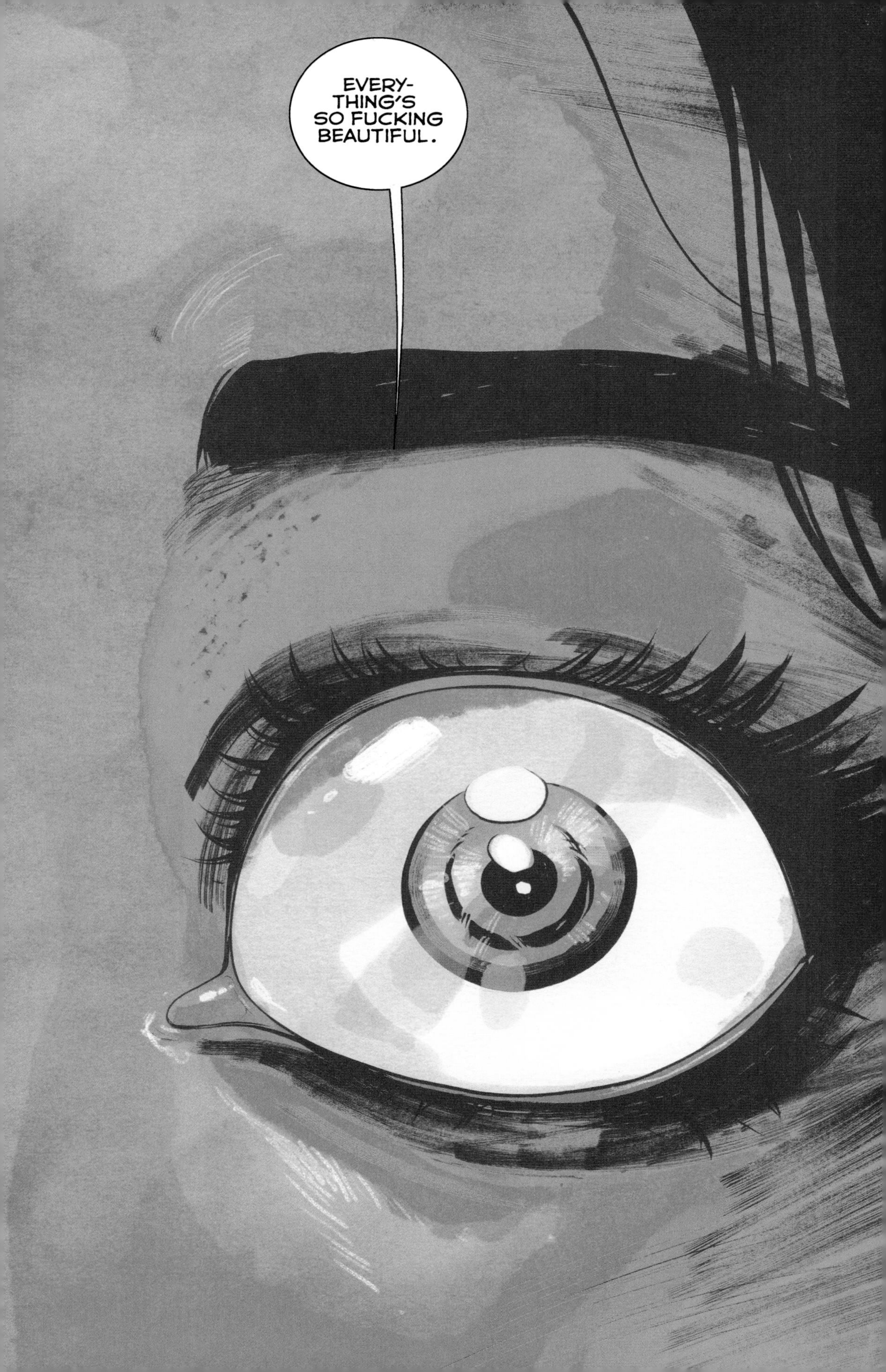
EVERY-THING'S SO FUCKING BEAUTIFUL.

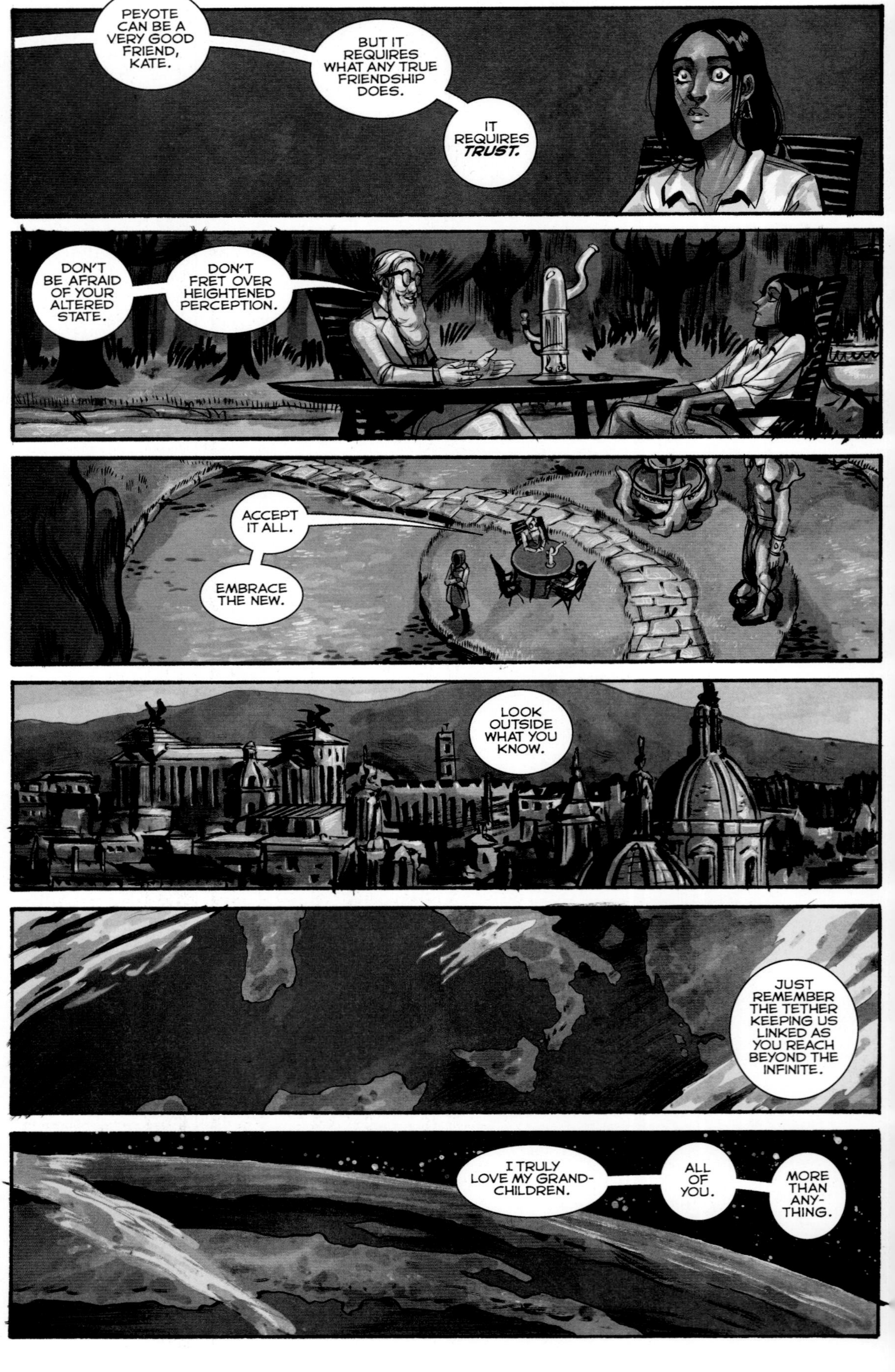
PEYOTE CAN BE A VERY GOOD FRIEND, KATE.
BUT IT REQUIRES WHAT ANY TRUE FRIENDSHIP DOES.
IT REQUIRES *TRUST.*
DON'T BE AFRAID OF YOUR ALTERED STATE.
DON'T FRET OVER HEIGHTENED PERCEPTION.
ACCEPT IT ALL.
EMBRACE THE NEW.
LOOK OUTSIDE WHAT YOU KNOW.
JUST REMEMBER THE TETHER KEEPING US LINKED AS YOU REACH BEYOND THE INFINITE.
I TRULY LOVE MY GRAND-CHILDREN.
ALL OF YOU.
MORE THAN ANY-THING.

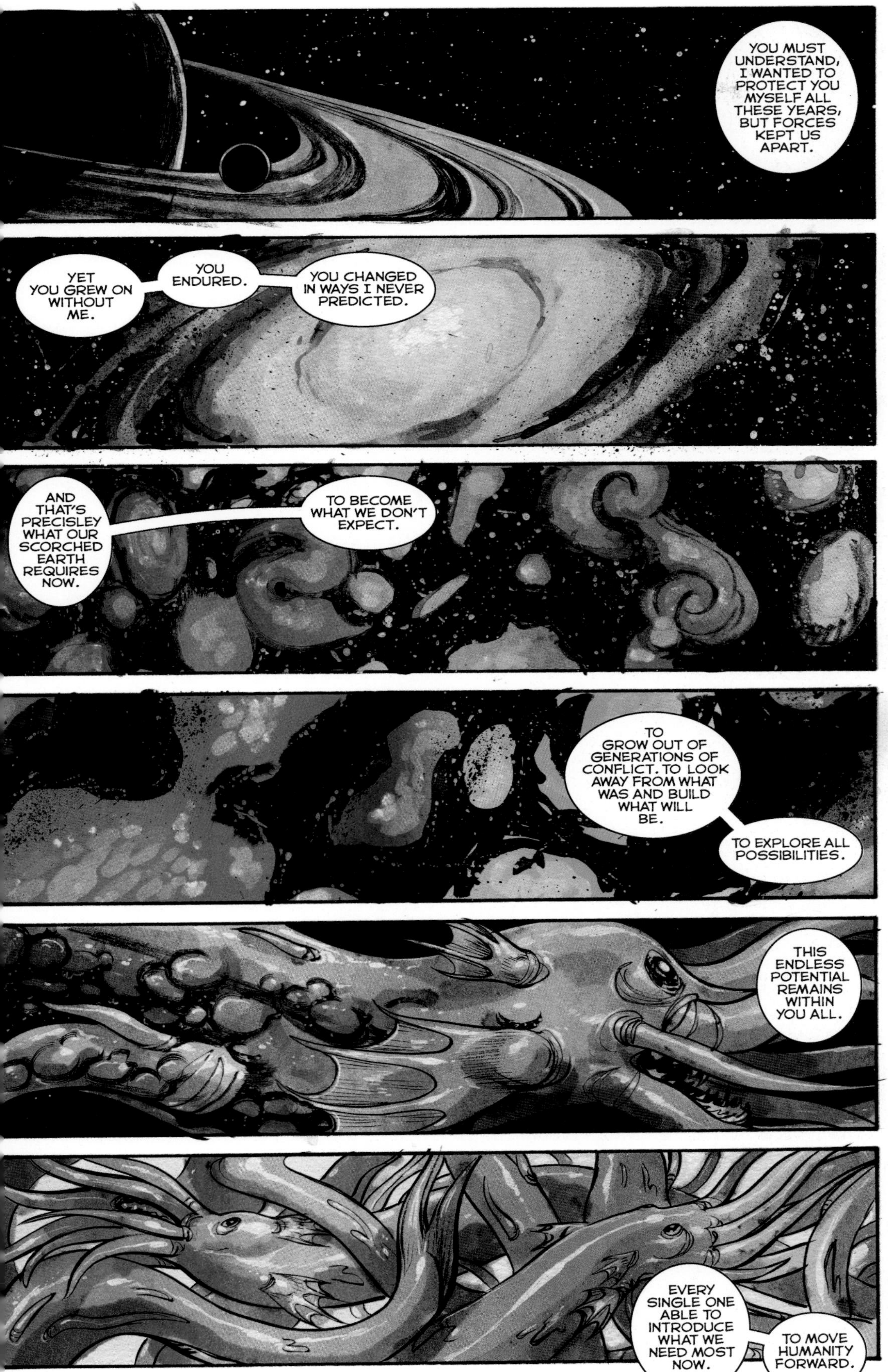
YOU MUST UNDERSTAND, I WANTED TO PROTECT YOU MYSELF ALL THESE YEARS, BUT FORCES KEPT US APART.
YET YOU GREW ON WITHOUT ME.
YOU ENDURED.
YOU CHANGED IN WAYS I NEVER PREDICTED.
AND THAT'S PRECISLEY WHAT OUR SCORCHED EARTH REQUIRES NOW.
TO BECOME WHAT WE DON'T EXPECT.
TO GROW OUT OF GENERATIONS OF CONFLICT. TO LOOK AWAY FROM WHAT WAS AND BUILD WHAT WILL BE.
TO EXPLORE ALL POSSIBILITIES.
THIS ENDLESS POTENTIAL REMAINS WITHIN YOU ALL.
EVERY SINGLE ONE ABLE TO INTRODUCE WHAT WE NEED MOST NOW.
TO MOVE HUMANITY FORWARD.

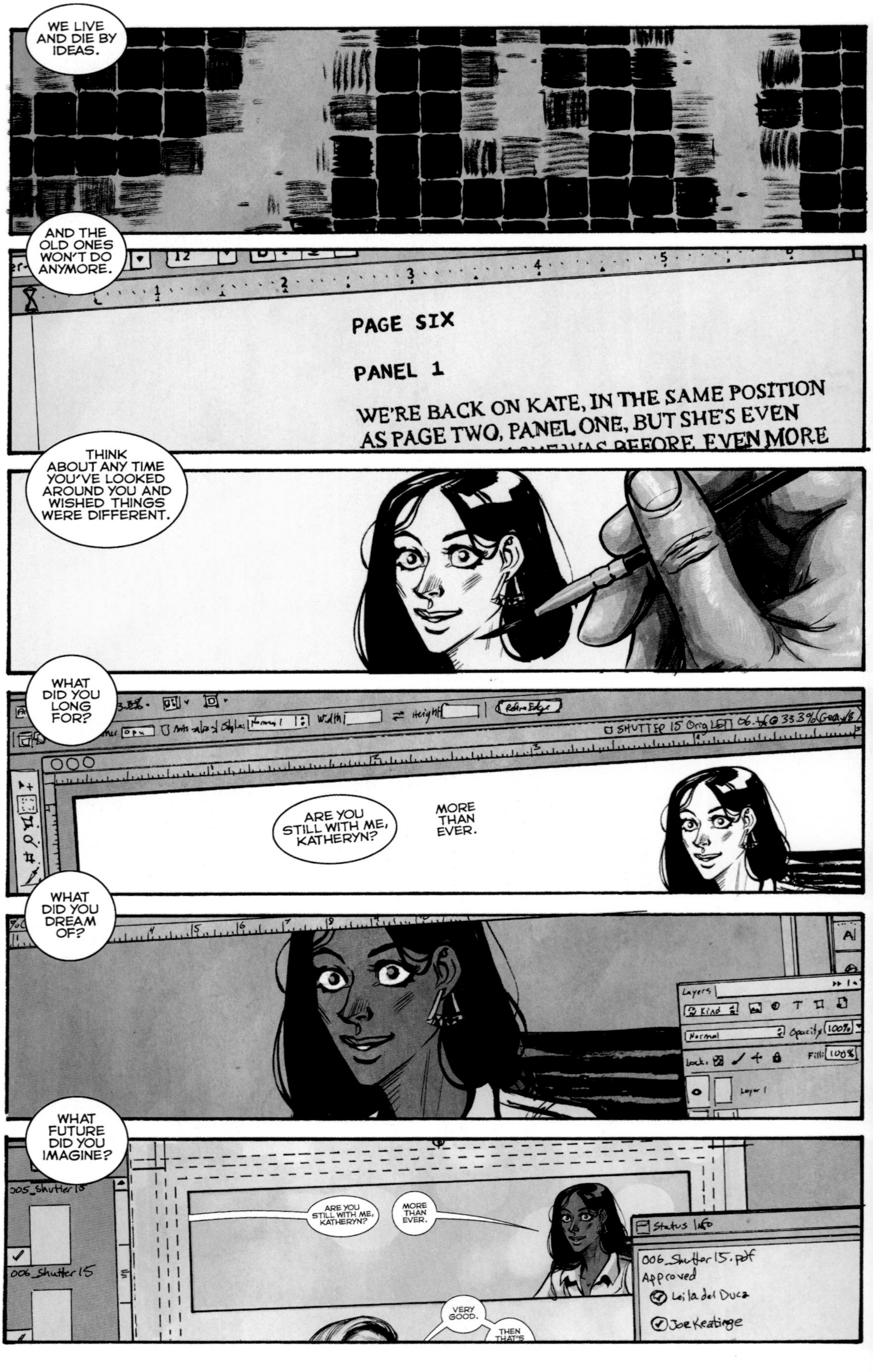
WE LIVE AND DIE BY IDEAS.
AND THE OLD ONES WON'T DO ANYMORE.
PAGE SIX
PANEL 1
WE'RE BACK ON KATE, IN THE SAME POSITION AS PAGE TWO, PANEL ONE, BUT SHE'S EVEN
THINK ABOUT ANY TIME YOU'VE LOOKED AROUND YOU AND WISHED THINGS WERE DIFFERENT.
WHAT DID YOU LONG FOR?
ARE YOU STILL WITH ME, KATHERYN?
MORE THAN EVER.
WHAT DID YOU DREAM OF?
Layers
Normal
Opacity 100%
Fill: 100%
Layer 1
WHAT FUTURE DID YOU IMAGINE?
005_Shutter 15
006_Shutter 15
ARE YOU STILL WITH ME, KATHERYN?
MORE THAN EVER.
Status Info
006_Shutter 15.pdf
Approved
Leila del Duca
Joe Keatinge
VERY GOOD.

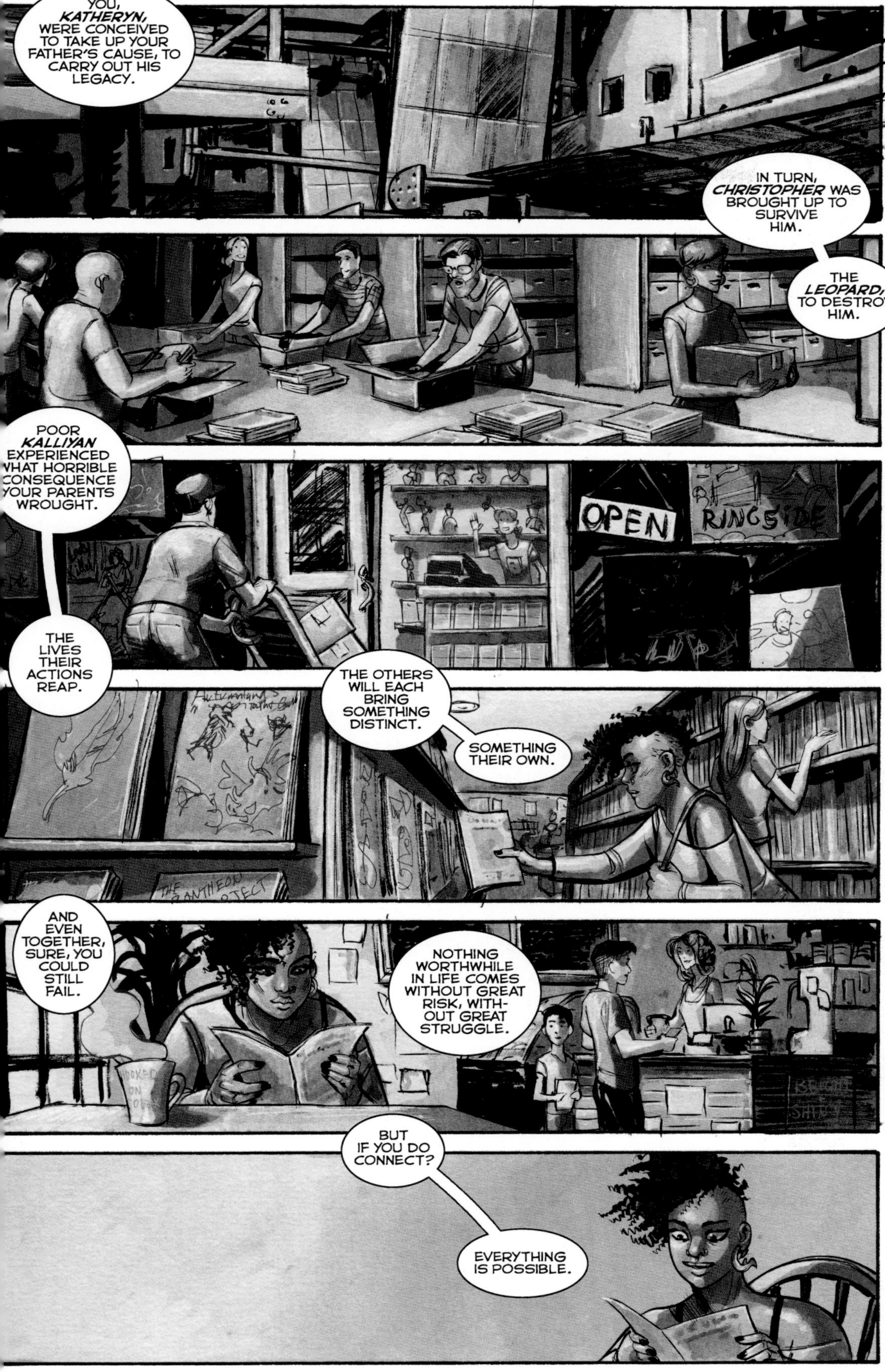
YOU, KATHERYN, WERE CONCEIVED TO TAKE UP YOUR FATHER'S CAUSE, TO CARRY OUT HIS LEGACY.
IN TURN, CHRISTOPHER WAS BROUGHT UP TO SURVIVE HIM.
THE LEOPARD, TO DESTROY HIM.
POOR KALLIYAN EXPERIENCED WHAT HORRIBLE CONSEQUENCE YOUR PARENTS WROUGHT.
OPEN
RINGSIDE
THE LIVES THEIR ACTIONS REAP.
THE OTHERS WILL EACH BRING SOMETHING DISTINCT.
SOMETHING THEIR OWN.
AND EVEN TOGETHER, SURE, YOU COULD STILL FAIL.
NOTHING WORTHWHILE IN LIFE COMES WITHOUT GREAT RISK, WITHOUT GREAT STRUGGLE.
BUT IF YOU DO CONNECT?
EVERYTHING IS POSSIBLE.

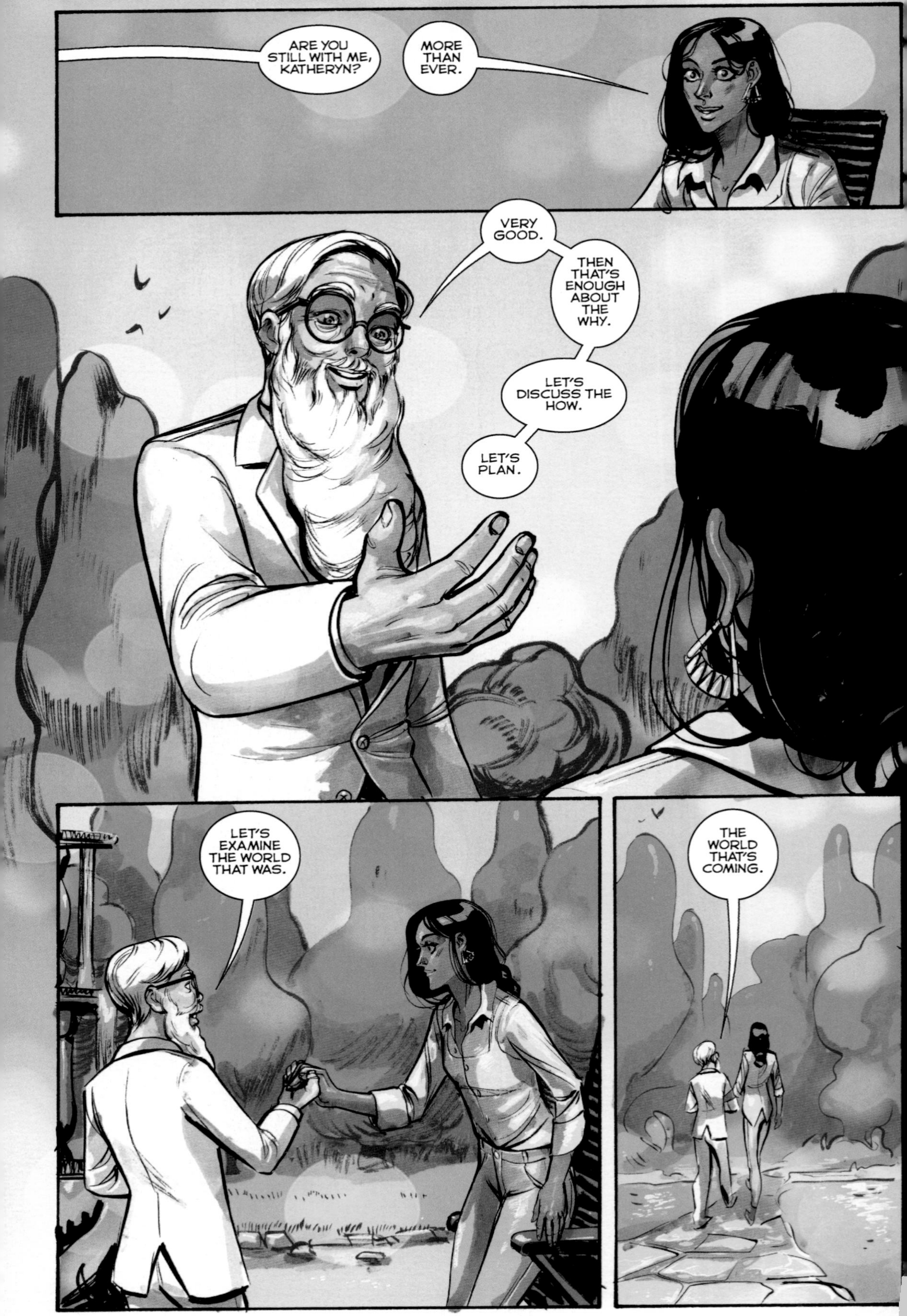
ARE YOU STILL WITH ME, KATHERYN?
MORE THAN EVER.
VERY GOOD.
THEN THAT'S ENOUGH ABOUT THE WHY.
LET'S DISCUSS THE HOW.
LET'S PLAN.
LET'S EXAMINE THE WORLD THAT WAS.
THE WORLD THAT'S COMING.

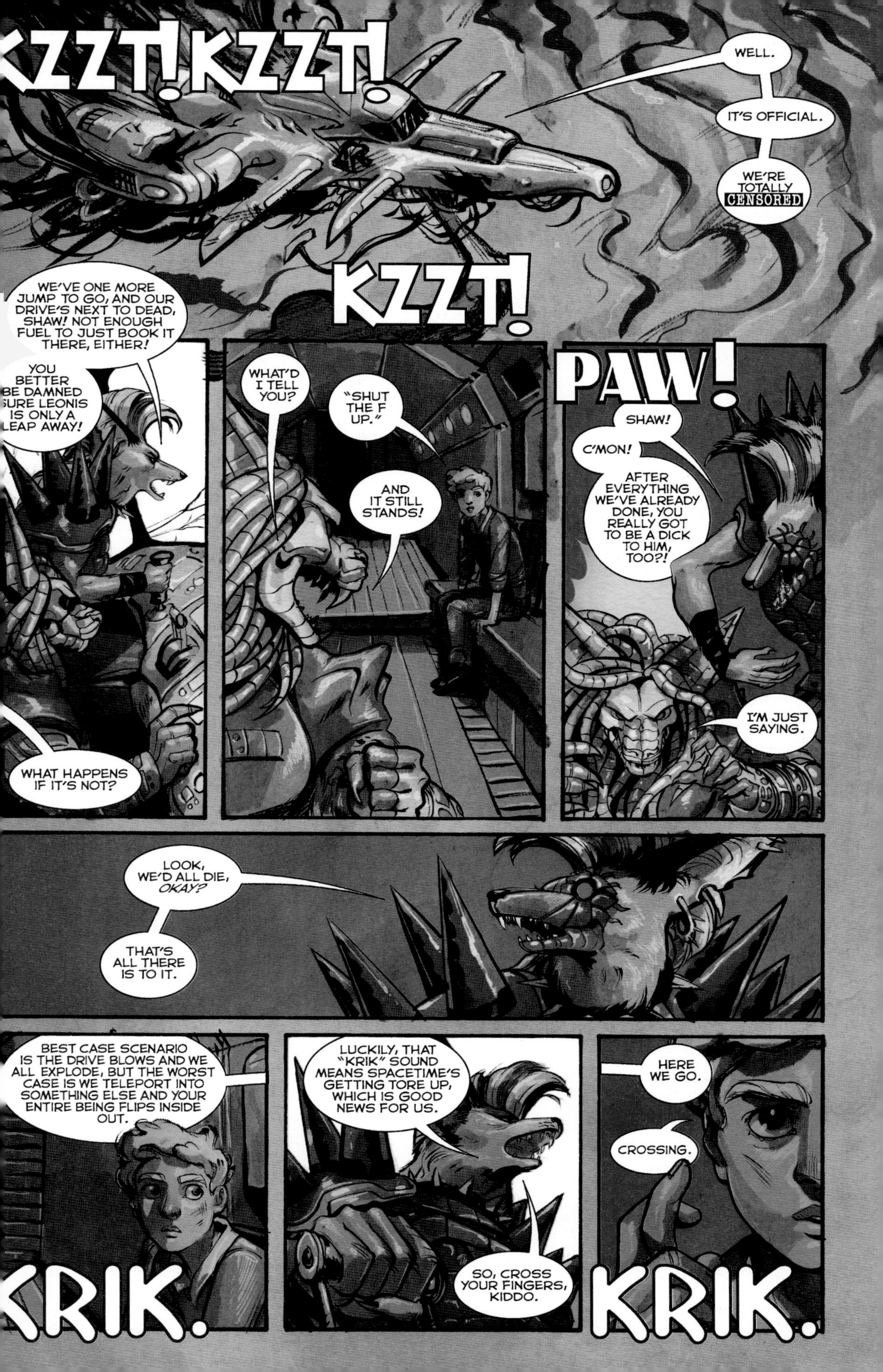
KZZT!KZZT!
WELL.
IT'S OFFICIAL.
WE'RE TOTALLY CENSORED
KZZT!
WE'VE ONE MORE JUMP TO GO, AND OUR DRIVE'S NEXT TO DEAD, SHAW! NOT ENOUGH FUEL TO JUST BOOK IT THERE, EITHER!
YOU BETTER BE DAMNED SURE LEONIS IS ONLY A LEAP AWAY!
WHAT HAPPENS IF IT'S NOT?
WHAT'D I TELL YOU?
"SHUT THE F UP."
AND IT STILL STANDS!
PAW!
SHAW!
C'MON!
AFTER EVERYTHING WE'VE ALREADY DONE, YOU REALLY GOT TO BE A DICK TO HIM, TOO?!
I'M JUST SAYING.
LOOK, WE'D ALL DIE, *OKAY?*
THAT'S ALL THERE IS TO IT.
BEST CASE SCENARIO IS THE DRIVE BLOWS AND WE ALL EXPLODE, BUT THE WORST CASE IS WE TELEPORT INTO SOMETHING ELSE AND YOUR ENTIRE BEING FLIPS INSIDE OUT.
KRIK.
LUCKILY, THAT "KRIK" SOUND MEANS SPACETIME'S GETTING TORE UP, WHICH IS GOOD NEWS FOR US.
SO, CROSS YOUR FINGERS, KIDDO.
HERE WE GO.
CROSSING.
KRIK.

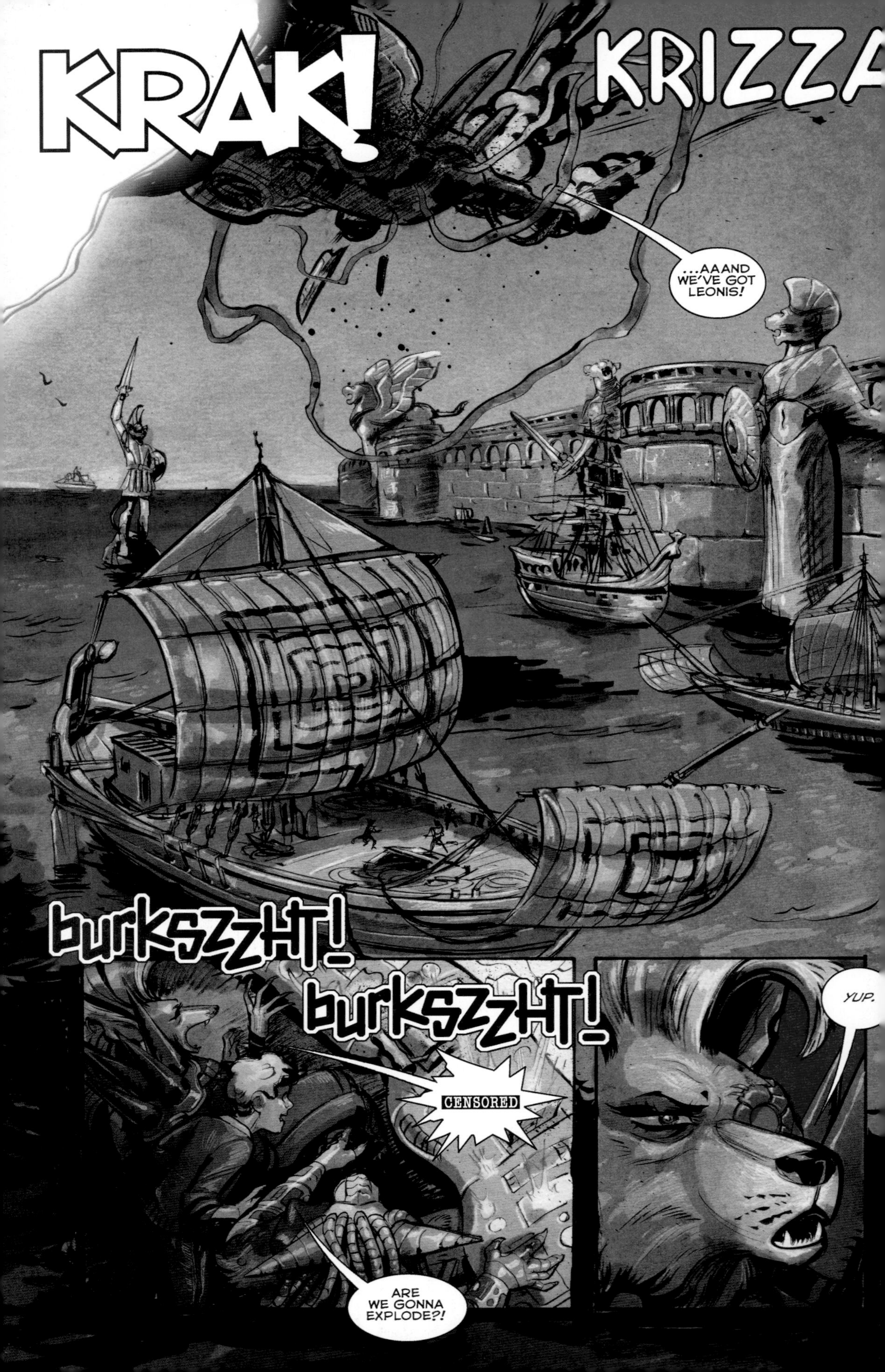
KRAK!
KRIZZA
...AAAND WE'VE GOT LEONIS!
burKSZZHT!
burKSZZHT!
CENSORED
YUP.
ARE WE GONNA EXPLODE?!

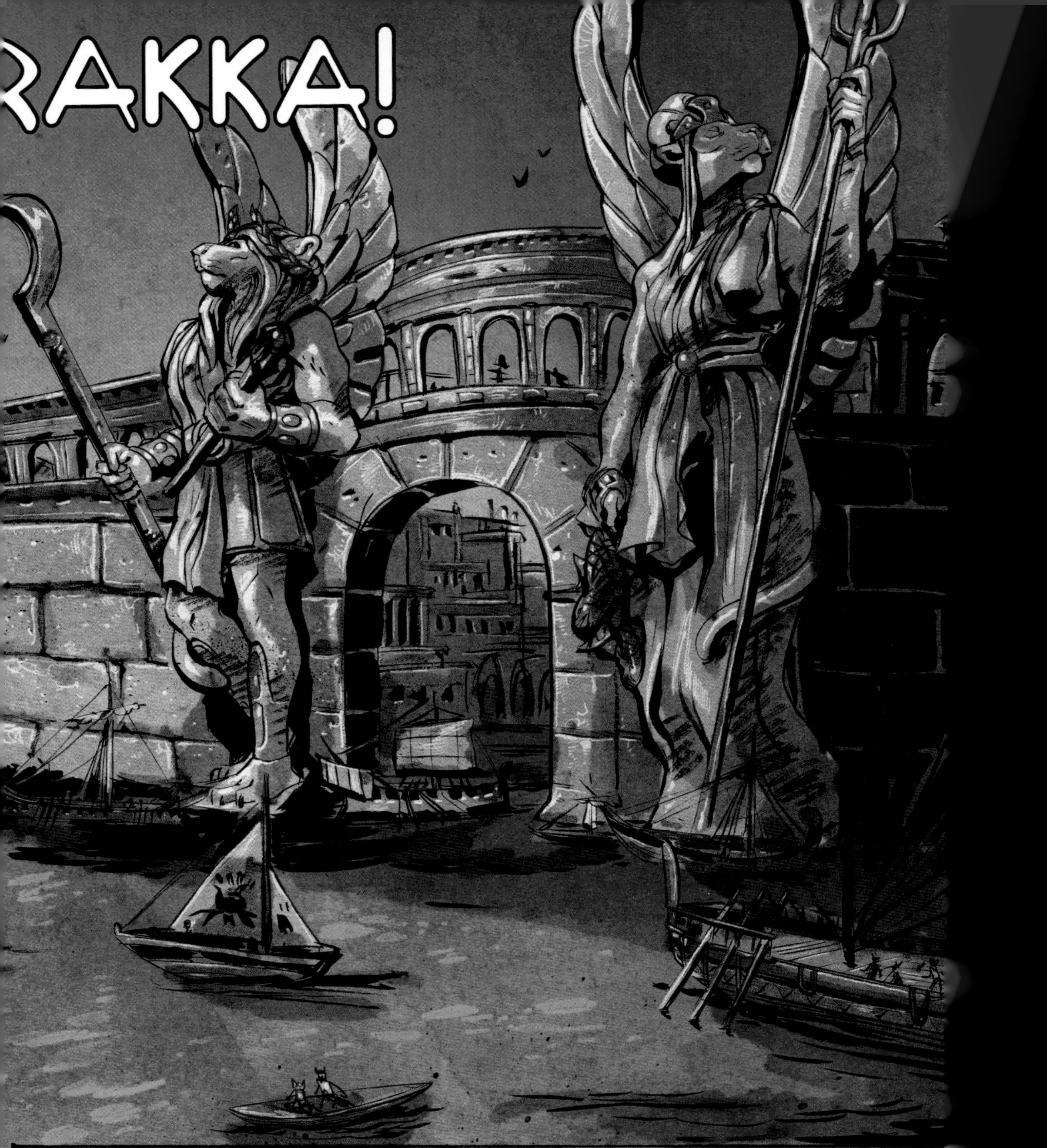
RAKKA!

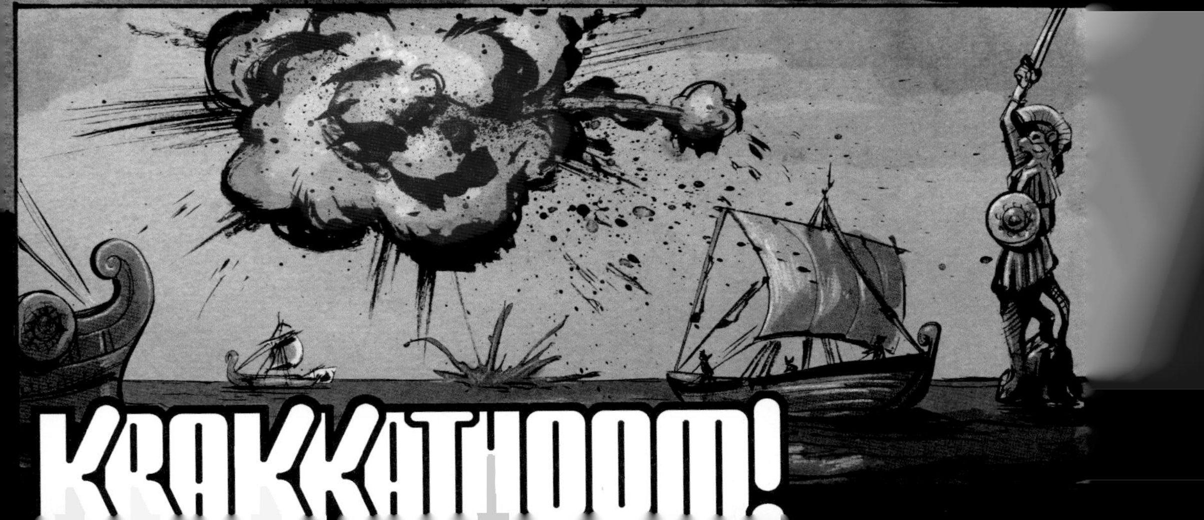
KRAKKATHOOM!

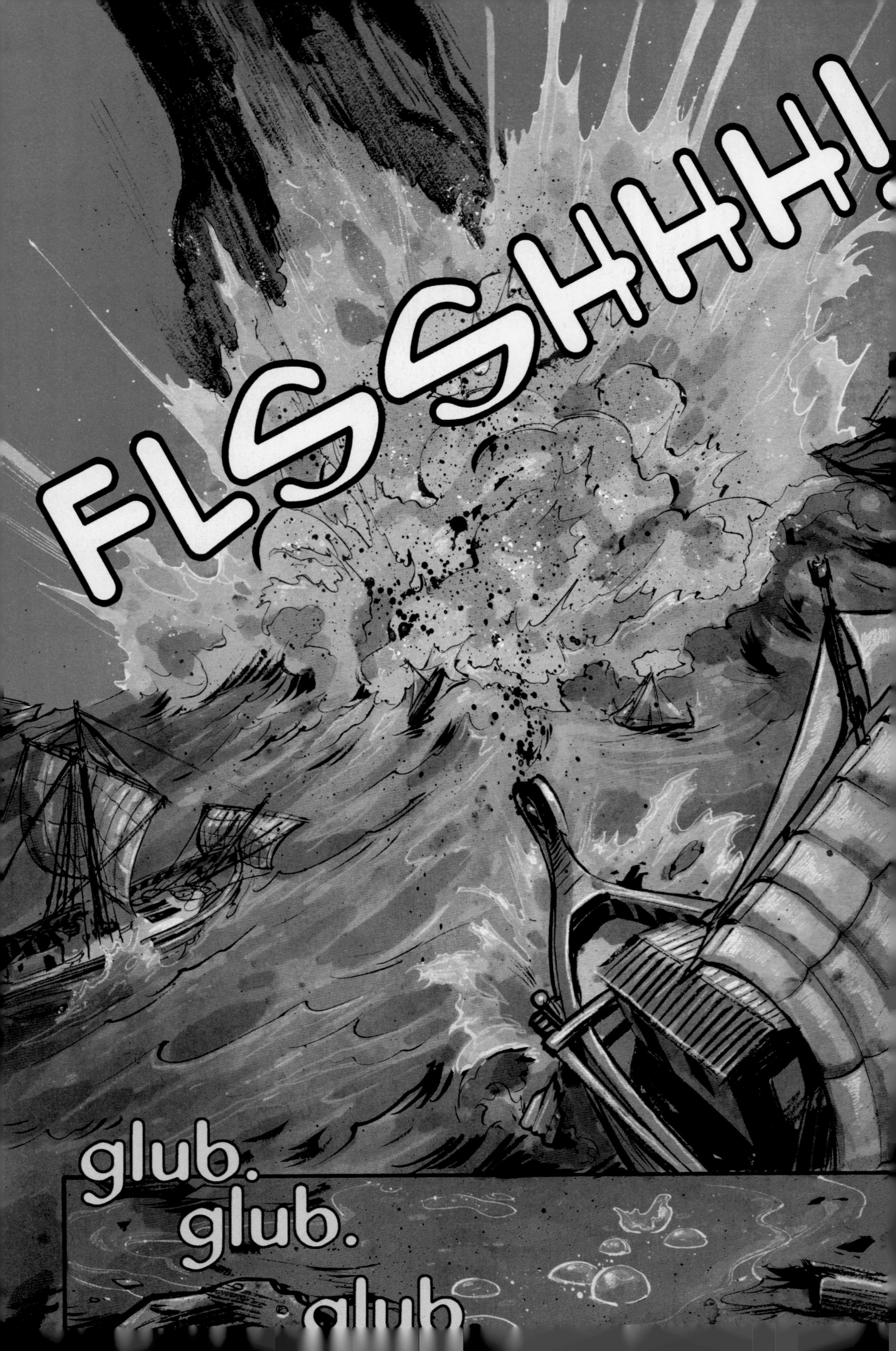
FLSSHHH!
glub.
glub.
glub.

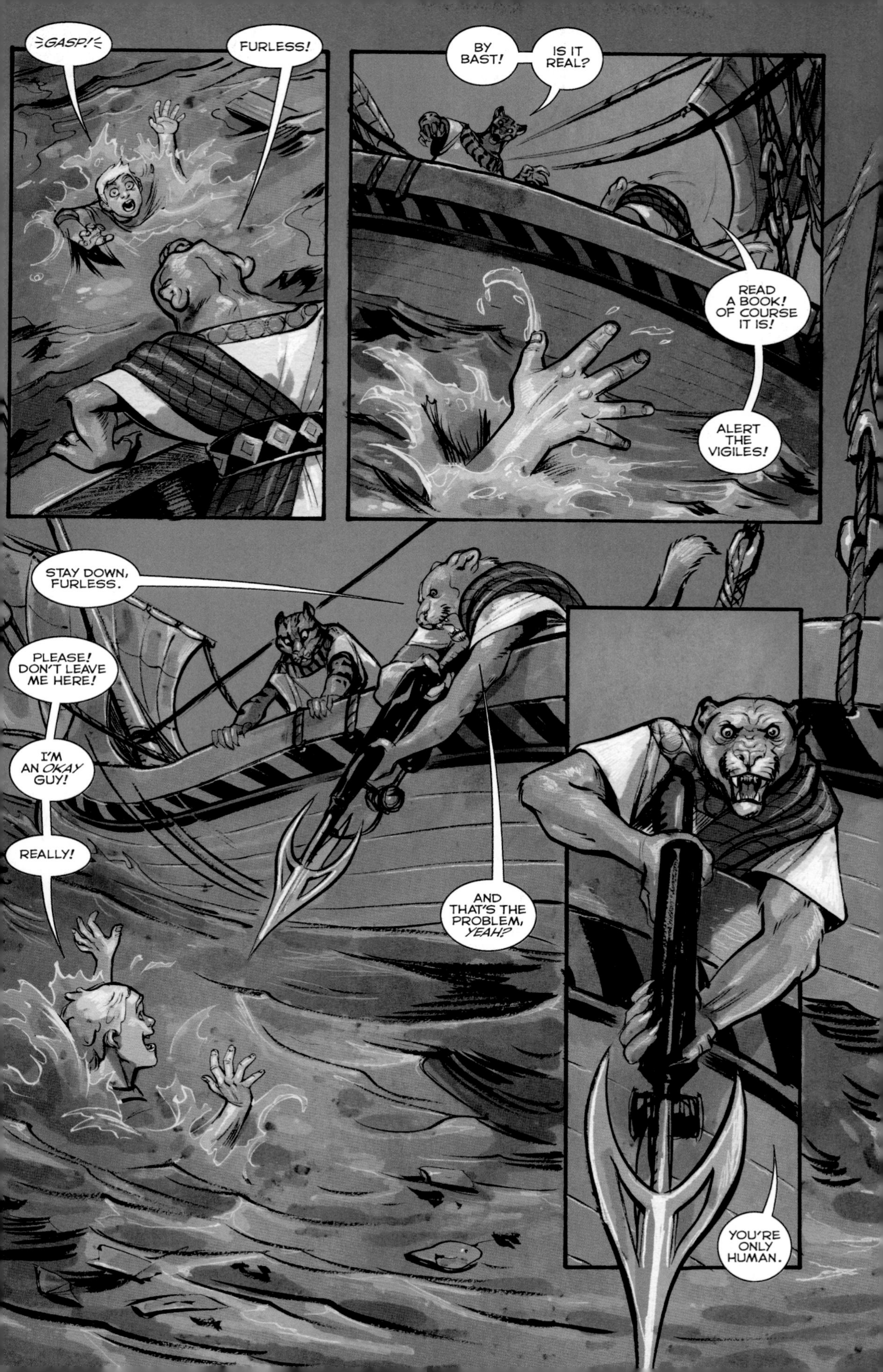

GASP!
FURLESS!
BY BAST!
IS IT REAL?
READ A BOOK! OF COURSE IT IS!
ALERT THE VIGILES!
STAY DOWN, FURLESS.
PLEASE! DON'T LEAVE ME HERE!
I'M AN OKAY GUY!
REALLY!
AND THAT'S THE PROBLEM, YEAH?
YOU'RE ONLY HUMAN.

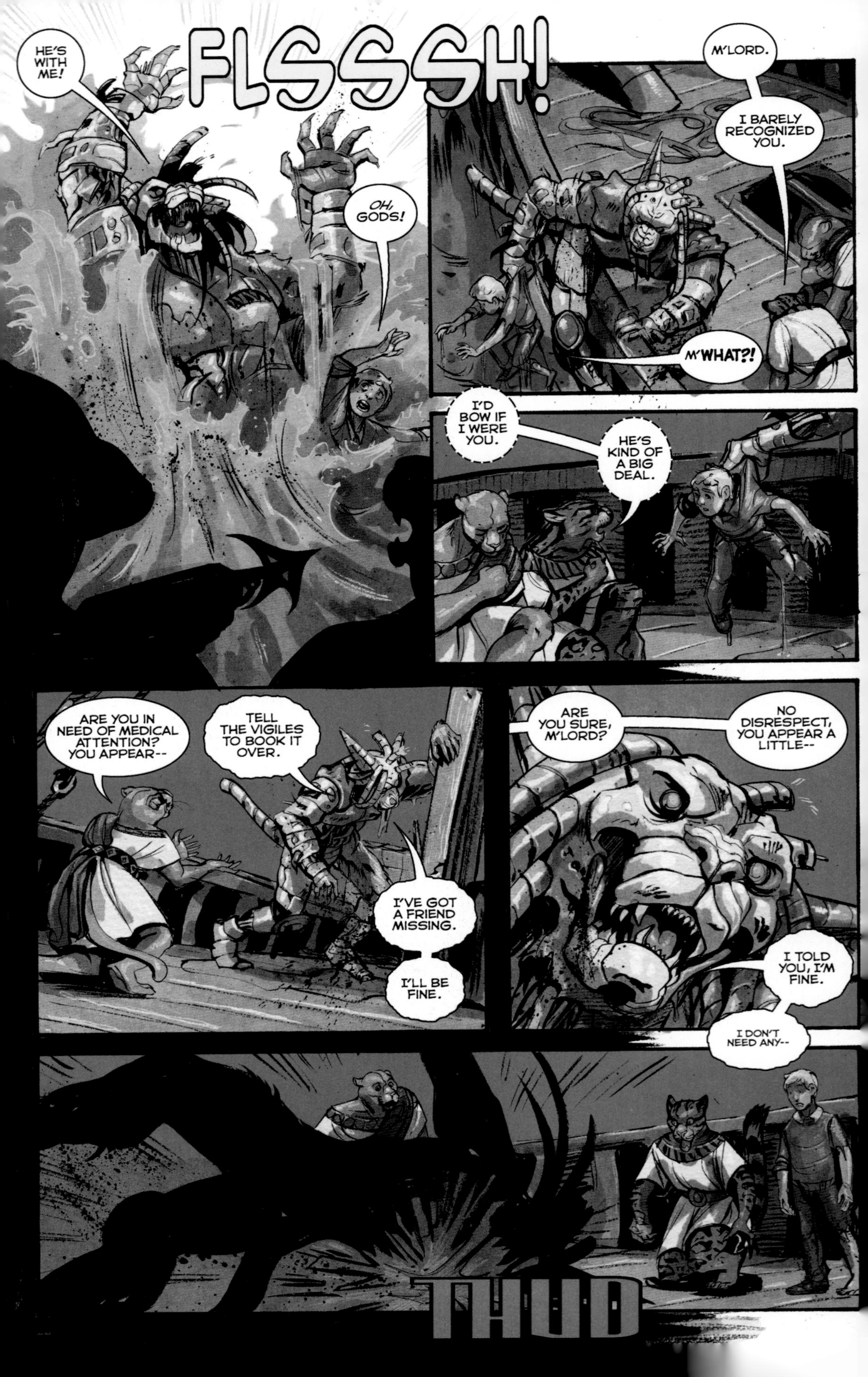
HE'S WITH ME!
FLSSSH!
OH, GODS!
M'LORD.
I BARELY RECOGNIZED YOU.
M'WHAT?!
I'D BOW IF I WERE YOU.
HE'S KIND OF A BIG DEAL.
ARE YOU IN NEED OF MEDICAL ATTENTION? YOU APPEAR--
TELL THE VIGILES TO BOOK IT OVER.
I'VE GOT A FRIEND MISSING.
I'LL BE FINE.
ARE YOU SURE, M'LORD?
NO DISRESPECT, YOU APPEAR A LITTLE--
I TOLD YOU, I'M FINE.
I DON'T NEED ANY--
THUD

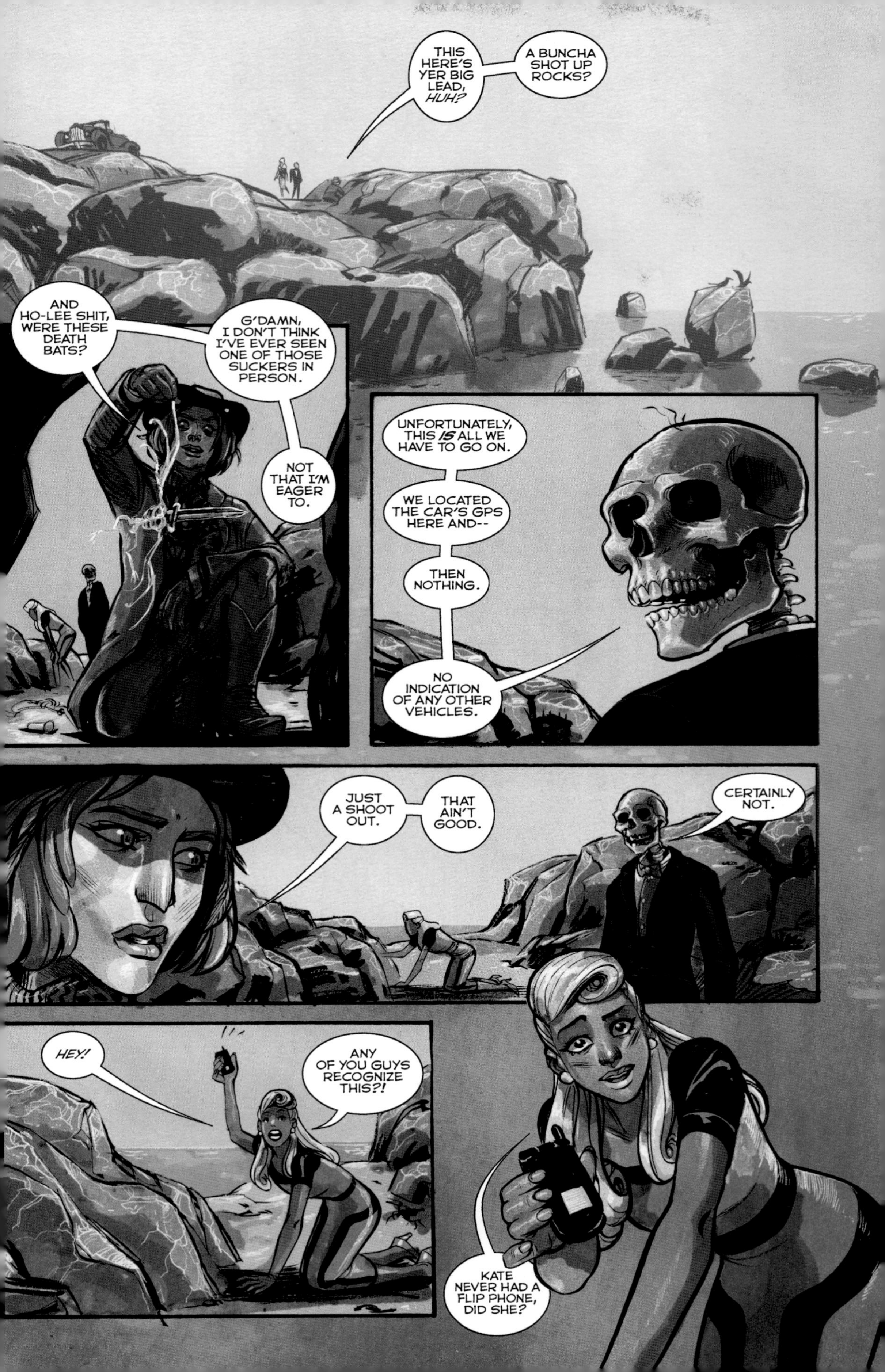
THIS HERE'S YER BIG LEAD, HUH?
A BUNCHA SHOT UP ROCKS?
G'DAMN, I DON'T THINK I'VE EVER SEEN ONE OF THOSE SUCKERS IN PERSON.
NOT THAT I'M EAGER TO.
AND HO-LEE SHIT, WERE THESE DEATH BATS?
UNFORTUNATELY, THIS *IS* ALL WE HAVE TO GO ON.
WE LOCATED THE CAR'S GPS HERE AND--
THEN NOTHING.
NO INDICATION OF ANY OTHER VEHICLES.
JUST A SHOOT OUT.
THAT AIN'T GOOD.
CERTAINLY NOT.
HEY!
ANY OF YOU GUYS RECOGNIZE THIS?!
KATE NEVER HAD A FLIP PHONE, DID SHE?

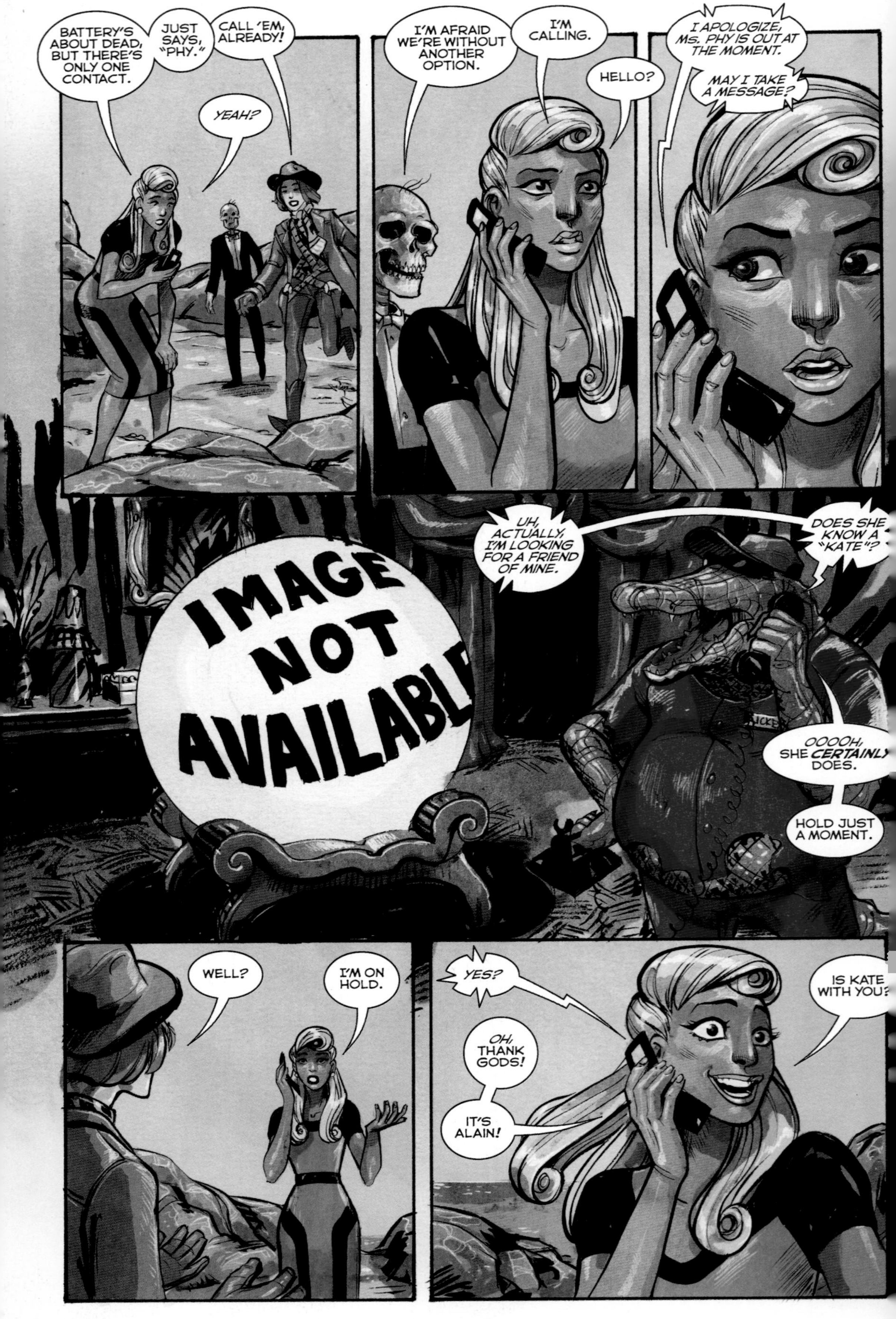
BATTERY'S ABOUT DEAD, BUT THERE'S ONLY ONE CONTACT.
JUST SAYS, "PHY."
CALL 'EM, ALREADY!
YEAH?
I'M AFRAID WE'RE WITHOUT ANOTHER OPTION.
I'M CALLING.
HELLO?
I APOLOGIZE, MS. PHY IS OUT AT THE MOMENT.
MAY I TAKE A MESSAGE?
IMAGE NOT AVAILABLE
UH, ACTUALLY, I'M LOOKING FOR A FRIEND OF MINE.
DOES SHE KNOW A "KATE"?
OOOOH, SHE CERTAINLY DOES.
HOLD JUST A MOMENT.
WELL?
I'M ON HOLD.
YES?
OH, THANK GODS!
IT'S ALAIN!
IS KATE WITH YOU?

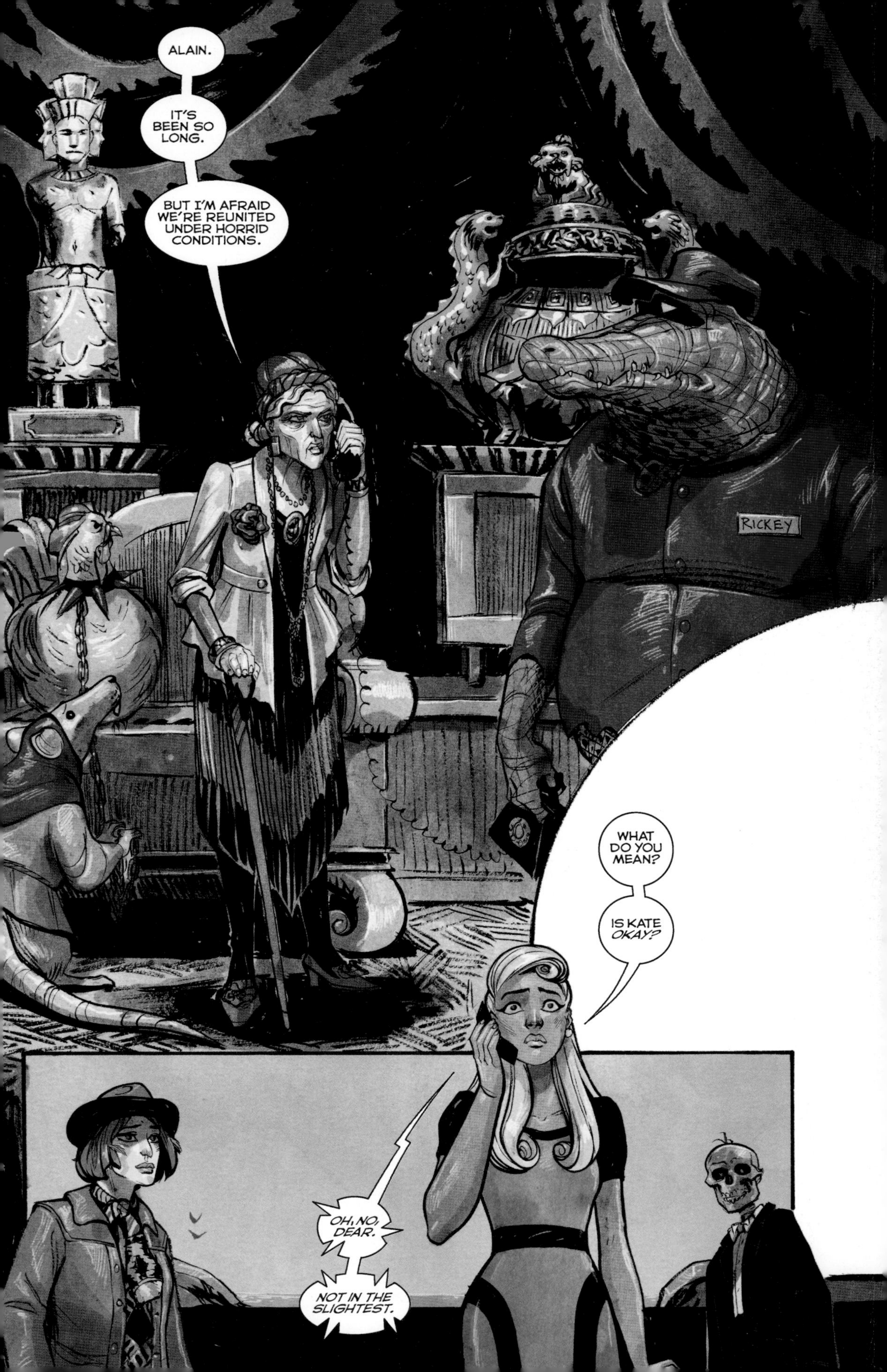
ALAIN.
IT'S BEEN SO LONG.
BUT I'M AFRAID WE'RE REUNITED UNDER HORRID CONDITIONS.
RICKEY
WHAT DO YOU MEAN?
IS KATE *OKAY?*
OH, NO, DEAR.
NOT IN THE SLIGHTEST.

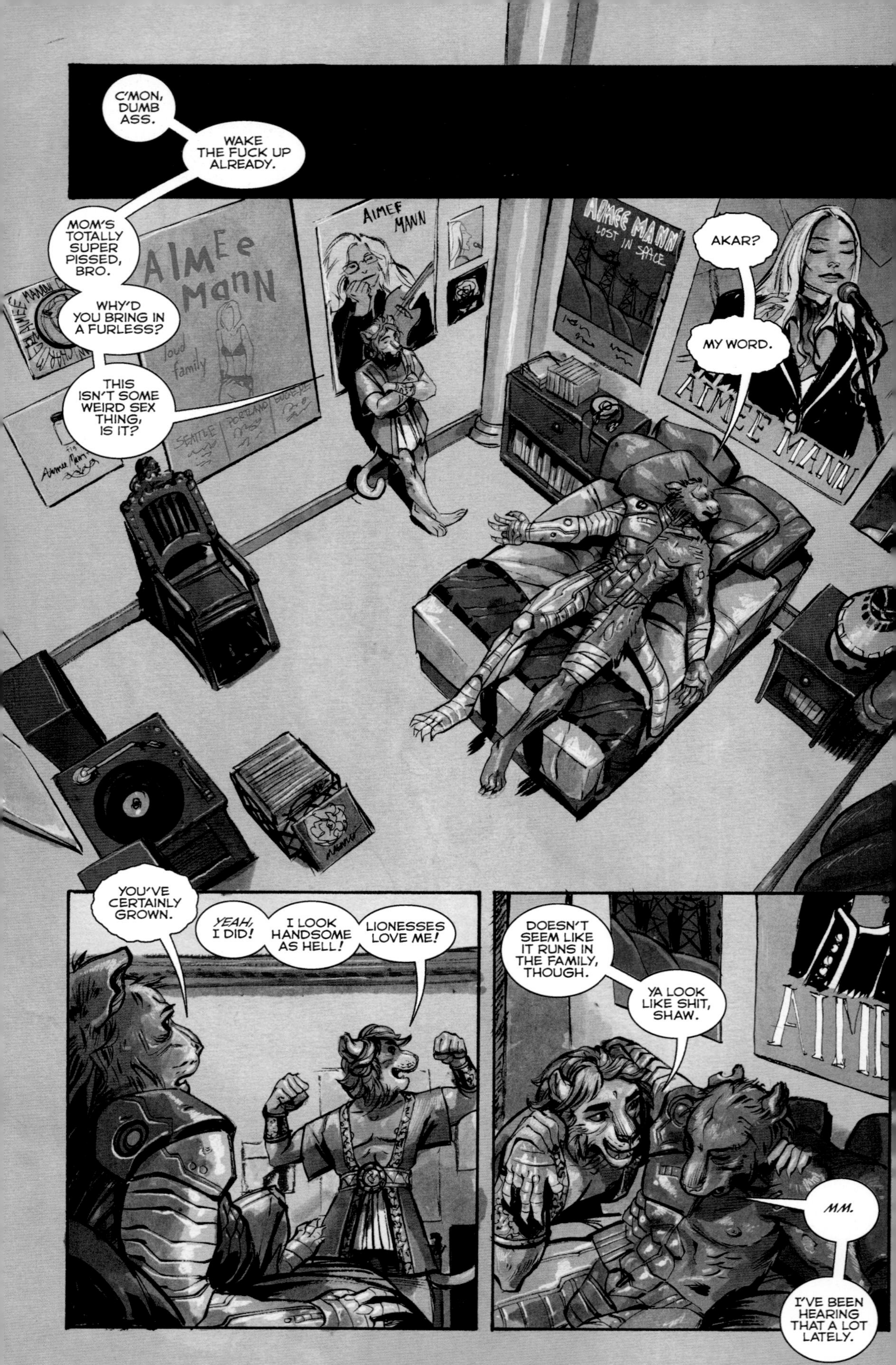

C'MON, DUMB ASS.
WAKE THE FUCK UP ALREADY.
MOM'S TOTALLY SUPER PISSED, BRO.
WHY'D YOU BRING IN A FURLESS?
THIS ISN'T SOME WEIRD SEX THING, IS IT?
AIMEE MANN
AIMEE MANN LOST IN SPACE
AKAR?
MY WORD.
AIMEE MANN
YOU'VE CERTAINLY GROWN.
YEAH, I DID!
I LOOK HANDSOME AS HELL!
LIONESSES LOVE ME!
DOESN'T SEEM LIKE IT RUNS IN THE FAMILY, THOUGH.
YA LOOK LIKE SHIT, SHAW.
MM.
I'VE BEEN HEARING THAT A LOT LATELY.

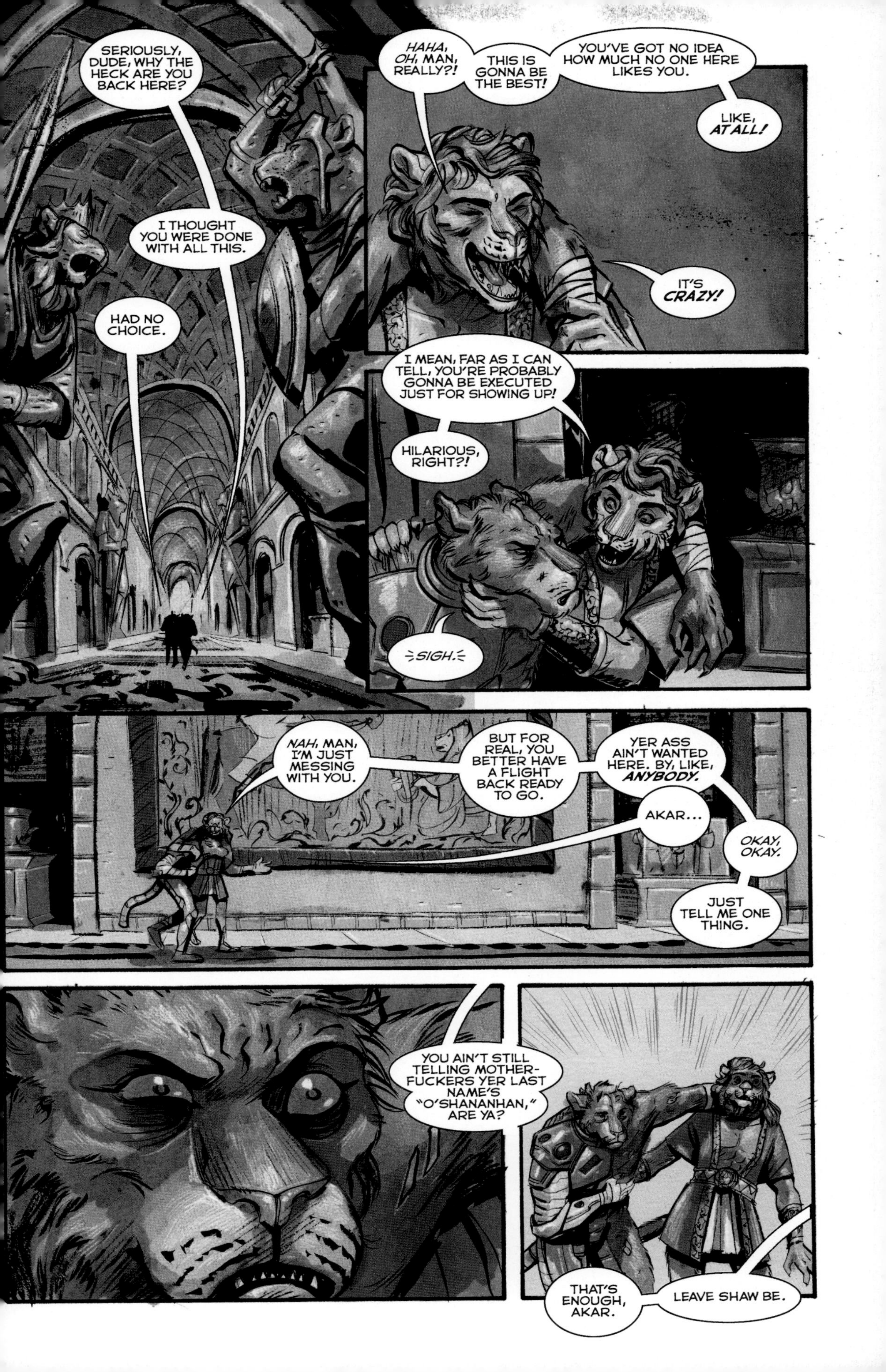
SERIOUSLY, DUDE, WHY THE HECK ARE YOU BACK HERE?
I THOUGHT YOU WERE DONE WITH ALL THIS.
HAD NO CHOICE.
HAHA, OH, MAN, REALLY?!
THIS IS GONNA BE THE BEST!
YOU'VE GOT NO IDEA HOW MUCH NO ONE HERE LIKES YOU.
LIKE, AT ALL!
IT'S CRAZY!
I MEAN, FAR AS I CAN TELL, YOU'RE PROBABLY GONNA BE EXECUTED JUST FOR SHOWING UP!
HILARIOUS, RIGHT?!
SIGH.
NAH, MAN, I'M JUST MESSING WITH YOU.
BUT FOR REAL, YOU BETTER HAVE A FLIGHT BACK READY TO GO.
YER ASS AIN'T WANTED HERE. BY, LIKE, ANYBODY.
AKAR...
OKAY, OKAY.
JUST TELL ME ONE THING.
YOU AIN'T STILL TELLING MOTHER-FUCKERS YER LAST NAME'S "O'SHANANHAN," ARE YA?
THAT'S ENOUGH, AKAR.
LEAVE SHAW BE.

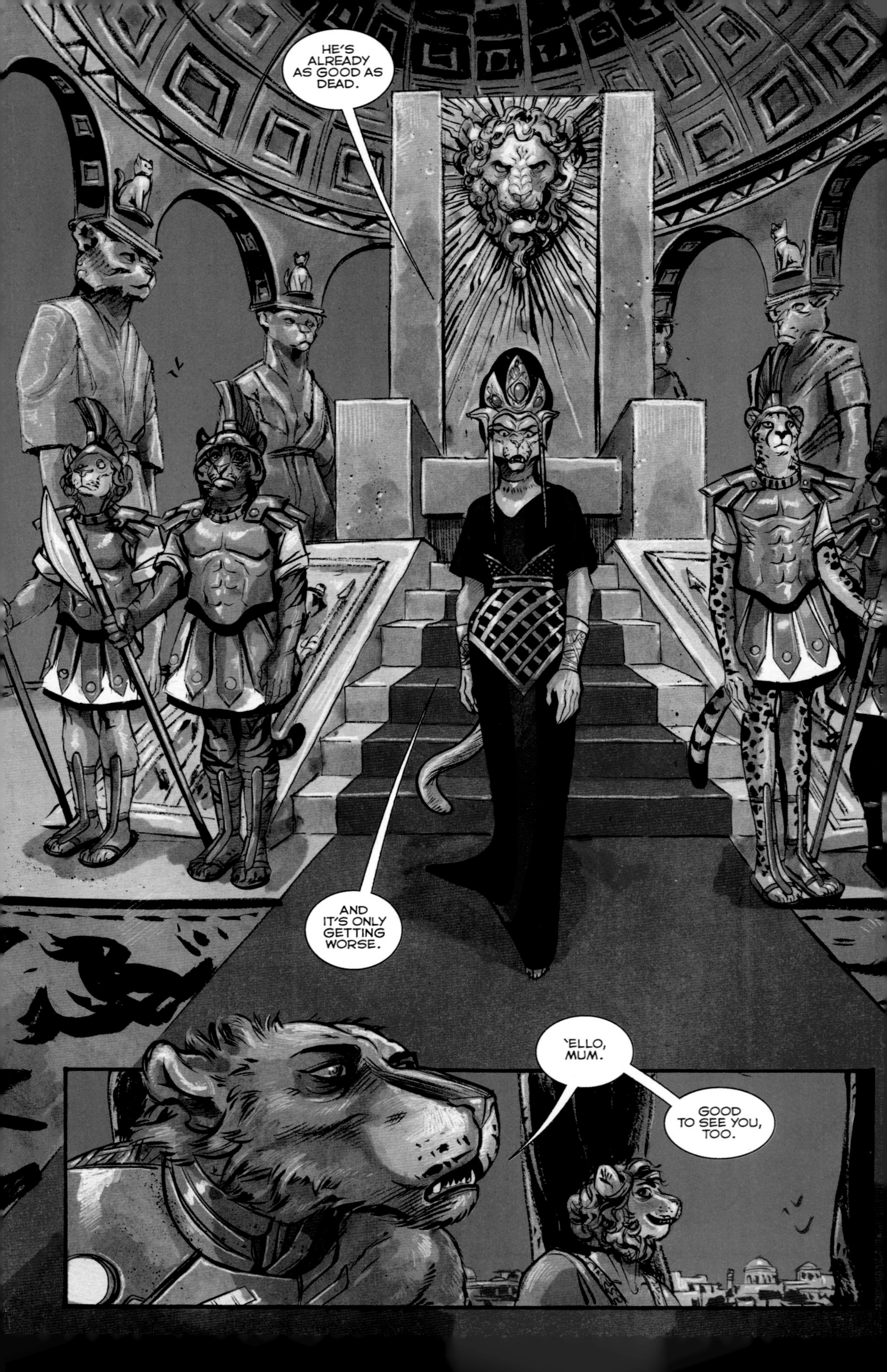
HE'S ALREADY AS GOOD AS DEAD.
AND IT'S ONLY GETTING WORSE.
`ELLO, MUM.
GOOD TO SEE YOU, TOO.

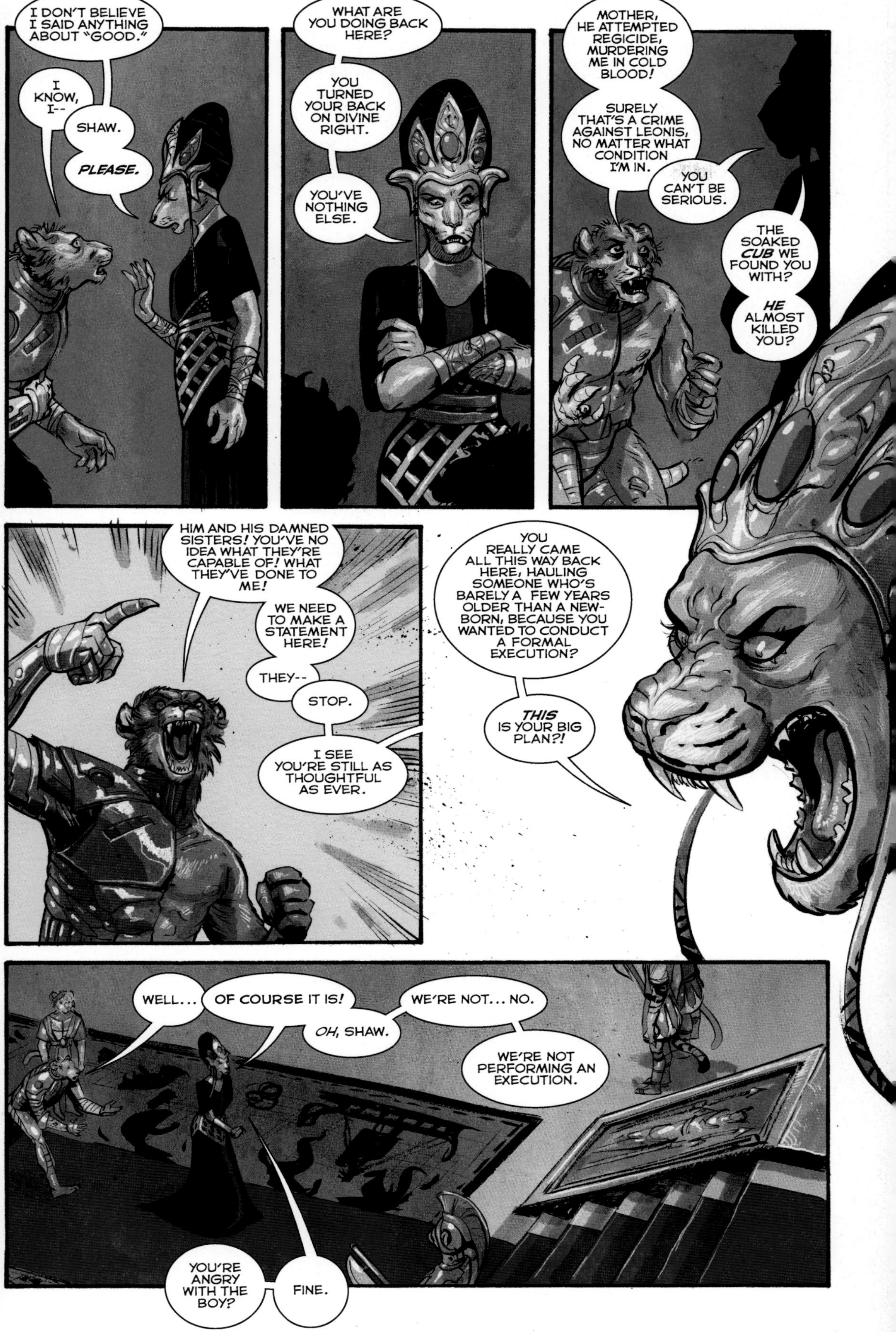
I DON'T BELIEVE I SAID ANYTHING ABOUT "GOOD."
I KNOW, I--
SHAW.
PLEASE.
WHAT ARE YOU DOING BACK HERE?
YOU TURNED YOUR BACK ON DIVINE RIGHT.
YOU'VE NOTHING ELSE.
MOTHER, HE ATTEMPTED REGICIDE, MURDERING ME IN COLD BLOOD!
SURELY THAT'S A CRIME AGAINST LEONIS, NO MATTER WHAT CONDITION I'M IN.
YOU CAN'T BE SERIOUS.
THE SOAKED CUB WE FOUND YOU WITH?
HE ALMOST KILLED YOU?
HIM AND HIS DAMNED SISTERS! YOU'VE NO IDEA WHAT THEY'RE CAPABLE OF! WHAT THEY'VE DONE TO ME!
WE NEED TO MAKE A STATEMENT HERE!
THEY--
STOP.
I SEE YOU'RE STILL AS THOUGHTFUL AS EVER.
YOU REALLY CAME ALL THIS WAY BACK HERE, HAULING SOMEONE WHO'S BARELY A FEW YEARS OLDER THAN A NEW-BORN, BECAUSE YOU WANTED TO CONDUCT A FORMAL EXECUTION?
THIS IS YOUR BIG PLAN?!
WELL...
OF COURSE IT IS!
WE'RE NOT... NO.
OH, SHAW.
WE'RE NOT PERFORMING AN EXECUTION.
YOU'RE ANGRY WITH THE BOY?
FINE.

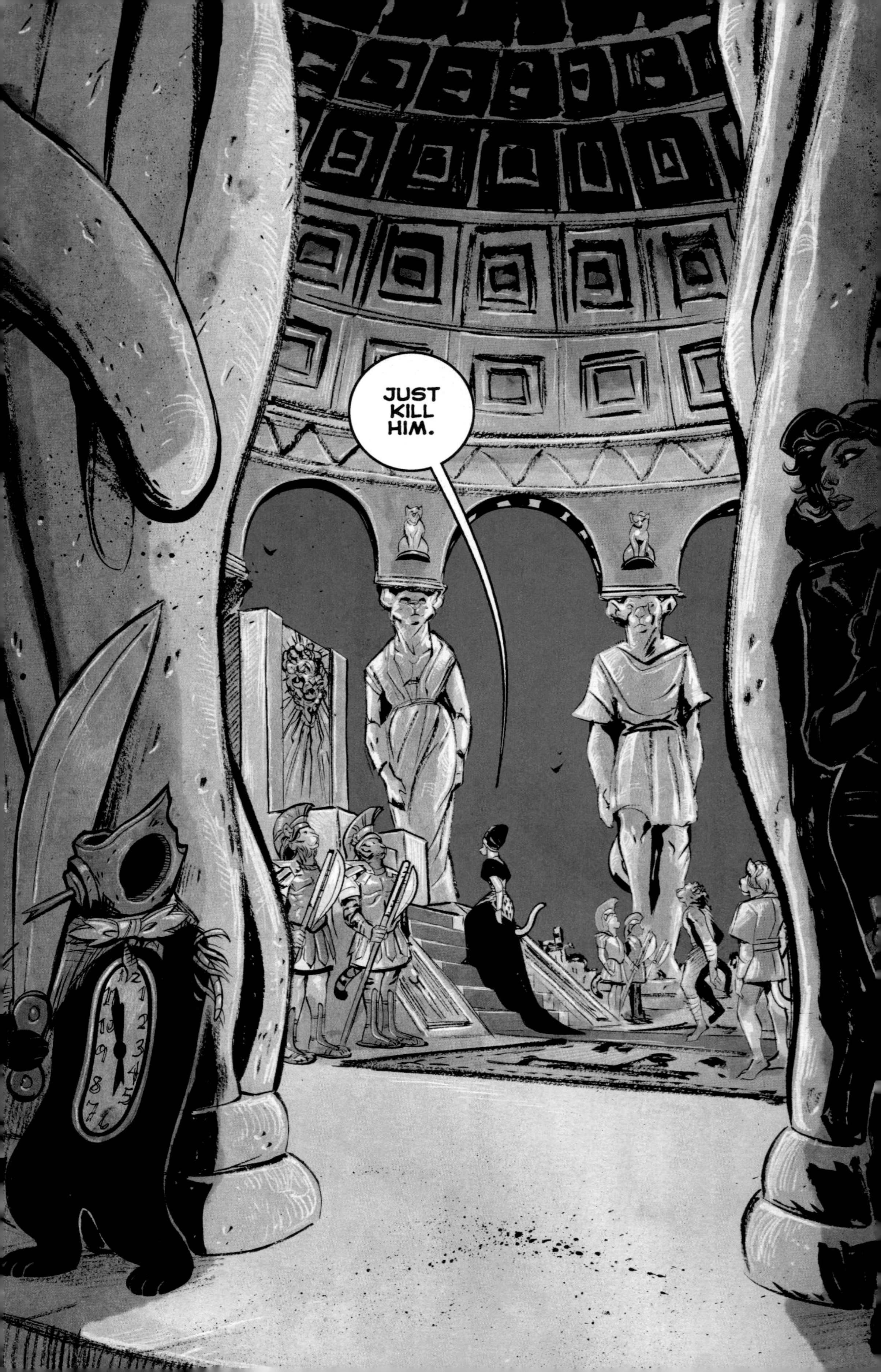
JUST KILL HIM.

CHAPTER 16

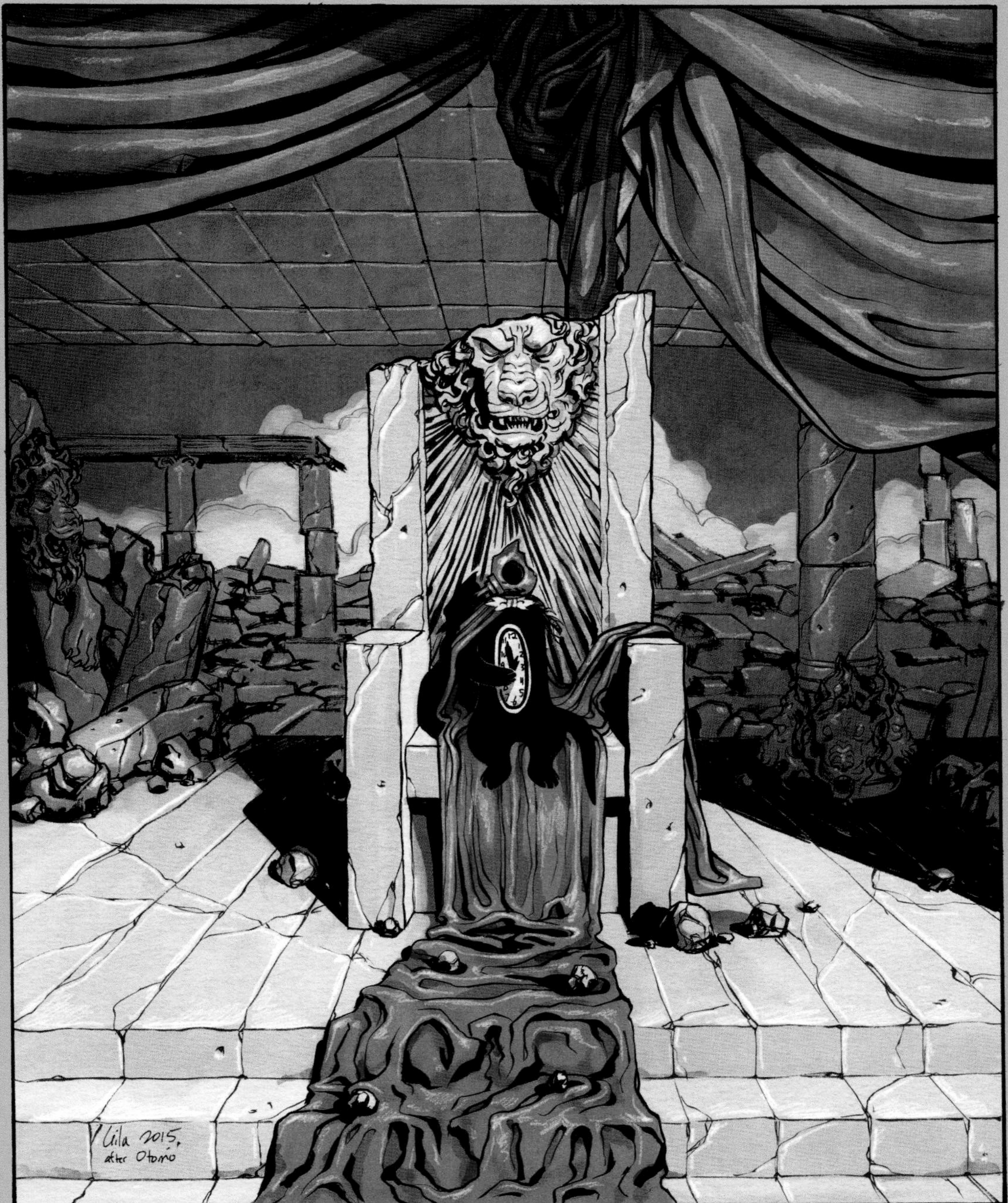
Lila 2015,
after Otomo

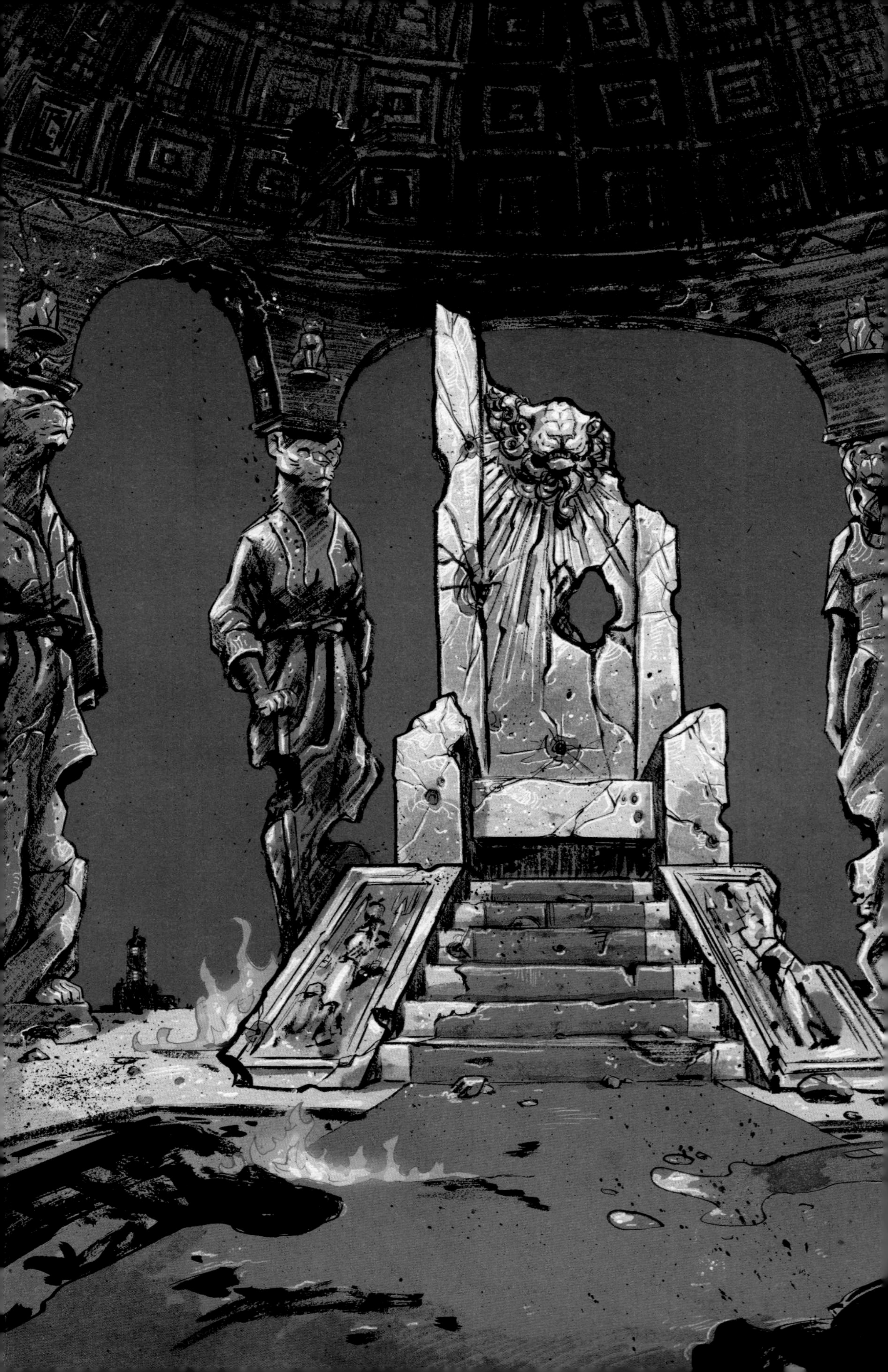

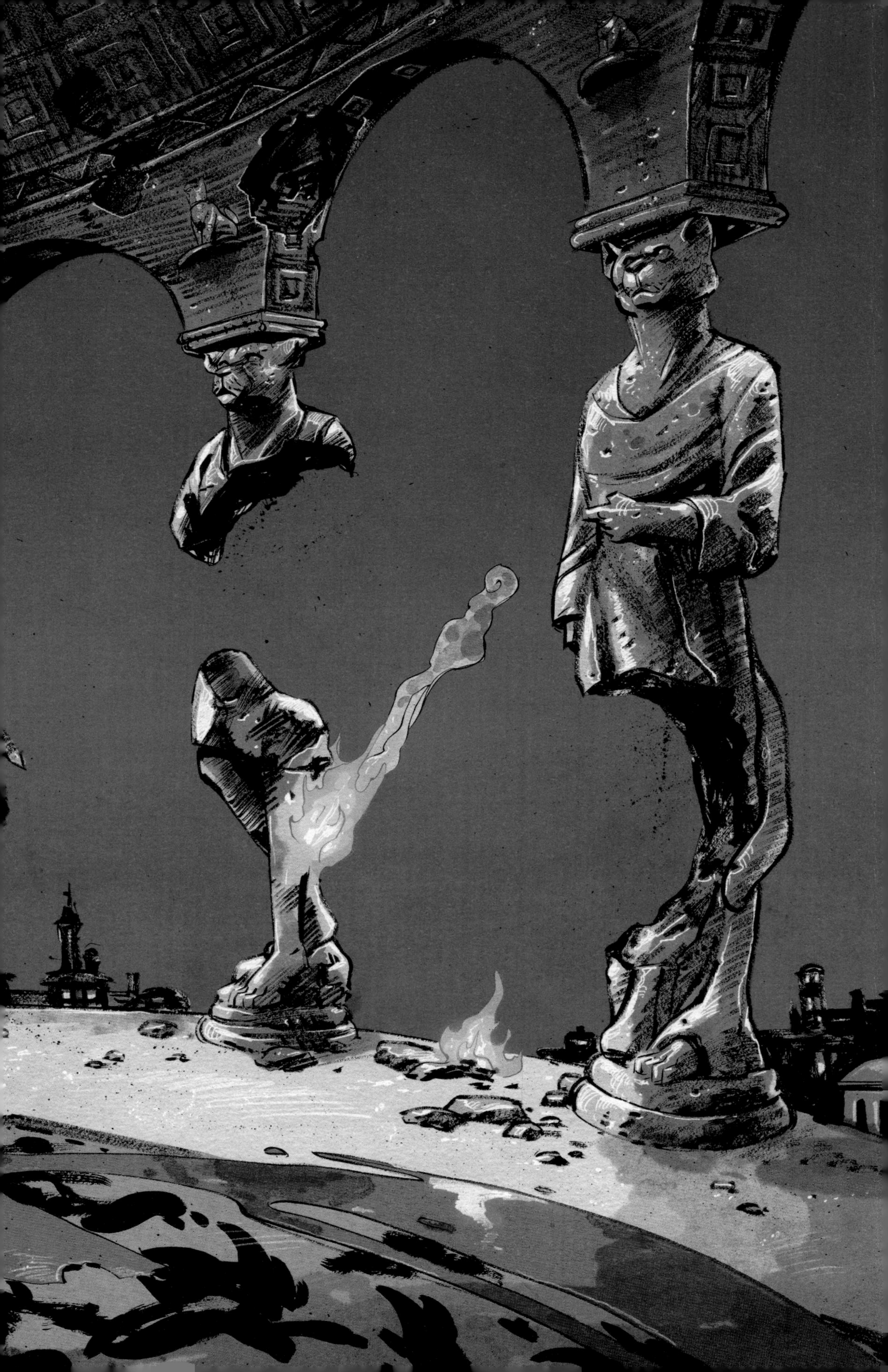

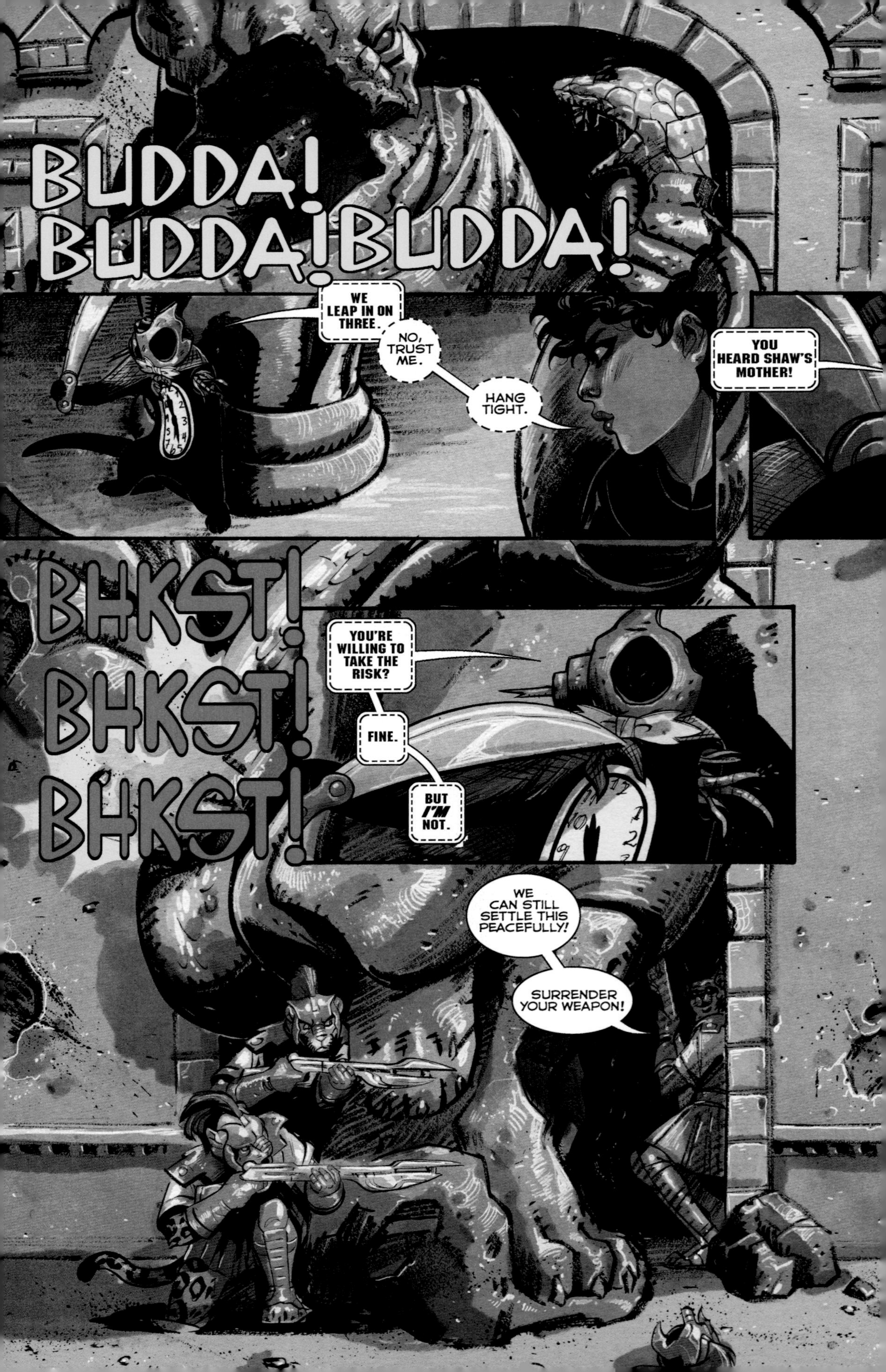
BUDDA! BUDDA! BUDDA!
WE LEAP IN ON THREE.
NO, TRUST ME.
HANG TIGHT.
YOU HEARD SHAW'S MOTHER!
BHKST! BHKST! BHKST!
YOU'RE WILLING TO TAKE THE RISK?
FINE.
BUT I'M NOT.
WE CAN STILL SETTLE THIS PEACEFULLY!
SURRENDER YOUR WEAPON!

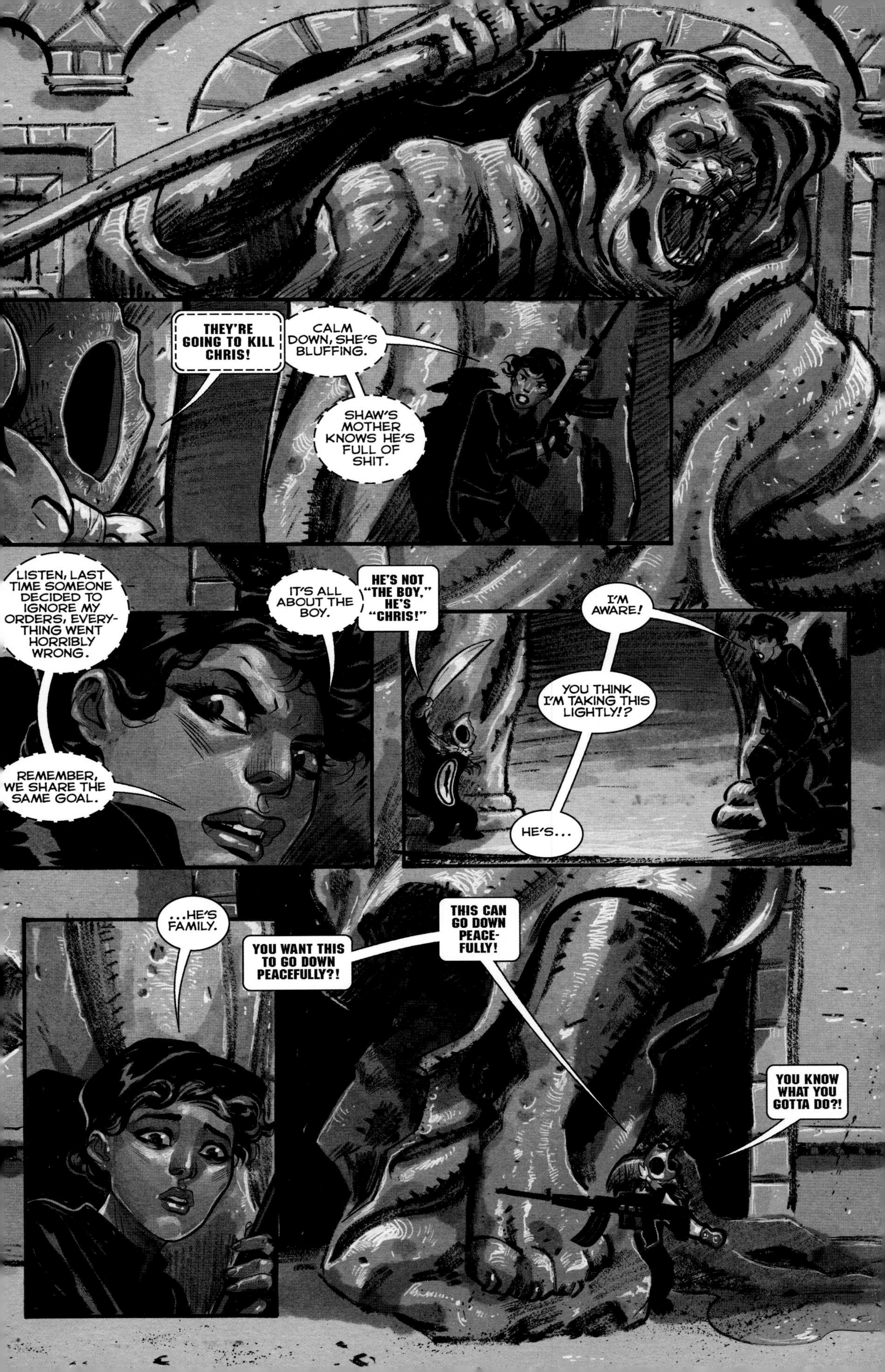
THEY'RE GOING TO KILL CHRIS!
CALM DOWN, SHE'S BLUFFING.
SHAW'S MOTHER KNOWS HE'S FULL OF SHIT.
LISTEN, LAST TIME SOMEONE DECIDED TO IGNORE MY ORDERS, EVERY-THING WENT HORRIBLY WRONG.
REMEMBER, WE SHARE THE SAME GOAL.
IT'S ALL ABOUT THE BOY.
HE'S NOT "THE BOY," HE'S "CHRIS!"
I'M AWARE!
YOU THINK I'M TAKING THIS LIGHTLY!?
HE'S...
...HE'S FAMILY.
YOU WANT THIS TO GO DOWN PEACEFULLY?!
THIS CAN GO DOWN PEACE-FULLY!
YOU KNOW WHAT YOU GOTTA DO?!

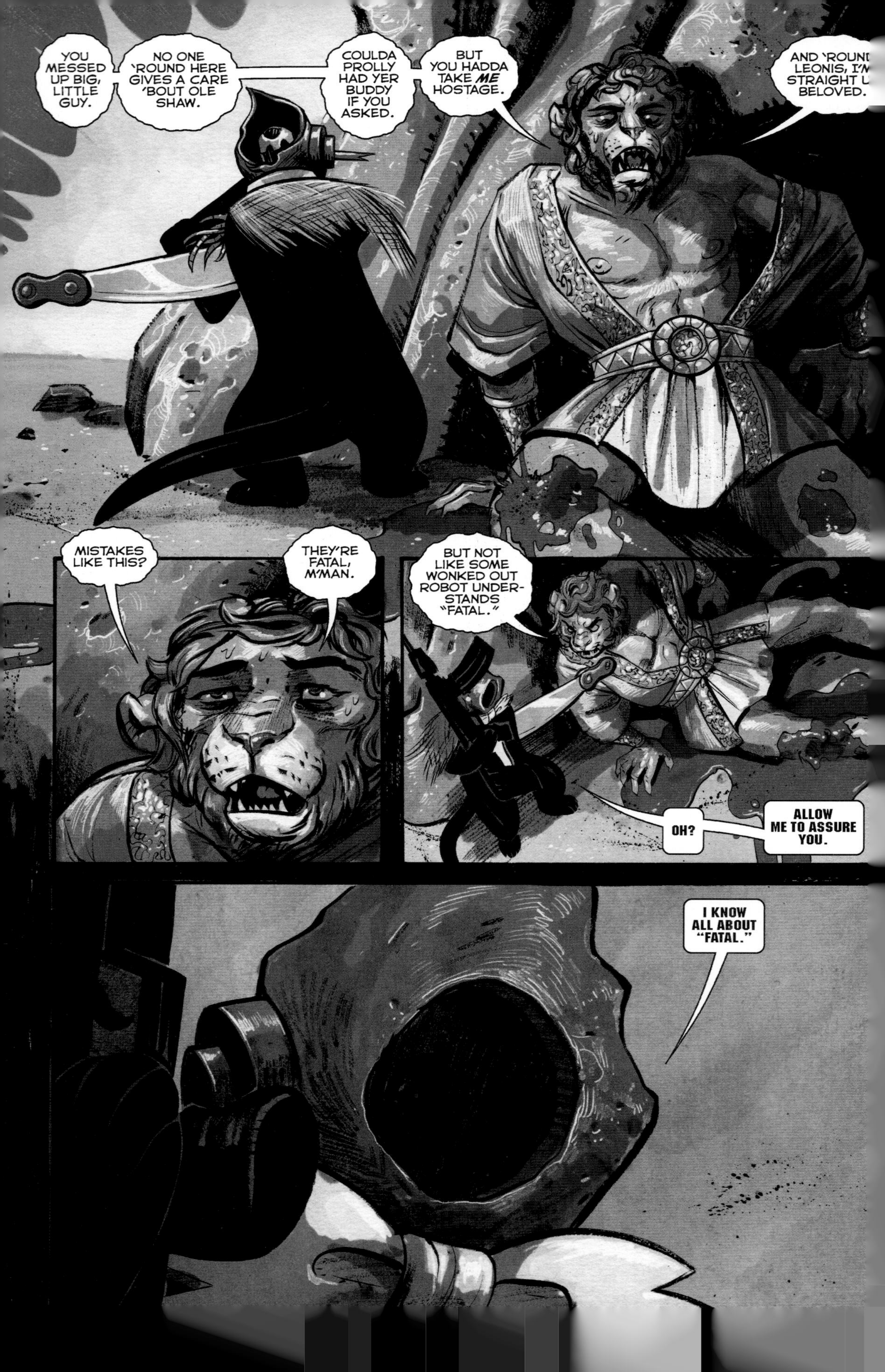
YOU MESSED UP BIG, LITTLE GUY.
NO ONE 'ROUND HERE GIVES A CARE 'BOUT OLE SHAW.
COULDA PROLLY HAD YER BUDDY IF YOU ASKED.
BUT YOU HADDA TAKE *ME* HOSTAGE.
AND 'ROUN LEONIS, I'M STRAIGHT U BELOVED.
MISTAKES LIKE THIS?
THEY'RE FATAL, M'MAN.
BUT NOT LIKE SOME WONKED OUT ROBOT UNDER-STANDS "FATAL."
OH?
ALLOW ME TO ASSURE YOU.
I KNOW ALL ABOUT "FATAL."

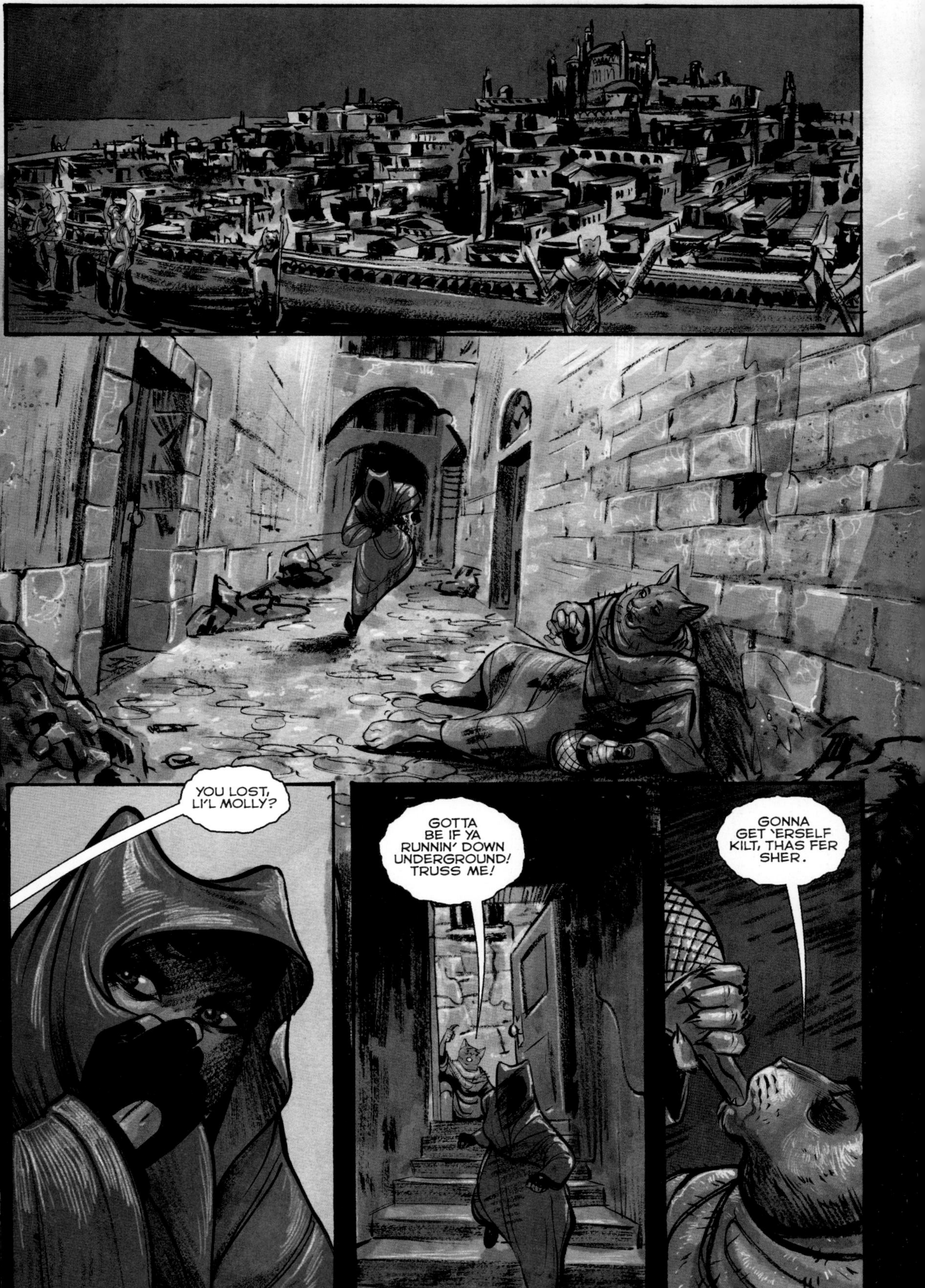
YOU LOST, LI'L MOLLY?
GOTTA BE IF YA RUNNIN' DOWN UNDERGROUND! TRUSS ME!
GONNA GET 'ERSELF KILT, THAS FER SHER.

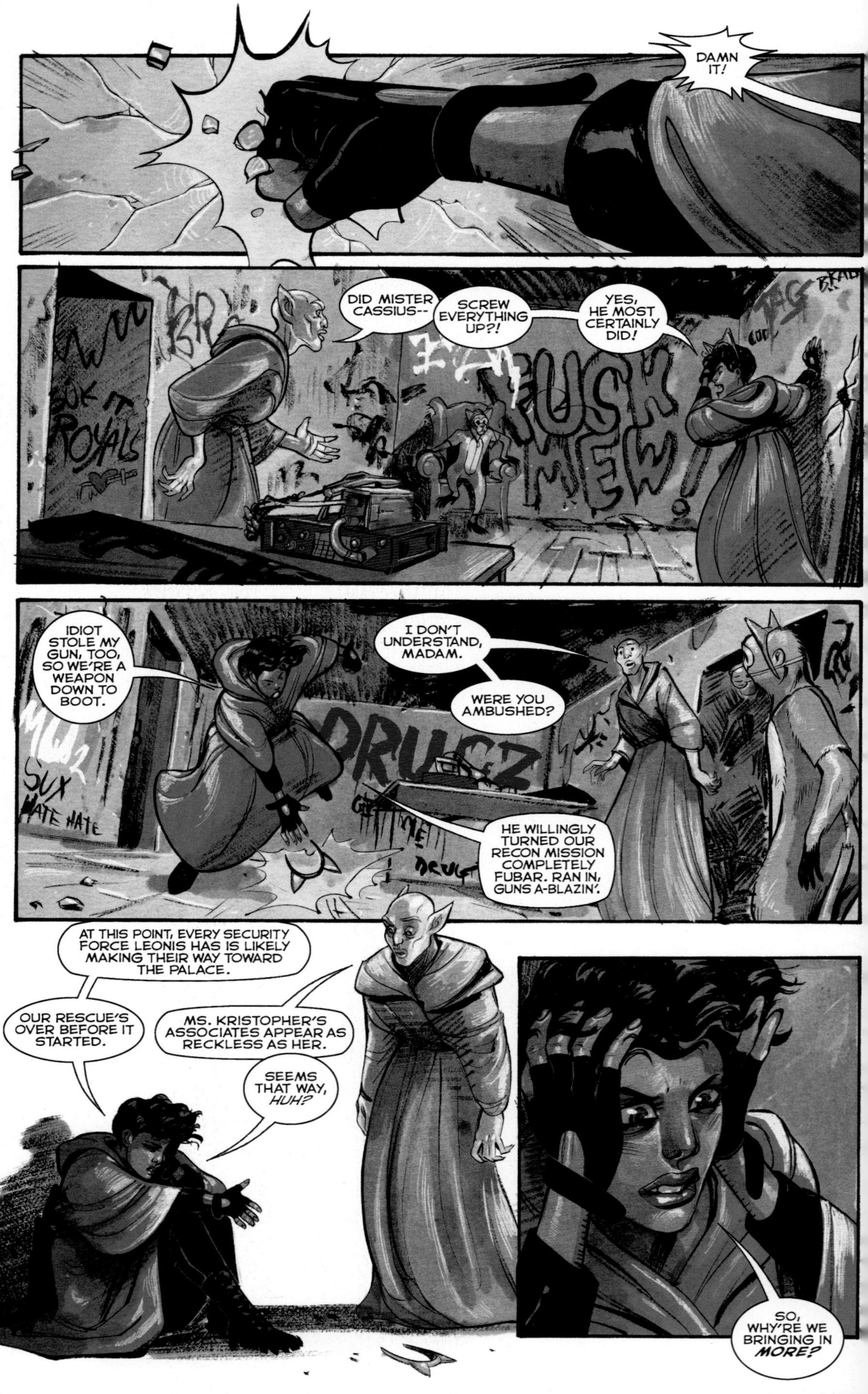
DAMN IT!
DID MISTER CASSIUS--
SCREW EVERYTHING UP?!
YES, HE MOST CERTAINLY DID!
IDIOT STOLE MY GUN, TOO, SO WE'RE A WEAPON DOWN TO BOOT.
I DON'T UNDERSTAND, MADAM.
WERE YOU AMBUSHED?
HE WILLINGLY TURNED OUR RECON MISSION COMPLETELY FUBAR. RAN IN, GUNS A-BLAZIN'.
AT THIS POINT, EVERY SECURITY FORCE LEONIS HAS IS LIKELY MAKING THEIR WAY TOWARD THE PALACE.
OUR RESCUE'S OVER BEFORE IT STARTED.
MS. KRISTOPHER'S ASSOCIATES APPEAR AS RECKLESS AS HER.
SEEMS THAT WAY, *HUH?*
SO, WHY'RE WE BRINGING IN *MORE?*

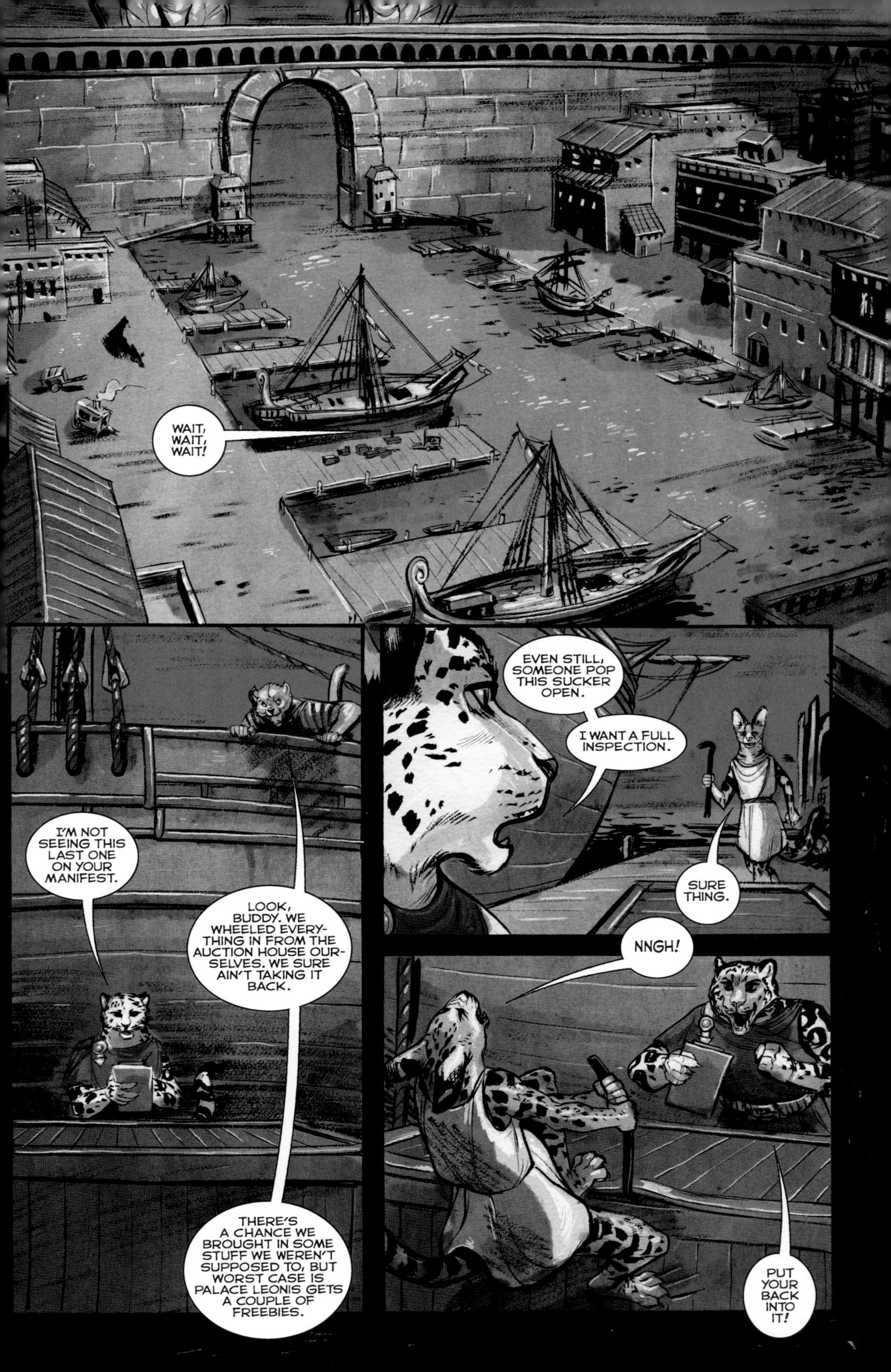
WAIT, WAIT, WAIT!
I'M NOT SEEING THIS LAST ONE ON YOUR MANIFEST.
LOOK, BUDDY. WE WHEELED EVERY-THING IN FROM THE AUCTION HOUSE OUR-SELVES. WE SURE AIN'T TAKING IT BACK.
THERE'S A CHANCE WE BROUGHT IN SOME STUFF WE WEREN'T SUPPOSED TO, BUT WORST CASE IS PALACE LEONIS GETS A COUPLE OF FREEBIES.
EVEN STILL, SOMEONE POP THIS SUCKER OPEN.
I WANT A FULL INSPECTION.
SURE THING.
NNGH!
PUT YOUR BACK INTO IT!

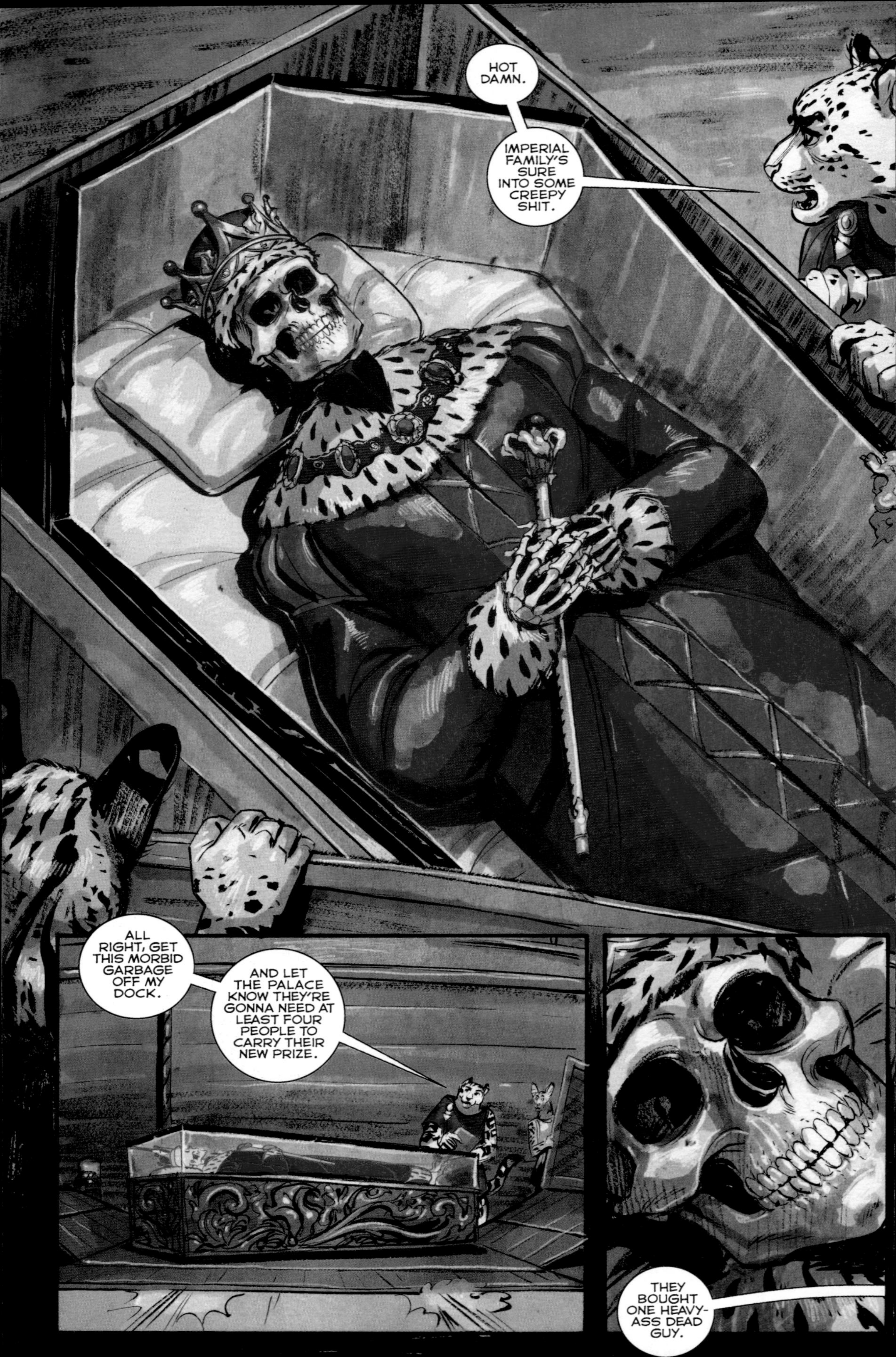
HOT DAMN.
IMPERIAL FAMILY'S SURE INTO SOME CREEPY SHIT.
ALL RIGHT, GET THIS MORBID GARBAGE OFF MY DOCK.
AND LET THE PALACE KNOW THEY'RE GONNA NEED AT LEAST FOUR PEOPLE TO CARRY THEIR NEW PRIZE.
THEY BOUGHT ONE HEAVY-ASS DEAD GUY.

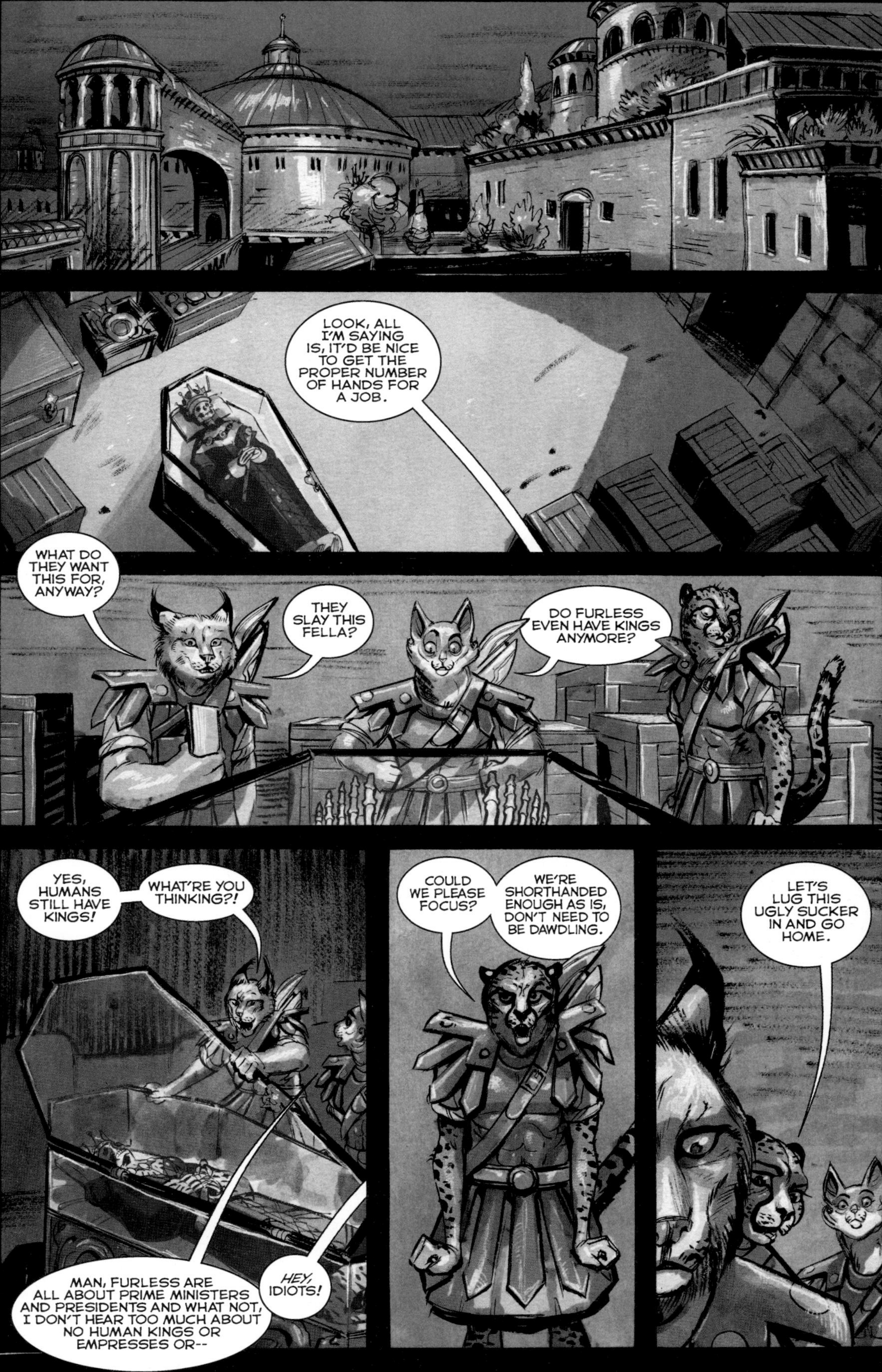
LOOK, ALL I'M SAYING IS, IT'D BE NICE TO GET THE PROPER NUMBER OF HANDS FOR A JOB.
WHAT DO THEY WANT THIS FOR, ANYWAY?
THEY SLAY THIS FELLA?
DO FURLESS EVEN HAVE KINGS ANYMORE?
YES, HUMANS STILL HAVE KINGS!
WHAT'RE YOU THINKING?!
MAN, FURLESS ARE ALL ABOUT PRIME MINISTERS AND PRESIDENTS AND WHAT NOT, I DON'T HEAR TOO MUCH ABOUT NO HUMAN KINGS OR EMPRESSES OR--
HEY, IDIOTS!
COULD WE PLEASE FOCUS?
WE'RE SHORTHANDED ENOUGH AS IS, DON'T NEED TO BE DAWDLING.
LET'S LUG THIS UGLY SUCKER IN AND GO HOME.

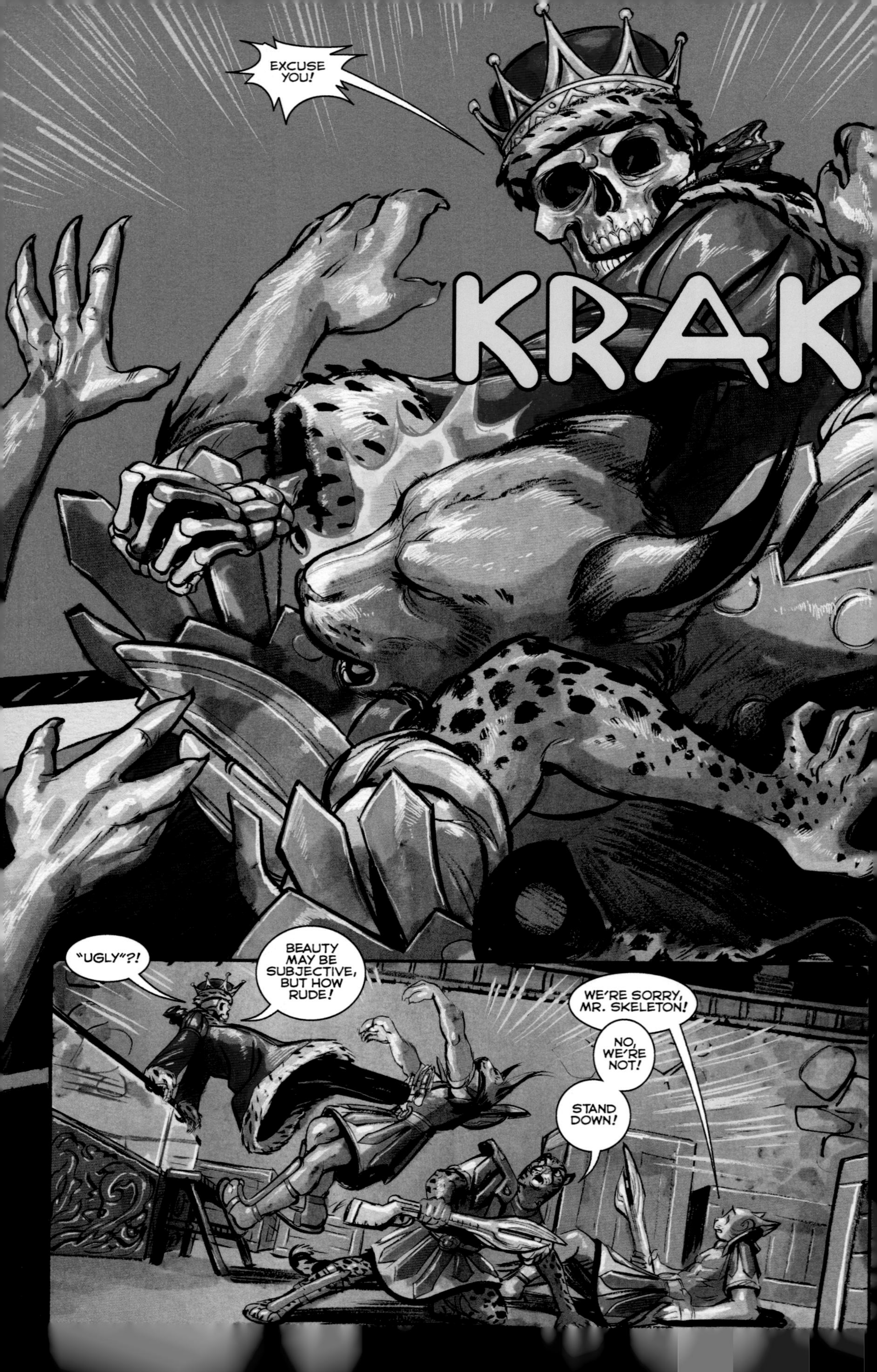
EXCUSE YOU!
KRAK
"UGLY"?!
BEAUTY MAY BE SUBJECTIVE, BUT HOW RUDE!
WE'RE SORRY, MR. SKELETON!
NO, WE'RE NOT!
STAND DOWN!

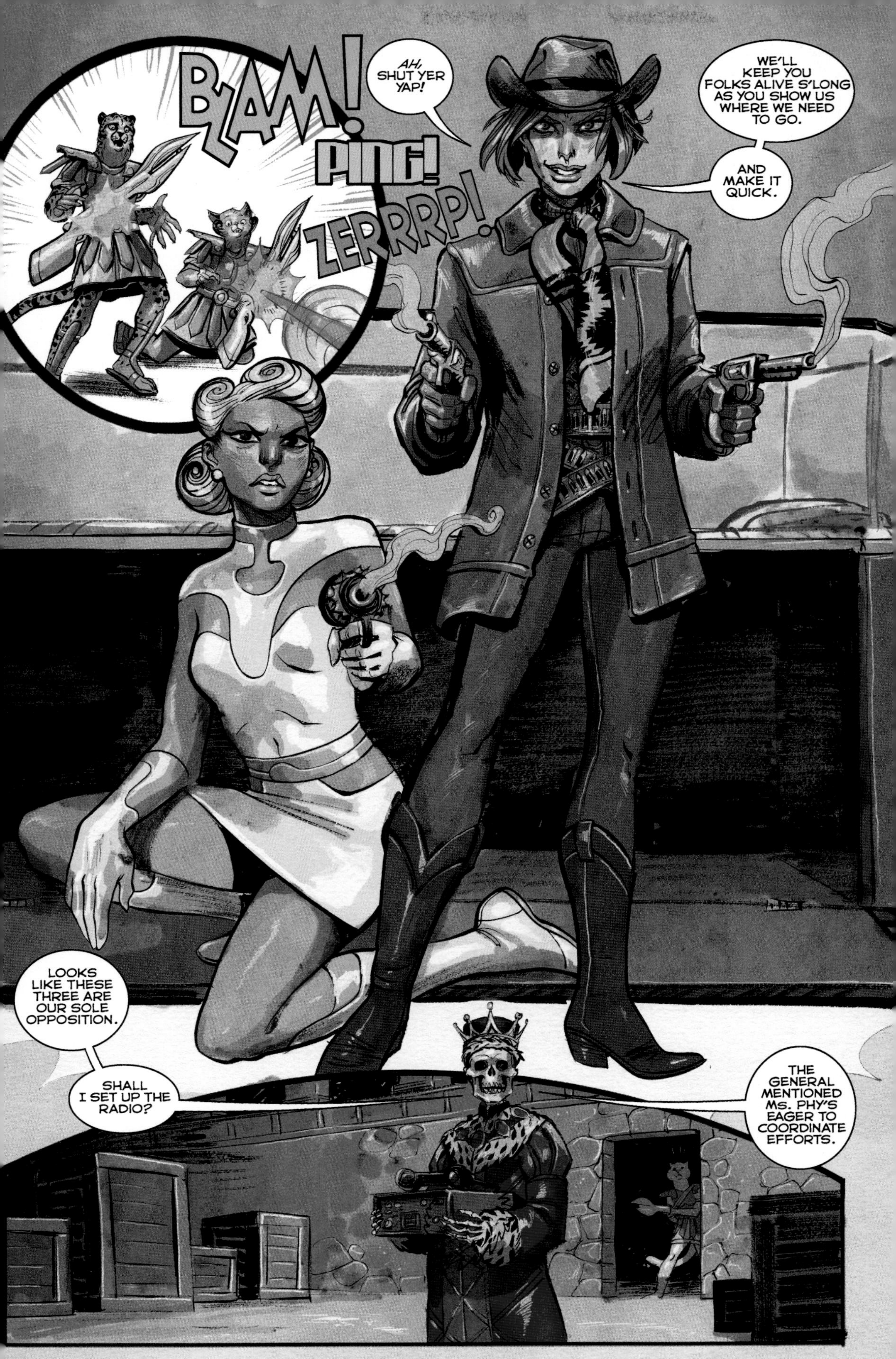
BLAM!
PING!
ZERRRP!
AH, SHUT YER YAP!
WE'LL KEEP YOU FOLKS ALIVE S'LONG AS YOU SHOW US WHERE WE NEED TO GO.
AND MAKE IT QUICK.
LOOKS LIKE THESE THREE ARE OUR SOLE OPPOSITION.
SHALL I SET UP THE RADIO?
THE GENERAL MENTIONED MS. PHY'S EAGER TO COORDINATE EFFORTS.

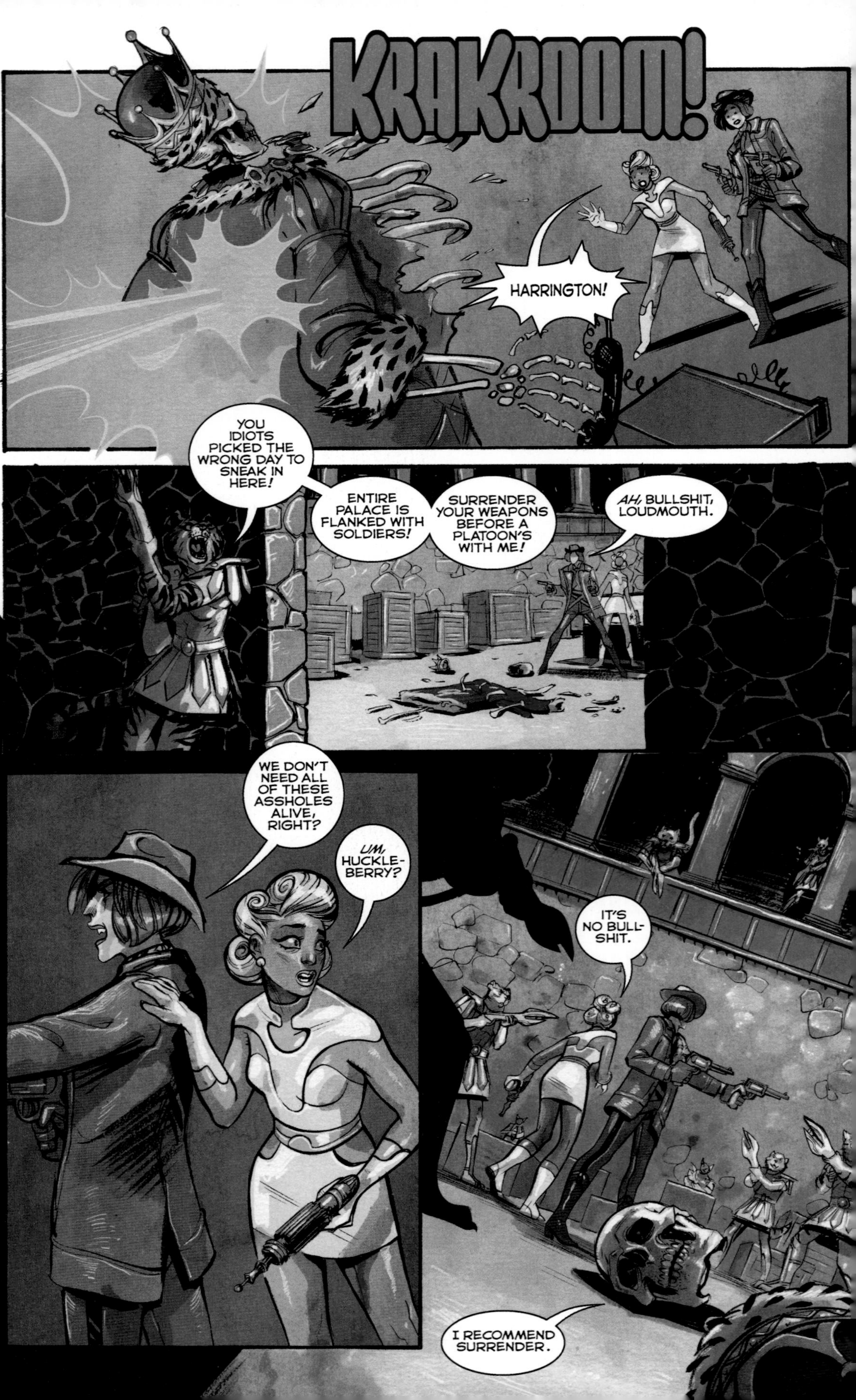
KRAKROOM!
HARRINGTON!
YOU IDIOTS PICKED THE WRONG DAY TO SNEAK IN HERE!
ENTIRE PALACE IS FLANKED WITH SOLDIERS!
SURRENDER YOUR WEAPONS BEFORE A PLATOON'S WITH ME!
AH, BULLSHIT, LOUDMOUTH.
WE DON'T NEED ALL OF THESE ASSHOLES ALIVE, RIGHT?
UM, HUCKLE-BERRY?
IT'S NO BULL-SHIT.
I RECOMMEND SURRENDER.

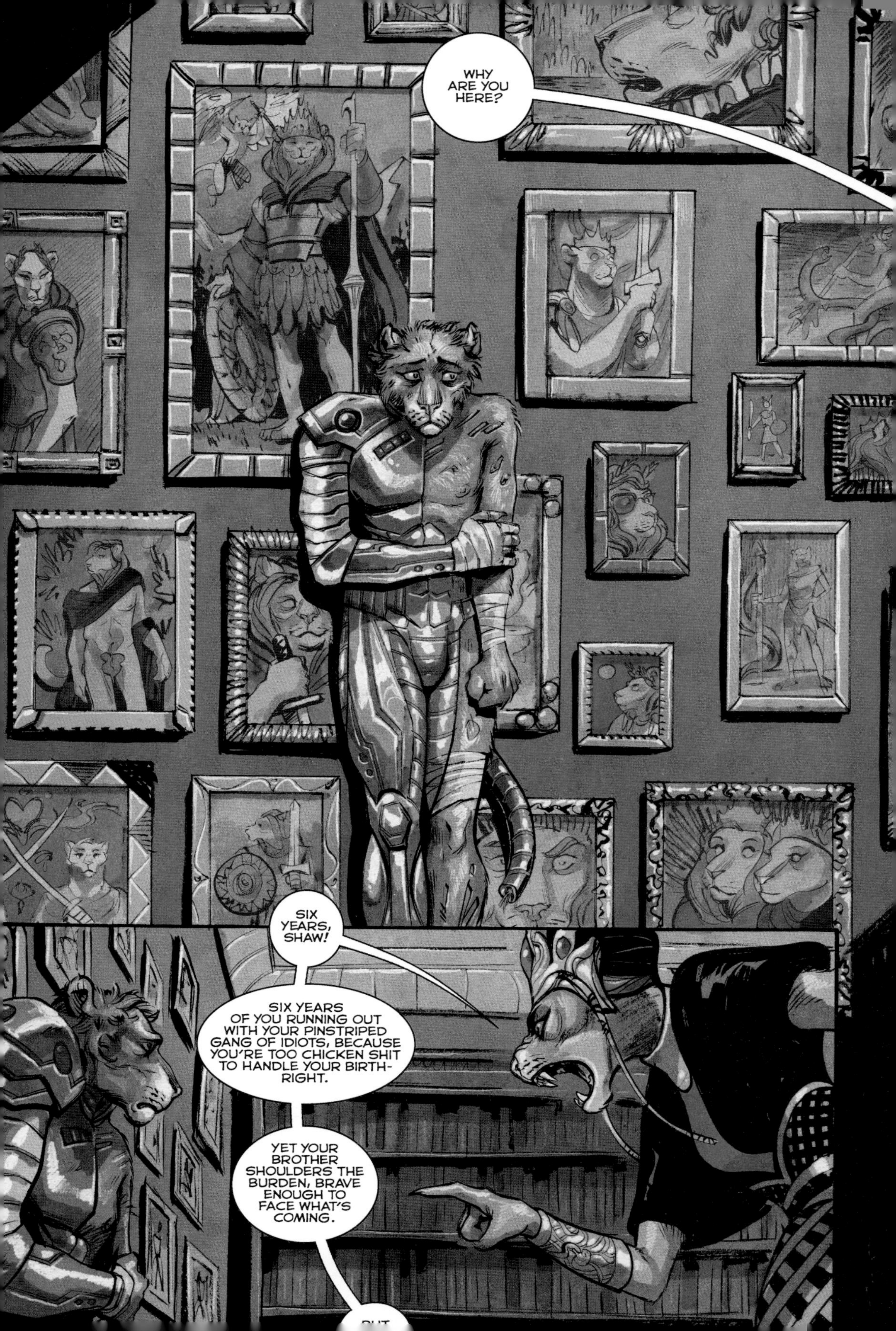
WHY ARE YOU HERE?
SIX YEARS, SHAW!
SIX YEARS OF YOU RUNNING OUT WITH YOUR PINSTRIPED GANG OF IDIOTS, BECAUSE YOU'RE TOO CHICKEN SHIT TO HANDLE YOUR BIRTH-RIGHT.
YET YOUR BROTHER SHOULDERS THE BURDEN, BRAVE ENOUGH TO FACE WHAT'S COMING.

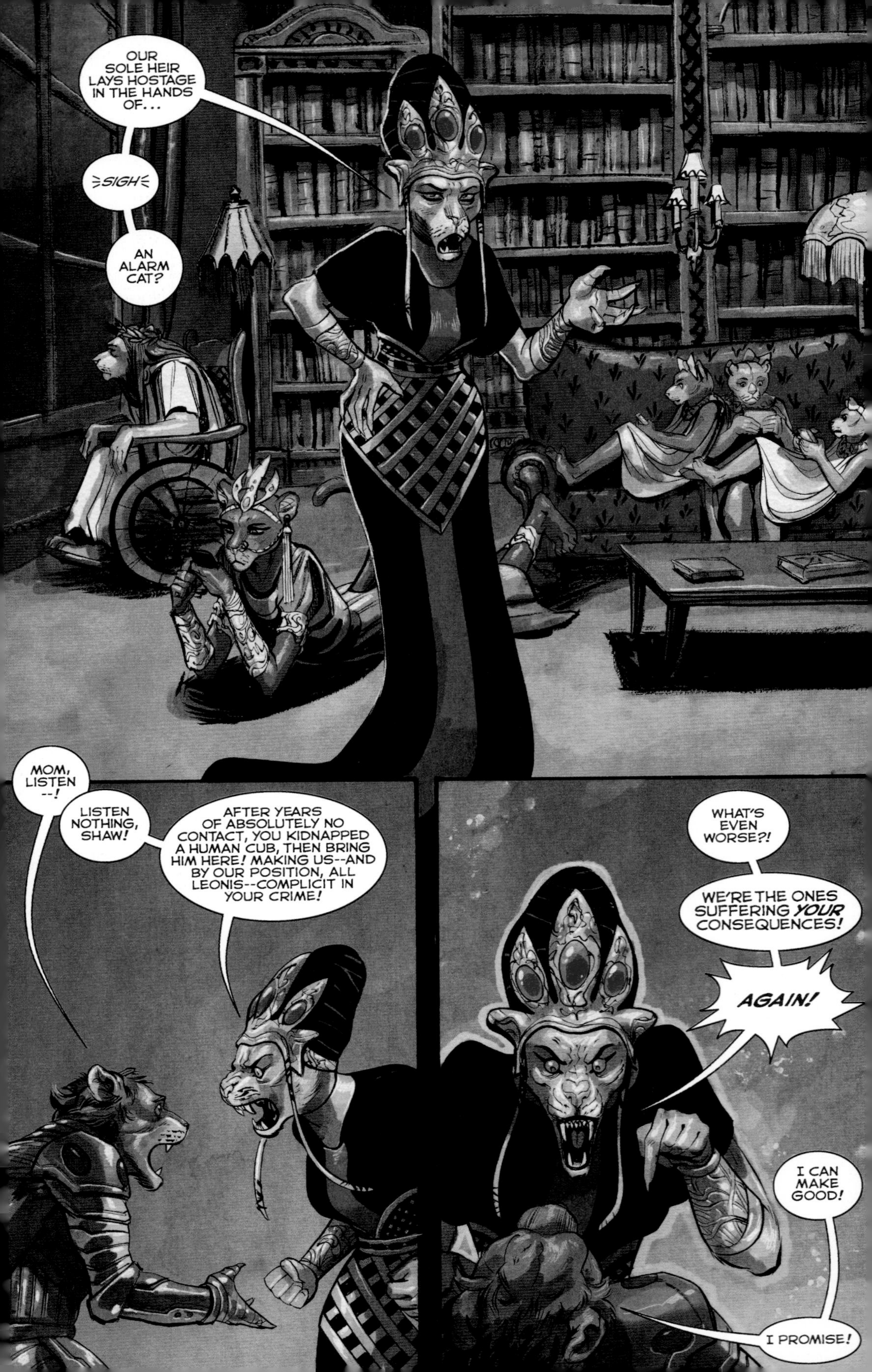
OUR SOLE HEIR LAYS HOSTAGE IN THE HANDS OF...
SIGH
AN ALARM CAT?
MOM, LISTEN --!
LISTEN NOTHING, SHAW!
AFTER YEARS OF ABSOLUTELY NO CONTACT, YOU KIDNAPPED A HUMAN CUB, THEN BRING HIM HERE! MAKING US--AND BY OUR POSITION, ALL LEONIS--COMPLICIT IN YOUR CRIME!
WHAT'S EVEN WORSE?!
WE'RE THE ONES SUFFERING YOUR CONSEQUENCES!
AGAIN!
I CAN MAKE GOOD!
I PROMISE!

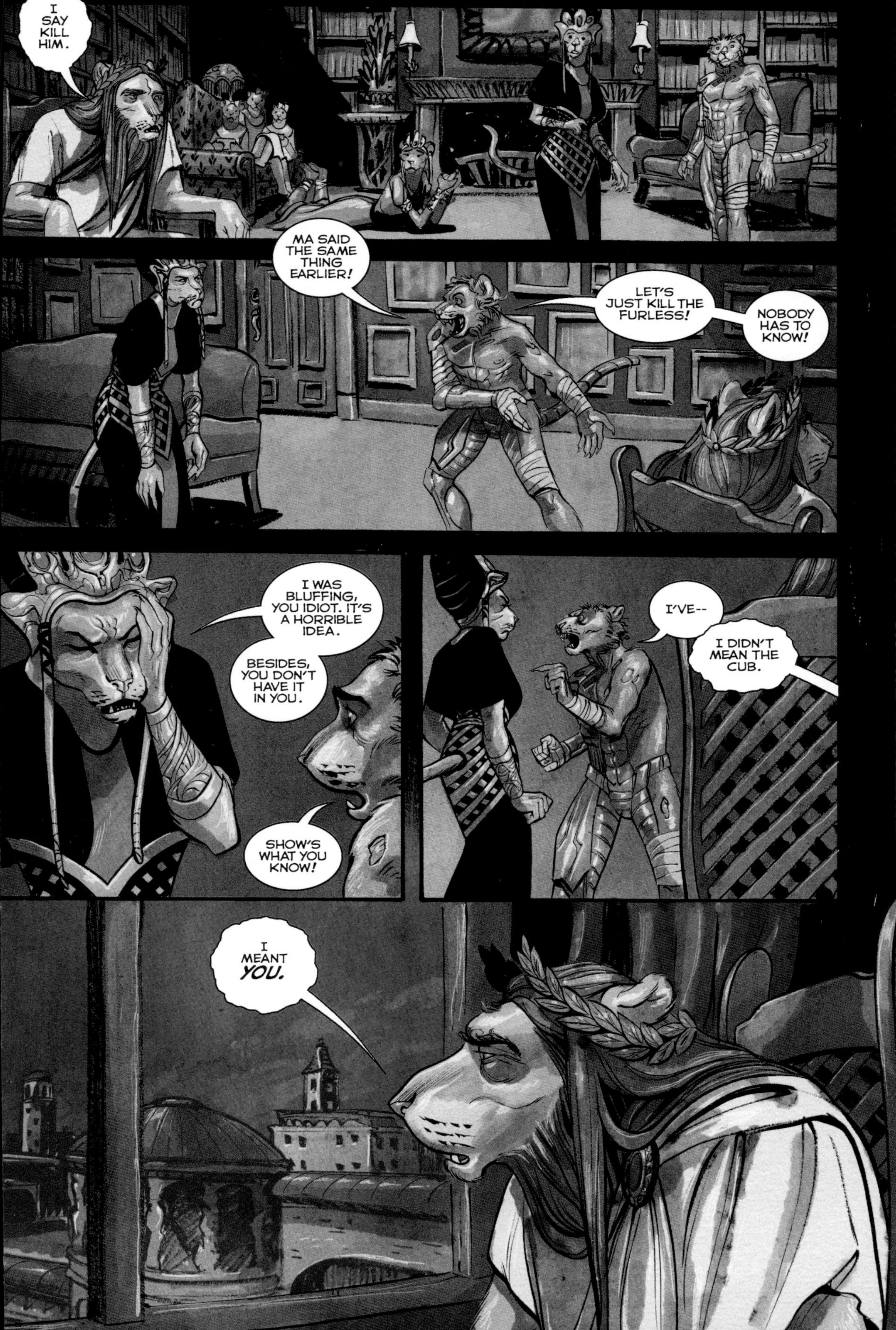
I SAY KILL HIM.
MA SAID THE SAME THING EARLIER!
LET'S JUST KILL THE FURLESS!
NOBODY HAS TO KNOW!
I WAS BLUFFING, YOU IDIOT. IT'S A HORRIBLE IDEA.
BESIDES, YOU DON'T HAVE IT IN YOU.
SHOW'S WHAT YOU KNOW!
I'VE--
I DIDN'T MEAN THE CUB.
I MEANT *YOU.*

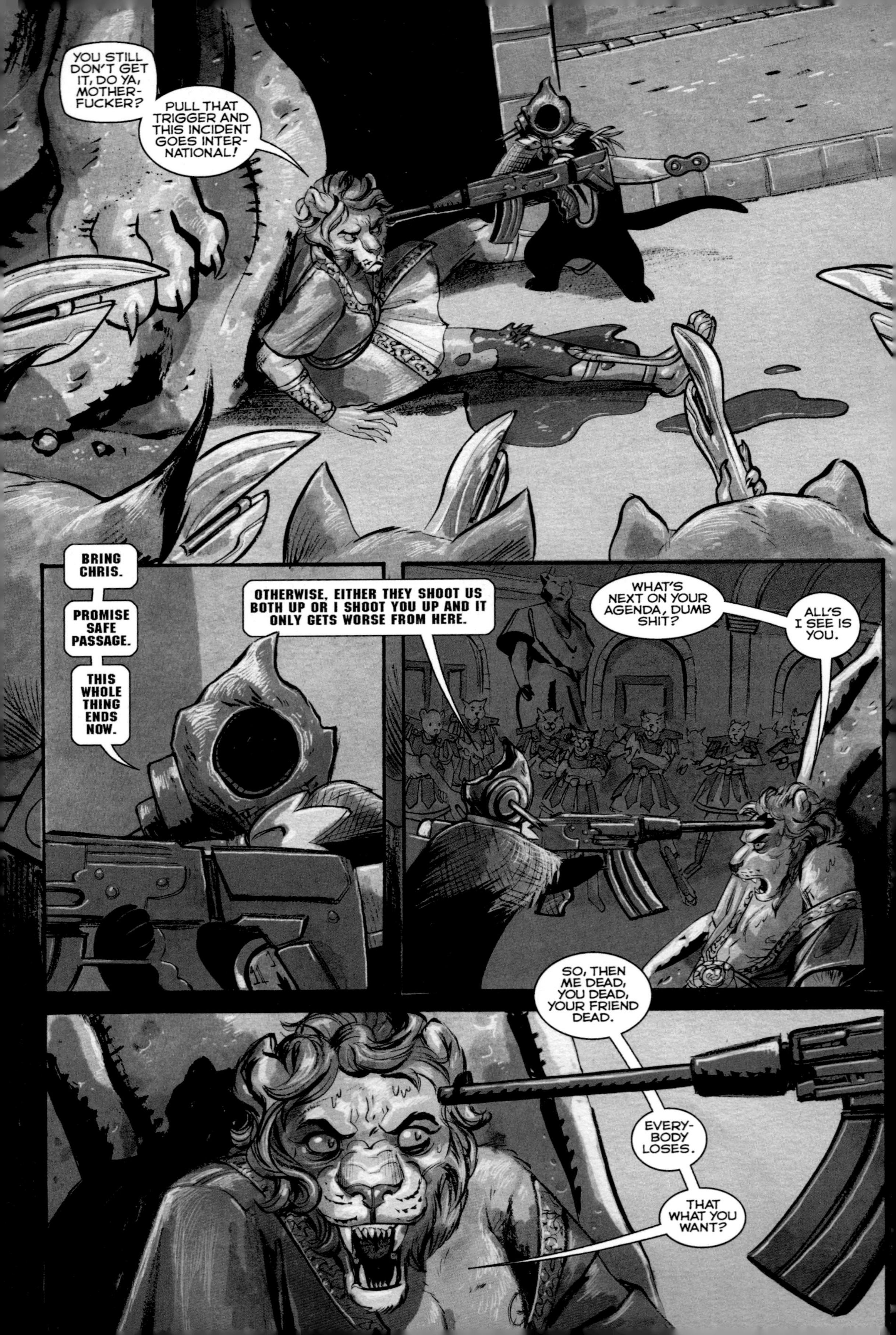
YOU STILL DON'T GET IT, DO YA, MOTHER-FUCKER?
PULL THAT TRIGGER AND THIS INCIDENT GOES INTER-NATIONAL!
BRING CHRIS.
PROMISE SAFE PASSAGE.
THIS WHOLE THING ENDS NOW.
OTHERWISE, EITHER THEY SHOOT US BOTH UP OR I SHOOT YOU UP AND IT ONLY GETS WORSE FROM HERE.
WHAT'S NEXT ON YOUR AGENDA, DUMB SHIT?
ALL'S I SEE IS YOU.
SO, THEN ME DEAD, YOU DEAD, YOUR FRIEND DEAD.
EVERY-BODY LOSES.
THAT WHAT YOU WANT?

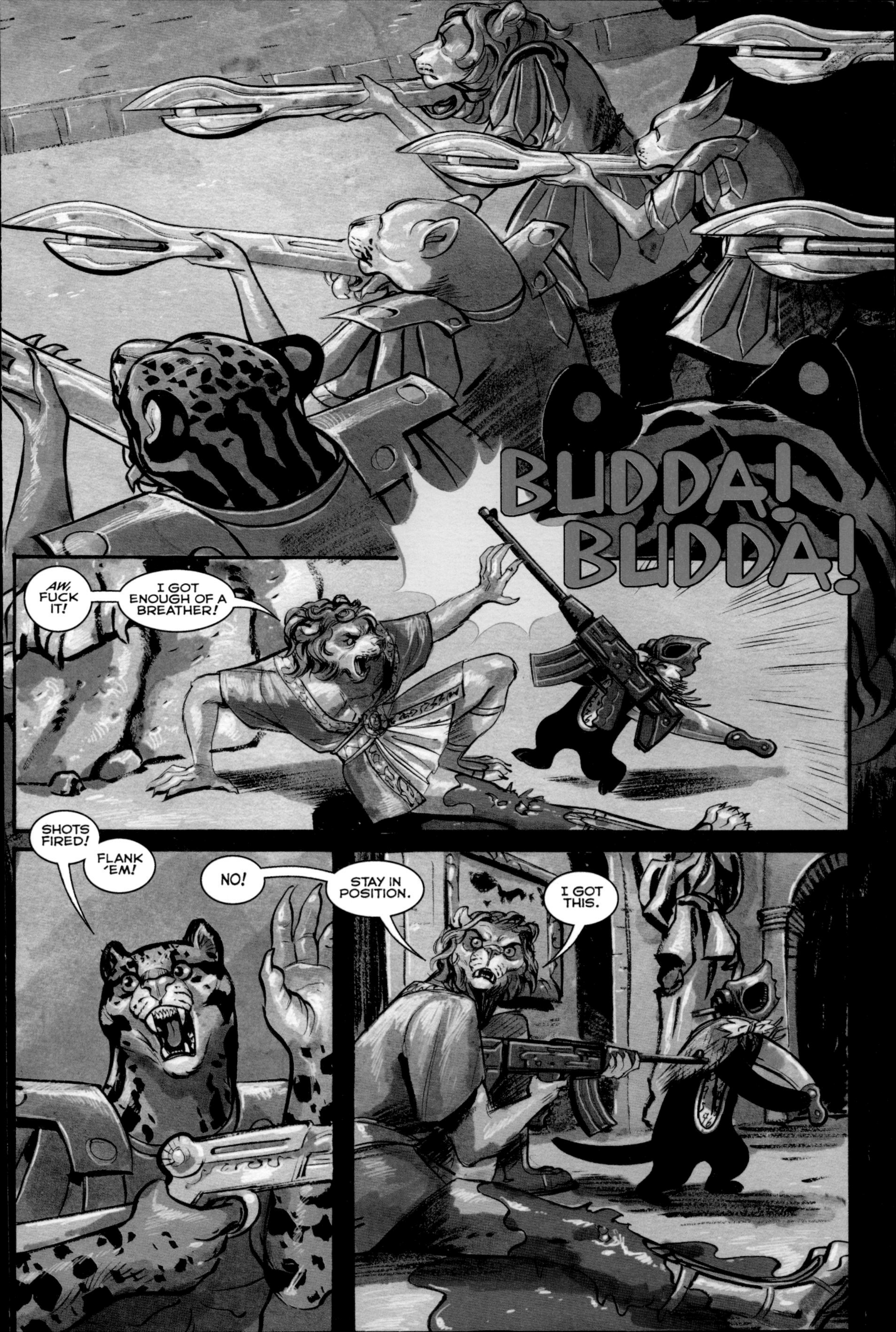
BUDDA! BUDDA!
AW, FUCK IT!
I GOT ENOUGH OF A BREATHER!
SHOTS FIRED!
FLANK 'EM!
NO!
STAY IN POSITION.
I GOT THIS.

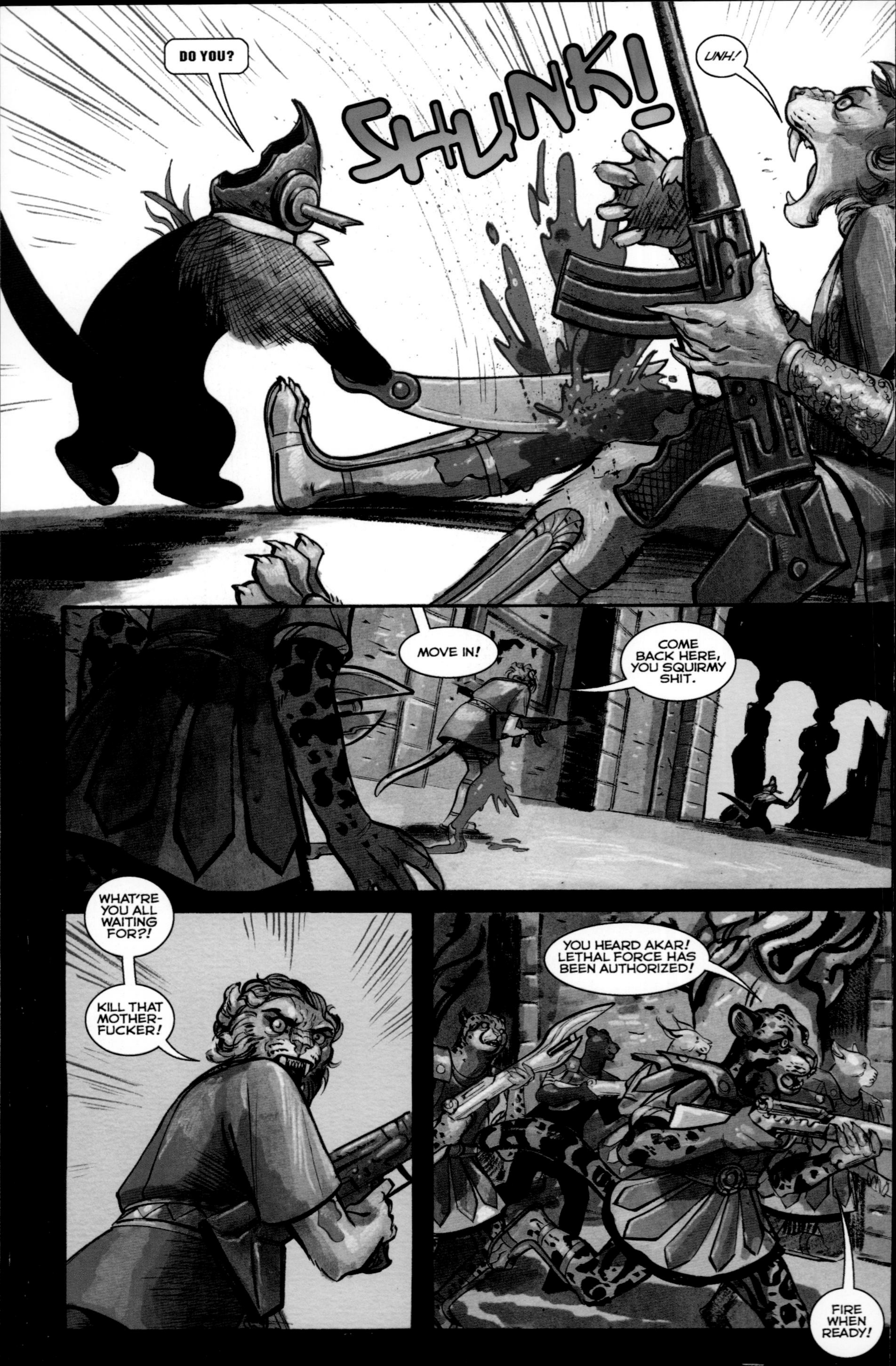
DO YOU?
SHUNK!
UNH!
MOVE IN!
COME BACK HERE, YOU SQUIRMY SHIT.
WHAT'RE YOU ALL WAITING FOR?!
KILL THAT MOTHER-FUCKER!
YOU HEARD AKAR! LETHAL FORCE HAS BEEN AUTHORIZED!
FIRE WHEN READY!

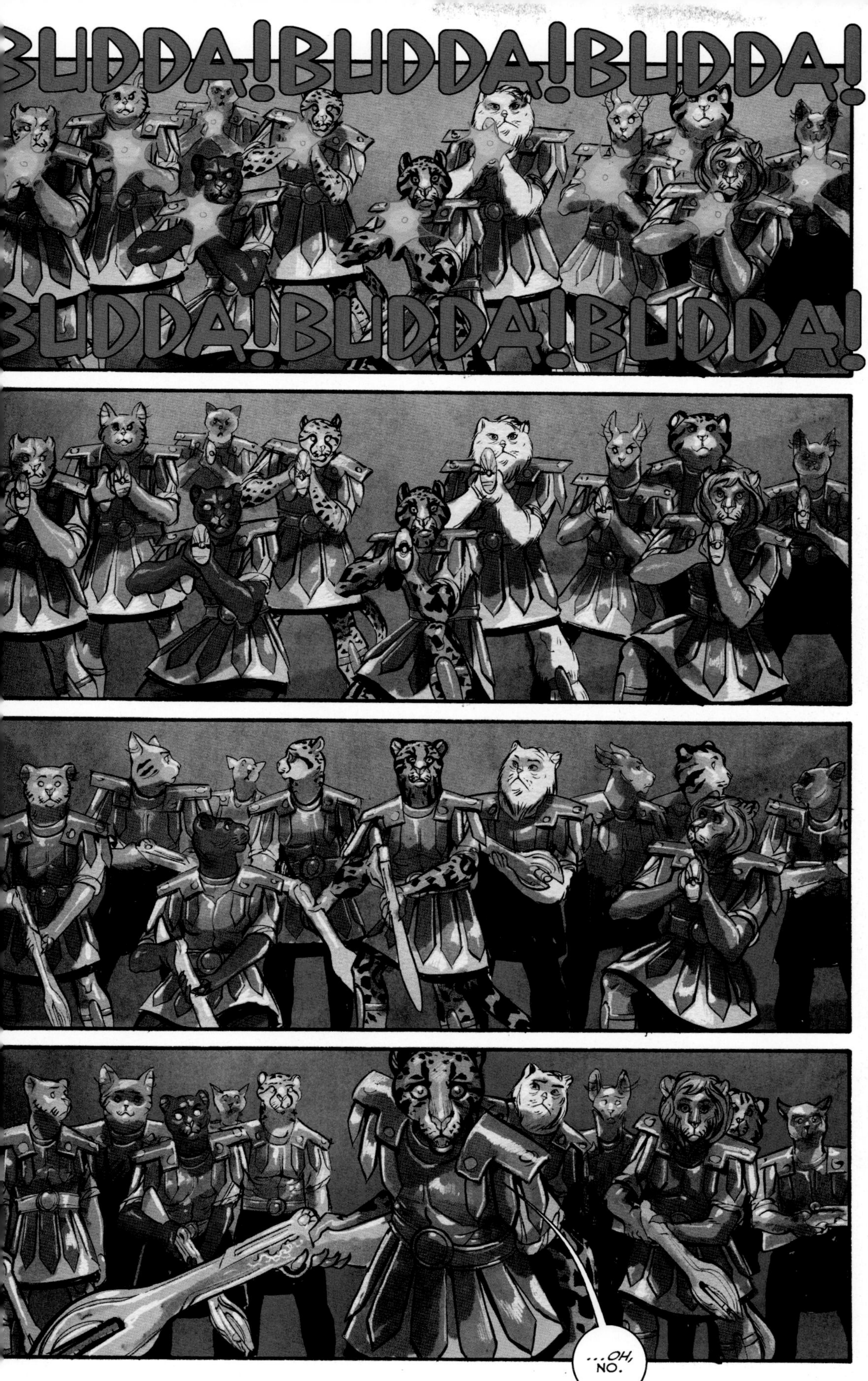
BUDDA! BUDDA! BUDDA!
BUDDA! BUDDA! BUDDA!
...OH, NO.

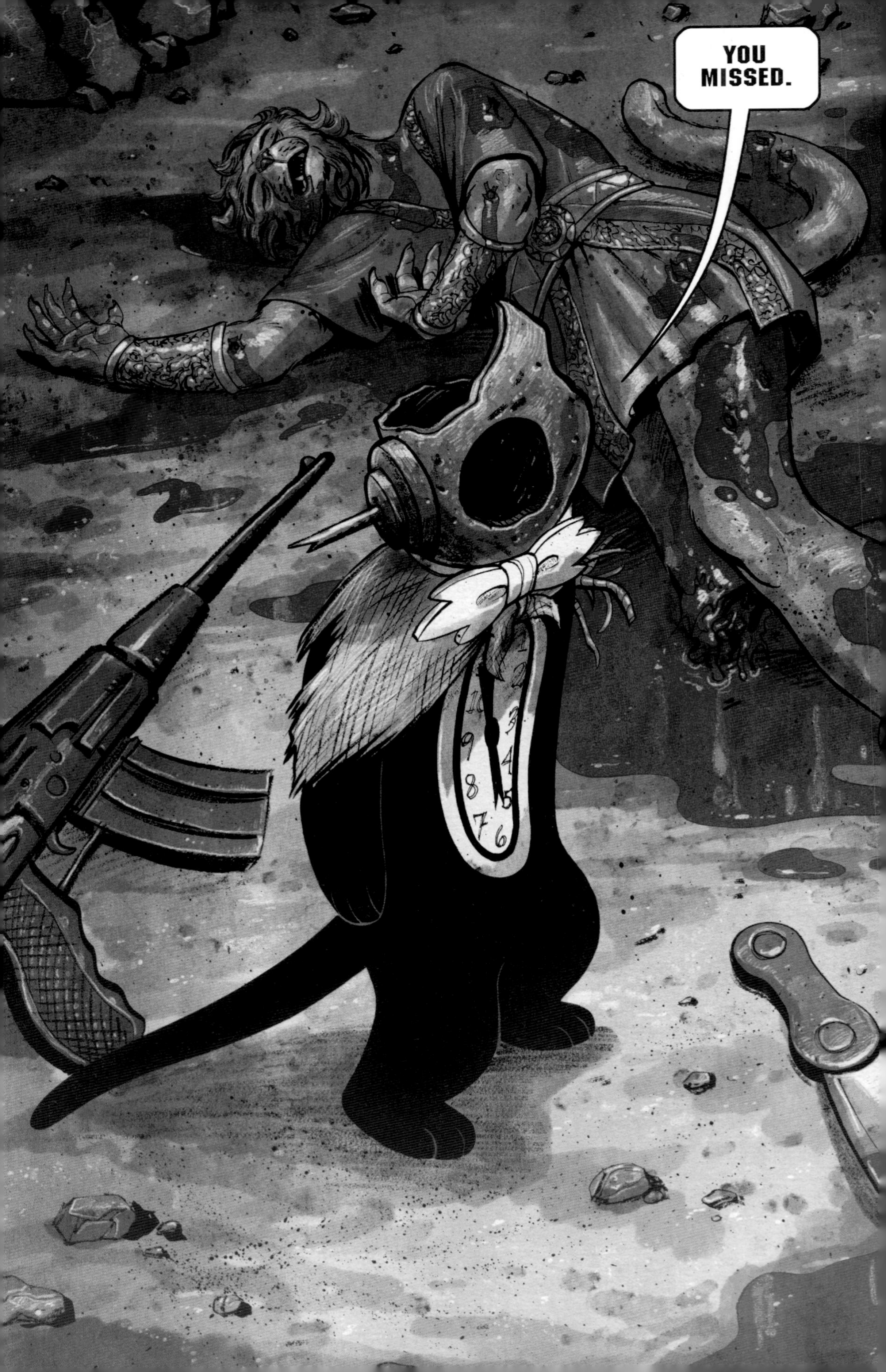
YOU MISSED.

CHAPTER

17

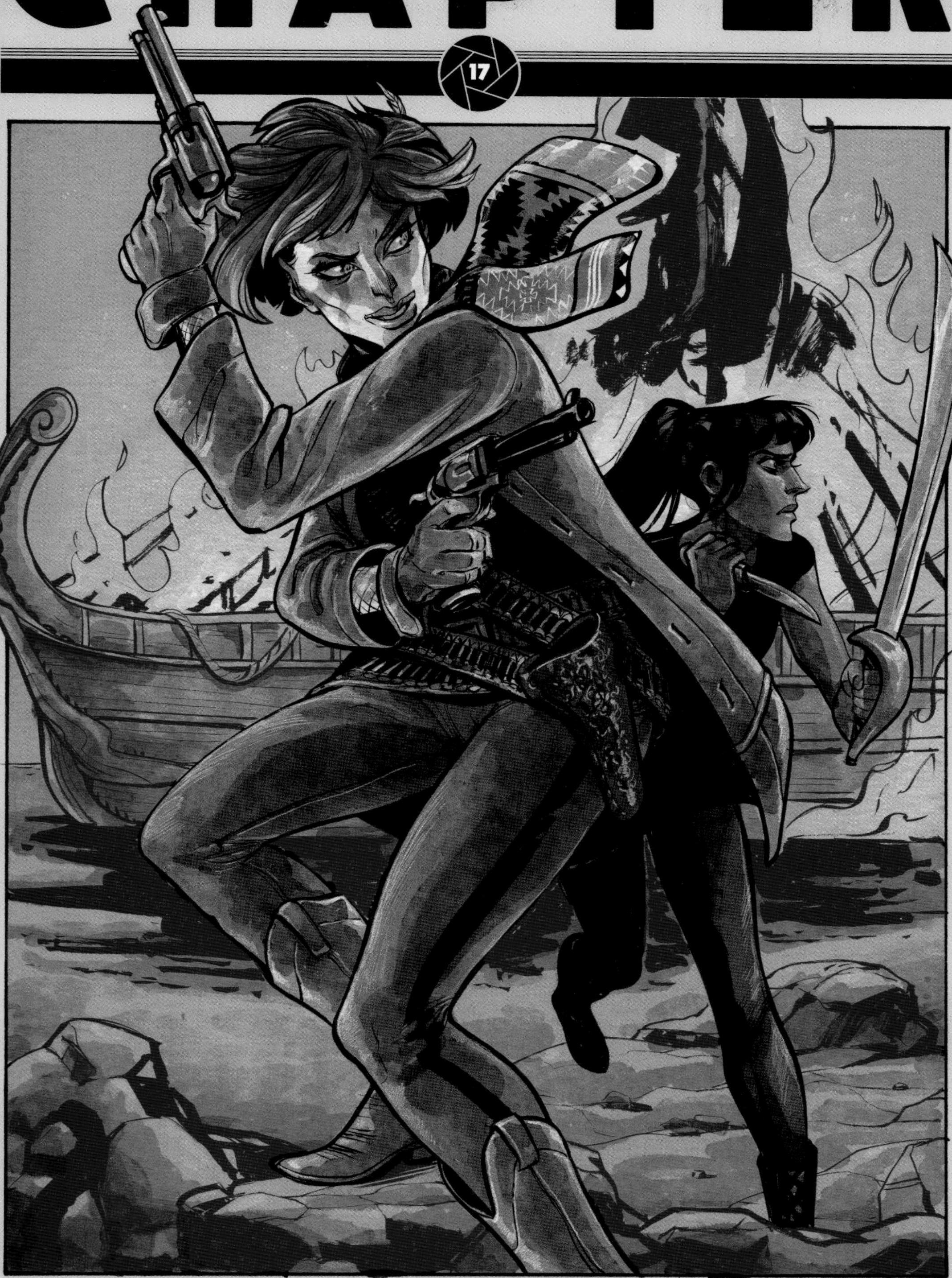

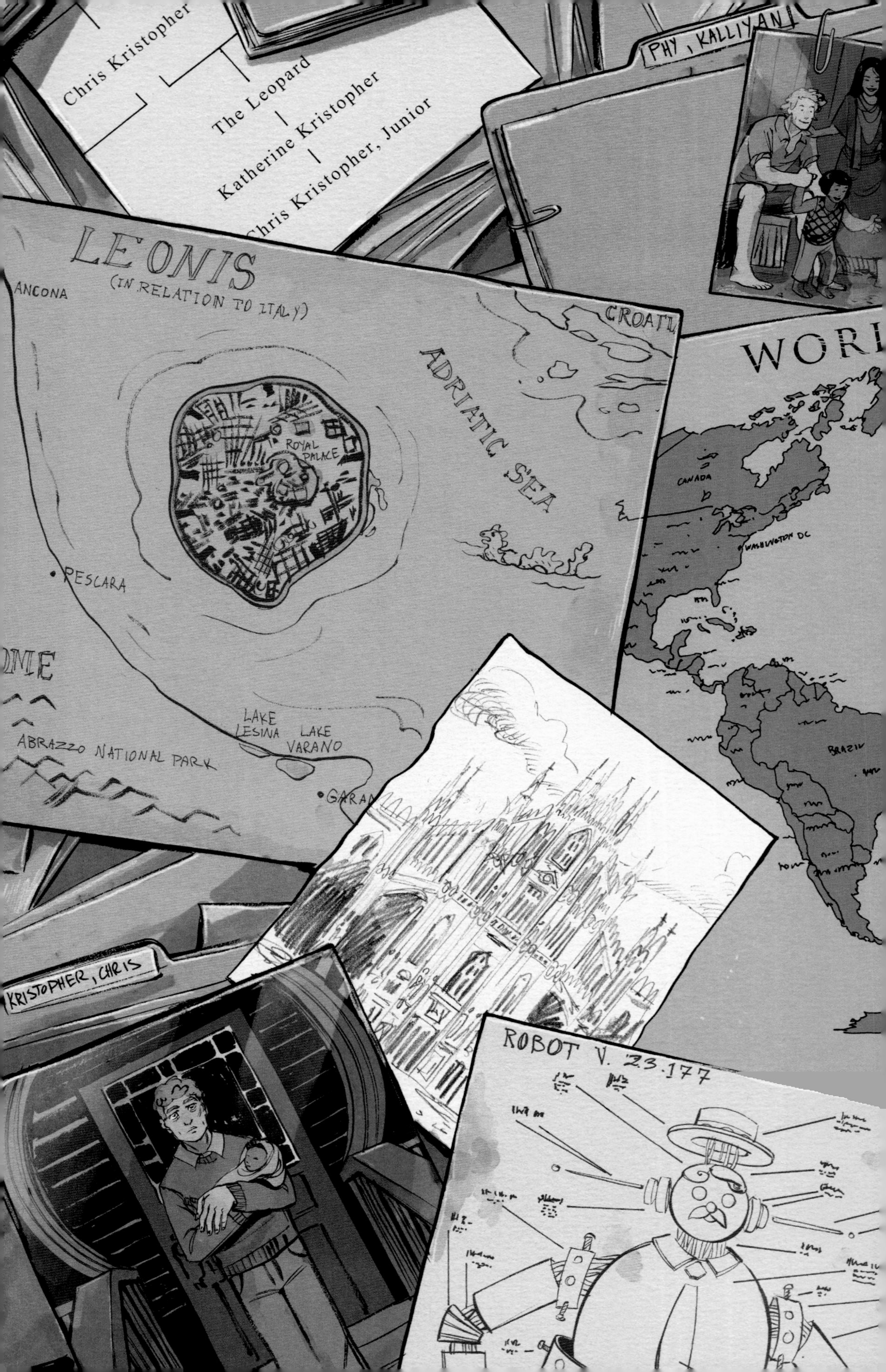

Chris Kristopher
The Leopard
Katherine Kristopher
Chris Kristopher, Junior
PHY, KALLIYAN
LEONIS
(IN RELATION TO ITALY)
ANCONA
CROATI
ADRIATIC SEA
ROYAL PALACE
PESCARA
LAKE LESINA
LAKE VARANO
ABRAZZO NATIONAL PARK
WORL
CANADA
WASHINGTON DC
BRAZIL
KRISTOPHER, CHRIS
ROBOT V. 23.177

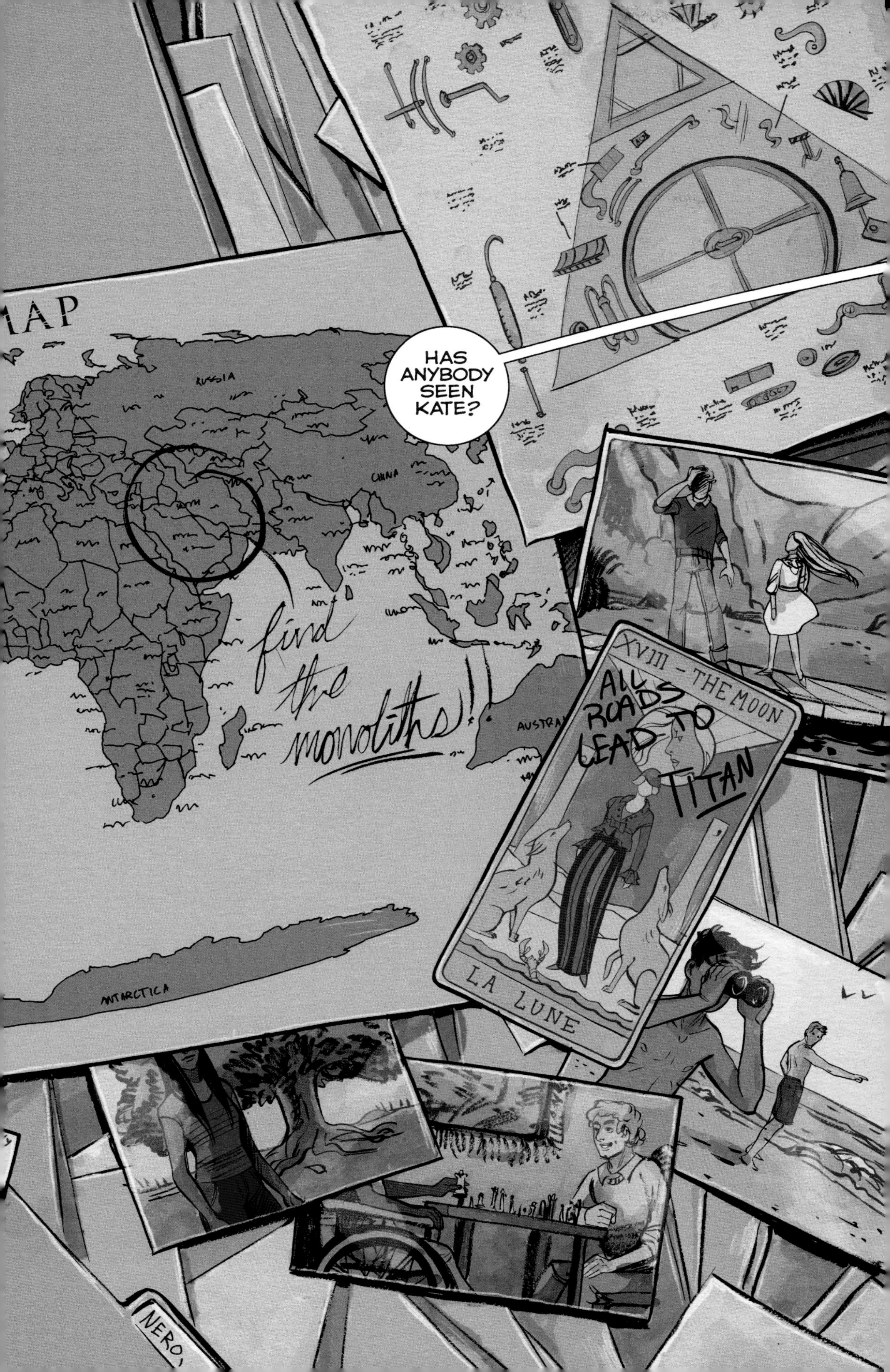
MAP
RUSSIA
CHINA
find the monoliths!
AUSTRA
ANTARCTICA
HAS ANYBODY SEEN KATE?
XVIII - THE MOON
ALL ROADS LEAD TO
TITAN
LA LUNE
NERO

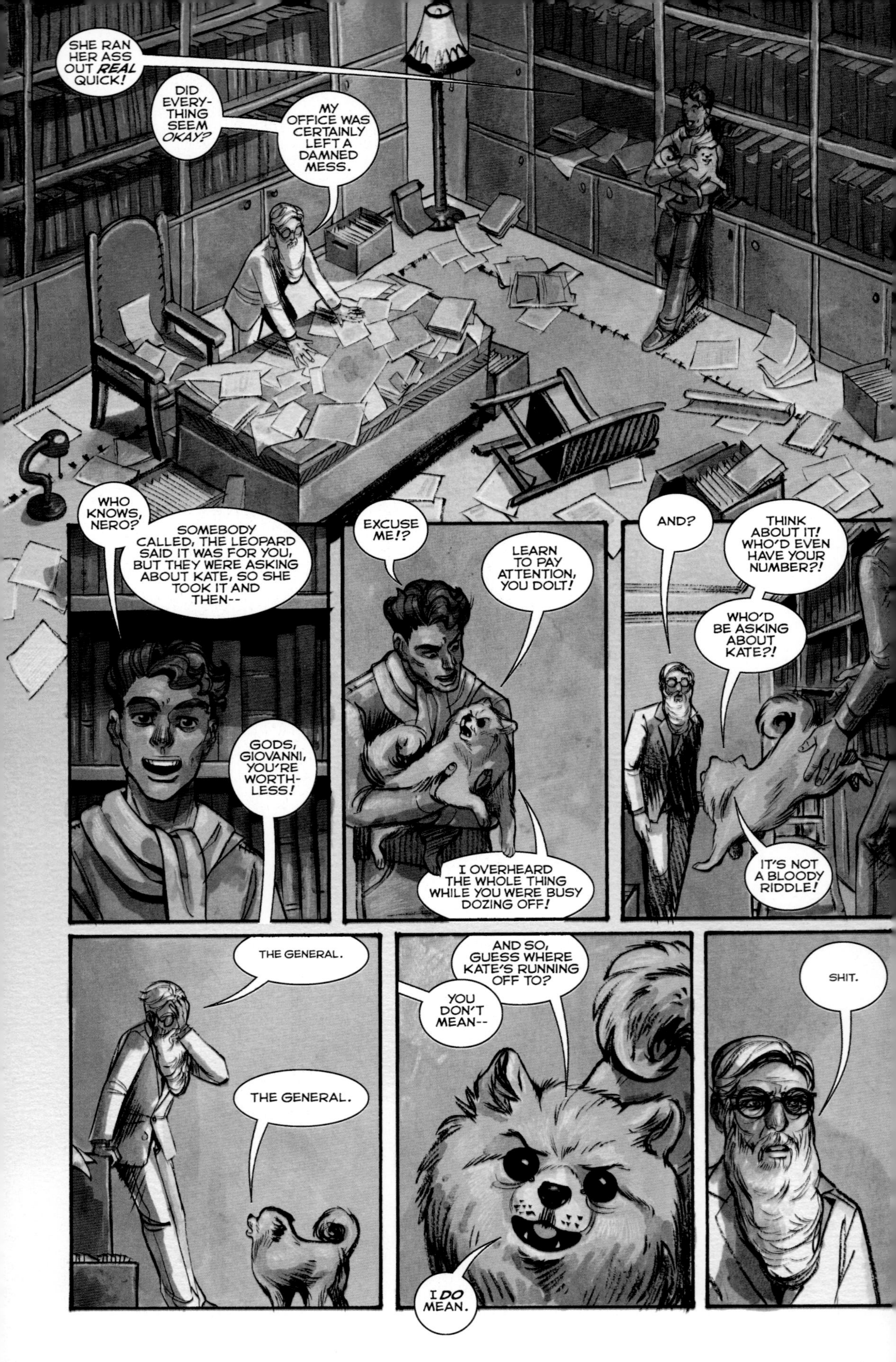
SHE RAN HER ASS OUT *REAL* QUICK!
DID EVERY-THING SEEM *OKAY?*
MY OFFICE WAS CERTAINLY LEFT A DAMNED MESS.
WHO KNOWS, NERO?
SOMEBODY CALLED, THE LEOPARD SAID IT WAS FOR YOU, BUT THEY WERE ASKING ABOUT KATE, SO SHE TOOK IT AND THEN--
GODS, GIOVANNI, YOU'RE WORTH-LESS!
EXCUSE ME!?
LEARN TO PAY ATTENTION, YOU DOLT!
I OVERHEARD THE WHOLE THING WHILE YOU WERE BUSY DOZING OFF!
AND?
THINK ABOUT IT! WHO'D EVEN HAVE YOUR NUMBER?!
WHO'D BE ASKING ABOUT KATE?!
IT'S NOT A BLOODY RIDDLE!
THE GENERAL.
THE GENERAL.
AND SO, GUESS WHERE KATE'S RUNNING OFF TO?
YOU DON'T MEAN--
I *DO* MEAN.
SHIT.

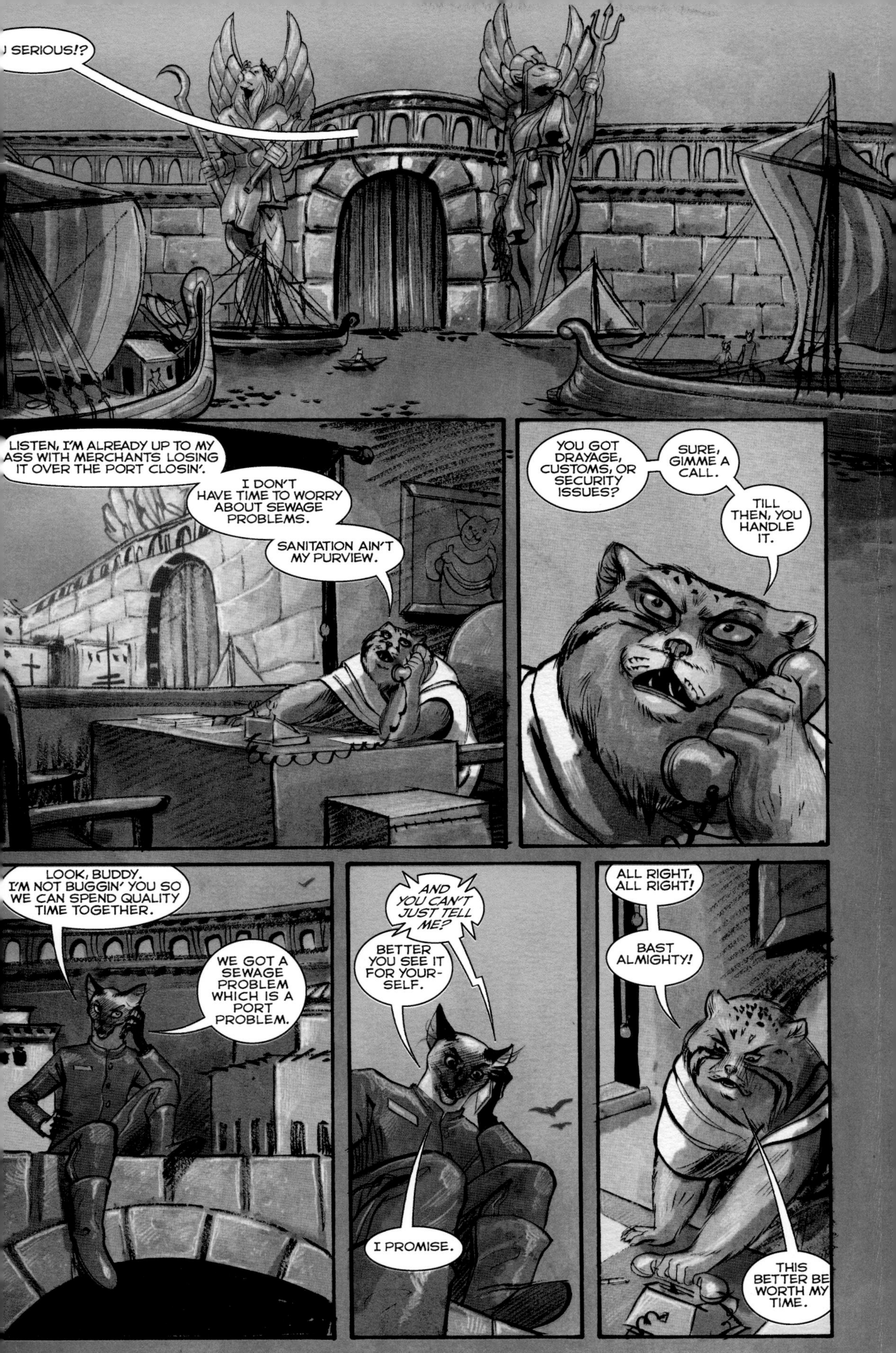

...U SERIOUS!?
LISTEN, I'M ALREADY UP TO MY ASS WITH MERCHANTS LOSING IT OVER THE PORT CLOSIN'.
I DON'T HAVE TIME TO WORRY ABOUT SEWAGE PROBLEMS.
SANITATION AIN'T MY PURVIEW.
YOU GOT DRAYAGE, CUSTOMS, OR SECURITY ISSUES?
SURE, GIMME A CALL.
TILL THEN, YOU HANDLE IT.
LOOK, BUDDY. I'M NOT BUGGIN' YOU SO WE CAN SPEND QUALITY TIME TOGETHER.
WE GOT A SEWAGE PROBLEM WHICH IS A PORT PROBLEM.
AND YOU CAN'T JUST TELL ME?
BETTER YOU SEE IT FOR YOURSELF.
I PROMISE.
ALL RIGHT, ALL RIGHT!
BAST ALMIGHTY!
THIS BETTER BE WORTH MY TIME.

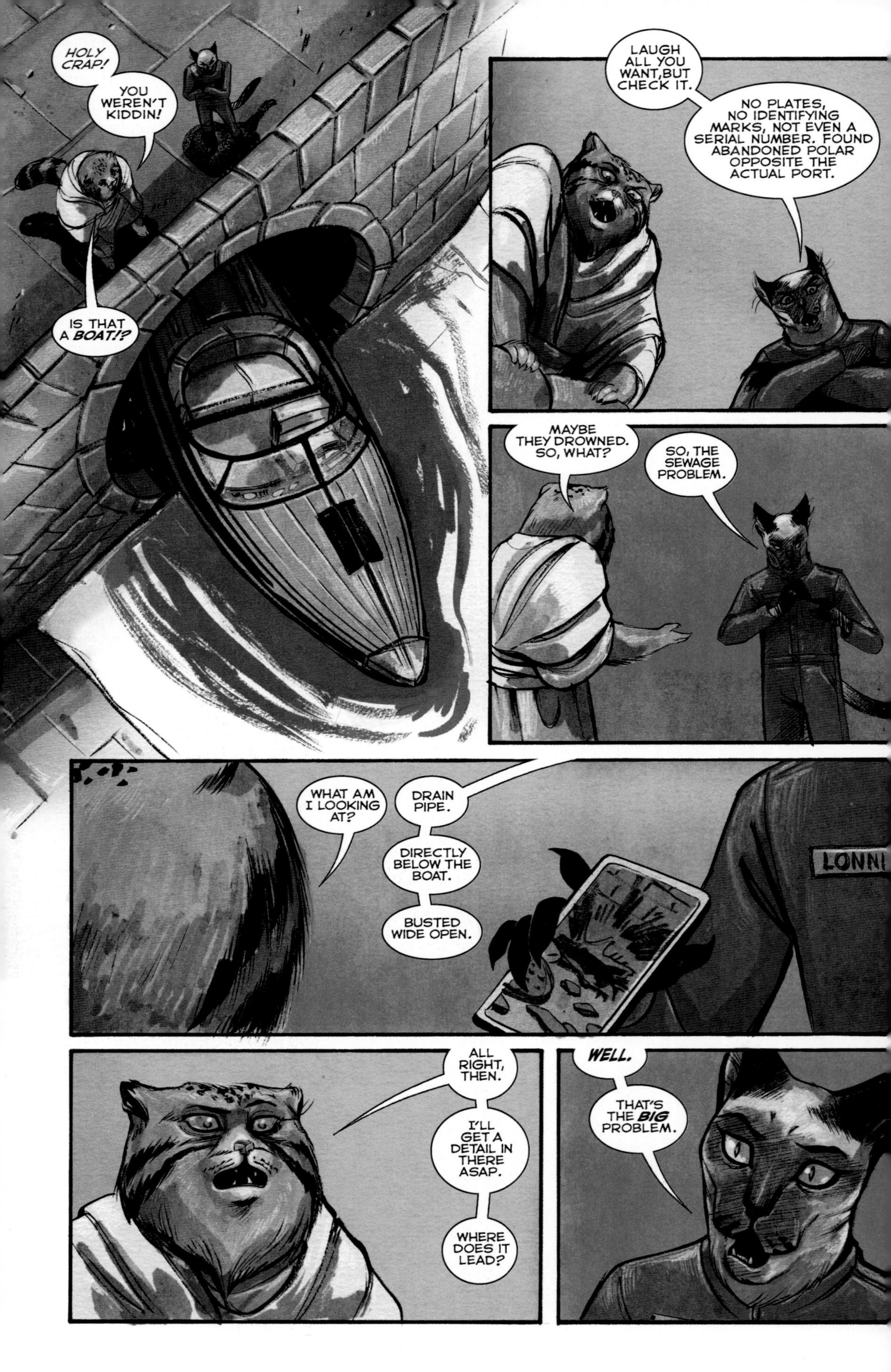
HOLY CRAP!
YOU WEREN'T KIDDIN!
IS THAT A *BOAT!?*
LAUGH ALL YOU WANT, BUT CHECK IT.
NO PLATES, NO IDENTIFYING MARKS, NOT EVEN A SERIAL NUMBER. FOUND ABANDONED POLAR OPPOSITE THE ACTUAL PORT.
MAYBE THEY DROWNED. SO, WHAT?
SO, THE SEWAGE PROBLEM.
WHAT AM I LOOKING AT?
DRAIN PIPE.
DIRECTLY BELOW THE BOAT.
BUSTED WIDE OPEN.
LONNI
ALL RIGHT, THEN.
I'LL GET A DETAIL IN THERE ASAP.
WHERE DOES IT LEAD?
WELL.
THAT'S THE *BIG* PROBLEM.

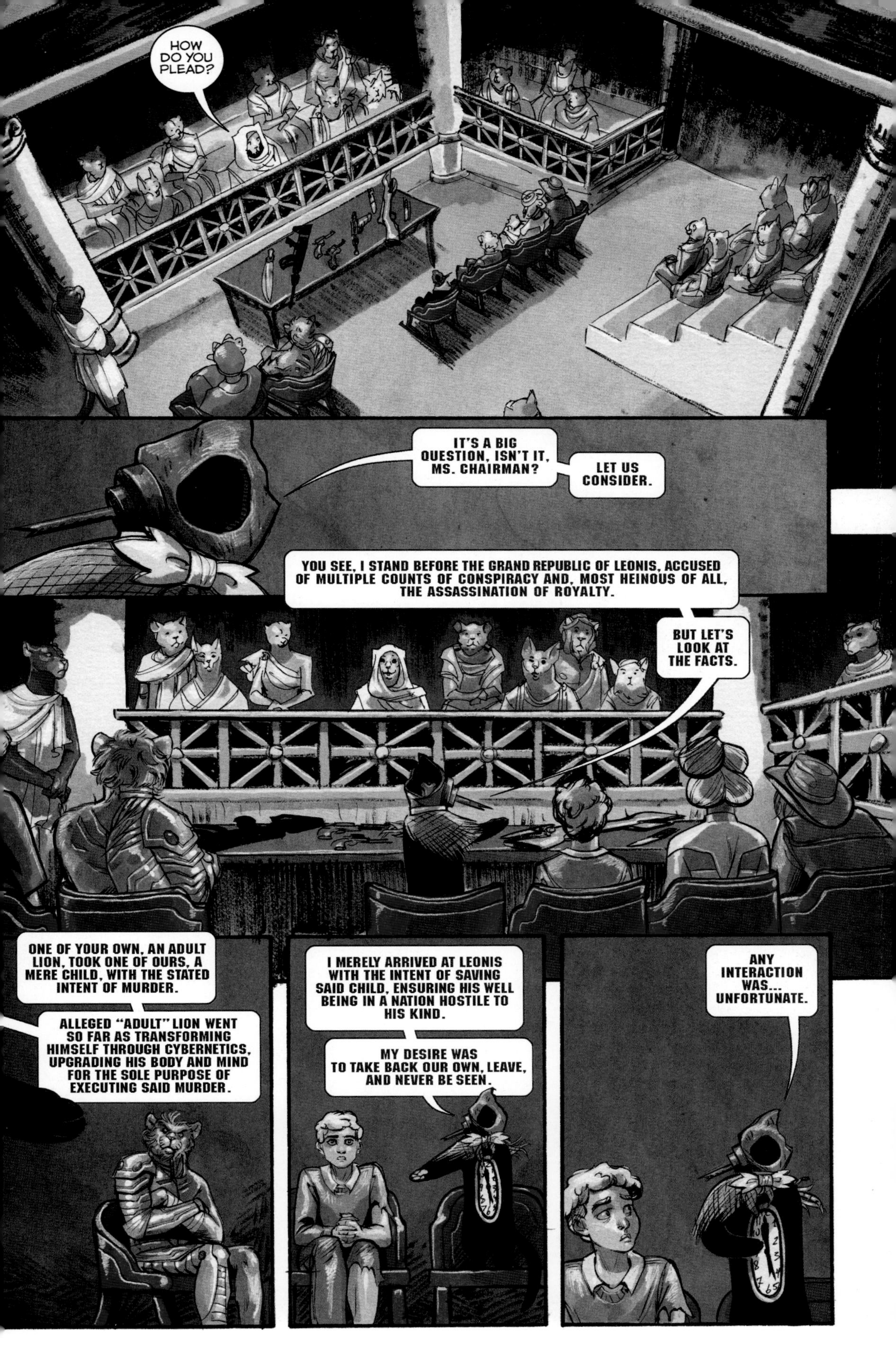
HOW DO YOU PLEAD?
IT'S A BIG QUESTION, ISN'T IT, MS. CHAIRMAN?
LET US CONSIDER.
YOU SEE, I STAND BEFORE THE GRAND REPUBLIC OF LEONIS, ACCUSED OF MULTIPLE COUNTS OF CONSPIRACY AND, MOST HEINOUS OF ALL, THE ASSASSINATION OF ROYALTY.
BUT LET'S LOOK AT THE FACTS.
ONE OF YOUR OWN, AN ADULT LION, TOOK ONE OF OURS, A MERE CHILD, WITH THE STATED INTENT OF MURDER.
ALLEGED "ADULT" LION WENT SO FAR AS TRANSFORMING HIMSELF THROUGH CYBERNETICS, UPGRADING HIS BODY AND MIND FOR THE SOLE PURPOSE OF EXECUTING SAID MURDER.
I MERELY ARRIVED AT LEONIS WITH THE INTENT OF SAVING SAID CHILD, ENSURING HIS WELL BEING IN A NATION HOSTILE TO HIS KIND.
MY DESIRE WAS TO TAKE BACK OUR OWN, LEAVE, AND NEVER BE SEEN.
ANY INTERACTION WAS... UNFORTUNATE.

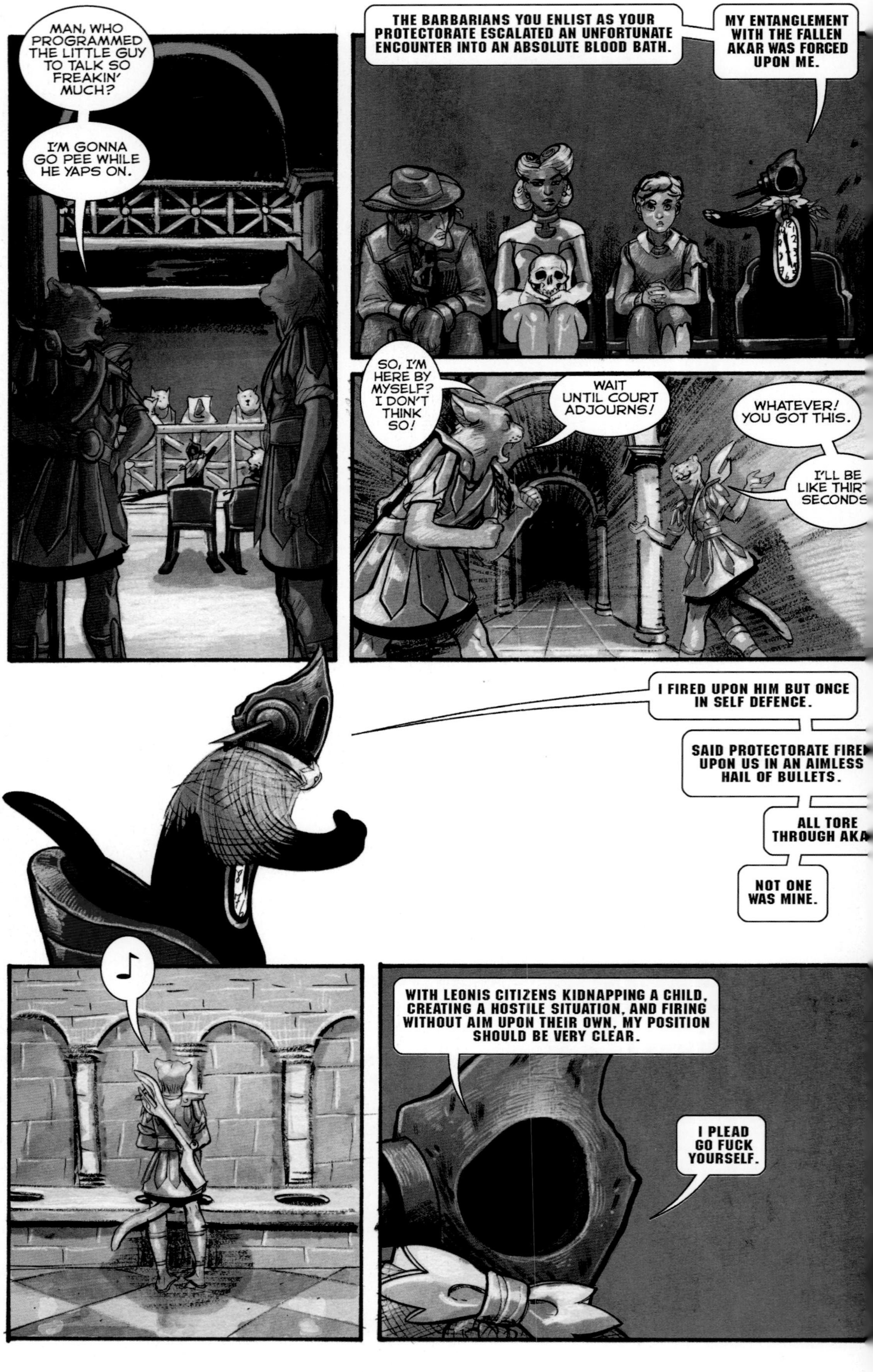
MAN, WHO PROGRAMMED THE LITTLE GUY TO TALK SO FREAKIN' MUCH?
I'M GONNA GO PEE WHILE HE YAPS ON.
THE BARBARIANS YOU ENLIST AS YOUR PROTECTORATE ESCALATED AN UNFORTUNATE ENCOUNTER INTO AN ABSOLUTE BLOOD BATH.
MY ENTANGLEMENT WITH THE FALLEN AKAR WAS FORCED UPON ME.
SO, I'M HERE BY MYSELF? I DON'T THINK SO!
WAIT UNTIL COURT ADJOURNS!
WHATEVER! YOU GOT THIS.
I'LL BE LIKE THIRT SECONDS
I FIRED UPON HIM BUT ONCE IN SELF DEFENCE.
SAID PROTECTORATE FIRE UPON US IN AN AIMLESS HAIL OF BULLETS.
ALL TORE THROUGH AKA
NOT ONE WAS MINE.
♪
WITH LEONIS CITIZENS KIDNAPPING A CHILD, CREATING A HOSTILE SITUATION, AND FIRING WITHOUT AIM UPON THEIR OWN, MY POSITION SHOULD BE VERY CLEAR.
I PLEAD GO FUCK YOURSELF.

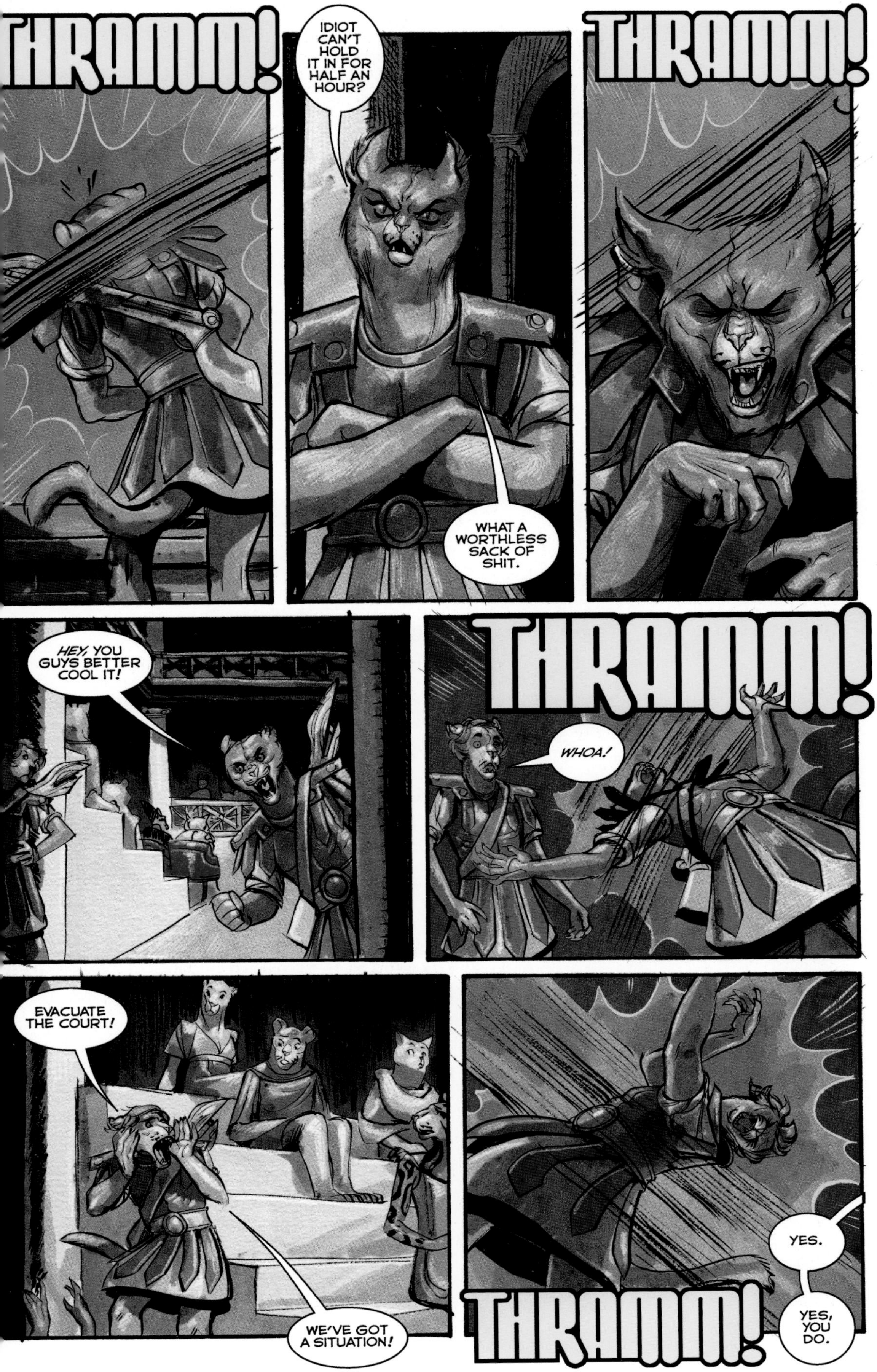
THRAMM!
IDIOT CAN'T HOLD IT IN FOR HALF AN HOUR?
WHAT A WORTHLESS SACK OF SHIT.
THRAMM!
HEY, YOU GUYS BETTER COOL IT!
THRAMM!
WHOA!
EVACUATE THE COURT!
WE'VE GOT A SITUATION!
YES.
YES, YOU DO.
THRAMM!

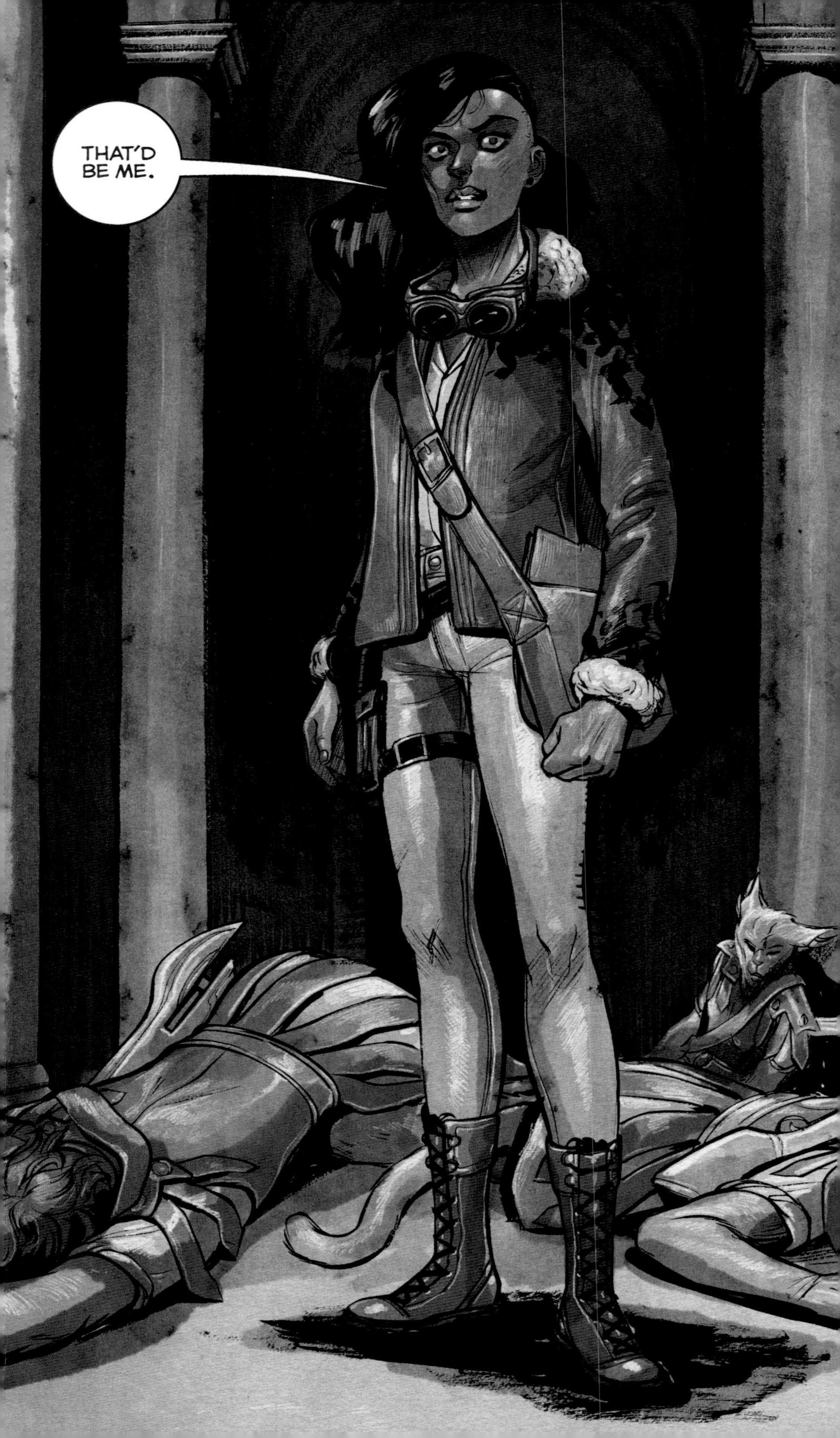
THAT'D BE ME.

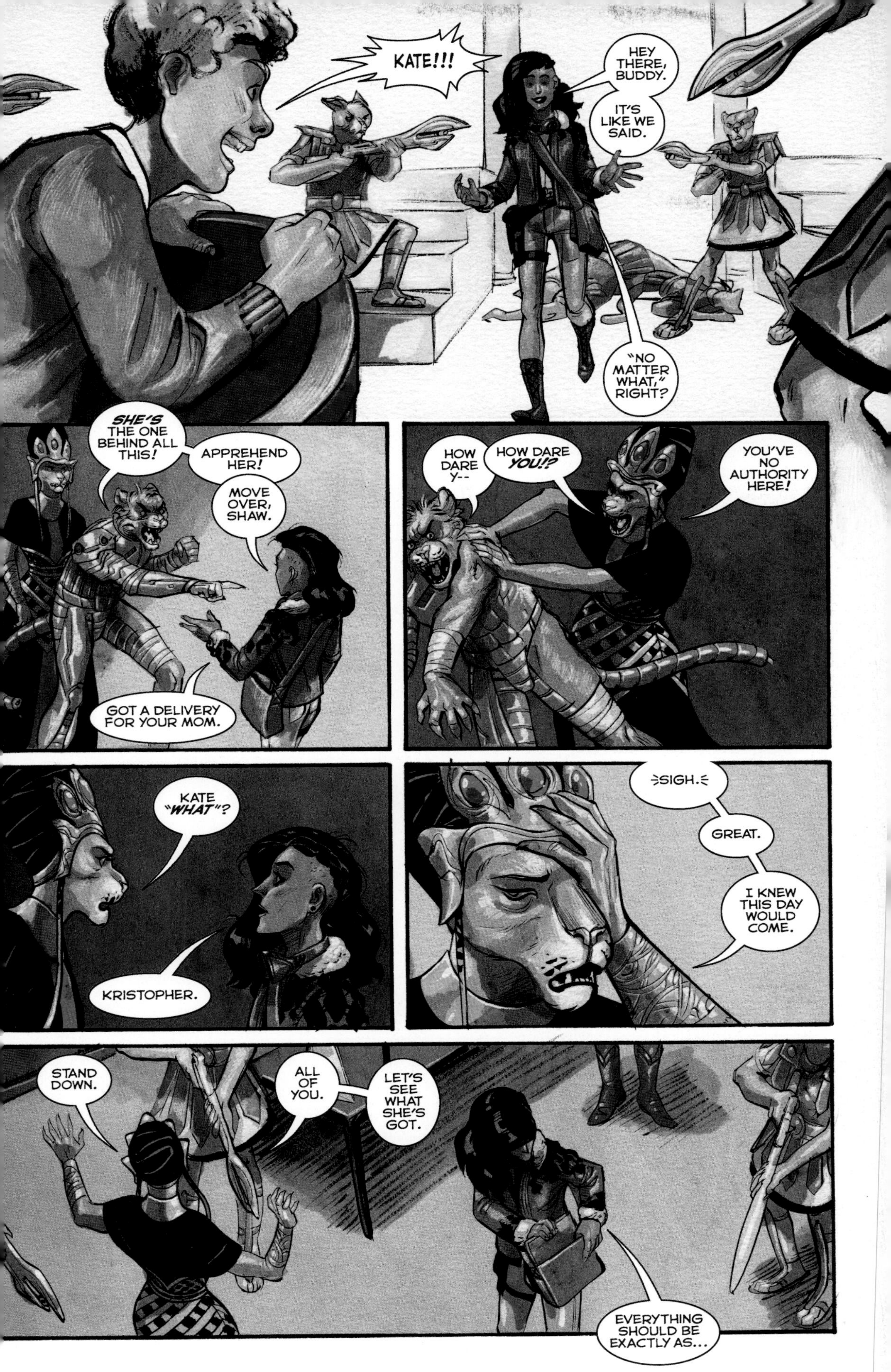
KATE!!!
HEY THERE, BUDDY.
IT'S LIKE WE SAID.
"NO MATTER WHAT," RIGHT?
SHE'S THE ONE BEHIND ALL THIS!
APPREHEND HER!
MOVE OVER, SHAW.
GOT A DELIVERY FOR YOUR MOM.
HOW DARE Y--
HOW DARE *YOU!?*
YOU'VE NO AUTHORITY HERE!
KATE *"WHAT"*?
KRISTOPHER.
SIGH.
GREAT.
I KNEW THIS DAY WOULD COME.
STAND DOWN.
ALL OF YOU.
LET'S SEE WHAT SHE'S GOT.
EVERYTHING SHOULD BE EXACTLY AS...

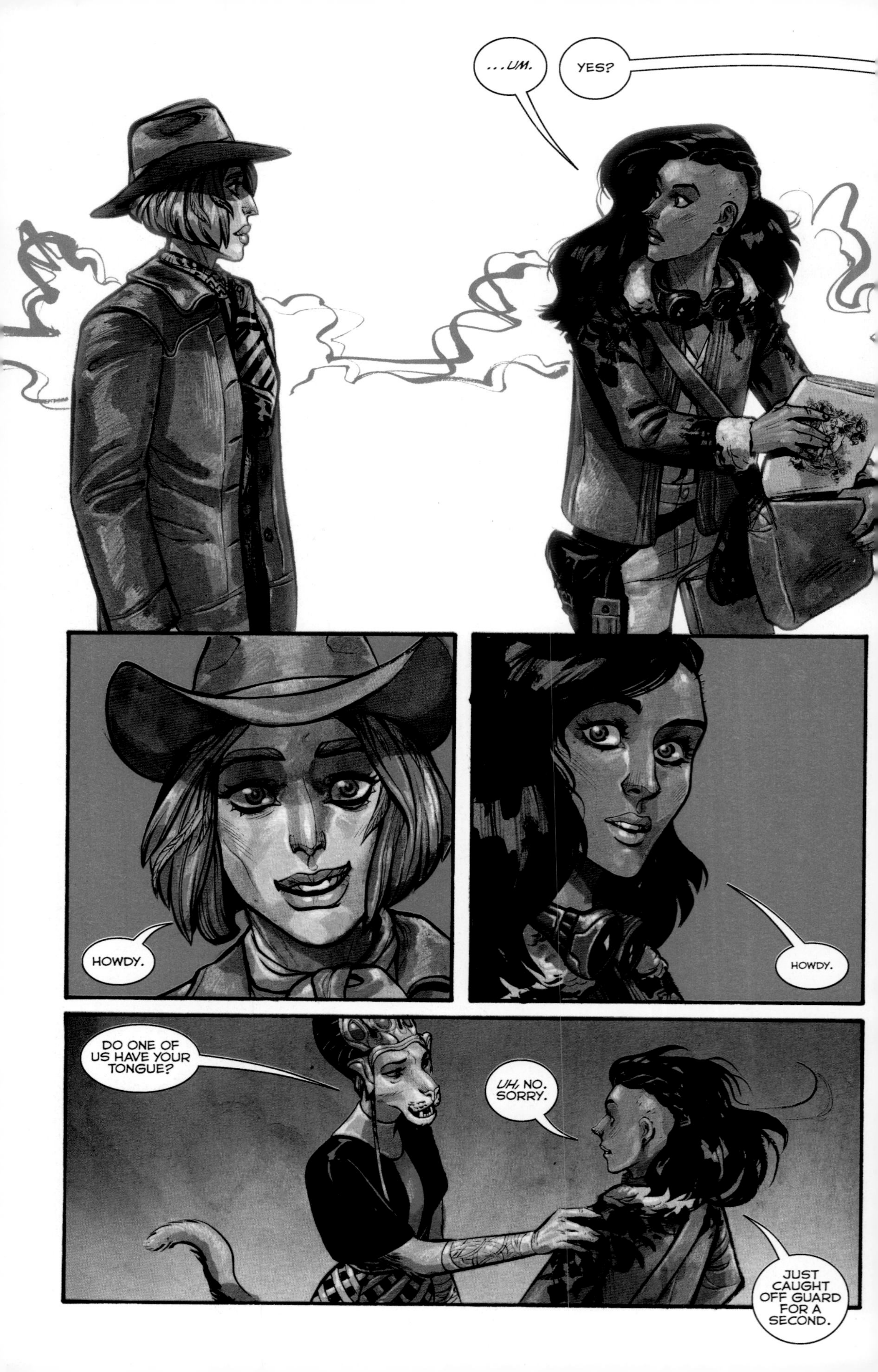
...UM.
YES?
HOWDY.
HOWDY.
DO ONE OF US HAVE YOUR TONGUE?
UH, NO. SORRY.
JUST CAUGHT OFF GUARD FOR A SECOND.

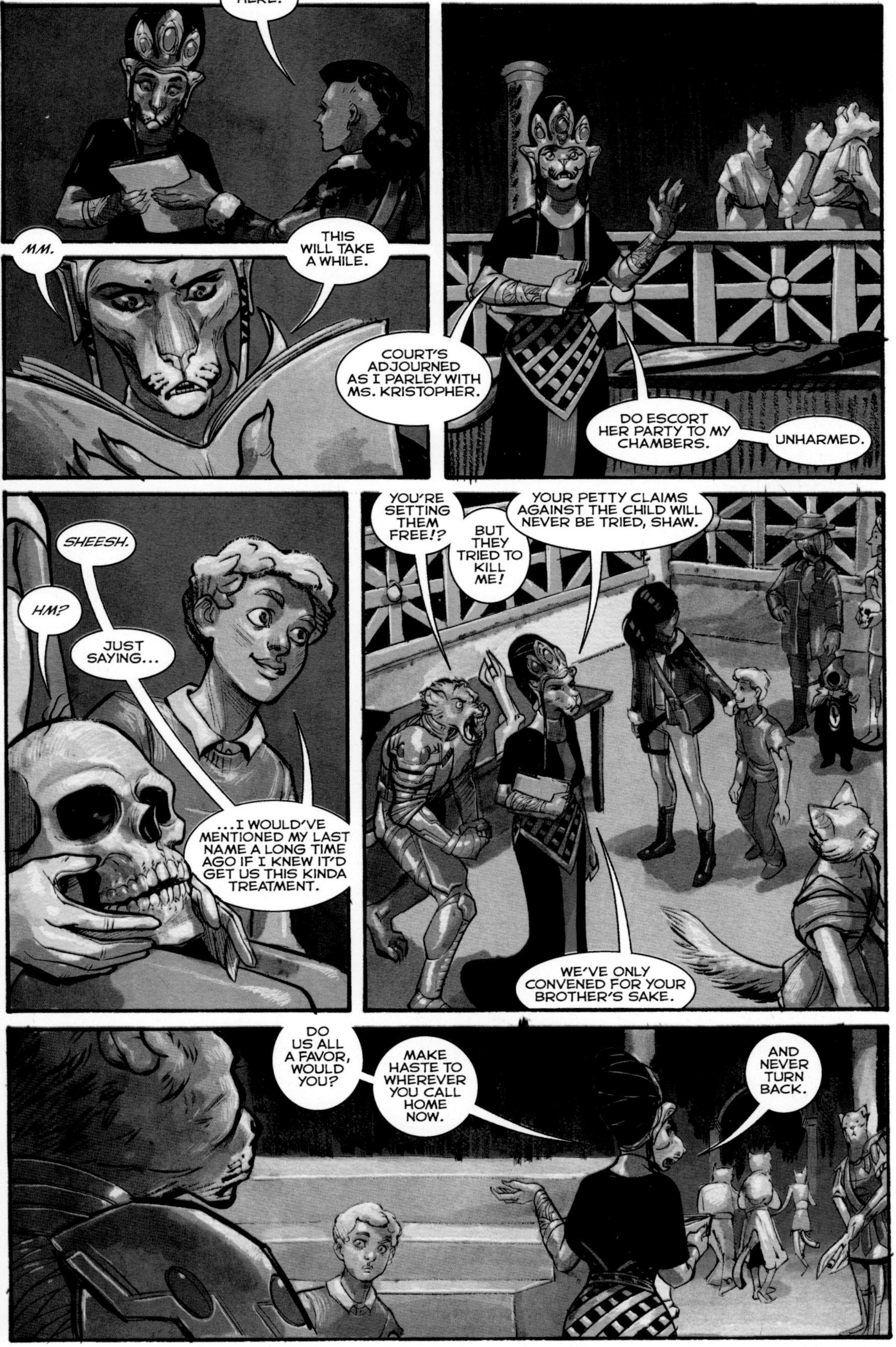
HERE.
MM.
THIS WILL TAKE A WHILE.
COURT'S ADJOURNED AS I PARLEY WITH MS. KRISTOPHER.
DO ESCORT HER PARTY TO MY CHAMBERS.
UNHARMED.
SHEESH.
HM?
JUST SAYING...
...I WOULD'VE MENTIONED MY LAST NAME A LONG TIME AGO IF I KNEW IT'D GET US THIS KINDA TREATMENT.
YOU'RE SETTING THEM FREE!?
BUT THEY TRIED TO KILL ME!
YOUR PETTY CLAIMS AGAINST THE CHILD WILL NEVER BE TRIED, SHAW.
WE'VE ONLY CONVENED FOR YOUR BROTHER'S SAKE.
DO US ALL A FAVOR, WOULD YOU?
MAKE HASTE TO WHEREVER YOU CALL HOME NOW.
AND NEVER TURN BACK.

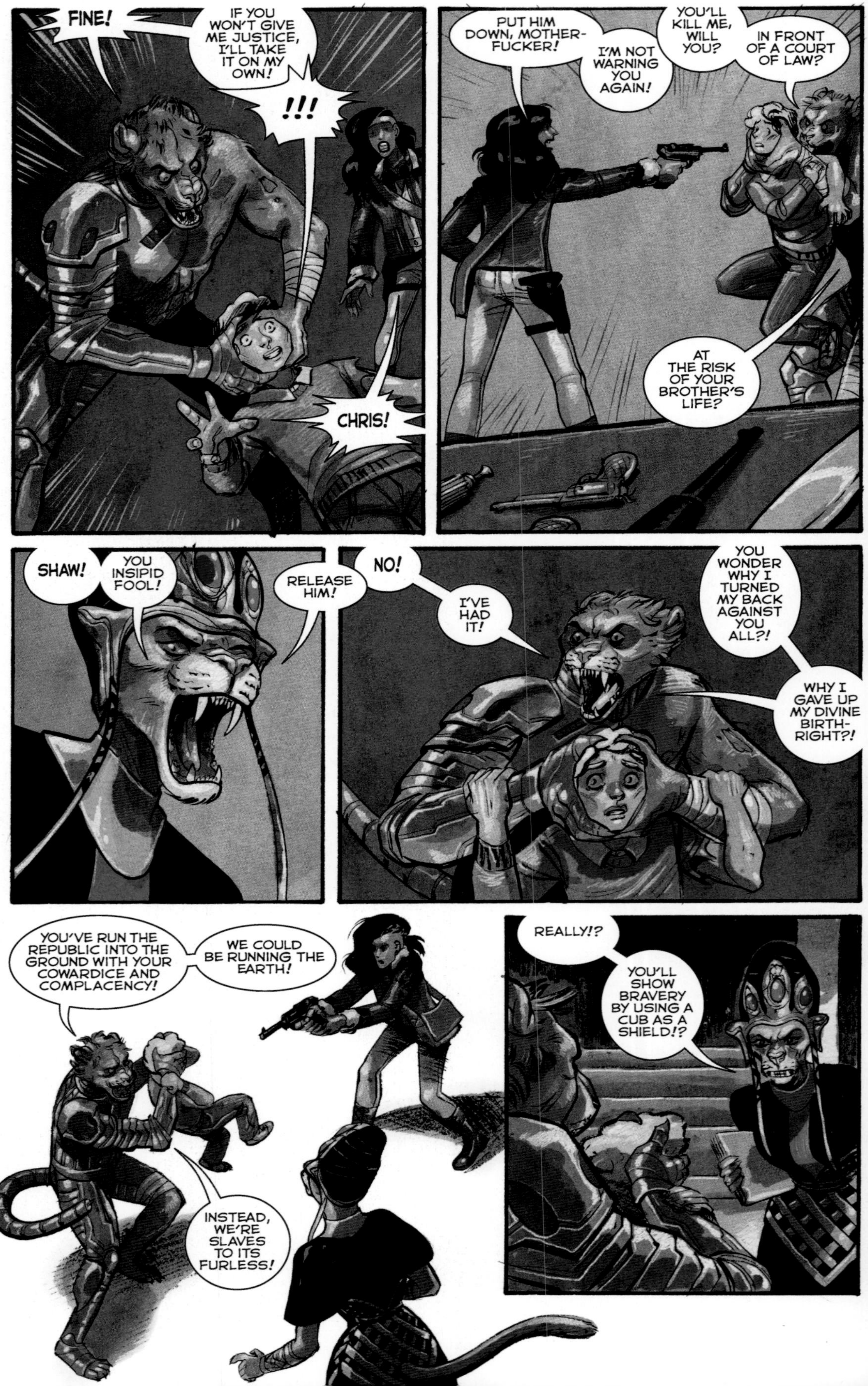
FINE!
IF YOU WON'T GIVE ME JUSTICE, I'LL TAKE IT ON MY OWN!
!!!
CHRIS!
PUT HIM DOWN, MOTHER-FUCKER!
I'M NOT WARNING YOU AGAIN!
YOU'LL KILL ME, WILL YOU?
IN FRONT OF A COURT OF LAW?
AT THE RISK OF YOUR BROTHER'S LIFE?
SHAW!
YOU INSIPID FOOL!
RELEASE HIM!
NO!
I'VE HAD IT!
YOU WONDER WHY I TURNED MY BACK AGAINST YOU ALL?!
WHY I GAVE UP MY DIVINE BIRTH-RIGHT?!
YOU'VE RUN THE REPUBLIC INTO THE GROUND WITH YOUR COWARDICE AND COMPLACENCY!
WE COULD BE RUNNING THE EARTH!
INSTEAD, WE'RE SLAVES TO ITS FURLESS!
REALLY!?
YOU'LL SHOW BRAVERY BY USING A CUB AS A SHIELD!?

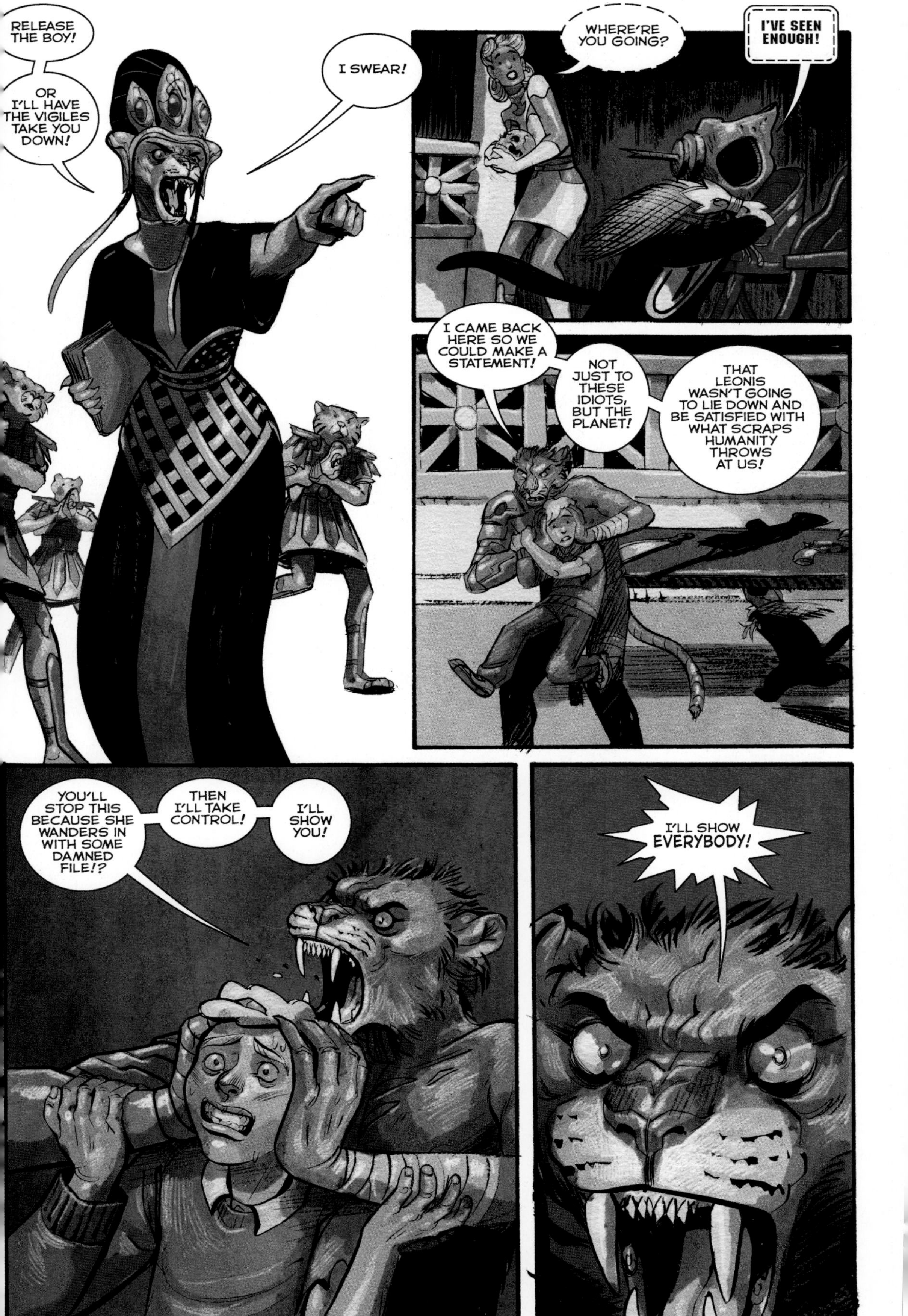
RELEASE THE BOY!
OR I'LL HAVE THE VIGILES TAKE YOU DOWN!
I SWEAR!
WHERE'RE YOU GOING?
I'VE SEEN ENOUGH!
I CAME BACK HERE SO WE COULD MAKE A STATEMENT!
NOT JUST TO THESE IDIOTS, BUT THE PLANET!
THAT LEONIS WASN'T GOING TO LIE DOWN AND BE SATISFIED WITH WHAT SCRAPS HUMANITY THROWS AT US!
YOU'LL STOP THIS BECAUSE SHE WANDERS IN WITH SOME DAMNED FILE!?
THEN I'LL TAKE CONTROL!
I'LL SHOW YOU!
I'LL SHOW EVERYBODY!

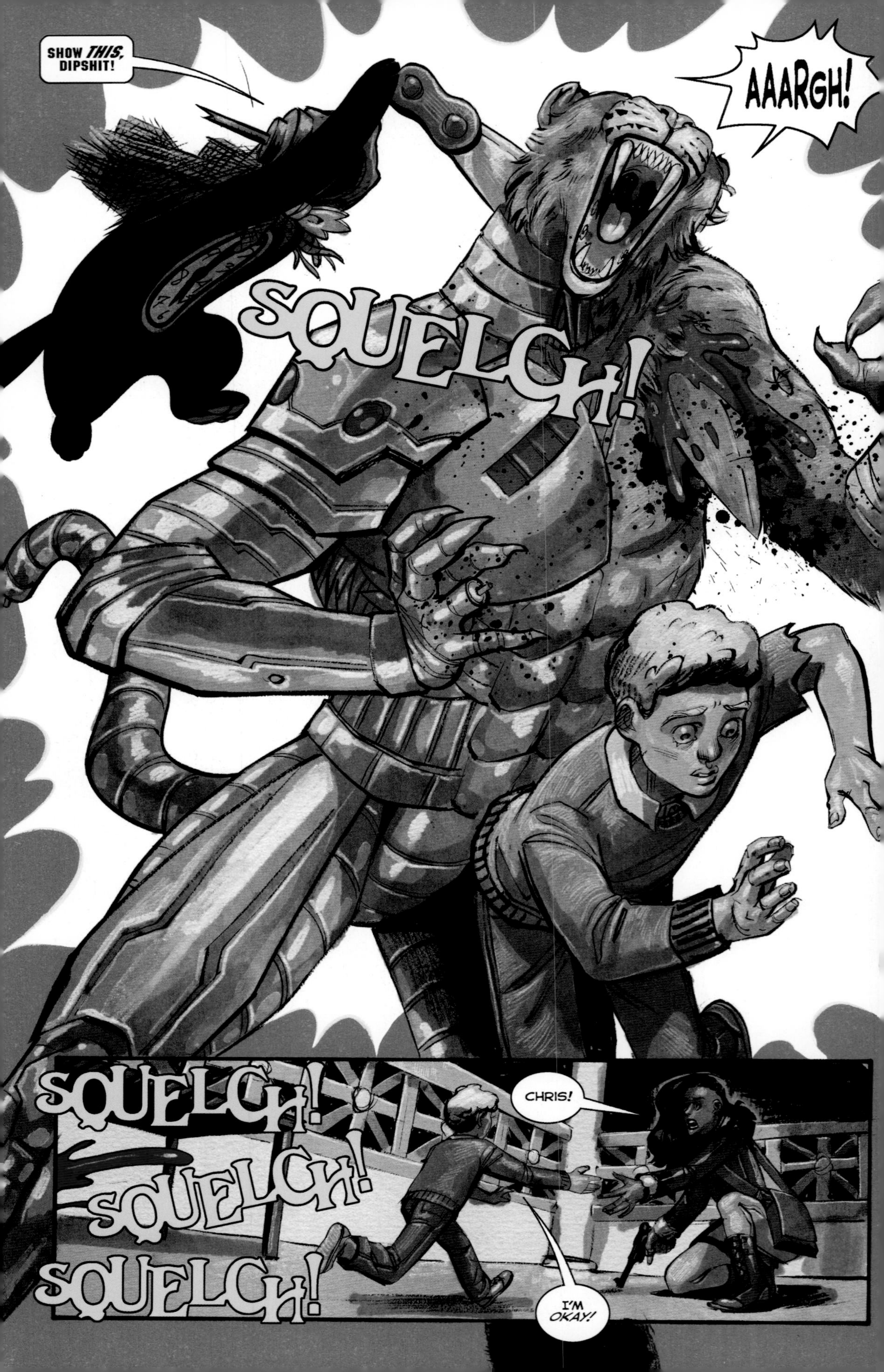
SHOW THIS, DIPSHIT!
AAARGH!
SQUELCH!
SQUELCH!
SQUELCH!
SQUELCH!
CHRIS!
I'M OKAY!

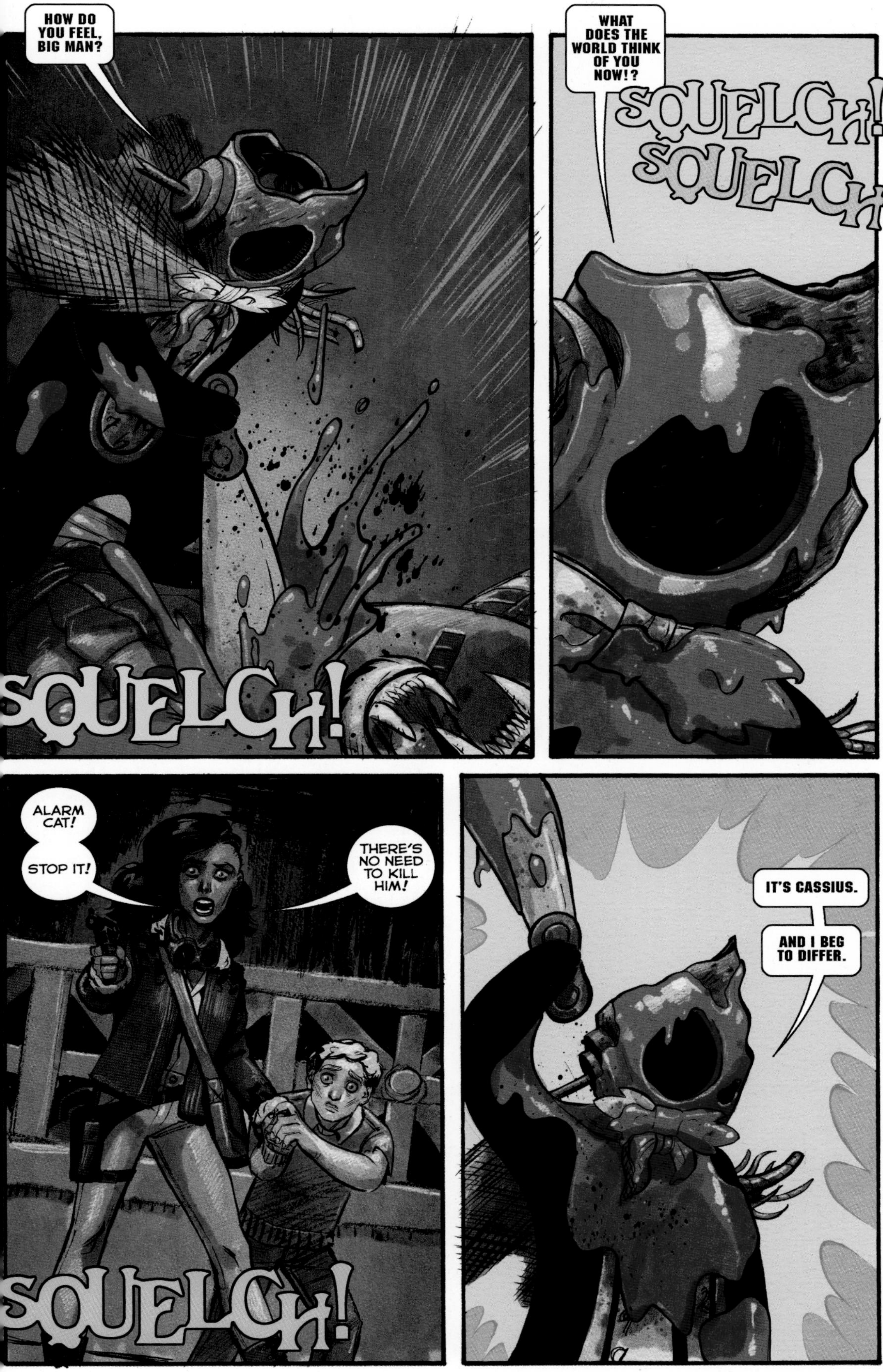
HOW DO YOU FEEL, BIG MAN?
SQUELCH!
WHAT DOES THE WORLD THINK OF YOU NOW!?
SQUELCH! SQUELCH!
ALARM CAT!
STOP IT!
THERE'S NO NEED TO KILL HIM!
SQUELCH!
IT'S CASSIUS.
AND I BEG TO DIFFER.

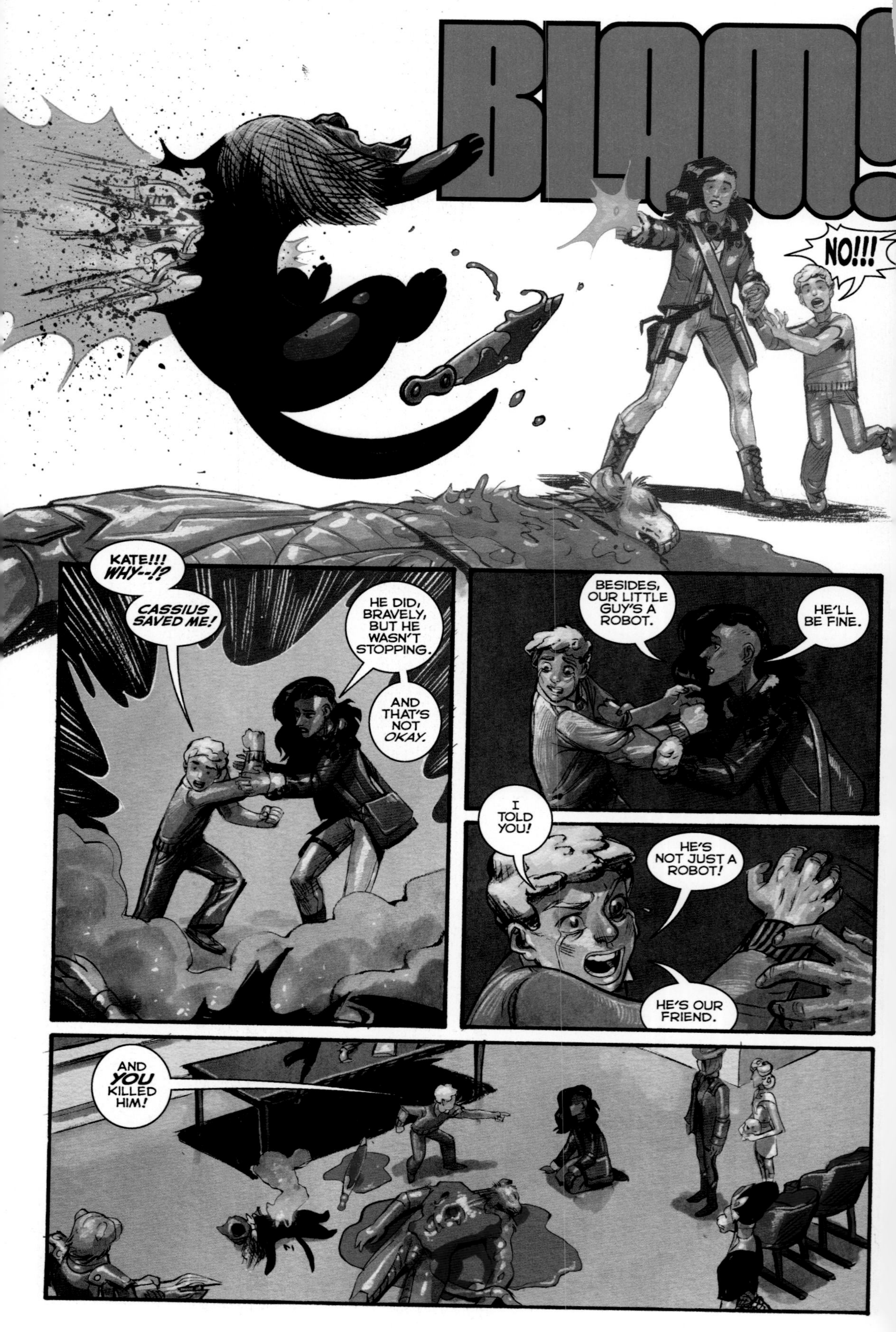
BLAM!
NO!!!
KATE!!! WHY--!?
CASSIUS SAVED ME!
HE DID, BRAVELY, BUT HE WASN'T STOPPING.
AND THAT'S NOT OKAY.
BESIDES, OUR LITTLE GUY'S A ROBOT.
HE'LL BE FINE.
I TOLD YOU!
HE'S NOT JUST A ROBOT!
HE'S OUR FRIEND.
AND YOU KILLED HIM!

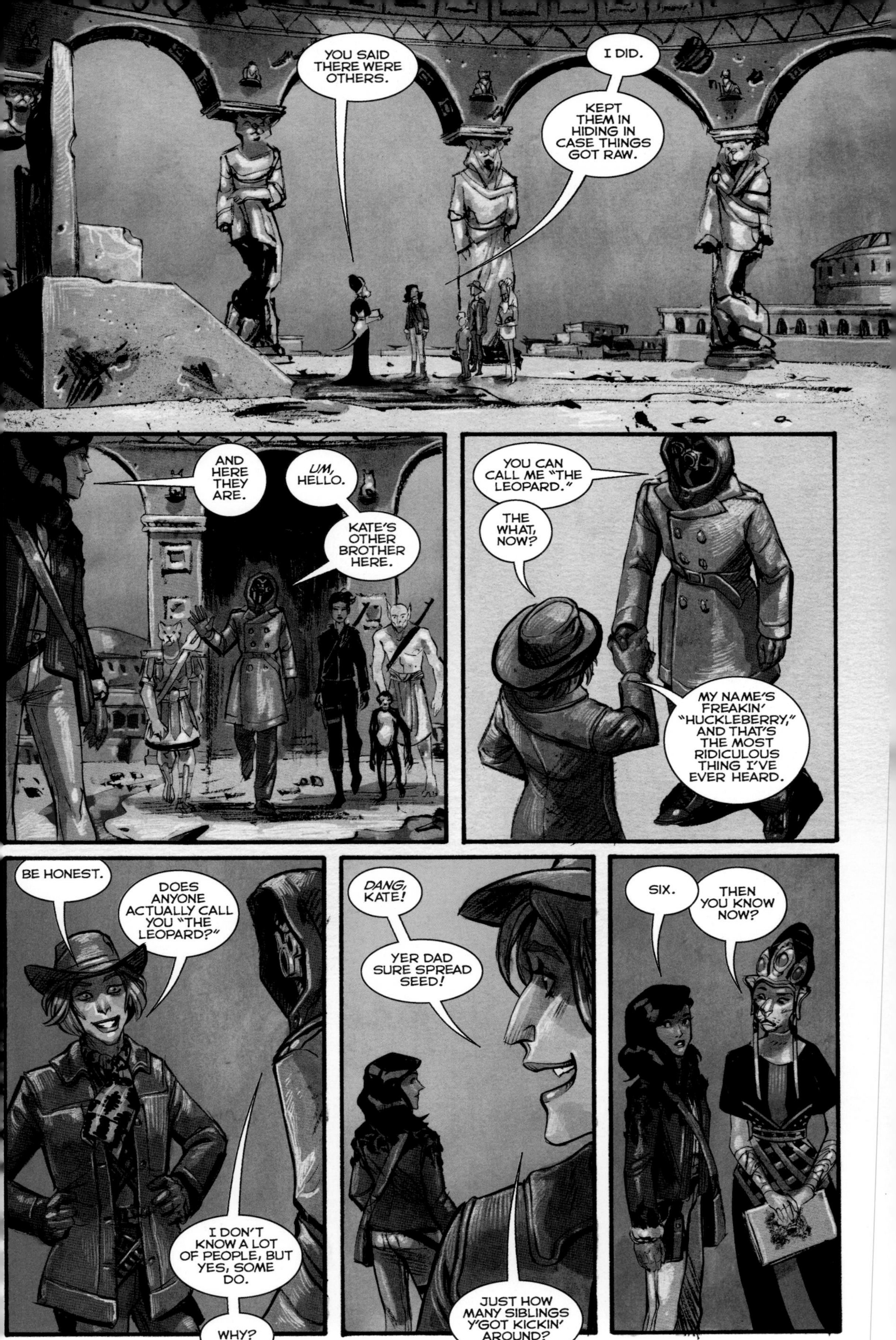
YOU SAID THERE WERE OTHERS.
I DID.
KEPT THEM IN HIDING IN CASE THINGS GOT RAW.
AND HERE THEY ARE.
UM, HELLO.
KATE'S OTHER BROTHER HERE.
YOU CAN CALL ME "THE LEOPARD."
THE WHAT, NOW?
MY NAME'S FREAKIN' "HUCKLEBERRY," AND THAT'S THE MOST RIDICULOUS THING I'VE EVER HEARD.
BE HONEST.
DOES ANYONE ACTUALLY CALL YOU "THE LEOPARD?"
I DON'T KNOW A LOT OF PEOPLE, BUT YES, SOME DO.
WHY?
DANG, KATE!
YER DAD SURE SPREAD SEED!
JUST HOW MANY SIBLINGS Y'GOT KICKIN' AROUND?
SIX.
THEN YOU KNOW NOW?

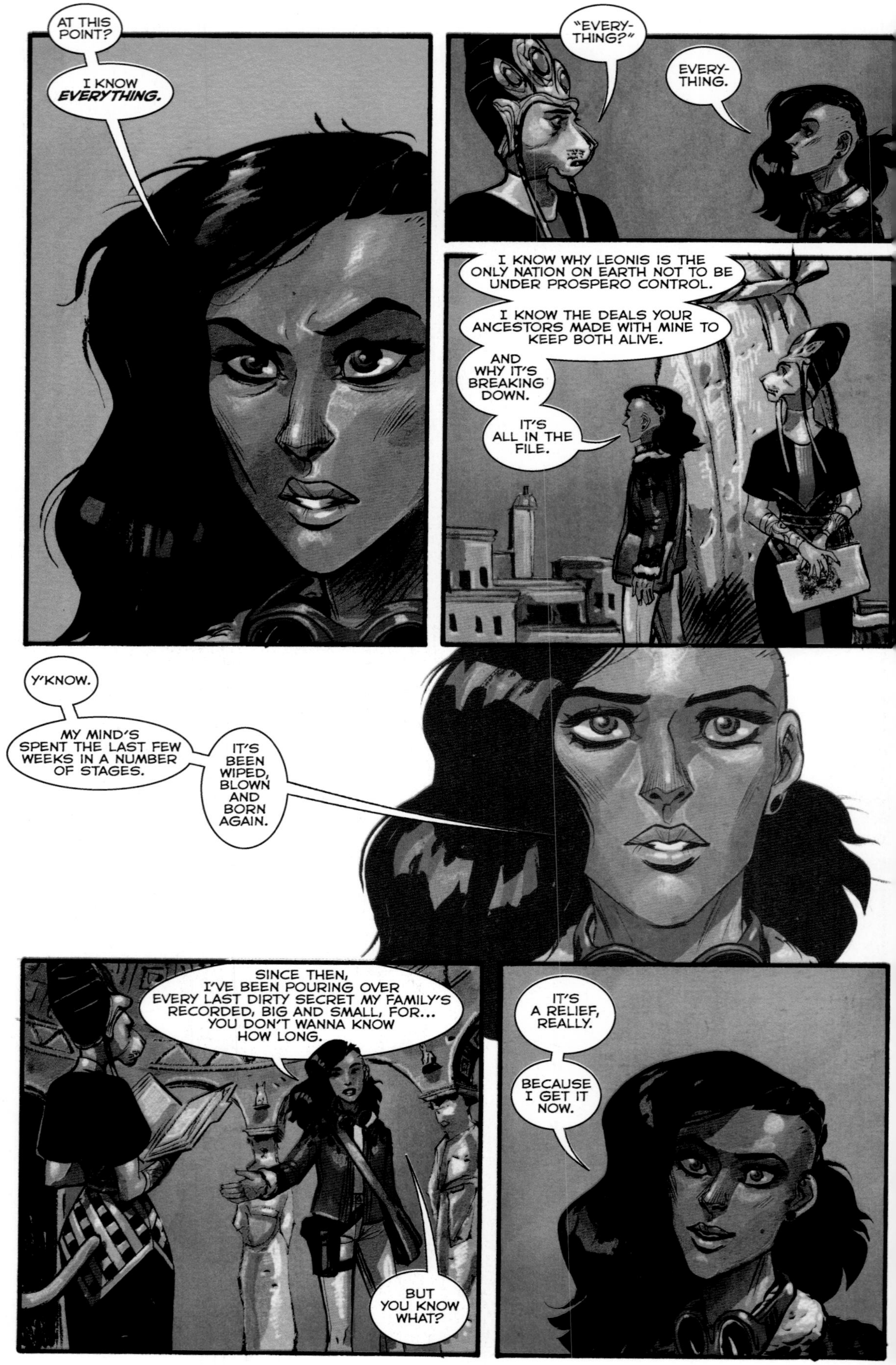
AT THIS POINT?
I KNOW *EVERYTHING.*
"EVERY-THING?"
EVERY-THING.
I KNOW WHY LEONIS IS THE ONLY NATION ON EARTH NOT TO BE UNDER PROSPERO CONTROL.
I KNOW THE DEALS YOUR ANCESTORS MADE WITH MINE TO KEEP BOTH ALIVE.
AND WHY IT'S BREAKING DOWN.
IT'S ALL IN THE FILE.
Y'KNOW.
MY MIND'S SPENT THE LAST FEW WEEKS IN A NUMBER OF STAGES.
IT'S BEEN WIPED, BLOWN AND BORN AGAIN.
SINCE THEN, I'VE BEEN POURING OVER EVERY LAST DIRTY SECRET MY FAMILY'S RECORDED, BIG AND SMALL, FOR... YOU DON'T WANNA KNOW HOW LONG.
BUT YOU KNOW WHAT?
IT'S A RELIEF, REALLY.
BECAUSE I GET IT NOW.

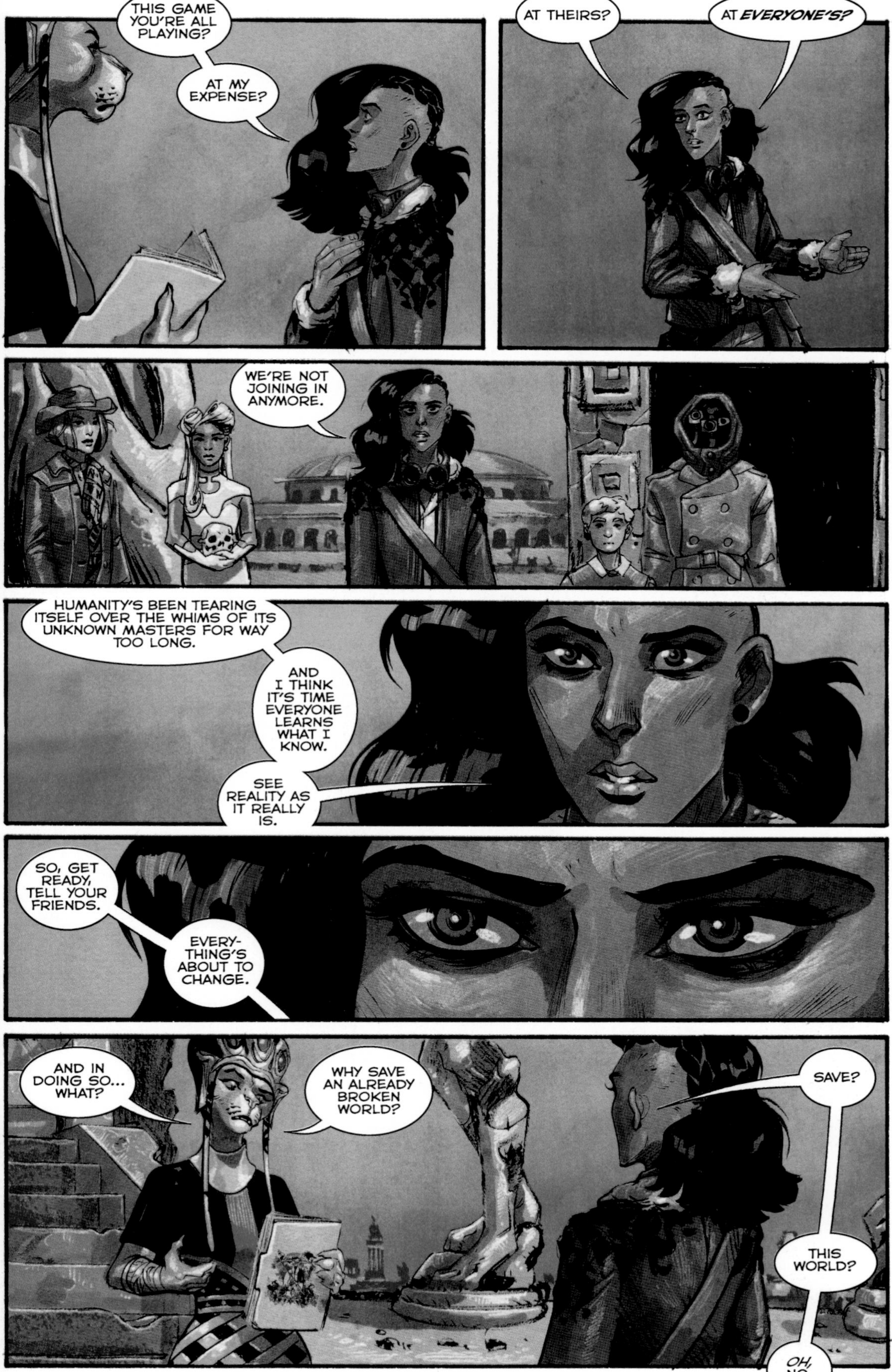
THIS GAME YOU'RE ALL PLAYING?
AT MY EXPENSE?
AT THEIRS?
AT *EVERYONE'S?*
WE'RE NOT JOINING IN ANYMORE.
HUMANITY'S BEEN TEARING ITSELF OVER THE WHIMS OF ITS UNKNOWN MASTERS FOR WAY TOO LONG.
AND I THINK IT'S TIME EVERYONE LEARNS WHAT I KNOW.
SEE REALITY AS IT REALLY IS.
SO, GET READY, TELL YOUR FRIENDS.
EVERY-THING'S ABOUT TO CHANGE.
AND IN DOING SO... WHAT?
WHY SAVE AN ALREADY BROKEN WORLD?
SAVE?
THIS WORLD?
OH, NO.

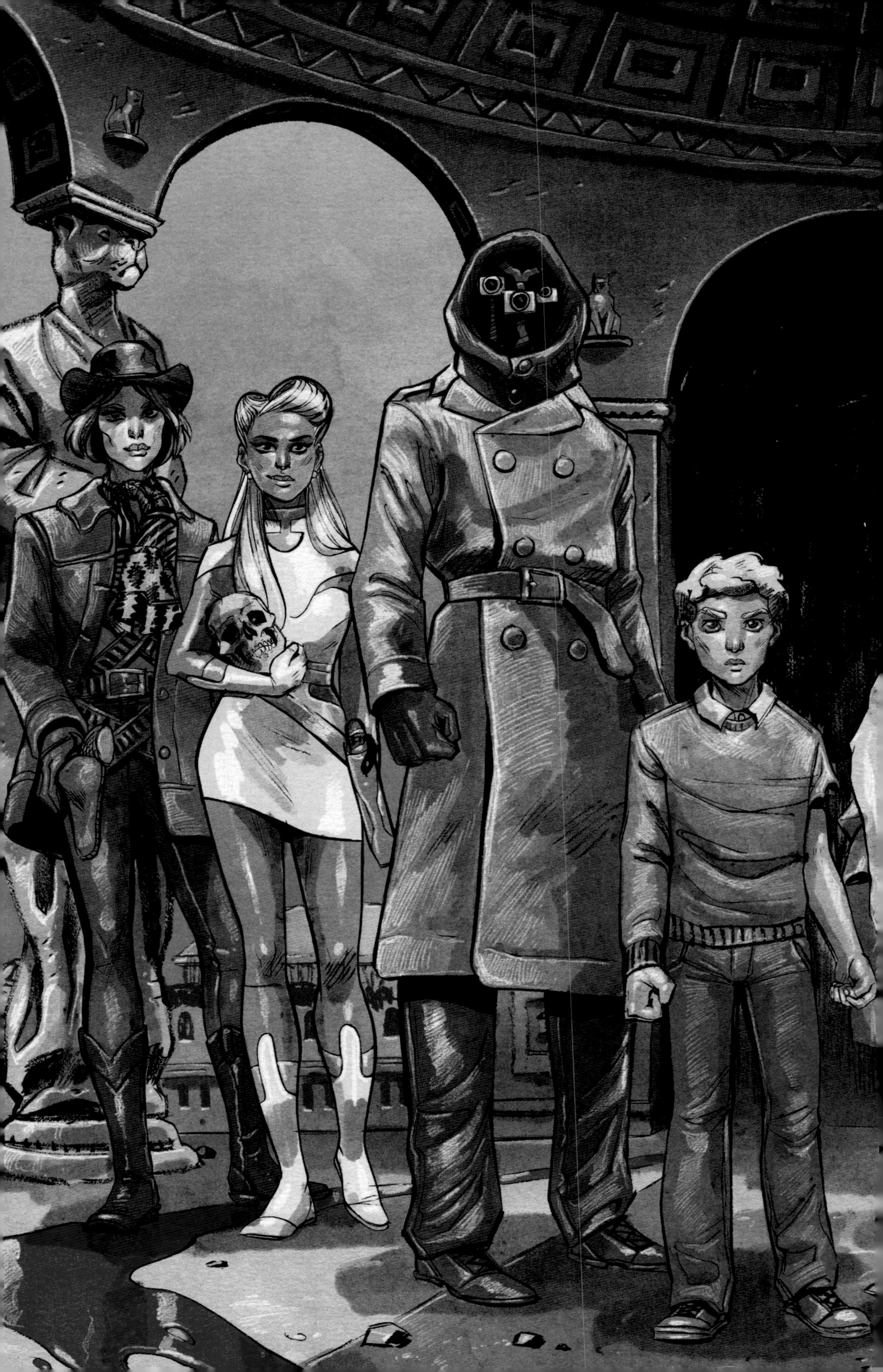

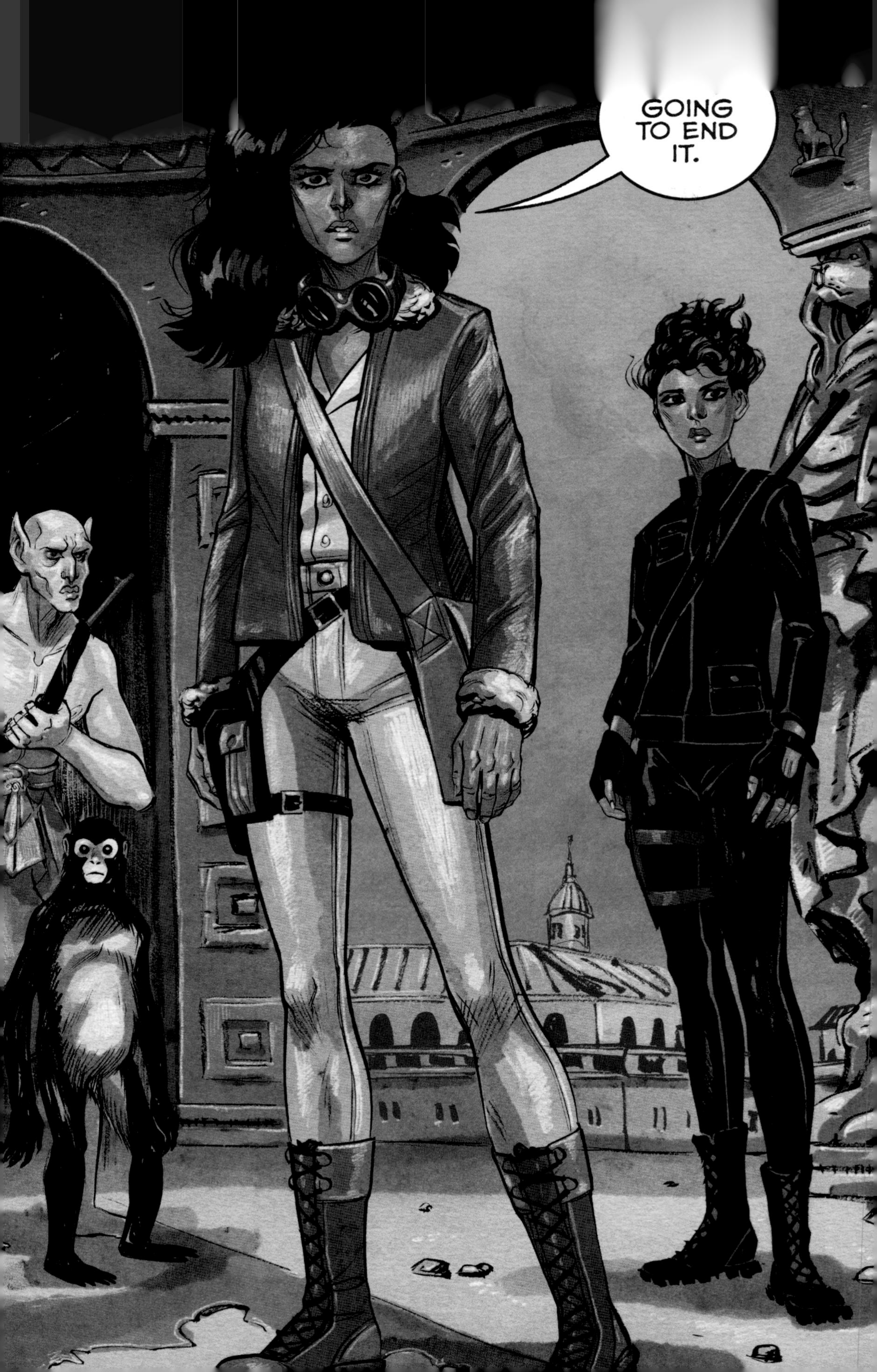
GOING TO END IT.

SKETCHBOOK

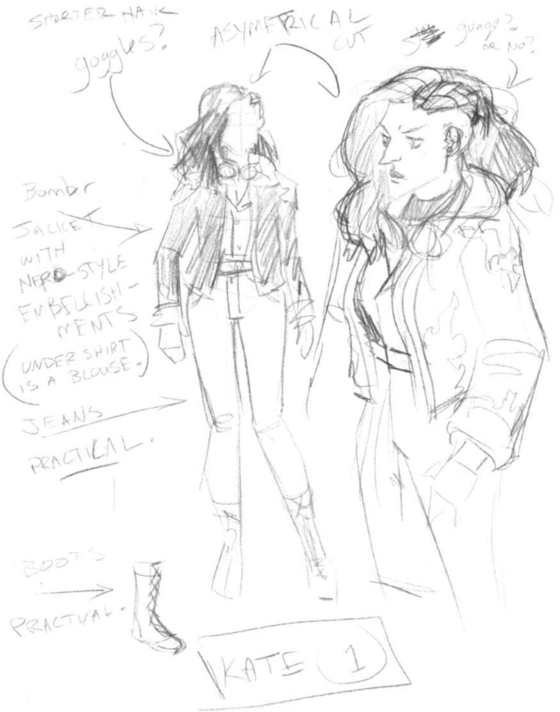
goggles?
ASYMETRICAL CUT
Bomber
WITH
EMBELLISH-MENTS
(UNDER SHIRT IS A BLOUSE.)
JEANS
PRACTICAL.
BOOTS
KATE 1

KATE CONCEPT SKETCH

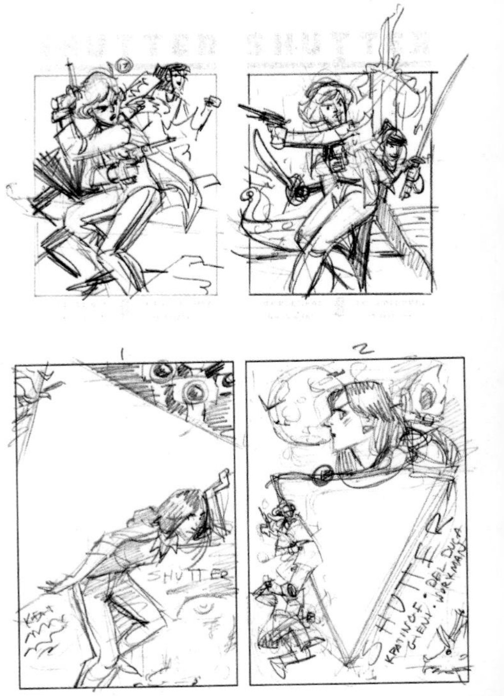
1
2
SHUTTER

SHUTTER 17 COVER & 13 SKETCH COVER LAYOUT

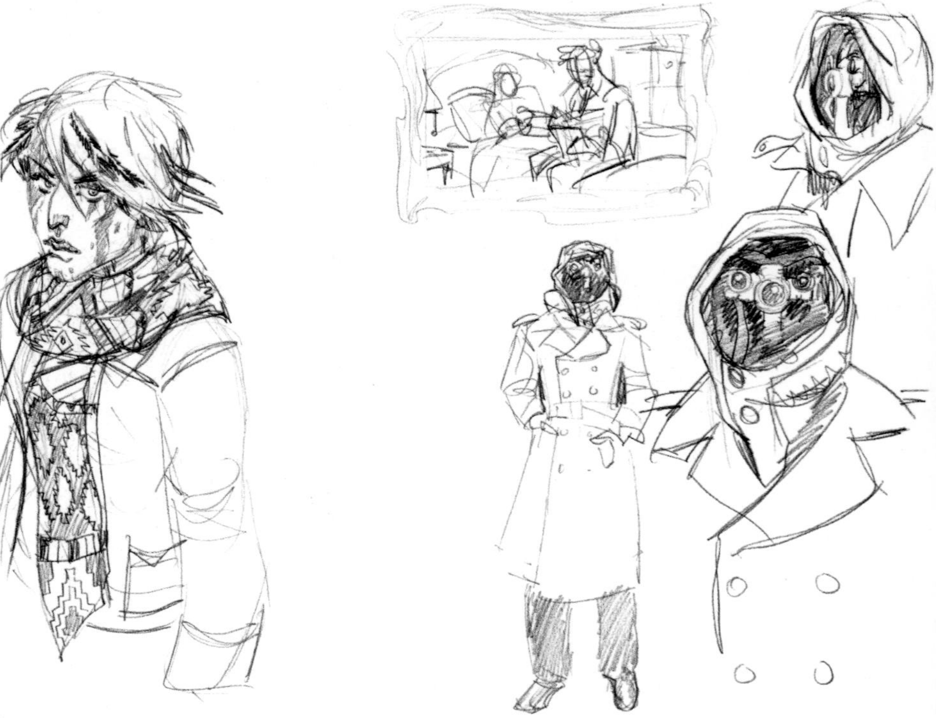

HUCKLEBERRY & LEOPARD CONCEPT SKETCHES

SHUTTER 14 COVER LAYOUTS & INKS

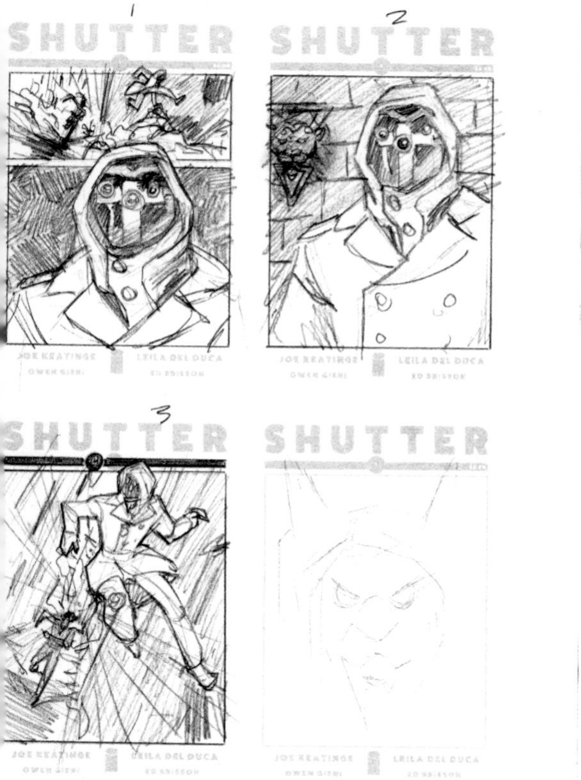
1
SHUTTER
2
SHUTTER
JOE KEATINGE
LEILA DEL DUCA
OWEN GIENI
ED BRISSON
3
SHUTTER
SHUTTER

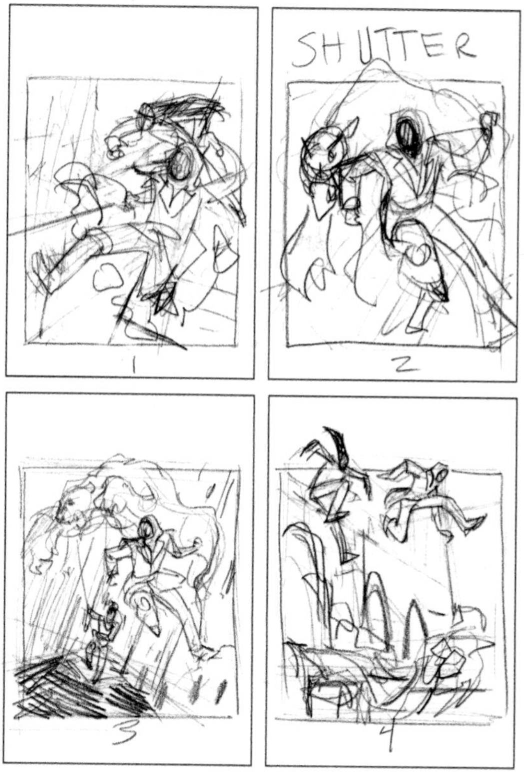
SHUTTER
1
2
3
4

11 x 17

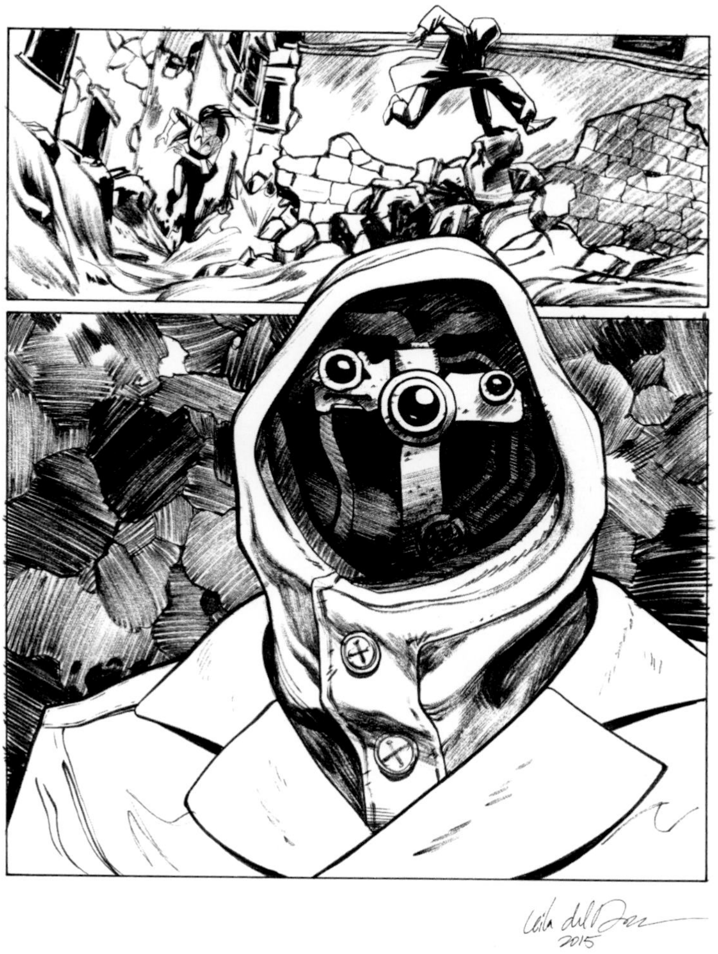
Leila del Duca
2015

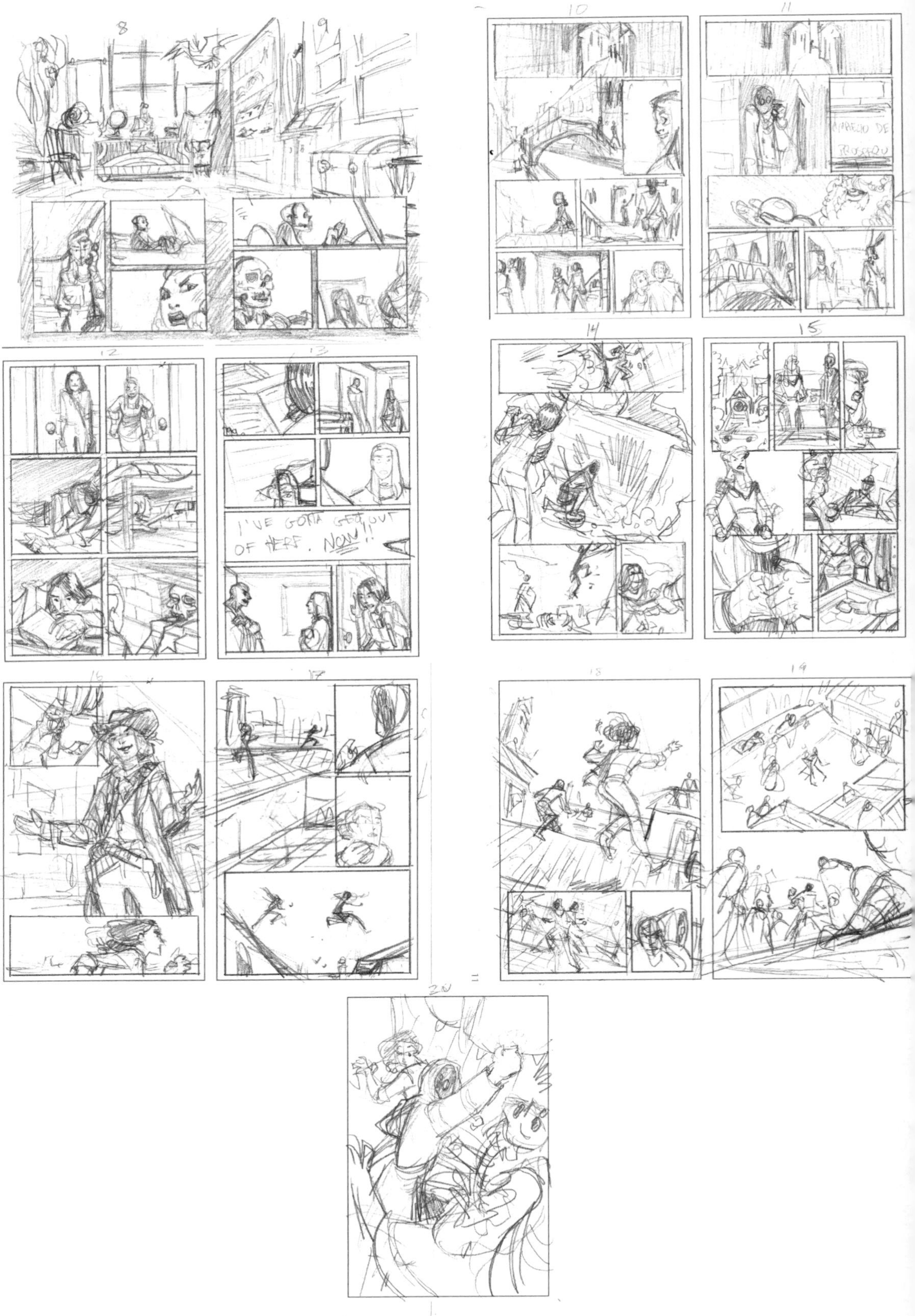
I'VE GOTTA GET OUT OF HERE. NOW!!

SHUTTER 13 PAGES 8-20 LAYOUTS

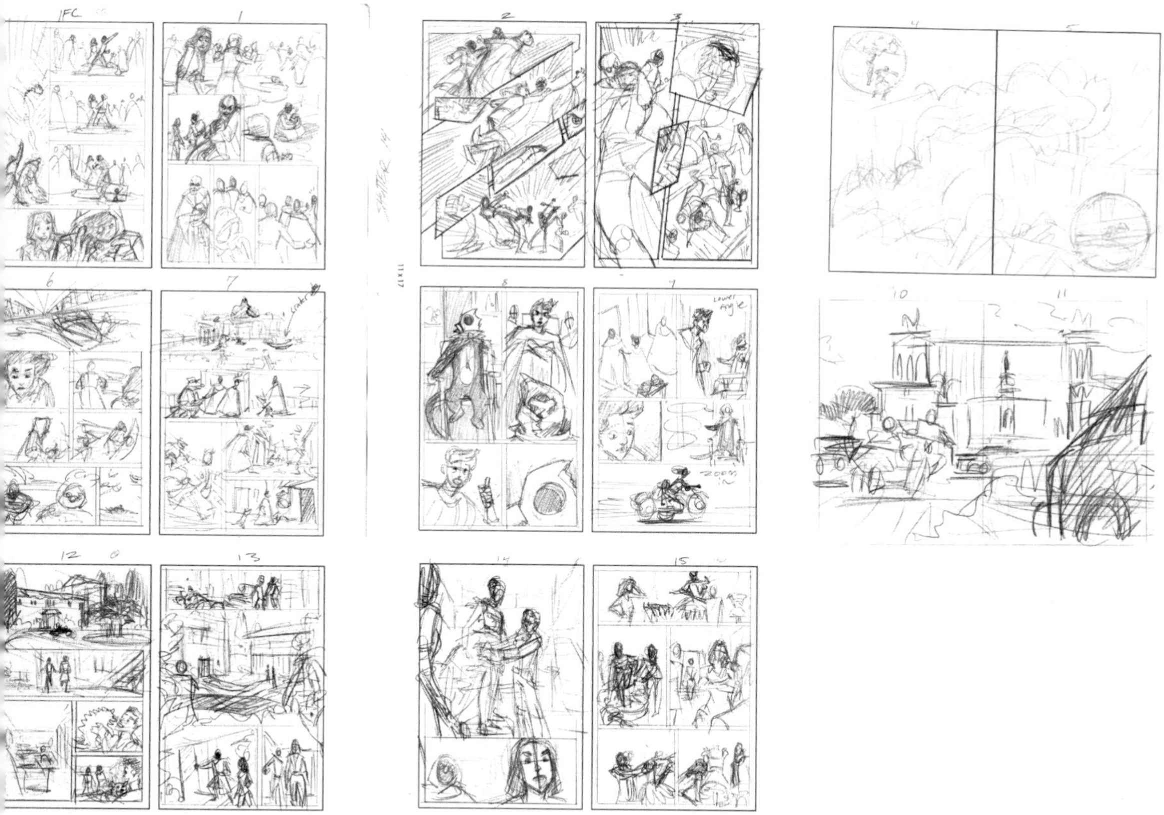

SHUTTER 13 PAGES IFC-15 LAYOUTS

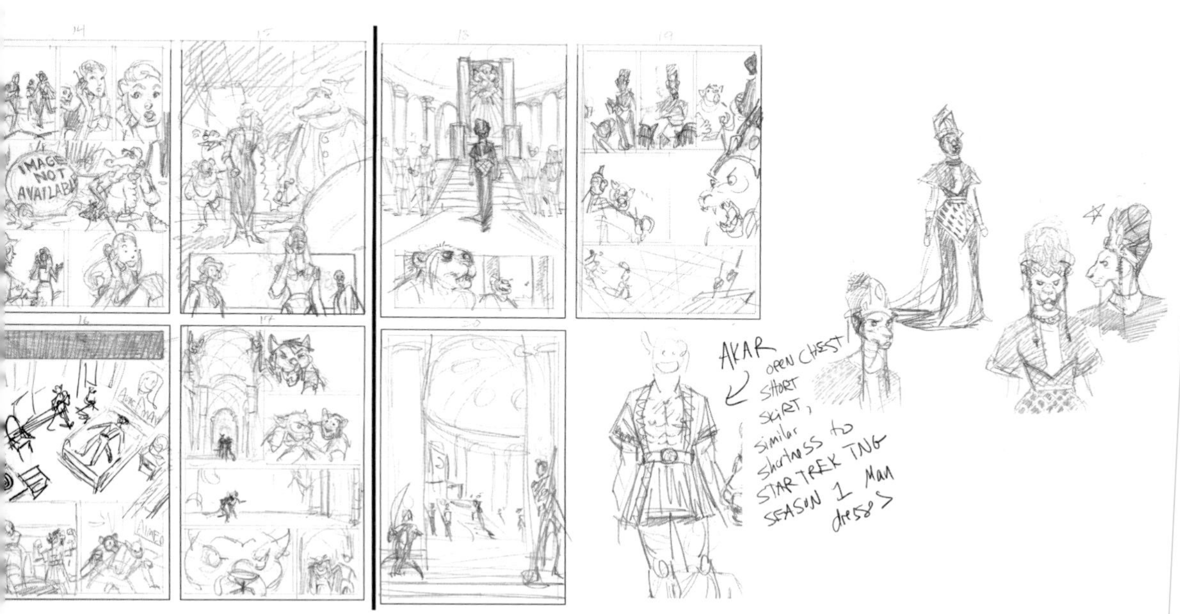
IMAGE NOT AVAILABLE
AKAR
open chest! short skirt, similar shortness to STAR TREK TNG SEASON 1 Man dresses

SHUTTER 15 PAGES 14-20 LAYOUTS

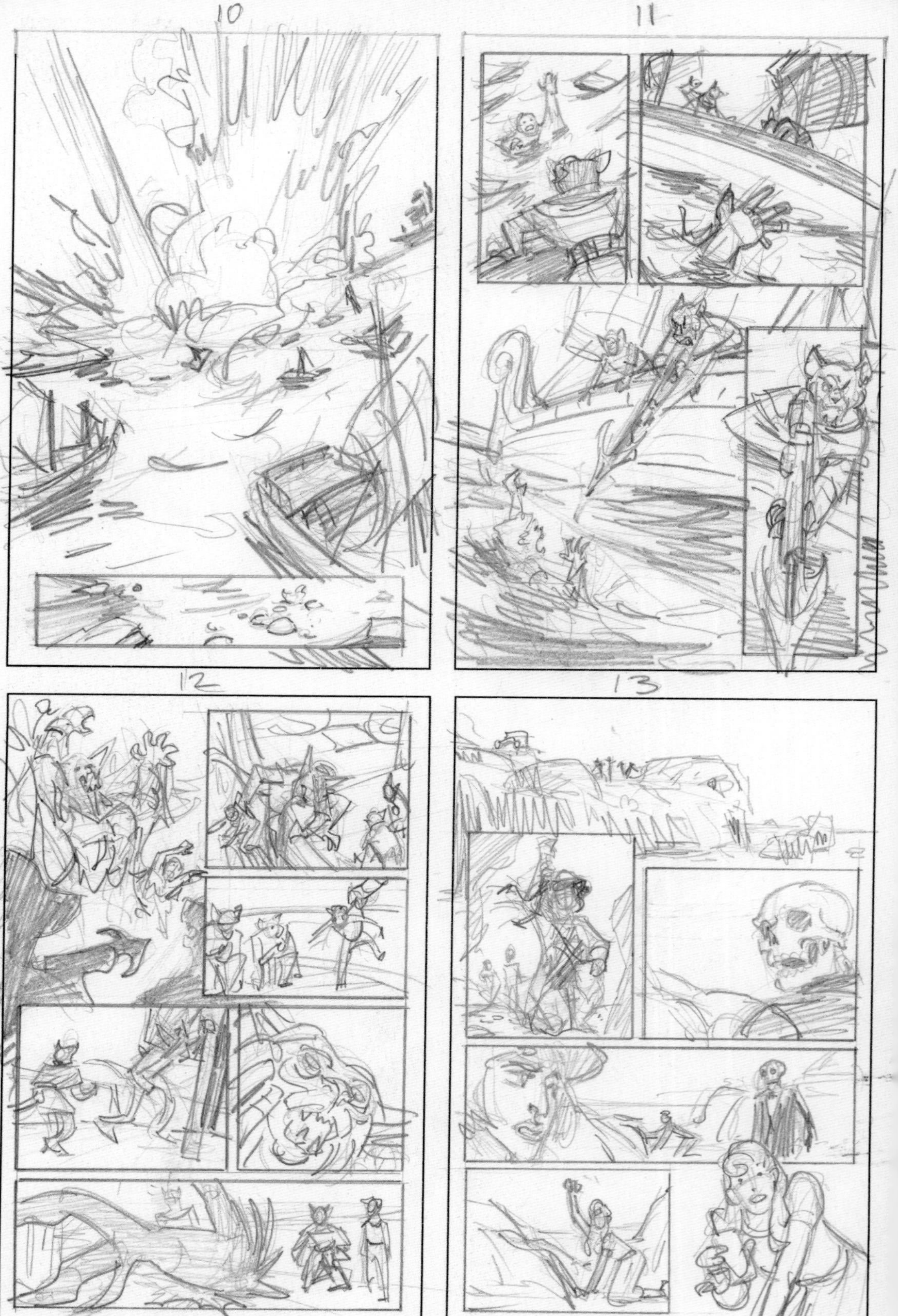
10
11
12
13

SHUTTER 15 PAGES 10-13 LAYOUTS

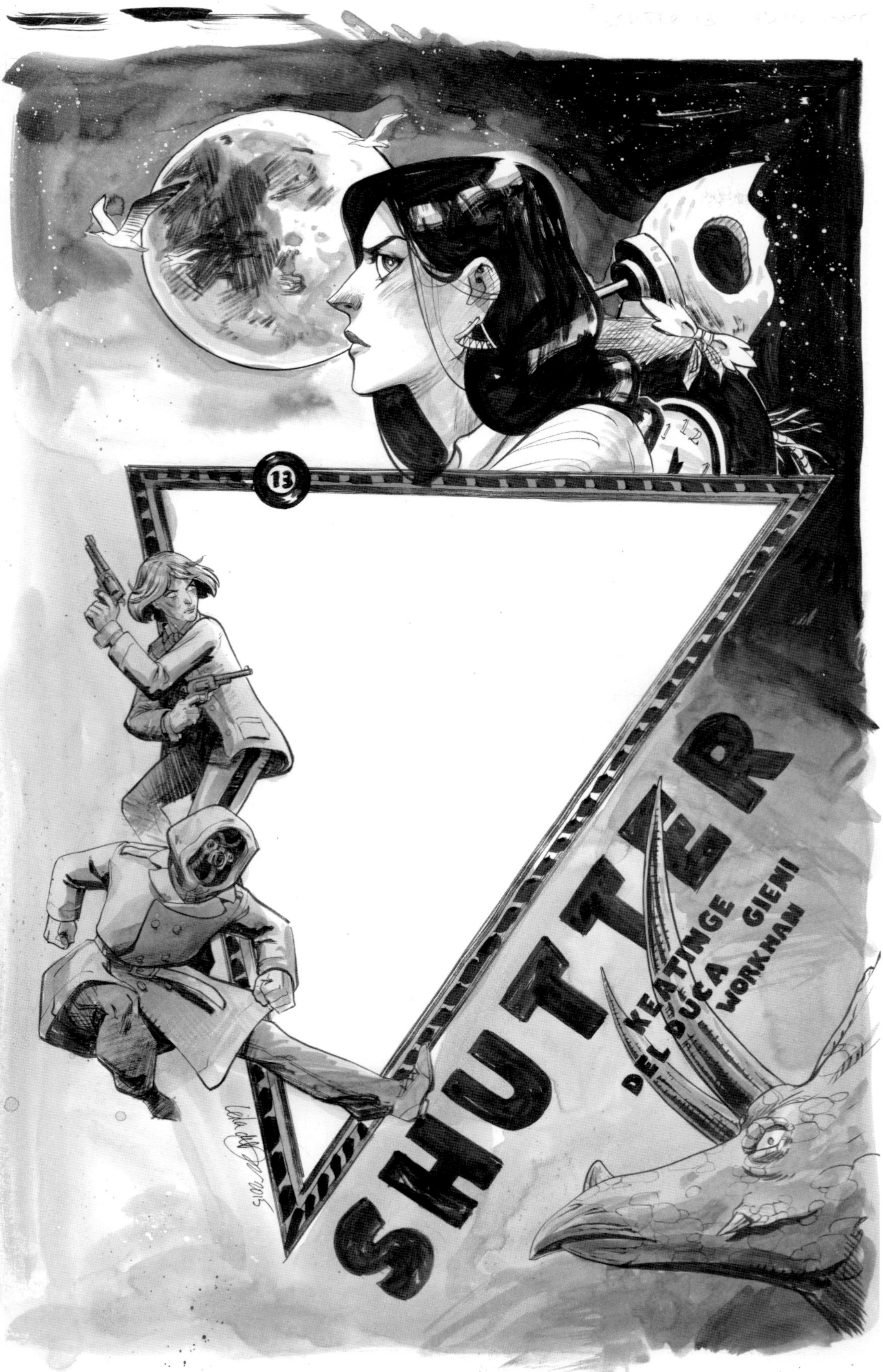
13
SHUTTER
KEATINGE
DEL DUCA
GIENI
WORKMAN

SHUTTER 13 SKETCH COVER INKS

SHUTTER

JOE KEATINGE is the writer of Image, Skybound, Marvel and DC Comics titles including SHUTTER, RINGSIDE, GLORY, TECH JACKET, MARVEL KNIGHTS: HULK and ADVENTURES OF SUPERMAN as well as the Executive Editor of the Eisner & Harvey award-winning Image Comics anthology, POPGUN, and the Courtney Taylor-Taylor penned ONE MODEL NATION. Keatinge, based out of the Portland, OR comics studio Tranquility Base, also writes for the premiere French-language magazine on American comics, COMIC BOX.

LEILA DEL DUCA is the penciller and inker for SHUTTER. She has worked with Image Comics, Vertigo, IDW, and National Geographic. Other titles she has worked on include THE WICKED AND THE DIVINE, THE PANTHEON PROJECT, ESCAPE FROM TERRA, and DEADSKINS. In 2015 she was nominated for the Russ Manning Promising Newcomer Award for her work on SHUTTER. She lives in Portland, Oregon, where she bikes around a lot, plays music for fun, and works out of Periscope Studio with a ton of other comics creators.

TEAM BIOS

OWEN GIENI is the colourist for SHUTTER, MANIFEST DESTINY, DEBRIS, and GLORY for mage Comics, as well as the artist of the Dark Horse series NEGATIVE SPACE. He loves comics. Really into hand painted European sci fi and old horror Manga lately. He lives in Vancouver, BC.

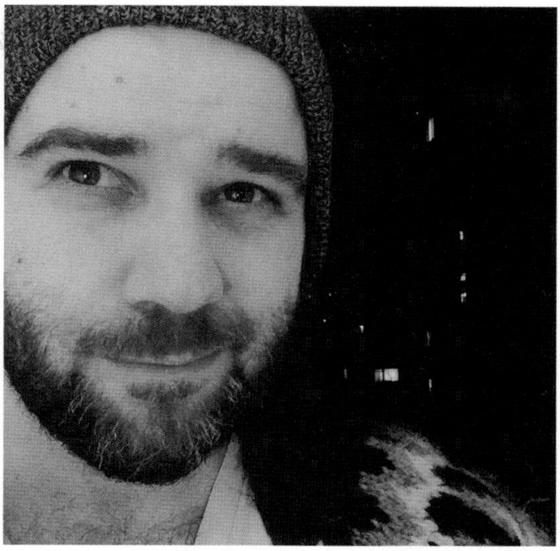

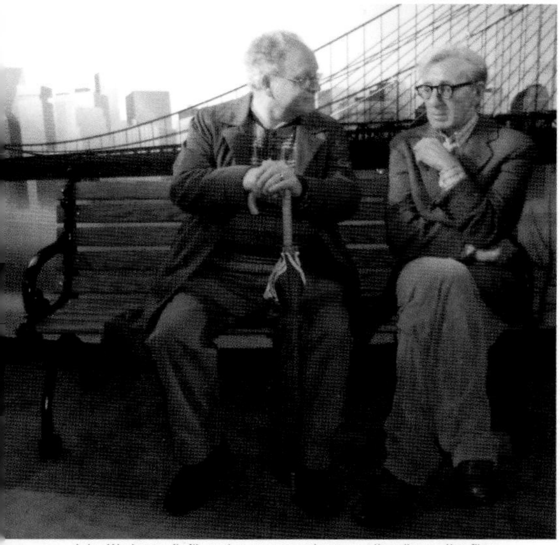

John Workman (left) and a young, unknown writer discuss the films "House of Wax" and "Mystery of the Wax Museum" in this photo by Kate Workman.

JOHN WORKMAN

Though he grew up in Aberdeen, Washington and has spent the last forty years in the New York/New Jersey area, John Workman was born in Beckley, West Virginia on June 20, 1950. Thirty-two years later, he slyly incorporated the date of his birth into the title of the JUNE 2050 feature that he created for Heavy Metal magazine during his tenure as art director for that publication. In the years both before and after that unique comics series, he had a hand in everything involved in the creation of comics as editor, writer, art director, designer, penciler, inker, letterer, and colorist. His comics material has been translated into several languages. Magazine covers that he designed or illustrated have won various awards. While still in high school, Workman began doing local and egional advertising work...almost always with a comics "hook" to the material. A well-received 1974 comics science-fiction story that he wrote and drew for one of the then-new "alternative publishers" convinced him to head for New York. There, he worked for two years in the production department of DC Comics before beginning a seven-year stint as Heavy Metal's art director. Since then, he has become known primarily as a letterer for dozens of different comic book titles from DC, Marvel, First, Pacific, Deluxe, Eclipse, Image, Dark Horse, Apple, Harris, Archie, Topps, Disney, and others. WILD THINGS, a collection of short features by Workman was published by S. Q. Publications. For Dark Horse Presents, Workman wrote and drew "The Adventures of Roma." He compiled, wrote, and designed the 2002 book HEAVY METAL: 25 YEARS OF CLASSIC COVERS and the later hardbound tome INNOCENT IMAGES. He has also written and/or drawn for DC, Marvel, Archie, Hamilton, Image, Apple, Deluxe, Fantagraphics, Heavy Metal, National Lampoon, and Playboy.

JOE KEATINGE - WRITER

LEILA DEL DUCA - ARTIST

OWEN GIENI - COLORIST

JOHN WORKMAN - LETTERER

COVER DESIGN BY LEILA DEL DUCA AND TRICIA RAMOS

CHAPTER BREAKS DESIGNED BY TIM LEONG AND ADDISON DUKE

IMAGE COMICS, INC.
Robert Kirkman - chief operating officer
Erik Larsen - chief financial officer
Todd McFarlane - president
Marc Silvestri - chief executive officer
Jim Valentino - vice-president
www.imagecomics.com

Eric Stephenson - publisher
Corey Murphy - director of sales
Jeff Boison - director of publishing planing & book trade sales
Jeremy Sullivan - director of digital sales
Kat Salazar - director of pr & marketing
Emily Miller - director of operations
Branwyn Bigglestone - senior accounts manager
Sarah Mello - accounts manager

Drew Gill - art director
Jonathan Chan - production manager
Meredith Wallace - print manager
Briah Skelly - publicity assistant
Randy Okamura - marketing production designer
David Brothers - branding manager
Ally Power - content manager
Addison Duke - production artist

Vincent Kukua - production artist
Sasha Head - production artist
Tricia Ramos - production artist
Jeff Stang - direct market sales representative
Emilio Bautista - digital sales associate
Chloe Ramos-Peterson - administrative assistant